DEPENDENCE

THE BELLATOR CHRONICLES BOOK TWO

CLARE LITTLEMORE

BRIT ALERT!

If you are reading this book and not from the UK, a brief warning that I am a British author and use British spellings throughout. In Bellator, the pavements have 'kerbs' rather than 'curbs', the students of the Danforth Academy may be disciplined for their bad behaviour (not behavior) and one or two of the characters might, on occasion, have to apologise (rather than apologize).

Happy reading!

Contents

CHAPTER ONE: NOAH

The trees rustled, disturbed by the brisk wind which hurried through the leaves as though it had somewhere better to be. In the distance, there was the sound of an owl hooting, and the occasional skittering of the smaller creatures which inhabited the forest floor. No doubt they were attempting to escape the piercing gaze of the owl, desperate to avoid becoming prey.

Noah knew how they felt.

Ever since the explosion at the hospital in Bellator, things in Eremus had been tense. Fearful that Danforth would seek swift revenge for Jacob's attack on the city, the entire community was on high alert. Defence had become their biggest priority, which was why Noah was now hiding up a tree in total darkness.

He was cold. Crouching in the branches of a sturdy oak, he shifted position for the hundredth time, trying to get comfortable. Guard duty was usually something he enjoyed. It provided an escape from the claustrophobia of the cave system, allowing him time outdoors and alone, surrounded by the peace of the forest. And, until recently, the chances of spotting a Bellator guard stalking through the area had been minimal.

But things were different now. This time, Noah was filled with a sense of dread. His body ached from the pent-up tension which had held his body hostage ever since the fateful raid. He knew he should be tired, but currently felt nothing but a creeping certainty that the recent actions of his community would bring the Bellator guards to the forest in droves.

Kidnapping the girls from Bellator had been a bad idea. They were valuable to the city, yes. But they were innocent. Victims of Danforth's system. The fact that they were currently huddled in one of the deepest caves in Eremus, fearing the worst, made his stomach churn. Knowing it was his involvement with one of those girls which had led, indirectly at least, to their capture, caused a wave of guilt to wash over him.

Faith. A Bellator citizen. A promising student of the Danforth Academy. A girl he should never have met, let alone spent any time with. But a girl he liked, nonetheless.

A girl who now hated him.

The crack of a twig close by startled him. Leaning forwards, he peered out into the blackness. A fox, probably, or perhaps a deer, made brave by the relative silence of the forest at night. His eyes had long-adjusted to the dark, and he could make out the general shapes of the things around him fairly easily. Sweeping his gaze in an arc across the surrounding area, he saw nothing unusual: the shapes of the branches were still the same, the outlines of the smaller bushes below remained unchanged. Still, something didn't feel right.

The noise had been made by something larger than a squirrel or a rabbit. He wished for a moment that Ruth was with him. Her presence always comforted him. But he was alone. It didn't help to know there were other Eremus citizens manning posts like this one in a large circuit all around the camp. He'd walked out here earlier with Dane, who'd quipped about communicating with him by imitating various bird noises.

But if a Bellator guard discovered him, he'd be dead before Dane could respond to any kind of distress call.

The cold steel of the pistol he'd been given pressed into his palm. It did not comfort him. Noah had relatively little training with guns, and he'd never actually pulled a trigger. He wasn't sure he was capable. He preferred helping people to hurting them. Working with his ma in what passed for the medical wing of the cave system Eremus inhabited. Healing wounds, not causing them. Faced with a Bellator guard, his life or hers, his brother Paulo always claimed Noah would fire, just to protect himself. Noah wasn't so sure.

He shook his head, trying to rid it of thoughts of his brother. They'd had no chance to be alone since returning from the raid. Things had been crazy, with the new prisoners to take care of and a growing sense of panic over Bellator's potential retaliation. But Noah had not forgotten Paulo's actions. The betrayal which had led to the girls' kidnapping: Paulo's idea, one he'd only considered because of his prior knowledge of the Danforth girls. Knowledge he'd been given by Noah, in confidence.

Noah couldn't let it go. But now wasn't the time to be distracted. In the day which had passed since the raid, there had been no sign of Bellator. But that didn't mean they weren't coming. Eremus' firepower was far more limited than Bellator's, despite the years of supplies Jacob had built up. Those on watch had been instructed to stay hidden, keep their eyes open and report back any unusual presence in the woods. If necessary, they could whistle a birdcall-style warning to other sentries. But their ammunition was to be conserved.

Hearing nothing more, Noah thrust the gun back into the makeshift holster on his belt. Hopefully, he'd never have to use it. Their community had gotten by for years by hiding. Right now, it was more important than ever to conceal Eremus' existence, or at least, pretend it wasn't large enough to pose a threat to Bellator. But like Flynn and his ma, Noah doubted they'd ever get away with that level of deception again.

Retreating to a position closer to the heart of the huge tree, Noah attempted to get comfortable again. He sat with his back braced against the trunk, a leg hanging down either side of the branch. He knew from experience that, within a few minutes, his legs would begin to go numb from the weight of his hanging feet, but for now, it worked.

He closed his eyes, thinking back to the last time he had seen Faith. Was it only a day ago? He had switched duties so he could guard the Danforth girls on their first night in Eremus, wanting desperately to explain himself. Although he had managed to get Faith alone, she hadn't accepted his version of events. He couldn't blame her.

When he'd given up and gone back to his post, he'd sat for most of the night pondering her appearance. She'd looked different than the last time he'd seen her. Thinner. Paler. He wondered what had happened since their chance meeting in the hospital. Had she been caught on her return? Punished, somehow?

He sighed. It was doubtful she'd confide anything in him, now that she blamed him for their kidnapping. Her eyes had glowed with resentment as he had tried to explain, tripping over words in his desperation to convince her of his innocence. When he'd run out of steam, she'd simply turned around and retreated into the depths of the cave. And he hadn't felt he had the right to follow her.

Instead, he had tortured himself all night, listening intently to the whispers which occasionally drifted from the girls' prison cell. Though he hadn't been able to make out individual words, he'd heard several of them crying, and various noises which signified others offering comfort. By the time someone came to replace him, he had been eager to leave. But his thoughts kept straying back to those sounds of fear and distress, and the stab of guilt which accompanied them was almost physically painful.

A flash of light in the distance caught his eye. He stiffened. Noises, he could attribute to animals. But he didn't know of any creatures that could use a flashlight. He kept his eyes fixed in the direction from which it had come. For a moment, all was dark. But then, there was another flash, closer this time. He sucked in a breath and retracted his legs as silently as possible. When they were tucked safely underneath him, he placed both hands on the branch and readied himself to leap down if he had to.

The brief flares of light between the leaves were becoming more frequent, and were soon accompanied by footsteps. There was definitely someone approaching. Noah considered climbing to a higher branch. The ones above him were thinner and less stable, but he wasn't heavy and he knew he'd have better cover further up the tree. Yet the beam of light was almost constant now, and definitely travelling in his direction. Any movement he made would create noise, attracting the attention of the person holding the flashlight.

He stayed where he was. Palms sweating, he clasped the branch as tightly as he could, willing himself to remain still. It was a single set of footsteps, he reasoned. Only one person approached. The odds of them being able to overcome him were vastly reduced by that fact alone. Yet he still wasn't confident he would be able to defeat a well-trained Bellator guard. He racked his brain as to the direction the light had approached from. The east, he figured. The nearest watch point in that direction wasn't too far. Had the citizen at that post seen the same figure? Were they already dead?

His entire body shook, though it wasn't cold. Whoever held the light was close now. The footsteps didn't sound especially heavy. Yet, if the intruder was a Bellator guard, she would be female, making it more likely she was slight. The thought didn't comfort him. Slightness was of little consequence if she was well-armed.

Noah's hand slid to his belt, easing the gun from its holster. Clenching his knees around the trunk to give him some stability, he trained the weapon on the ground below. He held his breath as a figure emerged from between the trees, making its way towards his hiding place. The stranger was not very tall and wore black clothing, which made her blend into the darkness. But the large weapon strapped to her back created an unmistakable outline against the pale moon which sliced across the clearing. This woman was definitely dangerous.

She passed beneath him, her pace slow and methodical. Nothing about her journey through the woods indicated a chase. She was alert, sure, but not focused on any specific prey. Not right now, at least. Noah wondered if she was on some kind of reconnaissance mission, sweeping the woods for signs of life.

If that was the case, she wouldn't be alone. Noah pictured his fellow citizens, hiding in various locations around the forest. Were large numbers of the Bellator guard stalking through the trees below them?

He waited for the footsteps to retreat, knowing he couldn't allow himself to move even slightly until the woman had gone. But just as she passed his tree, a brief, low pitched whine cut through the air. For a moment, Noah thought it had come from an animal, but then the woman paused, raising an arm to her face.

"Alpha 66. Copy."

She was speaking into her wristclip.

A strange, disembodied voice echoed from the direction of the device. "Anything to report?"

The woman had stopped just past the tree where Noah was concealed. Through the leaves, all he could see of her was the outline of her boots. Taking a chance, he leaned forward, until the rest of her came into view. The guard had turned to face the direction from which she had approached, and for a panicked moment, he felt like she was looking right at him.

"Nothing." Noah relaxed at her words. She couldn't see him, then. "If there are men in these woods, they're good at staying hidden."

"Copy that. Danforth's orders, though. We have to sweep the entire quadrant. Those girls didn't just disappear."

"Sure. I'll continue to walk this section, then report back for a new search area."

"Copy that. Over and out."

The woman glanced around her, the flashlight illuminating the nearby plant-life with an eerie glow. She directed the beam upwards, swinging it through the trees on both sides. Noah froze. He clutched the gun a little tighter. Forced himself to take a slow, deep breath. Re-aimed the barrel of the weapon at the guard standing below him. But she dropped the beam before it swept across his tree.

Abruptly, she stuck the flashlight into her belt and turned her attention to the tiny machine at her wrist again. After fiddling with it for a few seconds, she held it close to her mouth.

"Brady. Come in, Brady."

A few seconds later, a second voice echoed from the device. "What's up, Charlie?"

"Any problems on your end?"

"No. Nothing." There was a brief pause. "Why?"

"Not sure." The woman beneath him looked left and right again. "I can't see any sign of life out here, but I get the feeling that there's some kind of... presence. Is that stupid?"

A strange noise emanated from the device, making Noah jump. He cursed under his breath, anxious that the woman might have heard his movement. But she seemed more focused on her conversation.

"Don't laugh at me. I'm serious."

"I'm sorry, Charlie. But I really don't think there's anything out here. Not tonight, anyhow."

"Maybe not." The woman beneath him sighed. "Why we couldn't have done this search in daylight, I don't know."

"Yeah, you do. Stealth. Hammond said Danforth insisted. So we can take the Eremus *bogeymen* by surprise."

"Maybe." The woman turned in a slow circle beneath Noah. "Brady… you ever think… I mean, if they're so good at hiding… What if they already know we're here?"

There was a pause, as though the person on the other end of the strange device was considering their response. Just as Noah thought they weren't going to reply at all, the voice came again.

"Stop fretting, Charlie. You're armed to the teeth… *trained* for this. It's a search, that's all. Not a battle. Get the mission done and let's get back to base. The quicker we're finished, the quicker we're back home to hot food and a warm bed."

Charlie paused beneath Noah. For a moment, he thought she was going to argue with Brady. But eventually, she raised the clip again, her voice resigned. "Fine. I'll see you later, then."

Beneath him, the guard tapped the device once more, then dropped her arm to her side. With a final glance behind, she shook herself, then continued to pace through the woods, her flashlight sweeping from side to side.

Sagging back against the tree, Noah replaced the gun in its holster. The solid bark beneath his hands was reassuring, and as his heartrate returned to normal, he clung to it. The Bellator guards were sweeping the woods. There was more than one of them. They'd been instructed to look for signs of life. For the Eremus citizens. And it didn't sound like they were going to give up.

But he couldn't shake the feeling that the woman had sounded as scared as him.

CHAPTER TWO: FAITH

I t was dark. Faith woke up in the cave, as she had regularly over the past two nights. Again, the inky blackness threatened to engulf her. She didn't consider herself a coward. She had teased people in the past for what she deemed to be irrational fears: spiders and heights and thunder. But underground, the darkness was like an evil presence, ready and waiting to pounce.

Back in Bellator, her wristclip could have been relied on to cast a little light, but when the girls had woken from the drugs the Eremus folks had administered during their kidnapping, their wrists had been bare. Faith felt a stab of guilt, remembering how she had explained their purpose to Noah. Many of the girls had bitterly complained about the missing devices, stating how they might have been used to send an emergency alert to the city authorities. Speed up their rescue. Faith was torn about the idea.

Yes, they were prisoners, at least for now, but she had been a prisoner back in Bellator too. She had learned things, worrying things, about what the academy had planned for its students. She had even started to wonder if they might not be better off, in some ways, here in Eremus. Whether that was true remained to be seen. She hadn't confided these thoughts to the rest of the girls yet. It would have meant admitting her prior contact with Noah, and she knew some of them would blame her for their situation.

Stretching out, she felt for Sophia. Knowing her friend was there made things a little more bearable. For a moment, she searched blindly, her heart beginning to pound as her hand met only empty space and hard rock. But then it bumped against something soft and warm, and a moment later she felt a reassuring squeeze in return.

"Y'alright?" Sophia's voice was heavy with sleep.

"Yeah." Faith felt silly for a moment. "Just checking you were still—"

"I know." Sophia shifted her body sideways, wriggling closer. "S'okay."

"I hate that they barricaded the door."

When they'd arrived, Eremus had not been expecting them. A permanent guard had been posted just outside the cave entrance, which at the time had only been shielded by a thin curtain. Most of the girls had spent the first night cowering in the cave, terrified of what the man on guard might do to them. Bellator teachings ran deep.

Whilst not as frightened as the others, Faith had still found it difficult to fall asleep. When the guard was Noah, she found herself filled with such confusion and anger that she couldn't relax. And when it wasn't, she questioned whether the other Eremus men would be as gentle as Noah. Because, despite his betrayal, he had never hurt her. Not physically, at least.

The guard outside might not even have been necessary, if every Danforth captive had been submissive. But, defiant as ever, Diane had already tried to escape. Alarmed by their sudden and desperate capture, she was determined to get out of the caves. Every time she tried, Faith feared for her safety, but she had yet to succeed, and was always delivered back to their cell without harm.

Since her escape attempt, things had progressed. The morning after their arrival, several of the Eremus citizens had been sent down to construct a door of sorts, a wooden barrier fixed over the cave entrance which trapped them. None of them had spoken to the girls, though some shot curious glances at them while they worked. It had been a tense couple of hours, and Faith had huddled with the others as far from the strangers as possible until the job was complete and they had gone.

Once the barricade was in place, the guard outside was withdrawn. Not entirely, Faith didn't think. They were still there. Stationed further away, as there was no longer a need to watch the cave entrance like a hawk. But with the door in place, the light from the guard's lantern was no longer visible.

In the darkness, the contours of their cave became a mystery, and the girls had to feel around themselves to figure out who was where. Sophia had turned it into a sort of game, in an attempt to distract the other girls from their terror of the men who held them prisoner. It worked, most of the time. And as a result, they had been able to gain a better understanding of their situation.

Firstly, there were eight of them in the cave. All students from the Danforth Academy who had been at the hospital the night of the explosion. Aside from Faith, Sophia, and Diane, there was Avery and her friend Farrah, plus another senior girl, Helen, but Mary and Catherine, two of the girls taken, were only juniors. They had swapped stories about the kidnapping and come to the conclusion that all the other girls from the hospital had been left behind, and as far as they knew, were unharmed. They were working on the assumption they'd been selected at random, and that Eremus had no real knowledge of who they were, aside from the fact that they were Danforth students.

Secondly, the cave they were being held in was fairly small and contained nothing other than the girls, some blankets they had been provided with, and a bucket which served as a very basic bathroom facility. It was being emptied a few times a day, at least, but most of the girls had found the abrupt removal of even the most rudimentary of facilities very distressing, especially given that each time they had to endure the presence of a man in the cave. They were also being fed. Trays had been brought in three times the previous day with simple, but reasonable fare. Not what they were used to, of course, but enough to keep them alive and healthy.

What Faith really wanted was some light. And some exercise. Being cooped up had never suited her, and she was missing the outdoors, the chance to stretch her legs, to feel the wind on her face. She had tried to keep up some sort of stretching / movement routine as she had in her cell back in Bellator, but as the cave wasn't large and she couldn't see well, it was difficult.

"What time do you think it is?" Faith could hear Sophia yawning. "I mean, how are we supposed to even know if it's day or night down here?"

Again, Faith reached for her wrist, dropping her hand to her side when she realised it was bare. She wondered how long it would take to rid herself of the automatic impulse.

"No idea." She sat up, peering at the space around her. "Surely it must be time for a meal, though. I'm starving!"

"You're always starving." Sophia shifted a little closer. "Look, I think we need to be cautious about how we act with these people."

"You mean the bastards who kidnapped us?"

"Yes." Sophia's tone was earnest. "If we're pleasant, appear to cooperate, things will be better for us. I know it. They'll drop their guard a little, perhaps allow us more freedom, time outside of this," Faith could feel her gesturing around the cave, "hellhole."

"I suppose," Faith began, dropping her voice lower, "though we might have a hard time convincing some of the others to—"

"Hush!" Sophia hissed, as a telltale scraping outside signified someone was about to open the door. "Someone's coming."

The light from a lantern spilled into the cave as the large section of wood was pulled aside. Faith found herself blinking furiously. Once she had recovered, she glanced around at the others, automatically checking they were all okay. When she looked back at the door, a tall girl around Avery's age was standing there. One of her arms was bound up in some kind of sling. Faith found herself wondering why.

The girl placed a lantern on the ground and peered in at them. "We brought you some breakfast." She tapped the gun at her belt with her free hand and glanced over at Diane, who sat towards the rear of the cave, her eyes narrowed. "That is, as long as you're not going to cause me any trouble."

Faith shot a look at Diane. "We're not."

"Alright then." She turned to beckon to another figure behind her. "I'm Ella, by the way. This is Ruth."

A second girl, younger than Ella, entered the cave. Faith thought she looked familiar. She was carrying a tray filled with dishes, plus a large bowl which had steam rising from it. Placing it down on the ground, she ensured it was stable before backing away and regarding the girls with a suspicious expression. Ella ducked outside for a moment, returning with cups and a pitcher of water which she set down next to the first tray.

"Oats." She gestured to the bowl. "Not exactly luxurious, but they're warm and comforting, and they'll keep you going."

The first few trays of food had been brought in by male guards, who hadn't said much. The Bellator girls had been too frightened to speak to them, and Faith was pretty sure the very youngest girls were holding their breath until the men left. Every time, Catherine's eyes grew wide as saucers, and even the older girls, Farrah and Helen in particular, looked like they were about to pass out. Faith couldn't blame them. They were waiting for the men of Eremus to display the kind of violent behaviour they'd learned so much about back home. So far, none of them had.

But the new visitors were different. For a start, they were female, a fact which everyone except Faith found curious, given that they seemed to live alongside the men without complaint. Secondly, they were not much older than the Danforth girls. And instead of leaving immediately, they remained in the cave. The girl called Ruth did not look very friendly as she squatted on the ground and began doling out the porridge into bowls. Ella, however, smiled around at them.

"How are you all feeling this morning?" She took the first bowl of porridge from Ruth and passed it to Sophia, who took it with a shy smile. The girls exchanged nervous glances, but no one spoke. "I get that you probably don't trust us." She handed a bowl to Faith, meeting her gaze steadily. "I mean... I understand what we did must seem extreme, but you really don't understand what–"

"We don't *understand*?" Avery's voice was low and urgent. "We were kidnapped and drugged! Then we woke up here. Wherever *here* is. That seems pretty clear to me. What we don't know is what's going to happen next."

"That will become clear, in time." Ella's voice was soothing. "But I want you to know that Eremus means you no harm."

From the back of the cave, Diane scowled. "You're not going to let us go though, are you?"

"Not at the moment, no." Ella turned and smiled at Diane. "But we aren't going to hurt you." She waited while the remainder of the porridge was handed out, then gestured to the bowls of food. "Please, eat."

Having finished with the oatmeal, the girl called Ruth sat back on her heels. Her eyes swept the cave, peering through the dimness at each face in turn. When her gaze rested on Faith she stopped, her eyes narrowing. Faith paused, a spoonful of oats poised halfway to her mouth. She felt a sudden flash of anger. This was the girl who had knocked her out with the aerosol. The girl who had helped Noah to abduct her. Clearly, the Eremus females could be just as formidable as their men.

Lowering her head quickly, she thrust the spoon in her mouth and continued to eat. When she looked up again, the girl's eyes were still fixed on her, their expression unreadable. Noticing, Ella jabbed an elbow into Ruth's side and nodded at the door. With a brief frown, Ruth pushed herself to her feet and disappeared back out into the tunnel.

Ella busied herself pouring water into the cups on the tray. When she was finished, she pushed it towards the girls. "Help yourselves."

At that moment, Ruth returned, carrying a second lantern. It was an odd-looking thing, Faith thought, old-fashioned-looking. Ruth placed it just inside the entrance, and took a packet of matches from her pocket.

Ella smiled round at them again. "Look, we know you've been stuck in the dark and that can't be nice. We want to make sure you're comfortable. And feel... safe. I'm sorry we haven't done this before now... we... well, let's just say we didn't have much time to prepare for your arrival."

"Y' can say that again." Ruth lifted the glass casing from the lamp and struck a match. These were the first words she had spoken since entering the room and made Faith even more certain that this was the voice she'd heard shouting at Noah just before she had been attacked. The flame flared and Ruth waited until it had died down before holding it to the wick of the lamp with expertise. She turned to the girls, jerking her head at the glow. "Should be enough oil to last a few hours."

Beside Faith, Sophia shifted, turning her head towards the girl at the door. "Thank you, Ruth."

Surprise flashed across Ruth's face. She managed a tight nod at Sophia, but dropped her gaze. Following Sophia's lead, Faith turned to Ella and smiled, holding out her empty bowl.

Ella returned the grin. "You were hungry!"

"She's *always* hungry." Sophia joked, seeming determined to get the two Eremus girls onside. She rolled her eyes. "I've seen her devour a stack of ten pancakes in one sitting!"

From the door, Ruth snorted with laughter, then clapped a hand over her mouth, shifting her feet as though to cover her reaction. Faith exchanged glances with Sophia. For better or worse, her plan seemed to be working.

"Pancakes." Ella looked thoughtful. "*Ten* pancakes. I can see why you might not be impressed by the Eremus diet."

Faith felt a momentary stab of guilt. She'd never properly appreciated the plentiful supply of food they had in the city. There was a moment's silence before Mary, a timid girl of fourteen, crept forward with her empty bowl.

"Thank you." Ella stacked the bowl on top of Faith's. For a moment, Mary stood still, gazing at the Eremus girl with curiosity. "Are you alright? Something you wanted to ask me?"

"Are..." Mary's voice was barely audible, "...are they holding *you* captive in some way?"

Ella's forehead wrinkled slightly. "Captive?"

Mary took a step back. "I, I mean... you're living here with all these... *men*."

Ella shrugged. "Sorry, still not following."

"Did they kidnap you too?"

"She thinks we're the men's prisoners." Ruth's eyes were cold again. "That's what they teach you, right?"

Slowly, Mary turned to her. "Y-yes. I mean... you can't be living out here... with all these beasts... I mean... by choice."

Ella burst out laughing, the sound echoing too loudly around the cave.

Mary shrank away, turning to creep back to her spot at the rear of the cave, but Ella recovered herself and took a step towards the younger girl.

"Is that really what you *think*?" She paused, and when she spoke again, she had tempered her tone. Rounding on the group, she frowned. "It is, isn't it?"

"These men, though... they *keep* you here under the ground." Helen leaned forward. "Do they make you work for them? Do you get punished if you don't obey?"

"Not at all. We were born here. And the reason we live underground is because of the Bellator guards." Ella's eyes were kindly. "They hunt us... I mean, they used to. We had to hide."

"From the guards? But you're female!" Farrah burst out. "You'd be welcome in Bellator."

Ruth snorted, a loud, derisive sound. "Not likely."

Ella frowned at her. "But we don't want to live by Bellator rules. We choose to live here."

"Really?" Helen stared openmouthed at the two Eremus girls. "You choose..." she swept a hand around the cave, "this?"

"Well, you're not exactly seeing Eremus at its best." Ella flushed. "I guess... it seems like we have a lot to learn about each other."

"Not right now, though." From the doorway, Ruth cleared her throat and jerked her head at Ella.

"Ah yes. We have to go." Ella stood up and looked around, stooping to collect the last few bowls one by one. When she reached Avery's, it was was not quite empty. "You finished?"

"Yep." Avery said sullenly. "I'm finished.

"Not quite what you're used to?" Ruth's tone was pure sarcasm.

"It's not, no," Avery glared at her. "I'm still hungry, but I can't make myself eat any more of that... slop."

"I'm sorry we don't have any *pancakes*."

Ella stepped forward. "We *are* sorry. Sorry that this is not what you're used to. We live a much simpler life here in Eremus." Again, she seemed determined to calm the situation. "I'd learn to finish your meals, if I were you though." Faith caught a brief flash of uncertainty in Avery's eyes, but it was quickly quashed as Ella continued. "Look, it can take a while, but eventually living underground becomes second nature."

Faith glanced at the girls huddled around her. "I'm not sure we could ever get used to it."

"You'd be surprised." Ella shrugged. "It's far safer in here than out in the woods."

"It's not like we'll need to get *used to it*." Avery appeared to have regained some of her usual confidence. "The authorities will be here to rescue us soon. Bellator has all sorts of tech to track us down. You can't even imagine, hiding down here in your holes like... like *animals*."

From the door, Ruth scowled, and a shadow crossed Ella's face. "We're not animals."

"You're treating *us* like animals though."

Ella straightened. "I'm sorry you feel that way." She stacked Avery's bowl on top of the others and nodded at Ruth, who came over to pick up the tray. "We'll bring you a few more blankets later, maybe a pack of cards..."

"Cards?" Sophia questioned.

"Sure. Might help you to pass the time."

Intrigued, Ruth cocked her head at Sophia. "You don't have playing cards in Bellator?"

"No."

"They're used to play games." Ella smiled at their confusion. "For fun."

"Fun!" Avery snorted and turned away.

Ella's face darkened and Faith found herself wishing her fellow student would rein in her derision of the Eremus way of life. It wasn't doing them any favours.

Deliberately looking at Faith and Sophia, Ella went on. "If there's anything else we can do to make you feel a little more... comfortable... then let us know."

"Exercise?" Faith blurted out. "I mean... could we be allowed out of here for... a walk, or something?"

Ella and Ruth exchanged glances.

"I don't think so." Ella's tone was gentle. "Too much of a risk. I'm sorry."

Looking uncomfortable for the first time since she'd entered the cave, Ella moved towards the doorway. Ruth went out first, placing the tray on the ground outside the door. She returned a moment later to retrieve the waste bucket from the far end of the cave, wrinkling her nose as she replaced it with a fresh one.

Knowing they were running out of time, Faith tried again. "We could be supervised, of course. It would only have to be for a little while."

"Not right now. Maybe later, we could..." Ella turned, her expression kind, but firm. "Look, we have to go. We're needed elsewhere." She gestured to the cups of water. "We'll leave these here and come back and refill the pitcher later."

She slipped through the door and gestured to Ruth, who followed her. Taking hold of the heavy wooden barrier, she began to move it back into place. Faith marvelled at the strength in her arms, though they were fairly slim. Eremus citizens were certainly not weak.

"We'll be back later." Ella called through the receding gap. "Hang in there."

The two girls disappeared, and the cave seemed darker again, despite the addition of the lantern. As the barricade was locked in place and the sound of footsteps receded, Faith felt like they had been locked inside a tomb.

CHAPTER THREE: NOAH

As Noah wandered back through the woods, he felt exhaustion overtake him. The night had been long and draining. After his close shave with the guard, he'd spent the rest of his shift crouched on the tree branch on high alert. There had been no sign of anyone else, and Noah got the impression the Bellator patrol was a small one. By dawn, however, his body ached from the effort. When his replacement had arrived, he'd clambered down from the tree with barely a word.

He made it back to the caves without seeing anyone. Even slipping through the branches which covered the entrance was difficult, but once inside, he felt a sense of relief overwhelm him. He headed for the den, a tiny, hidden cave where he often met Ruth. If he went home, he'd have to endure some awkward questions from his ma. So far, he'd managed to avoid her since their return from the raid, but he knew eventually he'd have to face her. She'd been furious with the decision to kidnap the Danforth girls, and though he'd been against it, he knew she'd want to know why he hadn't fought harder to stop Paulo.

No. He couldn't cope with that right now. Picking up the pace, he rounded a corner and hurried past the tunnel which led to many of the smaller caves the Eremus citizens called home. He'd almost made it when he heard footsteps, and then a familiar voice.

"Noah?" His heart sank. "Noah, wait up!"

The only person he wanted to see less than his ma right now was his brother. Paulo was responsible for the girls' kidnapping. He couldn't even blame Jacob for the split-second decision which had forced Noah to bring Faith back here as his captive and turned her against him.

He watched his brother hurry towards him, trying to keep the scowl from his face. Refusing to begin the conversation, he waited as Paulo came to a stop in front of him, his face wary.

"You were on guard last night." It wasn't a question. Paulo had known the schedule, known where Noah would be. He wondered whether his brother had been hanging around waiting to speak to him. "Shift okay?"

The question was so normal it was infuriating. Noah managed to shrug. "I guess."

"You saw guards?"

"Just one."

"That's good."

Noah took a step back, his fists clenched. "There were others, though."

His brother nodded. "We've had the same report from several of our scouts. Just a small reconnaissance mission, by all accounts. Not too much of a threat at the moment."

"At the *moment?*" Paulo's lack of concern grated on Noah. "I heard the guard on the radio. They were sweeping the woods. Not too many of them, *yet*, but..."

"We're aware of the issue." Paulo brushed his concern aside. "It's being monitored." He stared at Noah. "You didn't let her see you, did you? Orders were to stay *hidden*. If she even–"

"I know what the orders were." Noah's words were choked out between gritted teeth. "Don't you trust me?"

Paulo shrugged. "Course I do."

"Well, you don't have to worry." Noah forced himself to take a slow, calming breath. "I didn't let you down."

"Good." His brother grinned. "Seems like you might be becoming a half-decent raider after all. Who'd've thought it?"

"So, we're joking now?" Noah clenched his fists by his sides. "You find the situation funny?"

Disgusted, he turned to go, but found Paulo's hand on his arm. "What's with you?"

"What's *with* me?" Noah spun to face him. "You really don't know? Your decision that night put our entire community at risk."

Paulo's face darkened. "Our community's *always* at risk. What I did was *strengthen* our position."

"Strengthen it?" Noah spat. "After all your training about caution on raids, following the rules while we're in Bellator, not risking the secrecy which has protected us for *years*... you do *this*."

"This?" Paulo glared at him. "You still don't see, do you? *This* was a good move. With those girls here, Danforth won't dare attack us. Risk her precious citizens? No chance. And you were a part of that. Your information helped me make that decision."

"Oh, don't remind me. You *forced* me to be part of this."

"*Forced* you?" For a moment, Paulo looked confused. "Don't you see? The intel you gathered was vital."

For a second, Noah was speechless. "Is *that* what I was doing? *Gathering intel?* I wish you'd told me."

"You know what I mean." Paulo scowled, as though Noah were being deliberately awkward. "The knowledge you were able to give me was vital... about the medical testing... the girls being from the academy... their value to Danforth..."

"You mean the innocent girls we dragged back here against their will?" Noah took a step closer to his brother. "How do you think *they're* feeling this morning?"

"This isn't about *them*." Paulo looked bewildered. "It's about–"

Noah cut him off. "I always thought being a raider meant I could protect our community. But I *never* wanted to do that at the expense of other innocent people." He stabbed a finger into Paulo's chest, aware of the formidable muscle there but, for the moment, not caring. "And right now, I think Eremus is more vulnerable than ever. Because of you."

"You're wrong."

"If you say so." Noah stepped away. "I have to go." Shaking with fury, he stalked away down the tunnel. He suspected it would take him a long time to calm down. But he had some apologising of his own to do.

He wanted, more than anything, to see his best friend. As he reached the entrance to the den, he prayed he was right about her whereabouts. Checking the tunnel was empty, he thrust himself through the gap in the rock. As he emerged on the other side, he spotted her lying on the blankets, her eyes closed. His heart thundered with relief, and he felt the anger of his meeting with Paulo begin to fade.

"Thought I might find you here."

She didn't respond. He knew she wasn't sleeping though. Wriggling through the tiny entrance was not an easy task, now that they were no longer children. It wasn't an activity done quietly, which was why they always made sure there was no one in the outer tunnel before entering. A person on the inside would have to be sleeping like the dead to miss it.

"Ruth?"

The silence seemed to go on forever. And then, she cracked open one eye and glared at him.

"I'm still mad at you."

"I know." He settled on the ground, attempting not to touch her in the limited space. Soon, he was looking up at the sky through the crack in the cave's roof. Today the weather was cloudy, the view far bleaker than it often was.

They were quiet for a moment. Noah stretched out his tired limbs, not knowing how to go about mending things between them. They had rarely fallen out in the past.

Eventually, Ruth rolled on to her side, closing the gap between them. "Don't you have anything to say to me?" Her tone was accusatory. "I mean... I get that you were worried about the girl and all... but you risked both our lives."

Noah sighed. She was right. When the time had come to follow orders and capture the Bellator girls, he had failed. Face-to-face with Faith, her trustful eyes gazing at him, he had been unable to administer the Sleepsol. He remembered her expression when she'd first spotted him. Flinging herself into his arms, she had looked on him for rescue.

The sudden embrace had both startled and thrilled him. In that moment, he'd been unable to act against her, and his inaction had put his own people in danger. But Faith wouldn't understand that. The expression in her eyes later that night had been one of disappointment and betrayal. He doubted she'd ever forgive him. But maybe Ruth would.

"I'm sorry." He turned to face her, propping himself up on one elbow. "Really. I risked our lives for a girl I hardly know."

"Yeah." She stared at him. "You did."

"I can't explain it." He cast his eyes down. "I just... couldn't help myself."

"You really like this girl, huh?" Ruth was staring at him, incredulous.

"Umm. I guess so." He paused, running a hand through his hair. "I don't think I realised how much... 'til..."

"You're telling me!" Her face softened. "It's okay."

He stared back at her. "It is?"

"Long as you promise to make it up to me." She leaned across and punched his arm.

"And how can I do that?" For a moment, Noah dreaded her response, until he saw the glint in her eye.

"Share your sugar rations with me next week."

He let out a breath. "Done."

"That was almost too easy." She grinned. "Should've asked you to share for a month."

"Can if you like."

"Don't be stupid." Her grin faded. "She made a big impression on you... this girl. I mean, you meet her once, then–"

"Actually, I've met her twice." Noah held a hand up to stop her protest. "I know... I should've told you."

"Damn right you should."

"I met her on that first raid... with Paulo... to the med centre?" Noah thought back to the first meeting. Of their mutual surprise at one another. How they had each been nothing like the other had expected.

"Sounds like she's a bit of a rebel, this girl."

"Yeah. I guess so." He shifted slightly, making himself more comfortable. "She had concerns about what the school was doing to them. They're fed some kind of line about being privileged to attend Danforth, like they're 'chosen' or special. Helping the entire community. But she thought the school was lying to them... putting them through some kind of testing."

Ruth shuddered. "Creepy."

"Definitely. I don't think the Bellator citizens have it as easy as we think."

"Maybe not." Ruth sat up. "But they definitely get better food than we do. They looked at the oatmeal we took them this morning like it was poisonous."

"You saw them?"

She nodded.

"And you waited 'til now to tell me?"

"Sorry." She didn't *look* sorry. "I was mad at you. Hey, I'm telling you now, aren't I?"

"Alright." Noah felt a stab of guilt. "They acted like it was poisoned? Guess we can't blame them for thinking that. We kidnapped them. We're keeping them prisoner."

"But why would they think we wanted to kill them? I mean... if that was our aim, why not just do it when we first saw them in Bellator?"

"Perhaps they're not thinking logically right now."

"It's not all of them." She chewed on her lip thoughtfully. "Some of them were grateful. Ate the porridge and were happy to be fed. But some of them are... stuck up." She made a face.

"They must be scared, though. I mean... wouldn't you be?"

Ruth thought for a moment. "I would, yes."

"There you are then. So..." He hesitated. "How is– I mean, how are they all doing?"

Ruth snorted. "I think you mean how is *she*, right? What's her name?"

"Faith."

"She seemed okay. She was pleasant towards Ella and I, at least. More than some of them were." She frowned. "We took them a lantern. They've been sitting in the darkness." She waved his protest away. "I know. It can't have been nice for them. Don't know if she recognised me... from the raid, I mean. She and her friend thanked us. We're taking them some more blankets later."

Noah thought how cold it could be underground, even in the summer. "That's good."

"Anything you want me to ask her?" Noah shook his head. "Perhaps you'll get to guard them at some point soon... you could try and talk to her then."

He laughed mirthlessly. "Already did."

"Really?" She smacked his arm. "There's a lot you're not telling me."

"Sorry." Noah shifted into a different position. "I went down there the night they arrived. Switched guard duty with Mick." The older raider had been only-too-happy to let him take the night shift.

"That fast? You are worried about her. Sneaky, too." Ruth looked impressed. "And?"

He picked up a small pebble from the cave floor and rolled it around his palm. "And she wasn't interested. She's mad at me. Feels like I betrayed her trust."

"So? You did."

"Huh?"

"You *did* betray her trust. Not on purpose, but..."

"Ah, that makes me feel a whole lot better." He tossed the pebble at the other side of the cave where it bounced off the rock wall and back towards them. "Thanks, pal."

"So... she's mad at you. I was mad at you, until a few minutes ago." She glared at him as though he was very slow on the uptake. "And now I'm not."

"Well, at least one of you forgives me."

"Ah, stop feeling sorry for yourself. She'll forgive you too. Give her time." Ruth sat up. "For now, we have bigger things to worry about." He shot her a curious look. "I heard a whisper that Jacob left Eremus late last night. And he's not back yet."

"Really?"

She nodded, her face serious. "According to Ella, who overheard Sarah Porter telling Harden." She shook her head. "I really don't trust that woman. Dawn never did either."

Ruth's adopted ma had always been suspicious of Sarah's relationship with Jacob. Since her death, it seemed like Ruth had inherited Dawn's qualms.

But right now, Noah was more interested in their leader's movements. "Where was Jacob going? And why go alone?"

"Not sure." Ruth shrugged. "I'm guessing he wanted to keep a low profile."

"Does everyone know he's gone?

"I didn't get that impression, no." Ruth paused before continuing. "As I said, Sarah was talking like Jacob had confided in her." She scowled. "Like she was one of the only ones *in the know*."

"I'm sure he told the other council members."

"I hope so." Ruth sat up, peering closely at him. "You look awful, you know."

"Gee, thanks."

She made a face. "You do though. So tired. Have you been on shift all night?"

He nodded. "Look-out duty in the woods."

"Ah." She raised her eyebrows. "How is it out there?"

He shrugged. "Honestly? Pretty scary."

"Bellator Guards?"

"Yep. A group, sweeping the woods." He shifted slightly to get comfortable. "I saw one up close. Right underneath my post."

"Really?" His best friend sat upright. "What was she like?"

Noah paused and thought about it. "Well, not terrifying, I guess. I mean... she had a gun and all. But..."

"But what?" Ruth prompted, with her usual impatience.

"Well, I overheard her speaking to another guard. Twice actually. The first one was... I don't know... like someone in charge. She was just reporting in. Not emotional. But the second time was different."

"How so?"

"Well... it kind of sounded like she was speaking to a friend. Her name was Charlie. She sounded, almost, nervous, I guess. I mean... she wanted to get back to Bellator. Go home."

Ruth frowned. "I guess they're following orders, just like us on a raid. Must feel as tense as we do."

"Really?" Noah stared at her.

"What?"

"Nothing! I mean... that's quite charitable of you. I thought you hated all Bellator citizens?"

She shrugged. "P'rhaps I'm changing my mind."

"I really didn't get the impression they were looking to attack," Noah said. "Not tonight, anyway. It was more like they were sussing us out. Trying to locate us. I guess it makes sense they'd be a little more cautious now that they know we have more firepower than they realised."

"And they don't want to come in all guns blazing because they know we have their citizens." Ruth looked thoughtful. "Paulo might have been more right than we gave him credit for." Noah scowled at her and she held her hands up in surrender. "I know, I know. You're angry with him. But if Danforth is being cautious about her next steps, perhaps the girls will give us an advantage."

He glared at her. "That's what Paulo tried to tell me."

She fixed him with a stare. "I don't mean we have to treat them badly. I just finished telling you how we were trying to make them comfortable, didn't I?" He relaxed a little. "But... if they're here, maybe Bellator won't just storm the woods, attacking anyone they see."

"I guess not."

"And maybe, if we treat these girls well, and if you're right about what Danforth does to them, we can even get them on our side?"

"Maybe."

They fell into a silence, but this time it was a comfortable one. Noah closed his eyes, finding that his mind had relaxed slightly. He'd been terrified Ruth would hold a grudge against him. Just knowing she was back on his side as usual made him feel better. But he didn't realise he was falling asleep until Ruth shifted.

"Sorry," he mumbled.

"You're starting to snore." He felt the weight of a blanket being pulled over him. "Get some sleep down here. It's probably more peaceful than anywhere else at the moment." He felt her wriggling over him to reach the exit. "I have to go. I've a shift starting soon and I'll never hear the end of it from Harriet if I'm late. I'll bring you some food down later... make sure you're awake, in case there's any news."

He tried to murmur a reply but wasn't sure any words came out. He heard his friend chuckling as she crept out of the cave, but it was the last thing he was aware of for several hours.

Chapter Four: Faith

She must have drifted off, but when she woke later in the day, Faith felt woozy. The lantern still burned in the corner of the cave, allowing them to see one another, but the shadows it cast were eerie and, in Faith's opinion, hadn't improved the situation.

Sophia was bending over her, a concerned expression on her face. "You alright?"

"What?"

"You're burning up a little."

"M'okay." Faith struggled to sit up. "At least, I think I am. The world's kind of... spinning."

Her friend placed an arm behind her and steadied her. "If you get any worse, we need to tell them."

"Tell them what?" They turned to see Diane, who hadn't spoken to anyone in hours. Now, she wandered across, leaning close to Faith. "Oof. You don't look too good."

"Get her a cup of water, would you?" Sophia directed her.

The older girl moved towards the pitcher, lifted it up and frowned. "Empty." She glared around at the others. "Who finished it?"

"I did." Avery was lounging against the wall close to the doorway. Catching the expression on Diane's face, she frowned. "What's the problem?"

"The problem is that Faith needs some," Sophia said. "She's running a temperature."

"Oh." Avery looked surprised. "Sorry."

Catherine, one of the younger girls, brought the lantern over to Faith. "Are you alright?" She cast a nervous glance at the door. "Should we call for help?"

"Stop overreacting." Avery yawned. "I'm sure they'll bring some more water in soon."

"What makes you think *that*?" Diane banged the pitcher down on the tray, making the others jump. "Down here, *nothing's* guaranteed. You might want to consider the way you speak to these people."

Anticipating trouble, Catherine left the lantern where it was and scurried back to her place.

Avery stiffened. "Well... they haven't let us go hungry yet, have they?"

"Maybe not." Diane glared at Avery. "But it's hours since they were last here."

Noting the fearful look on Mary's face, Sophia smiled. "So it stands to reason they'll bring us something soon."

"Ella *promised*." Mary's voice was quiet, but she managed to meet Avery's gaze.

"There you go then." Avery shot Diane a withering look. It wasn't in her nature to pay attention to the younger Danforth students, but right now she didn't have a lot of choice. Faith would have found it amusing, if she'd been feeling better.

"I have a little water left," Farrah brought her cup across and handed it to Faith. "You're welcome to it."

Faith sipped from the half cup of water gratefully. As the tepid liquid hit her stomach, she couldn't decide if it had improved things, but managed a grateful smile anyway. Bracing her hands against the rocky ground, she stretched.

"Thank you."

"No problem." Farrah hesitated for a moment, before gesturing to the ground next to Faith. "May I sit?"

"Sure." Faith nodded, surprised. Farrah was Avery's friend, and as such, didn't usually spend time talking to her.

Ignoring Avery's concerned glance, Farrah squeezed into the space next to Sophia and Faith. They sat in silence for a few minutes. To her immense relief, Faith felt her head begin to clear. Eventually, Farrah sat up straighter, turning to face Faith.

"I wanted to ask..." she faltered for a moment before continuing, "the night of the kidnapping, outside the hospital. You spoke to me?"

Faith nodded. "I remember."

"And then... well... Avery came over and you walked away, and..." Farrah paused, as though she wasn't sure how to phrase the question.

"That's when the attack happened, right?" Sophia prompted. "You were the first to be taken, weren't you?"

"We think so, yeah." Farrah was still regarding Faith with a wary expression. "Me... and then Avery. But before the man... men... attacked me, I saw..."

Faith's heart sank. She had wondered how long it would be before she had to confess her involvement with Noah. Farrah had been in a perfect position to see Faith embrace him. A reaction Faith very much regretted. But she shook her head: she couldn't think of that now.

She'd very much been hoping Farrah had been too frightened to pay attention. She knew Avery hadn't noticed, or she would have heard about it long before now. But Farrah, who was quieter than her friend, a follower rather than a leader, had clearly been more aware of the situation than Faith had thought.

Time to face the music, then. Faith took a breath. "What did you see?"

"I saw one of the Eremus men approach you. But he seemed... different from the others. And... you didn't react to him the way the rest of us did." Farrah's forehead creased, as though she was trying to phrase her next words very carefully. "It... it almost looked like you... umm... hugged him."

The cave seemed to shrink. Suddenly, all eyes were on Faith; all ears were tuned to what she might say next. She found herself grateful it was Farrah who had this knowledge, and not Avery, who would have brought it up in a far more accusatory manner. But now the information was out, everything was going to change.

Shrugging off Sophia's supporting arm, Faith faced the others. "Okay. I have to tell you all something. And I need you to listen to what I have to say before you react." She glanced around at the seven pairs of eyes in the cave, their expressions ranging from sympathetic, to curious, to a blazing anger.

Taking a deep breath, she continued. "A few weeks ago, I sneaked out of Danforth in the middle of the night." She held a hand up for silence as several of the girls began to speak. "Hear me out. I went to the hospital to investigate the so-called health supplements some of the senior girls were going to be given. The ones which..." she glanced at Diane, whose downcast gaze was the only one not fixed on hers, "we believe were responsible for Serene's death."

There was a collective intake of breath. Encouraged by the reaction, Faith pressed on. "Yeah, I didn't want to believe it either. But what I found at the hospital confirmed that Serene's death wasn't anything to do with a *naturally occurring* sickness, but directly related to a drug she was given that day in the hospital, when they sent us home without–"

"What does your little night-time escapade have to do with our kidnapping?" Avery interrupted, staring down at her fingernails, which had been a vivid pink but were beginning to look chipped. "I mean... some of us *knew* you'd been sneaking out. That Anderson... that *Danforth* didn't trust you." She levelled her gaze at Faith. "That you're a troublemaker."

Faith shot Avery a scathing glance. "Yeah, you're right. Some people did know. And that's what got me locked up in what was essentially a *prison cell* in Danforth for the past week." She acknowledged the gasps of shock, noting with interest that Avery's face did not change. "But that's not what I'm trying to tell you about right now."

"Well, what on earth *are* you trying to tell us, then?"

Faith cleared her throat. "The night I went to the hospital, I wasn't the only one sneaking in. While I was there, I came across a... well, a boy. He was from Eremus."

Farrah leaned forward, her eyes wide. "You mean... the male... you *did* fling your arms around him... you actually *knew* him?"

"Did you help them *plan* this?" Avery stared at Faith, a strange combination of horror and delight on her face. "Did you tell them where we'd be?"

"No!" Faith felt her face flushing. "I just... met him. We talked. Diane and I had suspicions about what the school tells us about Eremus. We thought they were lying to us about it."

"And they were." Faith felt a small amount of relief flood through her as Diane backed her up. "They tell us Eremus has been eradicated." She gestured at the caves around them. "Clearly, that's not the case."

"But..." Avery pressed her advantage, "they turned up at the hospital... just when we were all being brought outside..."

"...like it was timed just right..." Catherine continued.

"...so they could take us when we were easy to get at!" Mary finished off, exchanging an alarmed glance with her friend.

"The perfect set up." Avery raised an eyebrow and swept her glance around the rest of the girls in the cave. "An inside job."

"It *wasn't* an inside job." Faith protested. "I had no idea he'd be there. I met him at the hospital and spoke to him for a while. That was it. He told me a bit about this place…" She faltered now, admitting her guilt. "If I was guilty of anything, it was trusting him. But I swear, I- I never thought he'd…"

"So either you're in cahoots with him, or you're incredibly gullible." Farrah rolled her eyes. "I'm not sure which is worse."

"Look," Sophia spoke for the first time, defending her friend, "Faith met Noah, and–"

"Noah!" Avery raised an eyebrow. "She even knows his name!"

Sophia glared at her with uncharacteristic bravery. "Yes, she knows his name."

"As do you, it seems." Avery glared at Sophia, but she didn't flinch.

"Of course." Sophia sounded measured and rational. "Faith asked his name when they spoke. And afterwards, she told me about him. Don't you tell Farrah *your* secrets?" Giving Avery no time to respond, Sophia turned back to the others. "The point I'm trying to make is that Faith went to the hospital that night to find information she thought we all deserved to know… so we could understand what Anderson's really up to. What Danforth has her doing to us. The lies we're told every day." She nodded. "And she did find things out. Important things."

"Like what?" Mary's eyes were wide.

"Like the fact that Eremus exists, even though Bellator tells its citizens they eradicated the settlement years ago," Sophia continued. "And that these men might not be the beasts we've been taught they are. You've already seen that there are women here, by choice."

"Did you know they mostly live in family units here?" Faith added.

"What? With mothers and fathers?" Farrah's eyes were wide.

"Siblings too," Faith continued. "They all kind of look after each other. And no one's here by force."

"The old way of life," Helen whispered. "Before the virus. Before women rose up. But isn't it... wasn't it an awful way to live?"

Faith shrugged. "That's what they tell us. But do any of us know that's the truth?"

The astounded expressions around her demonstrated the other girls would be hard to convince. Faith was glad when Diane broke in. "The point is, we're lied to. Every step of the way. About Eremus. About men. About the academy. We're told we're privileged to be at Danforth, that we're lucky enough to be among the first to trial groundbreaking new inventions and technology. In reality we're nothing more than the lab rats we studied in biology. We're expendable."

"But why?" Helen frowned. "What are these drugs supposed to do to us?"

Sophia shrugged. "We don't know. That's what Faith was trying to find out. Only they locked her up, so she couldn't investigate any further."

"They really locked you up?" Mary whispered.

Faith nodded. "Didn't you notice I was missing from class those last few days?"

"They told us you were sick," Catherine said. "You do kind of... look sick."

"That's because they gave me the same drug they gave Serene."

"So you're going to die?" Mary recoiled from her.

"I hope not," Faith muttered.

"Presumably, the drug has a purpose. An end goal, so to speak." Sophia explained. Again, Faith was grateful for her calm intervention. "And it isn't to kill us. Serene's death was a mistake. They have to have made... amendments to the formula—the chemical make-up of the drug, I mean—before they administered it to Faith. Perhaps she..." she cast a worried glance at her friend, "is suffering *less severe* side effects to it."

"Either way," Diane's voice was far less calm, "we protected you all from it."

All eyes spun to the older girl. Helen was the first to speak. "What do you mean?"

"I mean," Diane strode back to her usual spot at the rear of the cave before turning to face them, "that on Monday night, when we were marched to Bellator Hospital, they were about to give us all the same drug. If Faith and I hadn't intervened, if we hadn't pulled the fire alarm, then—"

"You pulled the fire alarm?" Avery was also on her feet, her eyes blazing. "That's the reason we were all outside at *exactly* the right moment the Eremus people wanted to kidnap us?" She laughed bitterly. "And you want us to believe you're not on their side!"

Diane shot a poisonous glance at her, opening her mouth to retaliate, but Avery continued.

"How can we believe a word you've said?" She turned to Faith. "Either of you! When we know that you—" she stopped abruptly.

Faith narrowed her eyes. "*What* do you know?"

Avery seemed to flounder for a moment. "Well...y-you..." She regained control. "You've admitted that you knew this boy... Noah... and that you were the ones who caused us to be outside that night at the exact moment... in the exact place the Eremus beasts were waiting to capture us!"

"It wasn't like—" Sophia began.

"We were saving you!" Diane's eyes flashed.

"How can we—" "What are they—" "Didn't you—"

The explosion of voices in the previously quiet space was alarming. Feeling dizzy again, Faith slumped back on her elbows and tried to focus on drawing in a couple of deep breaths. How had it come to this? At the moment, there were two people on her side, but the other five girls were now staring at her with various degrees of mistrust. Admitting the truth had made things far worse.

She still had no idea what their purpose here was, and the fact that they had clearly been brought to Eremus on a whim, with no plan in place, made her nervous. With no clear objective, what might the people here do with them? And if the Eremus people were wary, even frightened of them, what else might go wrong? She exchanged a glance with Sophia, who had also given up on trying to calm the others. Her friend shrugged.

There was nothing they could do for now. They had to let the others talk it through, calm down. They'd been faced with a lot of information in the last few minutes. Once they'd had a chance to process it, she would speak to them again, find ways to convince them she was telling the truth. But now, with Avery stirring them into a frenzy, was not the time.

Over the cacophony of voices which continued to rage, she heard a sound from outside in the tunnel. Someone was coming in. She raised a hand to warn the others, but aside from Sophia, they were too busy arguing to notice. For a second, she found herself hoping it was Noah, that perhaps he had been telling the truth the night of their arrival here, and that he might offer her some kind of protection.

She didn't know why she was still allowing herself to believe such fairytales. Most of the evidence pointed to Noah using her as a source of information, only to betray her to his Eremus family when the time was right. Part of her didn't blame him. So far, she could see what he had told her about Eremus was true. It had to be hard to live like this. Who could blame them for trying to gain a better life? Still, the betrayal stung.

When the wooden panel was lifted from the door, the girls fell silent. All eyes turned to the entrance, faces part-hopeful, part-petrified of what this new intrusion might bring. As light flooded into the space, a pair of male eyes Faith didn't recognise appeared.

There was a collective intake of breath and the girls recoiled from the intruder. Sighing, the man stepped into the space. All eyes went to the gun he held, in his hand, and not on his belt, as Ella's had been.

"Come on then." He jerked his head in the direction of the tunnel, where Faith could make out other figures, standing in the shadows. "Get up! We've places to be."

Trying to stop her legs from shaking, Faith pushed herself to her feet and followed their guards, wondering where they were being taken, and what awaited them when they got there.

CHAPTER FIVE: NOAH

Gulping down a bread roll and some cheese which presumably Ruth had left for him at some point while he slept, Noah hurried back to the family's cave. More rested now, he'd woken to realise he desperately needed a change of clothing, so he had no option but to return home.

Hoping that at least one of them was out on shift, he was disappointed to hear conversation floating from inside the cave as he approached. He paused to listen, cursing his poor timing. Both Flynn and his ma were home, but he could also hear Paulo's voice. Fighting the urge to turn and flee, he took a deep breath and prepared to slip inside, hoping they wouldn't pay him much attention.

"How long has he been gone now?" Anna was saying.

"Several hours."

Obviously, Paulo was aware of Jacob's absence. But he'd kept it from Flynn and Anna. A fact Noah found worrying.

"What time did he leave?" Flynn was demanding of his nephew. "And why didn't you let me know earlier?"

"I was trying to find him myself." Noah could almost *hear* Paulo's scowl. Things between him and his uncle hadn't been good ever since they'd rowed over him taking Noah on a raid without permission. The fact that he had come to ask Flynn for help suggested Paulo was really concerned. "And I'm not sure when he left. He didn't tell me he was going."

"Welcome to my world," Flynn growled.

It seemed odd to Noah that Jacob had told Sarah about his little excursion, but no one else. Even Paulo had only found out by accident.

"I figured, wherever he'd gone, he'd be back this morning." Noah heard Paulo begin to pace. "But it's way past noon, and I've looked everywhere, and he's–"

Giving up on waiting for a pause, Noah ducked inside. The conversation inside ceased immediately, and three pairs of eyes bored into him.

"Don't mind me," he waved a hand at them as he passed through, making sure he didn't meet anyone's gaze. "I'm just getting changed."

He moved into the space which served as his sleeping area, knowing he'd failed to escape notice when his ma followed him.

"Where have you been?" she demanded.

"On duty. You know that." He bent down to rummage in the trunk where his clothes were stored.

"Not since first thing this morning," she admonished. "I was worried."

He shrugged. "I slept at Ruth's."

"Really?" She glared at him. "Look, that might have been okay when Dawn was living there, but I'm not sure that you should be–"

"Ma!" Noah felt himself blushing. "It's not like that, okay?"

She fell silent for a moment, but he could feel her eyes boring into his back. Digging out a fairly clean t-shirt and a pair of jeans, he stood up and raised an eyebrow at her. "Some privacy, please?"

"I'll bring you some water," she relented, wagging a finger at him as she left the space. "But don't think I'm done with you, yet."

As he shrugged off his sweaty shirt, he tried to tune into the conversation which had resumed outside. He was glad, at least, that Paulo hadn't tried to speak to him again. Clearly his brother was more concerned with Jacob's disappearance. He wondered if that was what Paulo had been eager to tell him about this morning, then decided he didn't care. He was still furious with his brother, but any discussion of their argument would have to take place well out of his ma's earshot. There were things he'd rather she didn't find out. Not just yet, anyway. The thought of his ma learning how Paulo knew about the Danforth girls filled him with dread.

The words coming from the outer cave were drowned out for a few minutes as his ma filled a bowl of water for him. When she reappeared, Noah caught a glimpse of Flynn through the gap in the curtain. He was sitting in his usual chair, but his entire body seemed tense and his usually calm features were creased into a deep frown.

"Thanks." Noah took the wash bowl and cloth and waited for his ma to leave, before running the wet cloth over his chest. It made him shiver slightly, and he sped up the process.

"People are frightened," his ma was saying. He could hear her moving around the cave, no doubt gathering things for her shift. "And I'm inclined to feel the same way."

"If they hear that Jacob's disappeared, the situation isn't going to improve any." Flynn sighed loudly. "Those girls..."

"Those girls will be the thing that keeps us safe from a Bellator attack!" Paulo hissed, his voice low. "If we hadn't taken them... if we'd come back empty handed after the explosion, they'd have hunted us down by now."

"They *are* hunting us down, Paulo." There was a creaking sound, and Noah knew Flynn had eased himself out of the chair. "They're just taking their time over it, that's all. Don't think we can escape reprisals."

"It's all about how we deal with them." Paulo's voice was lower, more urgent. "We just have to make sure we use the girls to get the result we want." There was another sound, footsteps this time. Noah thought his brother had begun pacing again.

He hurried to finish washing and ran a towel over his body, knowing he had to get out of the cave, and soon. Seeing the concern in Flynn's face and hearing his ma voice her fears had further stoked his anger. Their community was in more danger now than it had ever been. Danforth's people were sweeping the woods. Faith and her friends were languishing in a cave in the depths of Eremus. Torn from their ordinary lives, hating their captors. And still, Paulo talked about them like they were a commodity to barter with, to resolve Eremus' problems with Bellator.

Before shrugging off his jeans, he reached into the pocket and carefully removed the necklace he carried with him wherever he went. Faith's necklace, which he intended to give back to her, if she ever spoke to him again. He'd been carrying it around ever since he'd picked it up in the hospital storage room. He still didn't know what had made him keep it.

Tossing the jeans on the bed, he dragged on the new pair and fastened them, wincing as the zip bit into his skin. He slipped the pendant back into his pocket, hoping he'd have the chance to return it.

"We'll have to hope Jacob returns soon." Flynn was saying. "I'll spread the word that he's gone into the woods on a scouting mission for now, let people think it was planned. That should keep them calm for the time being."

"Thanks." Paulo's tone was begrudging, and Noah knew it had cost him to ask his uncle for help.

"What we're going to do when he does get back is another matter." Noah cringed at his ma's sharp tone. She had stopped clattering about and he could imagine her fixing Paulo with a fierce stare. *"Everything's* changed now. Don't think we can go back to living the way we did."

"But who says we should?" Paulo burst out. "Who would want to? Hiding away out here, pretending we don't exist. I'm sick of it."

"You've been spending too much time around Jacob," his ma ground out. "Don't you understand? At least, before, we were *safe*. We didn't spend every day afraid for our lives."

"You've never lived the way we used to." This was Flynn, who sounded weary. "When Bellator attacks were regular and devastating."

"Jacob has," Paulo grumbled.

"He has." Flynn sighed. "And I've no idea why he'd want us to go back to that. To risk so many lives."

"Not just Eremus lives, either." Noah heard the pain in his ma's voice. A previous citizen of Bellator, she had more sympathy with its inhabitants than most. "Think about those poor girls we have locked up down there."

Noah pulled a shirt over his head, deciding it was time to go. Running a hand through his hair, he brushed aside the curtain which led into the main space.

His ma continued to berate Paulo, barely even glancing at him. "And what do we do when we need supplies from the city? I mean... you're telling me they're not going to be on high alert now? After we kidnapped eight of their citizens?"

Noah stopped dead. "You're certain Danforth will come after us?"

Flynn frowned. "We've given her a good reason to come after us. But I don't think she'll attack right away."

Noah turned to face him. Flynn had always been like a father to him, and he trusted him to tell the truth. "How do you know?"

"You were in the woods last night, right? You saw the way those guards acted. Danforth sent them in to spy, to get the lay of the land." He shrugged. "I hate to admit it, but Paulo's right. She won't just come barrelling in and risk killing her own citizens."

Noah shot his brother a look. Unsurprisingly, Paulo's face was smug. Noah fought the urge to smash a fist into his face.

"She's preparing for *something* though." Flynn frowned. "We won't escape her forever."

"Just how valuable are these girls?" Noah saw his ma's gaze return to Paulo's. "And how did you know about them?"

Noah froze. Paulo shot a quick glance at him, before turning back to Anna.

"Saw something written about the school on a report in Jacob's files once."

His ma considered this. "But how did you know these girls outside the hospital were from the school?"

"Their... the uniform." Noah was thankful for his brother's quick thinking. "It has their crest and the school name on it."

Noah watched his ma closely. Her eyes narrowed, but she seemed to accept the lie, for now at least.

"Okay. I guess that makes sense." As she leaned over to grab her work bag from the table, Noah found he could breathe again. "Guess I'd better go. Have to be at the medcave soon."

"Thought you didn't have any patients other than Ella at the moment." Flynn took her hand as she passed him. "Her arm's almost better now, right?"

She bent to drop a kiss on his forehead. "Yes. She should be able to lose the sling soon. But I'm sure she's been using the arm more than she's supposed to." She gave a small shrug. "I'm checking the Danforth girls over today."

"Didn't you do that already?" Noah blurted out. "You saw them the night they came in."

"Why are you so interested?" His ma turned to him, curiosity sharpening her features. "I did. But only briefly. Just enough to see they had no broken bones or serious wounds that needed immediate attention. It was pretty dark in their cave and Jacob didn't let me have much time with them. Poor things."

"We have to show we're treating them well." Flynn agreed. "It's our best hope of Danforth showing us any kind of mercy, should things—"

But his ma interrupted, the sharpness returning to her voice. "I don't think we need to dwell on that right now."

"Maybe you're right." Flynn let the point go for the time being, turning to Paulo and Noah. "We've just sent some folks down to accompany them to the baths. Let them get clean."

Noah's heart jolted at the idea that Faith might be wandering the tunnels of Eremus at this very moment, bathing in the underground pool, coming across who knew which other members of his community.

"Will they be safe?"

His ma's gaze landed on him once again. "What do you mean?"

"I-I- well, there are a lot of Eremus folk who aren't too keen on the Bellator citizens being down here. They might—"

"They'll be fine. Dane's with them. And Beth." Noah relaxed. Both citizens were good friends of theirs, and he knew they would protect the girls from any of the less welcoming citizens. "They're going to bring them to the medcave afterwards, one at a time, so I can look them over properly. See if they'll trust me enough to talk to me."

"I don't suppose they'll tell you much."

"We'll see." His ma sounded intrigued. "Again, I don't really understand why you're so interested."

"I'm not." But Noah could feel Paulo's eyes boring into him. He stood up and turned away, feeling his face growing hot.

"Hmmm." He knew his ma didn't buy his protest, but she let it go. "Well, I'll have to get going. Hope you manage to locate Jacob."

Flynn nodded. "You and me both."

"Good to see you, Paulo. Stop by again sometime, won't you?" She moved towards the door. "Maybe when you don't need rescuing."

Noah turned to see his brother scowling, but his ma had already gone. Left with Flynn and Paulo, Noah felt a little awkward. The older man peered at him as he eased himself out of the chair. "I'd better get to work too." He peered more closely at Noah. "You don't look good. You sleep okay?"

Noah shrugged. "Not really."

"It was a hell of a night out there." Flynn shook his head. "I kept imagining Bellator guards swarming in through every entrance."

"I know what you mean." Noah shuddered.

Flynn shot him a smile. "Try not to worry." He turned to his nephew as he made for the door. "I'll see if I can find our missing leader. Or at least start spreading the word, try to keep people calm 'til Jacob gets back. I'll stay in touch."

He turned to go. As the sound of Flynn's footsteps faded, Noah bent to pick up a sweatshirt and pulled it on. Realising he'd left his boots in the other room, he hurried to grab them. He returned to find Paulo still standing there.

"Did you need something?"

"I was hoping you'd had the chance to calm down since this morning."

Noah resisted the urge to fling one of the boots at his brother. Hard. Bending down, he began pulling them on, hoping he would get the message and leave.

"Look," Paulo took a step towards him, "I want you to understand. My decision to take the girls was... spur of the moment. I thought it would give Eremus more to bargain with... more power." He paused, then went on, his voice quieter. "I still do."

Gritting his teeth, Noah pulled his laces tight, imagining they were wrapped around Paulo's neck.

"These girls…" His brother came closer, placing a hand on his shoulder, "they give us something we've never had before. Can't you see that?"

Breathing heavily, Noah glared up at him. "No. I can't."

"Jacob agrees with me." Paulo's expression was mulish. "He thinks our captives could be very useful."

"Useful?" Noah heard his voice, dangerously quiet. "Useful? They're not objects, here to improve things for us. They're *people*. Innocent girls, who we ripped from their lives and brought back here, where they're alone, unprotected, and terrified."

"Ah, I see," Paulo's face changed. "So this isn't about the good of the Eremus citizens. It's more about the pretty little *girl* you're so stuck on."

"It's not!" Noah stood, knowing his denial had come too fast.

"Not very convincing, little brother." Paulo's tone was mocking now. "Ahh, did I ruin your chances with her?"

Furious, Noah pushed past him, his heart pounding. He managed two steps before Paulo grabbed hold of his arm. "Don't walk away from me."

Noah shook him off. He stepped out into the tunnel, vaguely aware there were other people around, passing by on their way to their shifts. He managed two more steps before Paulo had his arm in a vice-like grip.

"Noah, listen to me." He leaned close, his tone harsh. "Just because this girl has told you a few secrets, don't think you mean anything to her. This is bigger than you and her. It's bigger than all of us."

Noah struggled against his grasp. "Don't tell me how important this is. Don't you think I know? But it's not just about them and us. It can't be."

Laughing, Paulo loosened his hold. "You're so naïve. You really think this Faith girl would ever look at the likes of *you*? A stuck up Bellator brat like her? I bet she was laughing at you with those friends of hers." He gave Noah a nasty grin. "Not laughing now though, is she?"

Something inside Noah exploded. He leapt forward, his hands thrusting against his brother's chest. With the element of surprise on his side, he managed to push Paulo all the way to the wall on the other side of the tunnel. When his brother's back hit the rock, Noah heard his yelp through a fog of fury.

Drawing back his fist, he launched it at the face in front of him with everything he had. In the background, he heard gasps of surprise and knew there were witnesses to the altercation. Paulo straightened, Noah's fury mirrored in his eyes. Tensing, Noah braced himself, knowing his brother would retaliate.

When he did, the world went dark.

Chapter Six: Faith

As they followed their guards through the tunnels, Faith was glad she was not alone. Their abrupt eviction from the cave that morning had left her feeling unsettled. Despite hating their prison cell, at least she knew what to expect from it. Their armed escort to who-knew-where was alarming.

Whilst she was glad to get a better look around Eremus, Faith yearned to hide away again as their group passed numerous citizens going about their daily business. They stared openly at the girls, aliens in their midst, not even bothering to hide their curiosity. Some looked openly hostile. And there were so many of them.

Faith had never been more aware of the dirt which encrusted her skin, the sheen of sweat which seemed to permanently stain her face, the hair which hung limply around her shoulders. She'd never been too focused on her appearance back in Bellator, not like some of the girls, but not even being able to keep clean seemed a step too far. She found herself praying she wouldn't see Noah, although she wasn't sure why she cared. Looping her arm through Sophia's, she huddled closer, grateful for the answering squeeze.

The others seemed to find the journey just as distressing. Diane stalked along stiffly; Mary and Catherine huddled together in the middle of the line, keeping as much distance between themselves and the men as possible; in front of them, Helen's shoulders were shaking so much, Faith wondered if she was actually crying. Even Avery walked quietly, her head bent close to Farrah's.

Their three guards guided them through the maze of tunnels without a word. The older man who had brought them out of the cave led the line from the front, keeping up a rapid pace, while a similar-aged woman and a boy around Avery's age brought up the rear. Under usual circumstances, Faith would have enjoyed the vigorous exercise, but after two days in cramped surroundings with no place to stretch, her legs were complaining.

She wasn't the only one in trouble. Much to the annoyance of the man leading the group, several members of the group were struggling to keep up. Faith suspected it was as much due to their terror of the men flanking them as it was their stiff, sore muscles. To her horror, Mary had stumbled several times, to the open amusement of the young male guard at the back. She had turned white as a sheet and clung to Catherine for the rest of the journey.

Faith estimated they had walked for around ten minutes, when they arrived at a large opening in the side of the tunnel. The man at the head of the line stopped abruptly. Turning to them, he gestured through it. "In there."

The line of girls halted, and Faith shot a panicked glance at Sophia. Where were they being taken?

The man at the front was just opening his mouth to repeat the command, when a voice from inside the cave interrupted. "You can bring them through. There's no one in here but me." Frowning, the man jerked his head at them and disappeared through the gap. Reluctantly, the girls followed him.

On the other side was a cave far larger than any Faith had seen so far. Their footsteps echoed oddly, and the light played across the ceiling in a mesmerising kaleidoscope. As she walked further in, Faith dropped her gaze, realising the illumination was caused by the large pool of water which filled more than half the cave. It was almost still, but the slight swaying of the liquid caused glints and shadows to play across the ceiling in glorious patterns. Faith was transfixed.

The gentle clearing of a throat brought her attention back to the people inside the cave. Standing beside the water, a pile of material on the ground at her feet, was Ella. The sight of the friendly older girl was a welcome one, and, around her, Faith felt the group relax a little. As one, they moved closer to Ella, clearly preferring her company to that of their intimidating bodyguards.

"Hello again." She smiled widely before turning her attention to the guards. "Alright, you can leave now. It's not like you need to stay while they bathe."

Faith's eyes widened. Bathing? She was desperate to get clean, but the thought of stripping off here, in front of everyone, was shocking. She wrapped her arms around her body defensively, noticing most of the other Danforth girls had echoed her movement.

"We've orders to guard them at all times." The gruff voice came from the young man.

"What exactly do you think they're going to do, Harden?"

"This one keeps trying to escape." He jerked his head at Diane. Clearly, all the guards had been told to watch out for her.

The older man at the front spoke up. "Ella, you know Jacob'd have us if we let them go."

Ella rolled her eyes at him. "Alright Dane, if it makes you feel better, why don't you stand guard right outside the door?" He still didn't seem comforted, and Ella took a step towards him, shooing him away. "Come on, give them some space! There's only one entrance to this cave."

"S'pose so." The older man shrugged cheerfully. "Alright, then. Holler if you need us."

He nodded to the other two, and they turned to go. Harden was the last to leave, and he swept a frustrated gaze across the group of girls before he did. "Don't try anything."

"They won't." Ella trilled, waving her fingers at him in a mocking goodbye. When he was gone, she turned to them and rolled her eyes. "So overprotective."

"You mean..." Avery frowned, "he's worried about you?"

"Well, *worried* might be a bit strong." Ella grinned. "Harden doesn't like to be argued with. He's probably concerned about the damage to his reputation if you jumped me and made your escape on his watch." She stared at their confused faces. "Genuinely though, he's looking out for me. We do that here."

"But he–"

Ella shot her a quizzical look. "He what?"

"Why does he care? I mean... you're *female*."

"Bellator really does a number on you, doesn't it? I mean, your opinion of men is pretty low." Ella raised her eyebrows. "Look, Harden's a little arrogant, defensive, but he'd protect me if it became necessary."

No one responded, and Ella gave up trying to explain their cultural differences. Instead, she waved a hand at the water in front of them. "So, this is how we Eremus folk keep clean." Eight pairs of eyes stared at her in horror.

This time, Avery voiced what they were all thinking, her expression horrified. "You mean we have to...?"

"Well, you don't *have* to, of course, but..." Ella stifled a smile, shooting a pointed glance at their less-than-pristine appearance. "It's probably not what you're used to, but this is our female bathing pool. There's a kind of sluice gate which means we're able to change the water every few days. It's fairly clean. I'm sure you'd feel better for getting washed."

Faith took a step forward and bent down, trailing a hand through the water. "It's cold."

"Well, yes. It's naturally occurring. We don't have the means to heat it, I'm afraid," she gestured to the large sections of material on the ground at her feet, "but you can get clean, and then dry yourselves with these when you're done. Ruth's hunting out some spare clothes for you to wear, so we can wash yours." She ran her gaze over their academy uniforms. "Not that they're particularly... practical for living down here." She waved a hand at the water. "Hop in, whenever you're ready."

Beside Faith, Sophia's eyes widened. "But what if—"

Ella followed her gaze to the door. "Don't worry. The guards won't come back in unless I ask them to. Everyone else is at work right now. We won't be disturbed."

No one moved. Perhaps noting their discomfort, Ella dropped her gaze to the ground. "Maybe I'll just... pop outside and have a word with them." Nodding as though she felt this was the right thing to do, she turned and walked towards the exit. "I won't go far. Call if you need me."

When she was gone, Faith stared at the others. "Would feel good to get clean... at least a little."

"Hmmm." Sophia crouched next to her friend and dipped in a finger. "Not sure I'm liking the temperature, but maybe it would do us all some good. You especially."

Faith's dizziness had abated since the walk, but she was still warm, and thought the water might help to cool her temperature. With a final glance at the entrance, she stepped forward, stripping off her outer clothing. In only a bra and her underwear, she sat on the side of the pool, dangling her legs in the water below.

"What are you doing?" Avery cast her a disparaging glance. "*Anyone* could come in."

"Ella said she'd keep them out."

"She might be lying," Mary whispered, keeping one eye fixed on the exit.

"Well, I'm desperate to get clean." Faith shivered at the cool temperature. "I won't take everything off. And I'll be quick." Shooting a rueful glance at Sophia, she pushed off the side. "Here goes nothing!"

Seconds later, she was completely submerged, forcing her body to remain underwater until she had grown accustomed to the chilly temperature. When she came up for air, she was gasping for breath.

"Is it–?"

"Cold?" She tried to prevent her teeth from chattering as she replied. "Um... yes. But it feels kind of nice too."

When Ella returned, this time with Ruth in tow, they were all standing in the pool, attempting to wash the grime from their tired bodies. After seeing the enjoyment on the other girls' faces, even Avery had given in. Ruth dumped a large pile of faded clothing on the ground close to the door and then stood still, her eyes averted from the pool area. Faith tried not to stare at her. The idea that the girl who had been directly responsible for her kidnapping was now helping her was difficult to reconcile.

In contrast to the more taciturn Ruth, Ella approached with a smile, seeming encouraged that they were all in the water now.

"Here." She passed bars of soap to the girls closest to her, then tactfully moved away. "This will help, though you'll have to share. Try not to be so modest. You'll have to get over that here."

Faith wondered about the difference in their living conditions. The strangeness she felt at seeing even Sophia in her underwear, when the Eremus folk must feel completely comfortable being naked around one another. Back at Danforth they'd had a private bathroom since the age of fourteen. To imagine large numbers of Eremus women in here bathing all at once, was enough to send a flush through her entire body.

Shyly, the girls passed around the scratchy soap, revelling in feeling clean for the first time in several days. The first to finish, Faith waded to the side of the pool, enjoying the sensation of the water on her skin now that she was more used to its temperature. At the side, she reached for what passed as a towel and attempted to wrap it round herself as she clambered out.

From her position at the door, Ruth raised her eyebrows. "You'll regret keeping those on later."

Ella shot her a glare and she quickly straightened her face.

"She's right, though." Ella shrugged, turning to Faith. "You'll be damp for hours."

"Sorry." Ruth frowned, coming a few steps closer. "I guess this must be hard for you all. Clothes are here." She pointed at the pile of material behind her. "When you're dressed, I'll take you over to Anna. She's waiting for you."

Faith felt a sense of dread creep over her. She wasn't sure she wanted to be alone with Ruth. She was even less certain she wanted to be taken somewhere alone.

"Anna's our resident medic," Ella shot at Faith as she waved an impatient hand at the others. "Time to get out now." They began to clamber awkwardly from the pool. "She saw you all the night you came in, but wants to check you over a little more closely, now that things have settled down a little."

Faith vaguely remembered the night they'd arrived, a pair of green eyes bending over her, gentle fingers probing her wrist and checking her body for injuries. For a moment, her mind flashed back to the tech from the medical centre in Bellator and she remembered the sudden injection and the sickness which had followed. A shiver ran through her. Would she ever feel like she could trust a medic again?

Sorting through the garments Ruth had laid on the ground, she tried not to panic. She selected a pair of worn but comfortable trousers, a t-shirt with some kind of faded slogan, and a sweater which was at least two sizes too big. As she pulled them on, she turned to Sophia, who was attempting to towel herself dry. Her friend raised her eyebrows.

"Stylish!"

"Well, they're not exactly high fashion," Ella grinned at them broadly, "but they might help you blend in." She nodded to Ruth. "Want to take Faith up there, now? Anna asked to see them one by one."

"Will do." Ruth nodded and beckoned to Faith.

"I'll wait 'til the rest of them are dressed." Ella turned back to the others. "Make sure you've all eaten something."

Casting a reluctant glance back at Sophia, Faith followed Ruth out of the cave. Outside the door, her new chaperone stooped to collect something from a tray on the ground. Turning, she tossed Faith an apple, nodding with approval when she caught it. A little further along the tunnel, the guards were waiting for them. The younger male stepped forward.

"You need company, Ruth?"

"Harden..." Ruth shot him a despairing glance as she swiped another apple for herself and moved off down the tunnel, "...the day I need help from you to escort an unarmed Bellator female from one place to the next is the day I give up my raider badge."

Harden scowled, but he stepped back against the wall. Faith felt his eyes on her long after she had passed him by. Though she wasn't especially comfortable with Ruth as her guide, she was a step up from the hostile young man they were leaving behind.

Ruth walked quickly, leading her prisoner in a direction she wasn't familiar with. Even as she hurried to catch up, Faith marvelled at Eremus' size and complexity. Bellator had no idea how many people were living under the ground just a few miles from its border. The maze of tunnels was far more organised than it seemed initially, and enabled a large community to thrive. It was basic, but catered to their needs well enough.

Faith was certain it was what had allowed the community to escape Danforth's notice for so many years. Now that Bellator knew of its existence, things here would have to change. The eight Danforth girls were stuck right in the middle of a potential warzone. She wondered if they stood any chance of escape. Not that she was desperate to return to Bellator. But she was far from comfortable with the thought of living underground for the rest of her life.

Quashing the disturbing thought, Faith realised Ruth was several steps ahead of her. Sucking in a deep breath, she focused on moving one foot in front of the other, trying to pick up the pace. Her head had begun to ache now, and the dizziness had returned since she had left the soothing coolness of the water. And she hated to admit it, but the Eremus girls had been right. Her underwear was still damp, and had started to chafe uncomfortably against her skin as she walked.

Seeming to sense that she was struggling, Ruth turned. "Sorry." She stopped, waiting for Faith to catch up. "Are you alright?"

Faith managed a nod, but she knew it wasn't very convincing.

"Don't you remember me?" The words were blurted out. "From the hospital? I was the one who..." Ruth stared hard at Faith, "...well, I knocked you out. With the spray." As Faith met her gaze, Ruth flushed. "I'm sorry." She hurried on. "It all happened so fast."

Faith dropped her eyes to the ground. "For us too."

"Paulo ordered us to..." Ruth took a small step towards her. "I was scared, if that makes any kind of sense."

Faith shrugged. "I guess."

"Look, we always work in pairs. We *rely* on one another for protection." Ruth stopped for a second and when Faith glanced up at her, she looked flustered. "Look, when Noah didn't–"

"Noah?" It hit Faith like a train. Of course, this girl knew him. She'd probably known him all her life.

"Yeah. Noah." Ruth rolled her eyes and her voice hardened. "See, *he* was supposed to knock you out, but then, when he couldn't... *I* had to. He let me down." Faith stared at the other girl, and the look of anger in Ruth's eyes faded. "At the time, I was furious with him. I didn't get why he couldn't do it. But now I can see that he–"

Faith tried to focus on Ruth's words, but her head was pounding. Suddenly, the tunnel walls seemed to be contracting around them and she was finding it hard to breathe. She took a step back, but Ruth grabbed hold of her arm. "Look, I know you probably hate Noah right now, but you should know he's not–" She stopped abruptly, peering into Faith's face. "Are you alright?"

Faith shook her head. "I- I need to..."

"You're very pale." Ruth's face was now creased with concern. "Look, the medcave isn't far." She loosened her grip, offering her arm for support instead. "Just a little further along this tunnel. Let me help you."

Tentatively, Faith accepted the offer of help. They began to walk again, making slow but steady progress. Faith was glad Ruth had, for now, stopped trying to excuse Noah's behaviour. It wasn't something she was ready to hear.

"You probably just need some rest," Ruth was murmuring as they shuffled along. "I'm not good at the caring thing. Ella's much better. But Anna'll know what to do. She'll look after you."

They had reached a bend in the tunnel and navigated their way around it. On the other side was a dead end, with only a single opening in the side of the tunnel. As was the custom in most of Eremus, a thin curtain covered the doorway, allowing some privacy for the people inside.

"Here we are. Just a few more steps." At the door, Ruth used her free hand to sweep the curtain out of their way. "Hey, Anna! I brought the first of the Bellator girls," she called out. "I have to say, she's a little–" She stopped abruptly. "What are *you* doing here?"

Faith had been focusing on the ground underfoot, concerned she might trip over. In her present state, she didn't trust her legs to hold her up. At the abrupt pause, she glanced upwards, finding herself standing just inside a medium-sized cave. It was fitted with storage cupboards and tables which held various old-fashioned-looking medical instruments.

In the centre of the room, there were a couple of cots, presumably for Anna's patients. One was empty. But the one closest to the door was already in use. A tall woman stood in front of it, bending over a patient. As they had entered, she'd twisted round to greet them, revealing the person she was attending to.

Sitting on the edge of the cot, his face bruised and blood pouring from a nasty-looking cut near his eye, was Noah.

CHAPTER SEVEN: NOAH

I t was bad enough that his ma was having to tend to him. But to have Ruth, and Faith, of all people, witness his humiliation, was too much. Noah tried to stand, but a firm push from his ma sent him right back on to the cot.

"Stay still." She glared at him. "Or I'll make you lie on this cot for the rest of the day."

He gave up. Slumping his shoulders, he refused to meet his best friend's curious gaze. Ruth knew better than to come closer, with his ma so angry. But he could tell she wanted to. At least she was looking at him. Faith's eyes had hit the ground the moment he'd appeared.

He sighed. The situation couldn't get much worse. His ma was furious with him. From the moment he'd stumbled into the medcave with their neighbour Dan Clark, she'd said very little.

"What happened?" Shock had widened her eyes and she had gasped, rather than spoken.

The older man, who'd been the one to separate Noah from his brother, had grimaced. "A fight, would you believe."

Horror had haunted Anna's features as she'd pulled her son further into the cave, rushing him to a cot and thrusting him down. Hurrying to one of the cupboards at the side of the room, she'd thrown it open, and begun searching through it.

She hadn't spoken again until she stood in front of him, peering at his rapidly-swelling eye. "Was this Harden?" She hissed at him, leaning closer.

"No!"

His ma had turned to Dan, who was still hovering in the doorway. "Who did this?"

He'd shifted awkwardly. "Paulo."

Anna had spun back to face Noah. "Your *brother*'s responsible for this?"

"Saw the whole thing. Or heard it, I should say." Dan had taken a few steps towards Anna, laying a hand on her arm. "Don't jump to the immediate conclusion." He jerked his head at Noah. "Paulo was provoked."

His ma had turned back to him. "You *started* it?"

"I did." Noah had felt his face heating up.

For a moment, Anna had lost the ability to speak. She had busied herself pouring ointment onto a clean rag and pressing it non-too-gently against the wound on Noah's face. He had tried and failed not to wince.

"I'd better go." The voice from the door had startled Noah. He'd almost forgotten Dan was there. Their neighbour shot a worried glance at his ma. "You'll be alright now?"

She'd given Dan a tight nod. After that, he had beaten a hasty retreat. Noah couldn't blame him. His ma, when riled, was a fearsome creature. And nothing would make her more furious than her son instigating violence.

It wasn't like him at all. And he didn't think he'd be quick to do it again. He was far better with his head than his fists. But for a fraction of a second, when Paulo's face had reeled away from the shock of his punch, Noah had felt vindicated.

Now, he just felt stupid. When Dan had left, he'd closed his eyes and let his ma clean him up, waiting for her to lay into him. And then Ruth had come in with Faith.

His head ached from Paulo's punch and the cut on his eye was stinging like crazy. Not to mention his fist, which was sore and bruised from his own attack. He hadn't known how much a punch could hurt the person delivering it. Noah suspected he'd be sore for days to come. But for now, the embarrassment of the situation was worse than the physical pain.

Seeing that he wasn't going to move, his ma turned to Ruth, nodding at Faith. "Put her on the other cot, please."

Noah watched as his friend led a pale and shaky Faith around his cot to the one behind. Still, she refused to look at him. Once the pair were out of his eyeline, he looked back at his ma. At least the appearance of the two girls had delayed her tirade. It was the only bright side.

"I'm sorry," she directed, over his shoulder, "that I'm not able to deal with you immediately. I didn't have any patients this morning and was just preparing for your arrival when Noah here," she shot him a poisonous look, "was brought in."

"We can wait." Ruth's reply came swiftly, and he knew she was desperate to stay and discover what had happened to him.

Faith did not reply. There was a momentary silence as his ma continued to dress his wounds. Eventually, the eyes which had been focused on his face glanced at the second patient over his shoulder.

"What's your name?"

There was a short pause.

"Faith." Her voice was clear, but quiet.

"Nice to meet you, Faith." His ma frowned. "Ruth, get her to lie down." Noah could hear Ruth settling Faith into the other cot. "You don't look good. Are you feeling well today?"

"She said she was dizzy, and she's a little warm."

At Ruth's answer, Noah found his heart pounding a little. He fought the urge to turn around.

Was Faith ill?

"Ok. I'll take a look at her in a minute." His ma sped up her actions, ignoring his wince as she swiped the antiseptic cloth over his final wound with vigour. "Ruth, can you go back to Ella, please? Tell her to escort the others back to their cave when they're done bathing and eating. I was hoping to see them all fairly quickly, but I don't like the look of Faith, and what with the delay caused by Noah, I might need a little longer before the next girl is brought down."

"Alright." Ruth's voice rang with disappointment, and Noah knew she'd have preferred to stay. But she knew better than to argue. Rounding the cot again, she shot him a final curious glance. "Talk to you later."

Noah managed to nod. As Ruth's footsteps faded away, his ma turned her attention back to him. "Okay. You're done. I just need to–" she paused, her face draining of colour. "Noah, where's Paulo?"

He stared at her. "Paulo?"

"Yes, Paulo." She sighed, pulling off the gloves she had been wearing. "Where is he?"

Noah winced, inwardly this time. By the time Dan had got hold of him, managing to trap him on the far side of the tunnel, Paulo had been long gone.

"Dunno." Noah felt sheepish as he tried to explain. "He ran off."

"Does he need me, too?" Her face horrified, his ma took a step away. "I can't believe I didn't think of it 'til now."

"Maybe." Though Noah had definitely come off worse, he had to admit he hadn't given his brother's condition much thought. "I only hit him once, though."

"Dammit!" His ma turned and hurried from the room, her voice echoing down the tunnel after her. "Ruth! Ruth, hold on a second!"

For a moment, Noah stayed where he was. He still had his back to Faith, and had no idea how she'd react when he turned around. He opened his mouth to speak, then closed it again. The silence stretched between them, and he had no idea how to break it.

Eventually, he heard her shifting on the cot behind him. "What happened?" Her voice was a whisper.

"A fight."

A small pause.

"With Paulo?"

He nodded.

"Isn't he your... brother?"

"Something like that."

Taking a deep breath which hurt his chest, he stood up and turned to face her. As her eyes came to rest on his face, she gasped.

"Looks worse than it is." He tried to smile, and winced. "I probably shouldn't try that again any time soon. Not that I've got much to smile about right now." She turned her head away and he felt like a heel. "Though I don't suppose you have either."

He walked around his own cot and came towards her. Her face was paler than he remembered, and she was shivering. Anger still burned in her eyes, yet her comments suggested she was concerned about his injuries. A tiny ray of hope ignited inside him. Perhaps the fight might do him a favour. The pain would be worth it if it began to repair things between them.

"You're cold." Hurrying to a chest at the side of the cave, he yanked it open, pulling out a blanket. He returned to her side and lay it over her gently, being careful not to touch her. "You look funny in Eremus clothing."

"Thanks." She cracked a small smile. "It's pretty strange to be wearing someone else's things."

Taking a chance, he leaned in, tucking the blanket more closely around her. "Are you ill?"

She shrugged. "I don't know. I've felt strange since I got here, on and off. Sophia thought I had a temperature. The bath cooled me down a bit, I guess, but now I can't stop shaking."

Noah laid a hand on her forehead and felt her start at his touch. Immediately, she broke their eye contact, glancing down at the blanket, her cheeks colouring.

"You're a little warm," he said gruffly. He moved to the table and found a thermometer. Returning to her side, he waved it at her, but she looked up at him blankly. "Um... could you put this under your tongue?"

She frowned. "What's it for?"

"Taking your temperature."

She shook her head. "That's not how you take a temperature."

"It is here." He proffered the instrument again. "Trust me?"

She raised an eyebrow. "That's not gone so well for me in the past."

He felt himself flushing but refused to look away. "You're right, it hasn't."

"Show me." He looked at her, puzzled, and she nodded at the instrument in his hand. "How does it work?"

He lined the slender instrument up with her eyes. "You place this end under your tongue for a few minutes." He opened his mouth and stuck out his tongue, demonstrating. "The sensor here will register how warm you are and the result will show up," he pointed, "here, on the scale."

She peered at it. "It doesn't administer any drugs?"

"Drugs?" He almost laughed. "We don't have many drugs here. And those we do have–"

"The ones you steal from Bellator?"

He nodded. "...we save them for those who need them."

She thought about this. "And when they run out, you..."

"We raid Bellator at night, as you know." He dropped his gaze. "I know, it seems like stealing to you, but..."

"It doesn't." He glanced at her in surprise. "Well," she clarified, "I guess it does. But I understand why you do it. You don't really have much choice."

Smiling in relief, he waved the thermometer at her. "So, can I...?" Nodding slowly, she opened her mouth. As he slipped the thermometer underneath her tongue, he felt her warm breath tickle his hand. "Now, close your mouth." Once her lips had sealed around it, he let go, trying not to blush. "That comfortable?" She nodded. "It just takes a few minutes."

But she could only stare at him now. For a moment, he wasn't sure what to say, but then he realised this was the perfect time to talk to her about the night of the kidnapping. She'd had time to calm down, to see Eremus wasn't planning to murder them. And, for a few moments at least, she couldn't open her mouth to argue.

"Listen," not breaking her gaze, he pulled up a stool next to the cot, "There's something I want to say." She raised an eyebrow, and he flushed. "I know, I'm taking advantage, talking to you when you can't argue, but I'm going to take my chances."

She shifted slightly on the cot, propping herself up on one elbow. Taking this as a positive sign, he ploughed on. "Look, I have no idea when I'll get to speak to you alone again, so..." he swallowed hard, "here goes.

"When I met you, there was no agenda. You have to believe that. It was my first raid—the first time I'd *ever* been to Bellator. We met by *total* chance. Eremus raiders have been going to Bellator for years. Hardly any of them have come across the ordinary Bellator citizens. D'you understand?"

Faith nodded, her eyes wide. "We come at night because there's less chance of being seen. The fact that we met *again*... at the hospital... well, that was a very odd coincidence." He leaned closer, willing her to believe him. "But you *have* to know there was no plan... at least not on my part... to snatch the girls from your school and bring them back here."

Taking a chance, he reached under the blanket and took her hand, emboldened when she didn't pull away. "We were at the hospital that night for a different purpose, but when things didn't go to plan, well..." He took a deep breath. "It was a split-second decision. Last minute. The only mistake I made was *telling* Paulo about you. That's how he knew Danforth students were important, see? He gave the order to kidnap as many of you as possible. And... well, you know the rest."

Suddenly shy, he let go of her hand, reaching out to take hold of the end of the thermometer. It gave him something to do, at least. Faith opened her mouth, relinquishing the instrument. He stared down at the reading for several moments, feeling her eyes on him but refusing to look at her. Why hadn't she spoken?

When he finally looked up, she was still staring at him. "I can't believe you haven't started to argue with me." He waved the thermometer at her. "You're free to speak now." When she didn't, he showed her the reading. "Look here. You've a bit of a temperature, but only a low one. See?"

She bent forward to look at it, her hair falling across her face. It smelled fresh and clean. He cleared his throat, backing away slightly.

"It's that number, right?" She pointed, and he managed to nod. "And that's low?"

"It is. I don't think you have too much to worry about." He shrugged. "Hopefully you just need some rest."

She sagged back on to the pillow. "Could I have some water?"

"Of course."

He stood up and moved to clean the thermometer in a basin of water. Returning it to the table, he poured a cup of water from the pitcher. As he carried it over, he took in a deep breath before holding it out to her. She struggled to sit up, so he moved closer, placing an arm around her waist and easing her into a sitting position before handing over the cup. Conscious of their closeness, he fought to keep his body steady as she began to drink.

She seemed to share his embarrassment, gulping down the water quickly. Some of it spilled down her chin, and she wiped a hand across her mouth as she handed back the empty cup. Noah lowered her to the cot again, relieved of the chance to put some distance between them before she became aware of his racing heart. When she was settled, he moved away swiftly, replacing the cup next to the pitcher to give himself something to do.

"Can I ask you something?" Her voice was soft, hesitant.

"Sure."

"Did you fight with your brother because of *me*? Because he betrayed you by using what you told him about our meeting?"

He tried to shrug. "It's a little more complicated than that... but yes, that was part of it."

She looked thoughtful for a moment, but didn't question him any further. "You don't think my temperature's anything to worry about, then?"

He shook his head at her rapid change of subject. "Well, I'm not an expert," he grimaced, "that's my ma's job. But a temp like yours isn't usually cause for concern."

"It's just..." she paused, shooting a nervous glance at him, "...back at school, before the kidnapping, I mean, something happened. After the night we met at the hospital."

"They caught you coming back in?"

"Not exactly. But they found out I'd been out and they separated me from the rest of my class. Locked me up. And... while I was there, they injected me with some kind of drug..." She shuddered. "I had a really bad reaction to it." She shot a brief glance at him, and her eyes reminded him of the woodland creatures the Eremus hunters caught in their traps. "Thought I was going to *die* for a while, but... in the end, anyway... I didn't. But I wondered if the temperature and dizziness might be linked to that?

"I don't know." Instinctively, he reached for her hand again. Fighting to control the anger building inside him. The thought of Faith having unknown drugs injected into her system made his blood boil. "You think," he took a breath, "they gave the same drug to you that they gave to the girl who died?"

"Not exactly, no." She closed her eyes, as though trying to suppress the memory. "But a version of it, perhaps."

"You need to tell my ma." He nodded. "She'll know what to do."

As a comfortable silence fell between them, Noah reached inside his pocket. His hands closed around the chain of Faith's academy necklace. He brought it out and stared at it, lying on his open palm. He looked at Faith. Her eyes were still closed and she seemed peaceful.

Taking a deep breath, he closed his fist around it and leaned forward. "Faith?" Her eyes fluttered open. "I–"

"What are you doing over there?"

Thrusting his hand back in his pocket, Noah spun round. His ma was standing in the doorway, a frustrated look on her face.

"Faith wasn't feeling too good. I took her temperature. It was only a little low, so I don't think–"

"Thanks for your help." His ma's tone was harsh as she strode towards him. "I'll take it from here." She glared at him, shooting a pointed look at the doorway. "Flynn said he could use your help down in the tunnels."

"Alright." Shooting a small smile at Faith, he turned to go. At the door, he paused, wondering if he dared to ask the question. "Is Paulo...?"

His ma was already bending over Faith, examining her. She didn't bother to look at him again. "He's gone AWOL," she shot over her shoulder. "Mick and Denton were just coming off shift. I've asked them to go out looking for him. You'd better hope he doesn't have a serious injury." She turned and stared pointedly at him.

Noah considered making a joke about how a single punch from him was unlikely to have caused Paulo any serious damage, but seeing his ma's face, decided against it. Exchanging a final glance with Faith, Noah turned tail and headed down the tunnel, wondering how Paulo would react the next time their paths crossed.

CHAPTER EIGHT: FAITH

Once Noah's footsteps had receded, Anna turned to Faith with a strained smile. "Let's see if we can make you a little more comfortable."

Faith nodded to the blanket. "Noah did his best."

"My son has done a lot of things today." Anna tutted. "Not sure any of it could be described as his best." She took a seat on the stool Noah had vacated. "But enough of him. How are you feeling?"

It struck Faith, now she could see Anna close up, how similar the mother and son were. Anna was tall, like Noah, and had a slender, willowy frame. Their colouring, too, was similar, especially the piercing green of their eyes. Anna's were kind, but shrewd, and as the older woman regarded her, Faith felt as though she were being assessed in more ways than one.

"Okay, I guess." She began, but then opted for the truth. "Actually, I've been feeling a little hot and dizzy on and off since we arrived here."

"Hmm. Could be related to the sleep solution, though I was certain it wouldn't have long lasting effects."

Faith thought back to the mist being sprayed into her face. "You designed that?"

"Yes. I'm sorry." Anna lowered her gaze. "I never intended it being used in the way it was." She leaned closer. "Mind if I move this?" She motioned to the blanket. "Just for now? I'd like to get a better look at you."

Grateful to be asked for permission, Faith nodded. Anna slid the blanket down to Faith's waist and began her examination. Intelligent eyes roamed over Faith's body, searching for clues about her condition. Despite having little in the way of medical equipment, Anna seemed capable and experienced, her careful movements reminiscent of the more sympathetic medtechs Faith had come across in Bellator.

She remembered Noah talking about his mother when their paths had crossed in the hospital supply room. He'd stolen the medical textbooks for her, despite the additional trouble it had caused him, mentioning how much she'd appreciate the additional knowledge they'd provide. The love and respect he had for her was quite alien to Faith. And, despite Anna's current anger, it was clear she cared about him very much.

She thought of her own biological mother, Grace. She had only played a small part in Faith's childhood, her job in the city often taking her away from their community for long periods of time. That wasn't unusual in Bellator. Although the women within a single community did care for one another, the bonds between them were far wider and encompassed more people than the traditional family of the old times.

Faith had never felt abandoned when there were so many other women around to address her needs. But witnessing the intense personal connection between Noah and his mother made her wonder how it might feel to have a proper family unit. Two or three people who loved you without question. Who protected you above all else. Who you would feel guilty for letting down.

Sophia's mother had attempted to retain a closer link with her daughter and suffered for it. When Bellator had identified what they had deemed a *problematic* relationship, they had simply removed Thea from her district, ensuring that she had no further contact with her daughter. And whilst she didn't have memories of Thea, Sophia had suffered as a result of what Bellator termed her mother's *abnormal* connection with her baby. But who were they to say the relationship between parent and child was unnatural?

Anna took hold of Faith's wrist. Her hands, though gentle, were ice-cold, and Faith gasped at the sudden contact.

"Sorry." Letting go, Anna rubbed her hands together. "I guess my fingers are a little chilly. I'm always that way. Never did get used to the cooler temperatures down here." She picked up Faith's wrist again, pressing two fingers to its outer edge.

"What are you doing?"

"Taking your pulse." Anna shrugged. "You have machines in Bellator for that, but here I have to do things the old-fashioned way."

Faith nodded, curious to know how much Anna might confide in her. "You have medical experience, then?"

"Of a fashion, yes." Anna replaced Faith's wrist on the cot and pressed the back of a hand to her forehead. "Mm-hmm. Noah said your temp wasn't too high."

"He was right, then?"

"Yes. He's quite capable of taking a temperature." Anna scowled. "I know it doesn't seem like it today, but my son is usually a very able young man." She closed her eyes for a moment. "In fact, I'm not sure what's gotten into him."

Faith took a deep breath. "And the man you called Paulo?" Anna's eyes snapped open. "Sorry. You seemed... I mean you're worried he might be injured?"

Anna sighed. "A little. But his disappearance isn't out of character. I suspect he'll turn up soon. And Noah would definitely come off worse in a fight between the two of them." She shot Faith a wry smile. "He's not really built for combat."

Remembering Noah's cryptic response to her question about the relationship between the two young men, Faith attempted to clarify. "Paulo's your older son?"

Ann shook her head. "He's not mine... biologically speaking, at least. He's my partner's nephew." Catching Faith's confused expression, she clarified. "His father was killed in a Bellator raid before I met Flynn. He's cared for him ever since."

"And you treat him like your own?"

"I try to." Anna smiled. "He doesn't always make it easy."

She moved the blanket down to Faith's waist. "Could you pull up your t-shirt?" She unhooked a snakelike instrument from around her neck. "I'd like to listen to your heart." Noting Faith's glance at the door, she patted her arm gently. "I hear everyone coming. It's why I chose this location for the medical area. Don't worry – I won't let anyone in while you're exposed."

Cautiously, Faith tugged the shirt upwards, shivering slightly as she was bared to only her bra. Anna leaned down and placed the circular piece of metal at the end of the tubing on Faith's upper chest.

"This is called a stethoscope. It helps me to– Oh!" Her fingers had brushed the strap of the undergarment Faith wore. "You're wet!"

"I know." Faith blushed. "Ella *said* we shouldn't bathe in our underwear, but..."

Anna nodded, understanding. "You're not used to stripping off in front of others. I remember–" She stopped herself. "Let me have a listen to your chest, then I'll find you something else to wear. You really will catch a chill if you wander around down here in damp clothing."

She returned to her task, listening intently to the stethoscope. Frowning, she moved it into several different places on Faith's chest. "It's quite fast. Can you sit up for me?" Faith heaved herself into a seated position, and Anna repeated the process with her back.

Eventually, Anna guided her back down to the cot and covered her with the blanket once more. Retreating for a second, she poured another cup of water and shook out a sachet of powder into it. A moment later, she brought it back. holding it out. Faith recoiled from the offer.

"I see." Without argument, Anna returned to the table, collecting the packet she had just emptied into the water. Returning, she thrust it at Faith. "It's just a vitamin boost. You have these in Bellator. In fact, that's where we get them from."

Faith recognised the sachet's distinctive yellow label. It was one of the branded vitamin supplements she'd seen many times back home. These were commonly used in the general population, and not the tiny purple pills the academy students had been taking more recently, which Faith no longer trusted.

"You need some energy," Anna confided. "And this is the best I can do for you, for now."

Again, she offered the cup. This time, Faith took it.

"I'm sorry," she apologized, when she had drained the cup. She sensed she could trust Anna, who, Noah had let slip, had been a fellow Bellator citizen at one point. If anyone understood, she did. "I just don't have much faith in mysterious medical treatments."

Anna accepted this, though her eyes glowed with curiosity. Taking a different tack, she asked, "Were you sick before you left the city? I mean, before we... took you? Was that why you were at the hospital that night?"

Faith wondered how much to tell her. Anna was a skilled medic, that much was clear. She'd come from Bellator, so her training would have been first-rate, even if she hadn't completed it. Chances were, she knew something of Danforth, of its purpose, its students. And Noah had told her to confide in his mother. But she'd trusted Noah before, and it had led to her current situation.

Having said that, something about his explanation had rung true. She could easily imagine it: the kidnapping being spur of the moment, Paulo making the abrupt decision, his knowledge of the Danforth girls coming from his brother. Faith found that, despite everything, she didn't want to land Noah in any more trouble. She'd have to confide what had happened to her without mentioning Noah's part in it.

Taking a deep breath, she began, making sure she considered each sentence carefully before it left her mouth. "I wasn't sick when I left the city. But I had been given a strong course of drugs a few days before we were taken from the hospital."

"Had you been ill?" Anna frowned. "Were you being treated for something?"

Faith shook her head. "Students at Danforth regularly test and trial new inventions... new technologies. It's an exciting part of our education. Being selected for the academy is a privilege. We're chosen because we're special..." She trailed off. "At least that's what they tell us."

Anna leaned closer. "You don't believe them?"

"Not anymore." Faith waited for Anna's reaction, but the older woman simply waited for her to continue. Figuring she couldn't get into any more trouble by confiding her story to Anna, Faith went on. "A few months ago, we were asked to start taking a new vitamin pill, to improve our focus and concentration in class... that kind of thing. Anderson seemed excited about the effect it was having on us all."

"Anderson?" Anna queried.

"Our principal." Faith explained. "Then, a couple of weeks ago, a small group of us were taken to the medcentre to be given another kind of health supplement. I don't know what, exactly... except they claimed it was good for us. One of the older seniors was the first to receive it, and..."

Anna frowned. "It made her sick?"

Faith nodded. "She had some kind of reaction, I guess. At least that's what we *think* happened. They whisked us away... wouldn't let any of us see her. And then, a couple of days later, they announced that she had died."

She glanced at Anna, whose face had darkened. "They told us she'd been ill to begin with, but... we didn't believe them. I sneaked out of school one night... headed for the hospital, to try and find out more. I found a medical storage room and searched the records on their digital system for Serene—that's the girl who died. I discovered that she'd been given a drug, not a vitamin supplement. And, according to the system, it hadn't been properly approved."

Anna's eyes widened, but she still didn't speak. Faith shifted slightly, easing herself upright. The story was an important one, and she wanted to tell it accurately. She glanced at the doorway, finding herself praying no one else arrived before she'd had the chance to finish. Unburdening herself, and to an adult who might be able to offer a more mature perspective, felt amazing.

"Anyway, I was caught... or someone saw me leaving and told the principal I'd been out. They took my wristclip from me. I'd snapped pictures of the incriminating information, so..." she shrugged helplessly, "well, I guess they didn't want people knowing. They locked me up that night, away from the rest of the students." She suppressed a shudder at the memory. "Eventually, they brought in a medtech who gave me the first dose of some kind of drug. I don't know what it was, but I suspect it was an altered version of what they'd given Serene."

"And you had a similar reaction?"

"I think so, yes." Faith shuddered. "I thought I was going to die for a while."

"I'm so sorry." Anna laid a hand over Faith's.

She looked away, finding tears pricking at her eyes. "Anyway, I lived, and recovered... mostly, at least. They were going to dose a larger group with it the night of the kidnapping."

"That's why you were there..." Anna stared at Faith, her keen eyes working through the chain of events. "In the middle of the night."

Faith shrugged. "I'm guessing they didn't want the general public knowing if something went wrong."

"I'll bet they didn't." Anna frowned. "So, was the drug given to the entire group?"

"No." Faith shook her head. "I managed to tell another girl. One I trust... she pulled the fire alarm. Got them to evacuate. That's why we were all outside when..."

"When Eremus arrived and took you all away." Anna nodded thoughtfully. Pushing back her stool, she strode to the rear of the cave. "I'll find you those dry clothes now." She grabbed a lantern and disappeared without another word into the darkness of what Faith presumed was a second cave.

Faith lay there, wondering if she'd done the right thing. Anna's abrupt departure seemed odd, like she was upset about something. But Faith didn't know what. Rotating her head from one side to the other, she realised she felt a little better. Perhaps the vitamin powder was working. She hoped so.

A moment later, Anna appeared from the other cave, proffering a handful of clothing. "Here." She motioned to a screen at one side of the cave. "You can change in there. They might not be quite the right size, but at least you won't risk making yourself ill." She helped Faith to her feet. "Can you manage?"

Faith tested her weight. "I think I'm okay."

"Alright." Anna nodded to the screen. "Change quickly now. We need to keep you warm."

Behind the screen, Faith removed her clothing as rapidly as possible and shrugged on the new, dry garments. They were similar to those Ella had given her, aside from the fact there was some new underwear which, although a little on the baggy side, felt blissfully dry next to her skin.

"I think," Faith could hear Anna clearing up on the other side of the screen, "you had a severe reaction to whatever they gave you, but you've recovered since. Or your body has adjusted to the new drug. The symptoms you have now... the dizziness, slight temperature, elevated heartrate, might be linked to it, especially if it's still in your system. I'd like to keep a close eye on you. Make sure you don't get any worse."

"Um, okay." Faith pulled the sweater she'd been given over her head. "Thank you."

"Can I ask you something else?" Anna's tone had changed, and for the first time since she'd been in the other woman's presence, Faith felt nervous.

"Ah, sure," she managed, as she pulled her shoes back on.

"The hospital you broke into... it was the same one you were taken for the midnight treatment, right?"

Faith hesitated for a millisecond. "Yes."

She could hear Anna's intake of breath even through the screen. "When was this?" Faith went still. Anna wasn't stupid. And Faith didn't want to give Noah away. But she didn't see how she could refuse to tell the medic, considering what she had already confided. "Don't you remember?"

"I do. Let me see, it was... a couple of weeks ago now. Maybe..."

"Was it a Monday night?" Anna's voice was distinctly cool now.

Faith didn't see any point in denying it. "Yes."

The silence that followed was lengthy. Faith didn't know how to break it, but it didn't seem like Anna was prepared to. Eventually, she crept around the screen and back into the main area of the cave. Anna was standing at one of the cupboards, her back to Faith.

"Thanks for these." Faith took a tentative step towards her. "I'm—"

"You'd already met Noah. Before he brought you here." Anna turned slowly to face her. Faith knew it wasn't a question. "In the hospital, that night. He was trapped for a while... in a medical storage room. You were there too."

Her eyes downcast, Faith nodded.

Anna regarded her closely. "Well, this changes things. And perhaps... clears up a few mysteries as well."

"I'm sorry I didn't–" Faith began, but Anna held up her hand. She stopped, wondering why.

And then, from the tunnel, a set of footsteps approached. Faith didn't know how Anna had heard them, but there they were. Both heads swung towards the doorway as the curtain was pulled back and a face peered in.

"Flynn!" Anna sounded startled. "What are you–?"

"Are you done here?" The older man beckoned to Anna. "Checking the rest of the girls over will have to wait."

"But I've only just started." Anna shot him a stubborn look. "Why?"

"Jacob's back."

Chapter Nine: Noah

As he entered the canteen cave, Noah could feel the tension in the room, though the podium at the front was currently empty. He scanned the crowd, nodding as he passed Jan and Dane, who stood talking with other more senior members of the community. Close by, his ma sat at a table with Flynn, deep in discussion. There was no sign of Paulo.

Spotting Ruth and Ella, he headed over to join them. The two sisters had grown much closer since the death of their mother a few weeks before. Killed in an attack by the Bellator guards, Dawn's death served as a reminder of how precarious life could be here in Eremus. Noah couldn't remember a time when his home had felt more vulnerable.

"Alright, Madden?" A voice to his right startled him and he turned to see Harden and Sil staring at him. Noah braced himself for a jibe, but there was no animosity in his gaze. Instead, the pair stared at Noah with open curiosity.

"What happened?" Sil asked.

Noah's hand went to his face, and he remembered his injury. He flushed. "I fell." Hearing the lack of conviction in his own voice, he added detail to the lie, trying to seem more convincing. "Last night, on guard duty. Smashed my face up."

"Really?" Harden raised an eyebrow. "'Cos I heard you finally stood up for yourself."

Deciding it wasn't a bad thing for Harden to believe he was tougher than he actually was, Noah opted to shrug. "You got me."

Harden laughed. "I'm waiting for you to tell me I should have seen the state of the other guy... but I already did." Beside him, Sil sniggered. Harden leaned closer, a little of the old bully resurfacing. "You look a lot worse than your brother."

Noah turned to leave, but found Harden blocking his way. He braced himself for the taunt, but Harden's words surprised him. "Even I'd think twice before taking Paulo on. He's–"

"Harden!"

Harden's expression clouded over. Noah turned to see Sarah Porter hurrying towards them. A formidable member of the Eremus council, Harden's ma was not a person to be ignored.

"Harden." Sarah reached her son's side. "What are you doing *here*?" Grasping his arm, she hurried him forward. "Council members stand up front."

Surprised to find himself pitying Harden, Noah continued towards Ella and Ruth. As he approached, they were deep in a heated debate he suspected was about him. His fears were confirmed when their conversation halted abruptly as he joined them.

"Woah! You wander down a dark alley by yourself, Noah?" Ella gestured to his wounds.

He dropped his gaze, wondering how many times he would have to deal with the same question. "Something like that."

"I told you. He and Paulo had a disagreement," Ruth said, leaning closer so she wasn't overheard. "But I've yet to hear the details."

"*Really? Paulo* did this? That's not like him." At Noah's nod of confirmation, she glanced around the room, her eyes searching for Noah's brother. She wouldn't find him. Paulo had been the first person Noah had looked for as he'd come in.

"Let's just say he was provoked."

"You mean *you* started it?" Ruth whirled to face him.

"Not my finest moment. I was..." he gritted his teeth, "...angry with him."

"Why?" Ella's eyes bored into him.

"Doesn't matter now. I was being stupid. Forget it." He glanced around the room, spotting his ma. She, too, was staring at him. And she didn't look happy. Desperate for a change of subject, he turned back to Ella. "Your arm all better now?"

"Pretty much." She glanced down at her arm guiltily. "The sling was driving me mad, so I took it off. Your ma won't be happy."

"Too right." Noah grinned. "Ruth tells me you've been taking food to the girls."

"Among other things."

"How are they?" Noah kept his tone even, trying to seem indifferent. "I mean... are they being taken care of?"

Ella's face darkened. "We're feeding them, if that's what you mean. But they're frightened. We haven't exactly given them a reason to trust us yet." She gestured at the podium. "If this meeting ever gets started, I'm going to bring it up today."

"Good for you."

"Well, I'm not the only one who feels like we haven't been treating them well, but there are others who..." she hesitated, glancing across at a group of Eremus citizens who stood to their left, "let's just say not everyone feels the same. I heard—"

The room fell silent and she stopped talking. Noah felt his heart jolt as he spotted Jacob striding towards the podium, Paulo right behind him. Wincing inwardly at the prominent bruise on Paulo's cheek, Noah was glad his brother looked otherwise unhurt.

As Jacob stepped onto the podium, all eyes were fixed on him. He stared at the crowd with his usual confidence, yet Noah thought he looked tired. Waiting until Paulo had joined him, he began to speak.

"Good afternoon." He smiled, but the sentiment didn't quite reach his eyes. "No one can deny the last couple of days have been a challenge. I know many of you are feeling... unsettled."

There was a general murmur of agreement. He waited until it subsided before continuing.

"Here's what we know. Two days ago, our attack on Bellator did not go as planned. The aim was to destroy the city's fertility unit. And we had managed to set up a good number of explosives, before the situation... altered." He shot a sideways glance at Paulo. "We were interrupted, and it became necessary to take alternative action."

Jacob had clearly decided to back Paulo's spur of the moment decision. He was presenting the situation as though the kidnapping had been just as much his choice as Paulo's.

"We did not *intend* to take hostages." Jacob swept an earnest gaze over the crowd. "However, we now find ourselves with several Bellator citizens here in our community.

"Obviously, our actions have not gone unnoticed. Last night, Danforth sent guards out into the woods looking for us. And now that they know we exist in fairly large numbers, they're unlikely to give up the search. For now, they appear to be searching cautiously, coming at night under cover of darkness. We can only presume this more... careful approach... stems from the fact they don't want any harm to come to their citizens."

"We must now attempt to protect our community at all costs, but use our knowledge of Bellator's vulnerability, and the hostages, to our advantage." Beside him, Noah felt both girls stiffen at his callous mention of the Danforth girls, but it was his ma who stepped forward to speak.

"Jacob, you can't simply dismiss these girls as bargaining chips." Anna's tone was horrified. "They're people, just like us. And no doubt terrified. We must ensure that we–"

"Of course, you'd defend them." Sarah Porter's words were loaded.

"And why shouldn't I?" Noah was proud of his ma for standing up for the girls. "They're frightened. Unused to living underground." She turned to Jacob. "Did you know they didn't even have a light down there until Ella took them one this morning?"

"Really?" Jan looked at Jacob, appalled.

Their leader flushed slightly. "I agree things could have been better organised. But we weren't expecting them. We'll improve as we go."

Ella raised her hand and Jacob nodded to her. "I'd like to propose a few things we could do to make them more comfortable."

"But why should we?" Sarah's tone was hard. "It's not like they've ever given much thought to the way we live, is it?"

To Noah's horror, there were murmurs of agreement from some among the crowd. Beside him, Ella drew herself up to her full height and continued.

"I'm not saying we throw them a banquet. But they don't even have the most basic facilities down there. Could we consider taking in some mattresses? Perhaps moving them into a larger cave? They don't even have any proper bathroom access."

From the front, Anna turned to Jacob. "Ella's right. They deserve better treatment."

"Like *we'd* get decent treatment if we walked into Bellator right now." Sarah snorted with derision, her comments stirring up the more negative side of the crowd even further. "Jacob," she turned to their leader, "these girls should be made to see how the other half lives. I don't think we should be wasting supplies on them. We all know how hard won our resources are."

Jacob nodded at her. "I take your point, Sarah."

"These girls aren't just ordinary citizens." Anna spoke again. "I've only managed to check one of them properly so far, but I'm concerned she might be suffering from a condition caused by some drugs she was given back in Bellator. It looks like the Danforth students were being experimented on."

"And the girl told you this, I presume? How can we believe her?" Sarah threw her hands up, glancing at the citizens surrounding her. "They're desperate. They'll say anything to gain our sympathy."

Paulo stepped up to the podium. "Anna's right though. They are valuable to Bellator. It's the very reason they were taken."

"How do you know that?" Beside his ma, Harden was cringing. For the second time in as many minutes, Noah found himself having sympathy for his old enemy. "How can you be sure it's not lies?"

"Because we knew who they were before we took them." Paulo's voice had grown in volume. "I assure you, Sarah, Danforth will not want them damaged."

"All the more reason to care for the girls' well-being." Anna resumed her previous argument.

"Does that mean we have to coddle them?" Sarah threw her hands to the sky. "They're a tool to us... that's all. A means to Eremus getting what it wants. Surely, all we have to do is keep them alive."

Without knowing he was doing it, Noah thrust his hand into the air.

"Yes, Noah?" Jacob looked curious. Noah wasn't one to speak in public.

Every eye in the room turned to him and he felt his cheeks colouring. "Look, if your aim is to *use* the girls to somehow..." his mind recoiled at the verb, but he pushed on, "...*reason* with

Danforth's government... then Ma's right. We *should* be treating them well." Ignoring the mutters that his words caused, he ploughed on. "What use will they be if we ill-treat them, or they become sick or..." he shuddered, "die even?"

"You seem very keen to protect these girls, Noah," Jacob said.

"You got a crush on one of 'em, lad?" Dane teased.

"No! I- I only mean... we need them." Noah dropped his gaze, the fight going out of him. "For... for Jacob's plan to work."

For a moment, the room was quiet. Then, slowly, Jacob smiled. "I suppose you have a point. It might be wise to make sure the girls know we won't allow them to come to any harm. And you," he eyed Noah slyly, "might be just the right person for the job. After all, you know them best."

Beside him, he heard Ruth's gasp. Once again, he felt the focus of the room shift to him.

"What do you mean?" Jan asked.

"Noah knows them best?" Sarah's beady eyes were now boring into him. "How does he know them at all?"

Paulo stood forward. "He came across one of the Danforth girls on a previous raid. He spoke to her, gained her trust. She gave him some very useful information, which he confided in me, and... well, you know the rest."

Noah hated the respect with which many of the citizens surrounding him were gazing at him. Paulo had made it sound like his aim in meeting Faith had been to take advantage of her. Harden and Sil were smirking openly. Even people he respected, like Jan and Dane, were nodding.

He stared at the ground as Jacob began to speak again. "Perhaps we can look at moving the girls to a different location. One which allows them closer," he shot a look at Anna, *"supervised,* access to a bathroom. And let's take them some additional supplies. It's no good them returning to Bellator talking of our abusive treatment."

At his words, there were reluctant nods from most citizens around the room. Even Sarah seemed to have given up arguing for now. She still eyed Noah sharply, though, and he knew she was unlikely to let this go.

"There is more interesting news from Bellator, though," Jacob said, and Noah was relieved when all the citizens turned back to him. "I'm sure you're all wondering where I disappeared to last night. I went through the tunnels to Bellator, hoping to speak to Madeleine. For those of you who don't know, she's an Eremus sympathiser who's helped us gain access to Bellator supplies for many years. She's also part of the resistance... a group of women in the city who don't, shall we say... see eye-to-eye with Danforth.

"Anyway, when I reached her home, I was unable to gain access. As many of you know, our raids are carefully planned." He gestured to his council members, most of whom nodded in agreement. "We usually get messages to Madeleine prior to entering the city. Last night, I hadn't told her I was coming. We have a system which she can use to warn us to take care when approaching her home. She'd used it last night. I was extremely concerned when I couldn't immediately speak to her, so I waited. Kept checking the tunnel to see if things had changed."

The crowd was silent now, hanging on his every word. It struck Noah how much power the older man had. As the creator of the Eremus cave system, he was widely respected by the community. If he decided the Danforth girls were to be used as pawns, it would be difficult to persuade people he was wrong. Thinking of Faith, potentially sick, lying in a dimly lit cave in the bowels of their community, he shivered.

"Did you manage to speak to her in the end?" Dane asked.

"I did. But I hung around for a full two hours before she was able to let me in," Jacob continued. "When I did get hold of her, she told me the city's under a temporary lockdown. Heavy patrols have been sweeping the streets, questioning citizens about the events of the night of the explosion. It seems Danforth knows she has more enemies than us. Madeleine believes she suspects there is rebellion within her own city. That's why she's had her guards questioning everyone. Especially those with links to the hospital."

"So she didn't immediately blame us?" Flynn asked.

"It seems not."

"Are Madeleine and the resistance under suspicion, then?" Flynn said.

"Perhaps." Jacob turned to his number two. "Madeleine's not too worried. Since the resistance had nothing to do with the explosion, Danforth can't find any evidence leading back to them, no matter how many questions she asks."

"Sounds like she's trying to frighten her own people," Cora said.

"It wouldn't be the first time." The voice came from the back of the crowd.

As people turned to look, Jan stepped forward. A council member, she was older and very much respected in the community. Noah remembered Sarah's insistence on standing up front to prove their association with the council. Jan didn't need any of that. People listened to her, no matter where she stood.

As she continued, every head in the room turned towards her. "It's typical of anyone who controls by fear. If Danforth's people are frightened, she can swoop in and rescue them. She'll wait a while, then she'll make a very public gesture: claim that the city is safe again, that she's gotten rid of the threat, that the lockdown was necessary. In the end, she'll make it look like she was the hero."

"Really?" Ruth exclaimed from her position next to Noah.

"Really." Jan nodded. "She's a very convincing speaker."

"It's the reason she's stayed in power for so long. I'm sure Jan's right." Jacob added, rubbing a hand across his chin thoughtfully. "Another point of interest, though. Danforth doesn't appear to have released the information about the Danforth girls' kidnapping to the public."

"How is she able to keep it a secret?" Sarah sounded surprised. "And why?"

"She controls most of the city's media," Flynn pointed out. "And her guards are very loyal, on the whole. It was probably easy to bury the students' disappearance in all the confusion and panic about the explosion."

"Flynn's right." Jacob agreed. "She has a huge problem dealing with the aftermath of the explosion as it is. The Bellator citizens will be concerned enough about the destruction of the fertility unit and any damage to the hospital. Danforth will want to carefully manage any reference to the city's defences being vulnerable."

"You think she'll try and keep the girls' disappearance under wraps for good?" Dan, Noah's neighbour, questioned. "Won't she try and stage some kind of rescue?"

Jacob shrugged. "I think she might. If the girls are as important to her as we think they are. Whether or not she tells the rest of Bellator about it is a different matter."

"She might tell them afterwards, once she has the girls back in the city." Anna's voice rang with sarcasm. "That way, she can play the hero yet again."

"Is there a chance these girls aren't as important as we believe them to be?" Mick, another more experienced member of the raiding team, said. "I mean... what if Danforth just writes them off... abandons them as a lost cause?"

Noah's heart pounded as he waited for Jacob's response. What would he do to the girls if they proved to be useless?

"I don't think that's the case." Jacob held up a hand as several citizens began to argue. "As I said, we have it from one of the girls' *themselves* that these tests they're undergoing make them of great value to the city."

"Let's hope she was telling the truth," Cora grumbled.

At the front, Jacob leaned forward slightly, as though he was about to confide the biggest secret of all. "There's more, though." He waited until all eyes were on him before continuing. "Just before I left, Madeleine told me the fertility unit we bombed was almost entirely destroyed."

"But we only managed to get half of the explosives in place," Mick, who'd been on Jacob's team during the raid, looked puzzled.

"True, but we destroyed their generator. Even in the section of the unit which was undamaged, the power to the freezers which stored the seed samples went out." He paused, dramatically. "And it wasn't restored for several hours."

Anna's eyes widened. "Wow. You mean they don't have any seed at all?"

Jacob shrugged. "We don't think so. And if the citizens find out, there'll be widespread panic. Danforth will have to cover it up, and fast."

He let his words hang in the air for a moment. No one seemed to know how to react. Eventually, Jacob gave a hint of his former smile.

"For us, this is great news. Without seed, Bellator cannot procreate. Eremus is filled with men who could assist them with resolving their problem, should we so choose. This situation can definitely be used to our advantage." He glanced down at Paulo. "And the Bellator hostages make us even stronger. Yes. I think," he steepled his hands at his chin, "that we might well be in a very strong position indeed."

CHAPTER TEN: FAITH

Having been delivered back to the cave by Anna with a promise she'd do what she could to improve their situation, Faith had hoped she could cheer the others up, but Avery had other plans. She was at her the moment the cave door was closed.

"Ah, the wanderer returns." Faith bristled at the older girl's sarcasm. "What took you so long?"

"You were gone a long time." Sophie whispered, as Faith settled back in next to her. "Avery thinks you've been plotting with your allies."

Faith rolled her eyes. "If you've something to say, Avery, let's hear it."

Pushing herself to her feet, the older girl stalked across the space. When she was looking down at Faith, she stopped. "We were all supposed to be seen by this... medical person, weren't we?"

"That *was* what she said," Helen said hesitantly, glancing between them.

"And yet, the only person to have received *treatment*," Avery drew exaggerated quotation marks in the air, "is you." Faith opened her mouth to interrupt, but Avery wasn't finished. She nodded at the others, who seemed far more agitated than they had been when Faith had left them. "Are you *sure* you don't know more about these people than you claim?"

Rubbing her fingers in small circles on her temple, Faith prayed for her headache to ease. "Look," she began, "it took a while because when I got there, Anna, the medic, was already busy fixing someone else up. And then, once she'd seen to me, she was called away to some kind of meeting."

"And you expect us to believe that? I mean, really–" Avery began, but Faith held up a hand.

"She said she'd be back to look over the rest of you later," Faith continued, determined to have them hear her out. "*And* she's going to speak to their leader about treating us a little better."

"That sounds... more promising," Farrah said, shooting Avery a pleading look.

"You think they'll let us go home?" Mary sat up, her face brighter than it had been in hours.

"I don't think that's going to happen." Faith felt bad as Mary's face fell.

"Maybe they'll give us better food!" Catherine grasped her friend's hand. "What I'd do for some pancakes with fresh strawberries... or blueberries."

"I'm not sure they have that kind of food," Diane said, before turning back to Faith. "This meeting. It was unexpected, by the sound of it."

"What do you mean?"

"Well, if this Anna had planned to examine us all today, it doesn't sound like she knew she had to attend a meeting, does it?"

Faith shrugged. "S'pose not. The message came when she was examining me. The guy just said that Jacob—I got the impression that he's their leader—was back. And he wanted to meet with the whole community."

"Back? Like he'd been away somewhere?" Helen exchanged glances with Sophia. "To Bellator, maybe?"

Sophia nodded. "Stands to reason they'd want to see the impact of the raid."

"And," Helen warmed to her theme, "if he called a meeting the second he got back, sounds like he has news."

The two youngest girls huddled closer together. "Bad news?"

"Maybe. But bad news for them might be good news for us." Sophia turned to Faith. "While you were gone some of us were talking. Most of us agree it might be wise for us to do as we're told... show them we're not going to cause any trouble." She shot a look at Diane. "Maybe even try to get to know them a little. Even the men haven't behaved as we expected them to."

"You're right. Kidnapping aside, we haven't been mistreated. Ella brought us the lantern, more food, we were allowed to bathe this morning," Faith ticked off the items on her fingers, "and Anna said she was prepared to speak up for us. Seems like at least some of them are on our side. For now, I think we need to follow instructions and behave sensibly."

"Then they're more likely to let their guard down." Sophia continued. "We might get to know them better."

"Speak for yourself," Avery muttered, her face pale. "I don't want to get to know any *men* better."

Faith rolled her eyes. "Did you ever consider they might not be as bad as we've been led to believe?"

"You would say that." Avery's eyes flashed, "If you were on their side." She turned on Faith. "I mean it! If you're somehow working with these people–"

"I'm *not*." Faith considered Noah's careful treatment of her in the medcave. He'd seemed thoughtful, genuinely sorry for passing on the information which had led to their kidnapping. But could she really trust him? She made her decision. "I'm not," she repeated, "and I agree with you. But there are some other things you need to know. About Bellator. About Dan-forth."

"Danforth?" Avery's voice had risen a tone. "What do you think you know about the chancellor that we don't?" She stalked back towards Farrah dismissively, lowering herself to the ground beside her friend. Faith couldn't help think she was going for safety in numbers. "Go on, then." She stared pointedly at Faith. "We're listening."

Faith took a deep breath. "I know you think I'm somehow in with the people here. And I suppose, in a way, I am... or I was... with Noah, at least. Look, I was naïve... foolish. I told him things about me... about the academy, information which he brought back to his community to be used against us. That's the reason we were taken." Ignoring Avery's stare, she pressed on, "But back in Bellator, things weren't great for me, and–"

"We *all* know things weren't great for you. Because you'd been caught *breaking the rules*," Avery scoffed. "Perhaps you deserved the sanctions you were suffering."

"I hardly think–" Faith began to defend herself, but Avery wouldn't let her.

"And now," she spat out, "now you're scared to go back and face the consequences of your actions. Well, the rest of us have done nothing wrong. We don't share your sentiments."

"But you *should*!" Faith sat up straighter. "Don't you see? *Yes*, I broke the rules. But I didn't deserve to be locked up. They barely fed me! And it's not a simple case of me being punished for something I did wrong. You're all being poorly treated. You just don't know it." Faith paused for a moment, considering her next words. "Did you *know*, for example, they were planning to inject us with an untested drug which has already killed one of our classmates?"

"That was an accident."

Faith turned to stare at Avery. "You knew about it?"

"Of course not." The older girl dropped her gaze. "I just meant that... obviously, her death was accidental. A tragedy.

To think it's linked to something the academy gave her... that's just absurd. And to suggest they were going to give it to you as well..."

"Not just me. *All* of us." Faith spoke through gritted teeth. "We are all at risk at the academy. You have to believe me."

There was a silence for a few minutes. Eventually, Diane spoke. "Alright. I believe that Danforth had some nasty things in store for us. But what are you suggesting? That we stay here forever?"

Sophia turned to her friend. "Do you *want* to be a prisoner here?"

"No, of course not."

"Then what?" Sophia's eyes begged Faith to be rational. She had been here with the others for several hours, and had clearly taken stock of the mood. Faith trusted her. She couldn't afford to alienate the group.

"I don't know." She sighed. "But you're right. There are people here who seem willing to help us. And no one has been violent towards us since the night we were taken. Let's do as you suggest—behave sensibly, don't act out. Then, in a day or two, we can consider what to do next."

There were various nods of agreement from around the cave. Even Avery seemed to have run out of arguments. Exhausted by the discussion, Faith slumped back on her mat, wrapping her blanket around her. She closed her eyes. A moment later, she was aware of a hand on her arm.

"Hey, you need to eat." Sophia crouched next to her, holding out a roll of rough-looking bread. "They left us this when they brought us back from the pool."

Accepting the gift, Faith chewed on the bread. It wasn't unpleasant, just a little tasteless. She found it difficult to choke down the food, but knew she had to eat.

"Are you feeling better?" Sophia laid a hand on her forehead. "You don't seem as warm now."

Faith swallowed a mouthful of the bread. "We got any more water?"

Sophia was already holding out a cup for her.

"Thanks." Faith took a long swig, hoping it would help the food go down. "I do feel better. I'm just a little tired, now."

"Did the medic think you were sick with anything serious?" Sophia's eyes were wide. "Because down here, if you're ill…"

Faith squeezed her friend's hand. "I'm fine. She thought it might have been an after effect of the femgazipane, but that has to be out of my system soon. I'll be okay."

Sophia smiled. "You really think she's going to argue for us to get better treatment here?"

"I do." Faith lowered her voice. "She came from Bellator. Originally."

"She did?"

"Uh-huh."

"How'd she end up here?"

Faith stifled a yawn. "She's Noah's mother."

"You mean, she was pregnant with a boy, and she…" Sophia's voice cracked slightly, "she ran away?"

"Yep." Finishing the bread, Faith took another sip of the water. "Brave, huh?"

"Definitely," her friend whispered.

Sophia took the cup and placed it neatly back on the tray with the other supplies. She looked troubled, and Faith wondered if she was thinking about her own mother. Too tired to ask her, Faith lay down.

"Get some sleep," her friend soothed.

Unable to keep her eyes open, Faith followed her advice.

Hours later, she woke with a start. The cave was quiet, aside from the sounds of the girls' even breathing as they slept. But something had disturbed her.

Stretching her stiff limbs, she peered around. Nothing seemed out of place, yet she could feel the hackles on her back rising. Holding her breath, she eased herself into a sitting position and waited. For several seconds, there was nothing.

And then, she heard it. A scraping sound, as someone fumbled with the wooden barrier which covered the cave entrance. Slowly, quietly, as though whoever was on the other side didn't want to be heard.

Moving into a crouch, Faith picked her way around the other girls to the door. Noah had visited her once before, the night they'd arrived. Could this be him? Helen was lying closest to the doorway, and as Faith stepped over her, she stirred. Faith froze, but the other girl merely groaned softly and rolled over.

As Faith reached the doorway, the barrier was removed. A lantern shone into her face, and for a moment, she was blinded. Recoiling, she shifted backwards, but her movement was halted as a large hand closed around her wrist. A hand which was certainly not Noah's.

"This one's awake." The male voice was somehow familiar.

"Take her." This one was not. The man sounded older, more gruff. This was someone used to giving orders. "I'll get one of the others."

Faith found herself being pulled out of the cave and into the tunnel. Before she could react, a hand covered her mouth.

"Stay quiet." That voice again. "We're not going to hurt you."

She managed to nod. The hand was removed from her face, but the one at her wrist remained. The man fumbled with something attached to his belt and seconds later, she found a rough scrap of material being pressed over her eyes. She struggled, and the fabric fell away. Cursing, the man let go of her wrist.

Faith considered running, but decided she'd only get lost in the maze of tunnels. She turned to look back into the cave and saw the second man bringing a sleepy Helen out after her. This man was older, his bulky frame almost filling the cave entrance. He frowned at the man holding her.

"Get on with it, then."

Again, the material was pulled over her eyes. Faith could hear the other man hissing a warning to Helen as a small cry escaped her lips. Then she, too, went silent. Faith assumed a rustling sound meant Helen had been blindfolded too. Blinded for the second time in as many minutes, she fought the urge to scream as a rope was secured around her wrists.

Screaming would get her nowhere, though. It wasn't like anyone would come to her rescue. Not down here. But the two men's stealth suggested they didn't want to be discovered. The irony of their earlier discussion about the men's peaceable behaviour towards them was not lost on her. She heard the wooden barrier being replaced over the cave entrance and then the man was at her side again. She felt his hands close around her shoulders and he began to guide her forward.

"Pick your feet up high as you walk," he hissed, his voice close to her ear. "That way, you won't fall."

And suddenly, she knew. Her captor was Paulo, Noah's brother. His voice was familiar because she'd heard it before, in the med centre, when she had first met Noah. But where was he taking her? Unable to do anything other than follow his instructions, she stumbled along, trying desperately not to trip on the uneven ground of the tunnel. She could hear Helen's faltering footsteps behind her. Wherever they were being taken, it was together. The thought gave her a small amount of relief.

They walked for what seemed like an hour. The men who guided them did not speak. Faith's heart pounded in her chest and her hands, awkwardly fastened behind her back, were clammy.

Eventually, there was a change in the air. It seemed cooler, somehow. Were they outside?

"Step upwards when we tell you." Paulo's hands grasped her elbows and she hated herself for feeling more secure. "Now."

Cautiously, she raised her foot high. When she lowered it again, the rock felt solid beneath her.

"Again."

She repeated the process, again, her foot hitting its mark. They continued up some kind of incline, until she felt the wind on her face. Her mind was racing. Where were they being taken?

For a moment, they paused, and Faith wondered if they had reached their destination. But after a moment of silence, Paulo rested his hands on her shoulders and guided her forward again.

They walked on for several minutes. Faith could hear rustling, like a breeze through leaves, and the alarmed flutter of a bird's wings as it took off into the air. After what seemed like a lifetime, Paulo's hand stilled her.

"Here?"

"Here," the older man confirmed.

Faith felt herself being turned and backed into something rough and solid: the bark of a tree, she thought. "Don't move." Paulo whispered. "Don't make *any* noise."

Seconds later she felt a warm presence next to her. The rapid, panicked breathing told her it was Helen. Stretching her bound wrists to their limit, she found the other girl's hand and clutched it tightly. The returning squeeze was tight, fearful.

"Shouldn't they be here already?" Paulo's voice was muffled, as though the two men had moved away.

"Relax. They'll be here." The older man's tone was tense, but more confident. "They know where we'll be."

"Couldn't we..." Paulo's voice trailed off.

"Using the walkie is too risky. Anyone could hear." The man sounded impatient. "We stick to the plan. It might take them a while to get one of them alone."

They lapsed into silence. Beside Faith, Helen whimpered slightly, then sucked in a deep breath, trying not to cry out. Faith shifted closer, resting the length of her arm alongside the other girl's, and she quieted.

A minute later, there was the unmistakable sound of footsteps. Several pairs, coming from somewhere to Faith's right. She felt Helen stiffen.

"Ready?" The older man again. "You stand with the girls. Let me do the talking."

Faith heard Paulo coming closer. "Stay still and quiet, and you'll be fine," he muttered, low enough for the other man to miss.

She nodded, not even sure if he was watching her.

The footsteps grew louder. There had to be at least three people approaching. A bead of sweat traced its way down her spine. She forced herself to breathe evenly, falling back on yoga techniques she'd been taught at the academy. As the footsteps stopped, she fought to control her breathing.

"This won't take long." The older man's voice had changed. It was colder, harsher in tone. Faith had no idea who his comments were directed at, but she could sense his hatred. "I'm sure you're aware that my associates here could already have killed you."

"They didn't because you are here to bear witness." He paused, allowing his words to sink in. "You will take my message back to Bellator and deliver it to Danforth. Understand?" He waited, as though he required a response. There was none, but when he continued, Faith assumed his target must have nodded their agreement. "Your chancellor suspects the students from Danforth Academy were taken by the people of Eremus. She is correct."

Faith felt Paulo tugging on her arm. She stumbled forward, aware she was being shown to whoever the older man spoke to. A Bellator guard, perhaps. Whoever it was, they didn't speak. Maybe they couldn't speak. Trembling, she tried to stay upright.

"Tell Danforth that Eremus is keeping her citizens as hostages." The man's voice increased in volume, and Faith felt him move closer. "We know their value. Tell her," he paused, "that we claim responsibility for the explosion at Bellator Hospital two nights ago."

Faith felt herself being pushed to her knees, and not by Paulo this time. She felt his hands clamp down on her shoulders, imprisoning her. "This. Girl." The older man punctuated his words with sharp pauses, "is one of eight. As you can see, she is still alive. So is her peer over there. The others are hidden. Somewhere you won't find them."

He moved his hand again, and a second later, felt something cold and metallic pressing against her temple. "As you can see, we are well-armed." Faith felt her entire body begin to tremble as the man continued. "I could kill this girl here where she stands, if it would make my point more clearly."

The blood roared in Faith's ears. Was this it? Was she going to die, here in the middle of a forest, without even being able to see her killer? She felt a scream building in her throat, but it lodged there, unable to break free. Frozen, she could do nothing as the man continued to speak.

"Danforth is in trouble. She used to hold all the cards, but now... well now let's just say that I have some cards of my own." The gun was removed from her head for a second, and she sensed he was aiming it elsewhere. "Tell her I want to talk. Tell her Eremus will no longer remain in the shadows. We will be heard. We will be recognised. She *will* listen to us."

Suddenly, the cold metal was at her temple again. Unable to stop herself, Faith let out a cry. The man holding her gave a humourless laugh. "As you can see, these girls are terrified for their lives. And they should be. Tell Danforth I'll be in contact. And I will want to talk. If she does not agree to meet with me, one of these girls will die. If she attempts to attack our community, one of these girls will die. Am. I. Clear?"

Again, there was no sound, but Faith assumed the person in question nodded their assent. The man behind her removed the gun once again as he continued.

"My associates here will take you back to where they found you. They will be keeping your comms device, so you're unable to contact your people until we are long gone. You'll be unharmed, but only... *only* because you are our messenger. You are our ransom note. Don't forget." He paused, and Faith felt the gun at her head once again. "Boom!"

He kept the gun in place until the footsteps had faded into the distance. Then, abruptly, she was released. She lost her balance and felt her body tumbling forward. With no hands to break her fall, her chin slammed into the ground. She cried out in pain. Rolling onto her side, she curled up into a ball as the world closed in around her.

Chapter Eleven: Noah

As Noah made his way through the tunnels, he felt a strange energy take hold of him. It had been an easier day. Work on the tunnel excavation was on hold for the time being, until the issues with Bellator were resolved. He'd had to operate the sluice gates to change the water in the bathing pools, and he'd helped out in the canteen for a while earlier but, other than that, his day had not been taxing. Not physically, at least.

With more time to think, he'd spent most of the day contemplating the situation with the Danforth girls. More specifically, he'd been thinking about Faith. How, now that she was here in Eremus, he might get to know her better. He didn't want to wait until their paths crossed by chance: he needed to know she wasn't angry with him anymore. But mostly, and he was honest enough to admit it, he just wanted to see her.

Ruth was on guard duty tonight, and he figured this gave him a far better chance. His friend didn't exactly approve of his relationship with Faith, if they even had one, but she understood its origin and could be trusted not to tell anyone. And she'd been far more accepting of the Danforth girls since she and Ella had begun getting to know them.

Smiling despite his nerves, he turned the corner leading to the girls' cave, immediately spotting his friend leaning against the wall. His heart sank: she wasn't alone. She had clearly just arrived for her shift and stood talking to Harden, of all people. He considered turning around and coming back later, but it was too late. They'd already seen him.

"Madden." Harden gave a brief nod. "What're you doing here?"

"Come to keep me company, hasn't he?"

Always quick on the uptake, Ruth knew Noah didn't want Harden questioning his presence. She shot him a look, and he realised he hadn't answered her.

"Um... yeah, that's right," he managed.

"You two needing some alone time?" Harden leered.

"Hardly." Ruth was quick to correct him. "We haven't had much chance to catch up recently, what with the raid, and all." She gestured to the closed door of the cave cell. "Anything else I need to know before you go?"

"Not really." Harden shrugged, losing interest in the conversation. "They've not eaten yet. Guess dinner will be sent down soon." He stooped to pick up a backpack from the ground. "Oh. And a couple of them are still with Anna."

"Still?" Noah frowned. His ma had gone down to the med-cave early this morning to make sure she could see each of the girls without further interruption. "The check-ups have taken all day, then?"

"Guess so." A dark look came over Harden's face, and a shadow of the old bully returned. "Maybe your ma's not up to the job, Madden."

Noah ignored the jibe and turned to Ruth. "You had dinner yet?"

She picked up on his change of subject, gesturing to her own pack. "Brought it with me. Grabbed some for you too." She swung it off her back and lowered it to the ground. "Hungry?"

"Starving." Noah made a big act of crouching down and unzipping the pack. "What'you got?"

"Bread, cheese, a couple of energy bars." Ruth sat cross-legged on the tunnel floor, tugging him down beside her.

A scowling Harden turned to leave. "I'll go, then. Leave you to your dinner for two. Said I'd meet Sil and Harriet anyway." When neither of them replied, he strode off. "Hey Madden," he tossed over his shoulder, "don't forget you won't have her alone for long. The others'll be back soon."

When he was out of sight, Ruth turned to Noah. "Didn't think he'd ever leave."

"Me neither."

There was an awkward pause. "Not sure why he's assuming we're–" Ruth stopped, biting her lip.

"Me neither." Noah knew he was blushing. His ma had suggested the same thing. "I mean–"

"I don't think about you *that way*." Ruth glanced sharply at him. "You know that. Right?"

Relief flooded over him. "Me neither. It's just that..."

"I guess people jump to conclusions 'cos we spend so much time," she gestured between them, "together."

"Guess so." Noah grinned.

"Glad *we* know where we stand, though."

"Me too." Reaching forward, Noah grabbed a hunk of cheese from the pack and bit into it.

"Oy!" Ruth snatched the bag back. "I was covering for you. I don't *actually* have a spare portion. You'll have to get your own."

Realising how hungry he was, Noah swallowed the mouthful and glanced at the wooden board covering the cave entrance. "Thanks for covering for me, anyway."

"S'okay." Ruth's mouth was similarly full. "I'm guessing your reason for being here has something to do with you not feeling *that way* about me."

Noah jerked his gaze back to his friend's. "What'd'you mean?"

She smirked. "You're here to see Faith, right?"

"Yeah," he admitted.

"Hmm." Taking another bite, Ruth regarded him steadfastly as she chewed. "You really are keen."

Once again, he felt himself flushing. "I just want to make sure she's alright... that she doesn't blame me."

"I think it's 'cos you feel *that way* about her." Ruth grinned at his discomfort. "Alright. Let me finish this and we can open it up. I can't guarantee she'll want to speak to you, but... I guess we can ask."

Noah waited impatiently while she ate the remaining cheese. When she leaned forward to pick up the hunk of bread, he groaned.

"Wow. You really are desperate." Relinquishing the food, she dusted off her hands and stood. "Alright. Let's get this open."

Ruth pulled out the bolts holding the wooden board in place and together, they hauled the slab aside.

"Hey," she called out, "it's only me." Her words were greeted by silence. Shooting a puzzled look at Noah, she peered inside the cave. "You all sleeping, or something?"

As she stepped inside, Noah made to follow her, but she held up a hand to stop him. Sensing she didn't want to startle the inhabitants of the cave, he stayed out of sight.

"Is something wrong?" he heard her ask, her voice unnaturally calm.

A murmuring followed her question, but Noah couldn't make out what was said.

"Aren't they–?" Ruth sounded confused. "I was told they were with Anna, our medic? She was supposed to check you all over in turn."

The murmuring continued. All Noah caught was "...middle of the night."

"What–" Ruth sounded shocked, "*both* of them?"

Whoever was speaking continued at the same low volume. "...not back yet..."

Noah could stand it no longer. Ignoring the gasps of fear from a number of the girls, he followed Ruth inside. As his eyes adjusted, he glanced around, straining his eyes in the dim light. One... two... three, four, five... six.

There were only six girls in the cave. And one half of the missing pair was Faith.

Ruth whirled to face him. "Noah! I asked you to wait outside."

He opened his mouth to reply when a voice to his left made him stop. "You're Noah?"

Turning, he spotted a slight girl around the same age as Faith. Her voice shook slightly, but she seemed determined to speak.

"I am."

She relaxed slightly. "I'm Sophia. Faith's friend?"

He smiled in what he hoped was a non-threatening way. "Hey, Sophia."

"Do you know where she is?"

"She's not here?" Noah asked, concerned. She shook her head. "She could be with my ma... except that doesn't make sense..." he turned to Ruth. "She already saw Faith... yesterday. Unless..." He spun back to Sophia. "Is she sick?"

Sophia shook her head. "She seemed fine last night. But when Diane woke me..." she pointed at one of the other girls, "not sure when, but it was still nighttime, she was gone."

Diane stepped forward. She was an older girl, the one who had tried so desperately to escape when the girls had first arrived. "Someone came in here during the night. I'm sure of it. I woke up, too late." She shook her head. "All I heard was the sound of the door closing over."

"And the girls were gone?"

"Faith... and Helen too." She nodded. "That's when I woke Sophia."

Emboldened by Diane's speech, Sophia leaned closer. "After that, we couldn't sleep. We waited... it seemed like hours. A man brought some food in this morning." Noah noticed some of the girls shiver at the mention of their visitor. "We've heard nothing since."

Ruth bent down next to Sophia. "The man this morning... you didn't know him?"

Sophia shook her head. "I tried to ask him." Noah thought it brave of her to question a man, given the girls' background. He respected her for it, and knew it showed how much she cared for her friend. "He wouldn't answer."

"He wouldn't speak to you at all." This voice came from the rear of the cave. Noah turned to see an older, blonde girl he hadn't noticed before.

"He wasn't like you and Ella." This came from the youngest-looking girl in the room, her voice no more than a whisper.

"He was one of the citizens who continue to treat us like animals." The blonde girl's voice was far more strident. Noah thought her face might have been pretty if it wasn't marred by a scowl.

"Anyway, now it's... what time is it, anyway?" Sophia peered at Ruth.

"Evening." Ruth explained. "Dinner time."

"Okay. So... a whole day." She chewed her lip, her eyes haunted.

"And they haven't been brought back?" Noah's frown deepened.

"No one's been in here at all." This time when Sophia spoke, her voice rang with hopelessness.

Noah's heart began to race. Where were the girls? And why had they been gone for so long?

"Is this how it starts, then?" The blonde girl piped up again. "We disappear, a couple at a time?"

"Avery!" Sophia frowned at the girl who'd spoken, gesturing at the two younger girls. They were huddled together, twin expressions of terror on their faces. The girl named Avery simply glared.

Ruth cast a look of concern at Noah. Two girls missing, and no clue as to where they'd gone. He jerked his head towards the exit, and Ruth nodded.

"Give us a minute." She reached out and squeezed Sophia's hand. "I'll come right back, I promise."

Outside, Noah turned to Ruth. "Where the hell are they?"

"I don't know. But I'd be willing to bet Jacob does." She grimaced. "All that talk of Bellator's weakness... how we have a chance to act..."

Noah's heart sank, but he knew she was right. "What do we do?"

She glanced back at the cave. "I'll try to reassure them. You head out and see if you can find out where they've been taken. Ask Jacob, Flynn, Anna, Sarah... anyone on the council."

"And when I find them?"

Ruth shrugged. "Not sure. I guess check that they're alright. Bring them back, if you're allowed to?"

"You really think the council–"

"I suspect they don't *all* know what's going on." Ruth gestured back to the cave. "Your ma and Flynn wouldn't be happy about this."

"After all Jacob's talk of treating them well–" Noah grasped his friend's hand. "D'you think he'd–?"

Ruth shrugged. "I think he's obsessed with gaining power over Bellator."

"Alright." Noah squeezed Ruth's hand, then let it go. "Take care of the rest of them, right? I'll head to the canteen first... ask around."

"If you see Ella, can you let her know they still need food to be sent down?"

"Sure."

"And Noah?"

He turned back. "Yeah?"

"Don't do anything stupid, will you?"

Gritting his teeth, he shook his head.

"See you later." Frowning, Ruth turned back to the cave.

Noah set off back up the tunnel at a jog. He had to find Faith, and fast. But he found nothing amiss in the canteen, just an ordinary mealtime, and none of the council members present. The only person he felt might know something was Harden, who sat at the far side of the cave, tucking into a plateful of stew. Thanking his lucky stars that Harden was alone, at least for now, Noah made his way across.

"Harden?"

He looked up, a flash of surprise on his face. "You followin' me, Madden?"

"Hardly. I just wanted to ask you something."

Harden sat back on the bench. "Can't keep away from me, huh?"

Gritting his teeth, Noah pushed on. "When you said the girls weren't all in the cave, did you mean they'd been in and out all day, visiting my ma for checkups?"

Harden's smirk disappeared. "Why d'you ask?"

"That doesn't answer my question." Noah pushed on as Harden shoved another forkful of food into his mouth, chewing determinedly. "You said there were still some girls in the medcave. That part was true, right?" Harden nodded. "Have the same girls been in there all day?"

Swallowing his food, Harden leaned towards Noah. "Why do you care so much?"

Harden's refusal to respond was as telling as a stuttered denial might have been. Not bothering to answer him, Noah turned away, heading out of the canteen. His heart pounding, he hurried towards the medcave, wondering what he would find when he got there.

He didn't have to wait long. As he rounded the corner which led towards his ma's place of work, he could already hear angry voices. Slowing his pace, he listened.

"I told you, it's unforgiveable." His ma. "We *agreed* to treat these girls well."

"...an accident..." Jacob's voice, and quieter than usual, so much so that Noah couldn't catch every word. "...didn't want to... send a message..."

Noah crept closer, straining to hear more.

"You've taken *all day* to come and speak to me about it." He'd never heard his ma so furious. "How can we expect these girls to trust us if we do *this?*"

"It was necessary." Jacob seemed to have run out of patience now. "You must see that. Our position is–"

"Our position is all you seem to care about." His ma sounded disgusted. "But these girls–"

"These *girls* have not been harmed."

"I beg to differ."

"Alright." Jacob sounded frustrated. "None of them were harmed *purposefully.* "

"But one of them was injured, all the same."

Noah's heart began to pound. Which girl was injured? How badly? He forced himself to remain where he was, wanting to hear the rest of the conversation.

"I think we might have to agree to disagree on the matter of our captives." Noah could hear every word Jacob said now, as the volume of his voice rose with his anger. "Yes, we shouldn't *mistreat* them, but if these girls are the key to gaining an advantage over Bellator, then we cannot be sentimental about them. Of course, we don't want to hurt them, but last night it was necessary to make a strong statement of our intention. Having the girls with us made it more powerful. And I think," he paused for effect, "many of our community would agree with me on this."

"Not *all* of your community," Anna spat out.

"But enough that you'd struggle to outvote me on this. You know that." Noah heard movement inside the cave as Jacob barked a final order. "Look, get them back to their cave now. They've been in here long enough. We've other things to do."

Hearing heavy footsteps coming towards him, Noah jumped. He had just enough time to straighten up and make like he had just begun walking towards the medcave, when Jacob strode around the corner, almost bumping into him.

"Watch what you're–" their leader stopped. "Noah!"

Judging himself incapable of speaking in a civil tone, Noah nodded, and stood to one side to let Jacob pass. The older man stared at him for a long time before returning the nod and continuing on his way down the tunnel. Sucking in a deep breath, Noah walked on towards the medcave, now dreading what he might find.

As he pulled the curtain open, his ma was standing only feet from the entrance, one hand over her face. She jumped at his entrance, her eyes jerking to the second treatment space behind her almost guiltily. When she saw him, she seemed to relax.

"Noah! Why aren't you at dinner?"

He took a step towards her, desperate to see the patients in the room beyond. His ma remained stubbornly where she was, and he knew she was attempting to keep him from the other room.

"I heard," he hesitated. "I haven't had much work today, so when I heard some of the girls were still down here with you, I came to see if you needed any help."

She raised her eyebrows. "A likely story." She sighed. "Look, I'm not sure what you heard. Things haven't exactly gone as I'd planned, today. The girls in there," she nodded towards the inner room, "were brought to me first thing this morning... for *treatment*, not a check-up."

"What happened to them?"

"It seems that Jacob and Paulo took them out... outside last night." His ma twisted her hands together absentmindedly. "The Bellator guards were patrolling again, looking for signs of our whereabouts. Jacob had... well, I'm not sure who, but someone captured a Bellator guard and brought her to Jacob. I guess, well, I guess he took two of the girls with him as some kind of proof... collateral... to show Danforth he meant business."

Noah struggled to find words. "He *literally* used them as bait?"

His ma nodded, sadly. "Blindfolded them and tied their hands as well." She shuddered. "Goodness knows what they thought was going to happen to them."

"Are they alright?"

"Mostly. One of them, Helen, is in quite a severe state of shock. I think she'll be okay, but I want to keep a close eye on her. The other... well," she placed a hand on his arm, "see for yourself."

She backed away, and Noah walked towards the inner cave. His ma only kept her patients in the space beyond if they were seriously ill, or if she wanted to keep them away from prying eyes. Noah wasn't sure which explanation applied here.

In the other room, the first bed was occupied by an older girl with long, black hair. She lay stretched out on the cot with her eyes closed, but he didn't think she was sleeping. Her face was extremely pale, and he could see abrasions on her wrists, where no doubt the ropes had cut into her.

He walked around the first cot, his eyes drawn to the figure in the one behind. It was Faith. Several bruises bloomed on her cheeks and her temple, and there was a large cut on her chin which had been sewn up recently, no doubt by his ma. Her eyes, too, were closed, but as he walked closer, they flickered open.

"Hey," he said, trying for a smile. "How're you feeling?"

Her eyes were filled with fear and mistrust. He hated that his people had caused her to look that way.

"I'm great." She choked out, raising a hand to her face. "Can't you see?"

He shook his head, hating the hard edge in her voice. "I'm sorry."

"Me too." She exhaled loudly.

"Faith?" From behind him, Noah heard his ma enter the room. "I'm afraid you'll be sore for a while, but you'll live. The wounds will heal, eventually."

"*Eventually*." Faith's words were laced with bitterness.

"Noah, would you escort the girls back down to the cave with the rest of their friends, please?" His ma kept her voice even, but Noah could tell she was struggling for control. "I have to find Flynn."

"Sure." He watched his ma help Faith into a standing position, wondering if the girl from Bellator would ever trust him again.

CHAPTER TWELVE: FAITH

As they walked along the tunnel, Faith's mind was racing. Her head hurt, a lot, but the fury she felt at the events of the previous evening was keeping her going. Yesterday she had been starting to feel like they might actually make a fresh start here in Eremus—that the people here might accept them, perhaps even offer them better treatment than they had back in Bellator.

Noah's apology had seemed sincere, his explanation of what had happened, genuine. Ella, Ruth and Anna had all treated the girls with care and respect. But now this.

Faith didn't believe that Noah was involved. The horror on his face when he'd seen the state of her had been real enough. But Paulo was his brother, his family. Paulo had been the one to instigate their kidnapping, based on information he'd received from Noah. Now, along with Jacob, it seemed he'd been willing to abuse them simply to demonstrate Eremus' newfound power.

She knew she'd never forget the terror she had felt stumbling blindly through the forest, her wrists chafing against the ropes which bound her. With no idea of where she was being taken and for what purpose, she'd been assaulted by myriad thoughts, each more disturbing than the last. She was being led towards the kind of assault Bellator claimed was in a man's nature, to some kind of agonising torture, to her death. And no, in the end they hadn't been planning to hurt her, but they'd had no problem allowing her to believe that they might.

When they had first returned to the tunnels, the girls had been taken in a direction they'd never been before, ending up at a set of caves which seemed like someone's home. Faith had idly wondered why no one was asleep there in the middle of the night, and eventually came to the conclusion that the cave had to belong to Jacob himself. The inner cave had been sparsely furnished with a couple of low camp beds, and a table with a couple of personal items laid out on it. The outer cave had chairs and a second table, which held a small lantern and a set of small rectangular cards with symbols on that she suspected were the playing cards Ella had mentioned.

Paulo had tried to patch her face up, pressing material over the wound and muttering to himself about stemming the flow. His treatment had not left her feeling any more comfortable. Eventually, he had left her and Helen to rest, retreating to the other room to talk with Jacob.

Once he left, Helen had started to cry. Faith had attempted to comfort her, until the other girl had passed out, exhausted, on her shoulder. Unable to sleep herself, Faith had tried to listen in on the conversation in the other room. But the men had purposely kept their voices low, and she'd only been able to catch parts of it.

Jacob had said something about allowing the *captives* more freedom. This morning, Faith knew, she might have found the idea more appealing. She would've welcomed the ability to move around the cave complex more freely, to exercise and get to know the Eremus people better. After tonight's events, she was more wary. There were citizens here who felt it was acceptable to abduct and terrify them in the dead of night.

Those were not the type of people she wanted to get closer to.

More worryingly, she heard Jacob mention the Danforth girls *helping* him with his plans. She couldn't catch any specifics, but if tonight's excursion was anything to go by, it didn't bode well.

When he had come back in to check on Faith's wound early this morning, Paulo had cursed.

"Problem?" Jacob had asked from the doorway.

"It's still bleeding." Paulo pointed to Faith's chin. "Slowly, I think, but she might need stitches. We don't want it to get infected."

Jacob had scowled, but nodded. After that, the two girls had been moved once again. But they hadn't been returned to their usual cave. Faith wondered what the others were thinking. Sophia had already lost her once, back in Bellator, and Faith didn't relish being the cause of her friend's misery yet again.

There had been very few people about as Paulo had led them through the camp. Those they did come across had mostly nodded deferentially to Jacob and averted their eyes from Faith and Helen. When they had reached the empty medcave, Jacob had left immediately. Paulo had stayed with them, guarding the door, but they had still had to wait an hour or so for Anna.

Once she'd arrived, she'd set to work treating Faith and Helen immediately. As she worked, she demanded an explanation from Paulo which she seemed to find unsatisfactory. She had sent him away, with strict instructions not to return without Jacob.

After cleaning out the wound thoroughly with an antiseptic wash which stung, she'd leaned close to Faith, peering at the cut.

"I need to sew this up." She had walked over to one of the cupboards. Taking a familiar-looking canister out of it, she returned. "This is Sleepsol." Faith recoiled, and Anna placed a steadying hand on her arm. "I know this was used *against* you previously. I won't use it if you don't want me to, but trust me, the needle's going to hurt more without it."

"Trust you?" Faith's voice had shaken as she spoke.

"I know." Anna had taken a seat on the stool next to the bed. "You don't have a lot of reason to trust us right now. We haven't given you that, and I'm sorry. It's your choice. But if you agree to it, I promise I won't use much, so you won't be knocked out for long. Believe me, the pain you'll feel as a result of this," she'd held up a long, slender needle, "will be far greater than if you agreed for me to use a small amount of the Sleepsol."

In the end, Faith had given in, nodding and closing her eyes as Anna administered the solution. When she'd woken up, her face felt sore, but it was no longer bleeding. Anna had brought her an old, cracked mirror, and she had winced at the state of her face, but it was clear her wound had been well taken care of. She was glad she had trusted the medic.

The rest of the day had been spent resting and recovering from their ordeal. Helen hadn't said a word since they'd been brought back from the woods. Usually quite talkative, she had been shaky and silent, so far only managing to nod to confirm Faith's story. Anna said she was in shock, and had administered lots of hot, sweet tea, but she seemed more concerned with Helen's mental state than Faith's physical injuries.

When Jacob had finally come to discuss the events of the previous night, Helen had curled up in a ball on her cot, shrinking away from the man who had abducted her. After he left, she had lain with her eyes closed until Anna had instructed Noah to take them back to their cell.

Now, as they walked along the tunnels, Helen's head was bowed and her arms wrapped tightly around her body. So far, they hadn't come across anyone else, but Faith feared what might happen when they did. Noah, who also hadn't spoken since he'd left the medcave, walked in between them.

"I'll bring you back a different way," he said, suddenly. The comment was directed at Helen, and Faith could tell he was trying to set her at ease. "It'll take a little longer, but we'll be less likely to pass by other people." Helen's gaze remained fixed on the ground. Noah turned to Faith, lowering his voice. "They were waiting on dinner being brought down when I left. Perhaps some food might help."

"Really?" Faith raised her eyebrows. "You think food will fix everything?"

"I'm sorry." Noah's shoulders slumped. "I don't know what else to say."

"I don't think there's much you can say."

"I didn't know. I mean–" he pounded a fist into his other hand. Helen cowered at the sudden movement and his face fell. "Sorry. I'm sorry." He held up his hands in surrender. "*We* didn't know. That this was what Jacob had planned." Faith fixed her eyes on the tunnel ahead, refusing to meet his gaze. He fell silent again.

They walked on, a cruel silence circling them. For a moment, Faith felt guilty. She opened her mouth to say she didn't blame him, then closed it again. Like it or not, he was a part of Eremus, and Eremus had treated them terribly last night. After the promise to take better care of them, the community had betrayed the girls once again. She had been injured as a direct result of Jacob's actions, his desperate need to send a message to Danforth. And the damage to Helen, whilst not physical, was just as severe.

They approached a crossroad in the tunnels. Glancing both ways, Noah directed them down a narrow passage to their left. Faith was sure she hadn't been down it before. As they turned the corner, Noah held out a hand to stop them, narrowly avoiding a collision with someone who was hurrying in the opposite direction.

"Noah!" It was Ella. Her expression was tense and anxious, but relaxed when her gaze fell on Faith and Helen. "Oh, thank goodness." And then, leaning closer to Faith, "What happened?"

"They had a bit of a disturbing encounter in the woods last night." Noah shot Ella a warning look. "I'm just taking them back down to their cave."

"Ah. I see. Want me to come?"

"If you like." Noah seemed grateful for the offer. Faith wondered again if she'd been too hard on him.

"Sure." Ella turned to Helen, her eyes filling with concern. "Are you alright?"

Helen stared at her for a second, her eyes wild. Ella reached out and took hold of the other girl's hand, as though she sensed her fear. For a second, Faith thought Helen would struggle, lash out, turn, and run. But instead, she clutched Ella's proffered hand like a lifeline, her entire body starting to shudder. Ella took a step closer, sliding an arm around Helen's shoulder. Faith wasn't sure what happened, but seconds later, Ella was standing with both arms circling Helen's body as the other girl sobbed silently into her shoulder.

"We can't take her back there like this." Ella frowned at Noah.

"No."

Keeping her arms wrapped around the weeping Helen, Ella glanced left and right. "Where could we take them?"

Faith watched Noah's face as he searched for a solution. Eventually, he nodded back down the tunnel they'd come from. "Your place?"

Ella looked worried.

"It's just there. And we needn't stay long." Noah's tone was reassuring. "Who'll even know?"

"Okay." Ella agreed.

Noah turned to Faith. "Are you okay with us taking a detour? Just until she's calmer?"

"Sure." She shrugged, despite her anger, grateful for the care he was showing Helen.

They turned back and walked in the direction Noah had suggested, Ella supporting Helen all the way. In contrast, Faith made sure to keep a distance between herself and Noah. In minutes, they were entering Ella's home. Faith thought it far more welcoming than Jacob's had been, with colourful, woven blankets on the cots and chairs and a stove in the corner. Someone had even gone to the trouble of collecting flowers to put in a chipped vase on the table.

"Make yourself comfortable," Ella said, easing Helen onto a bench at one side of the room. She crossed the room and poured a glass of water. Returning, she passed Helen the glass. "Sip it slowly."

Without a glance at Noah or Faith, she settled herself beside Helen, taking her free hand and sitting with her.

Noah gestured awkwardly to the only other seats in the room, a pair of wooden chairs next to a table which contained a couple of aging books. Faith walked across and sat down, wincing as she did.

"Sore?" Noah had followed her, but hesitated as he got closer.

"Yeah." Faith gestured to the other chair. "Go ahead."

As Noah lowered his frame into the seat, it struck Faith how tall he was. Stretched out, his legs reached all the way under the table, almost touching hers. His hands reached for one of the books, turning it over in his hands absentmindedly.

Faith glanced over at Ella, who was still bending close to Helen, whispering comforting words in her ear.

She turned back to Noah. "I know you had nothing to do with it." The words were out of her mouth before she knew she was going to say them.

Noah froze, the book still in his hands. "You do?"

"Yeah. Your ma's right — your face gives away your every feeling. When you saw me in the medcave, you were shocked... stunned. There was no way you could have been involved."

"I- um..." he placed the book on the table again and trailed off.

"Anna was the same way. So angry." Faith shrugged. "I could tell. What Jacob and Paulo did... I'm guessing only a few people knew about it."

A look of relief spread over Noah's face. "I honestly had no idea. And I don't think many others did either." He clenched and unclenched his fist and he picked up the book again. "We had a meeting yesterday. Everyone agreed we needed to treat you decently, and then he goes and–"

His fingers gripped the spine tightly. Too tightly. His knuckles were turning white. Faith found herself reaching out a hand to cover his. He stiffened slightly at her touch but didn't withdraw. Encouraged, Faith squeezed his hand gently, working her fingers into his palm so she could release their hold on the volume. He stared down at their hands.

"Poor book," she murmured. "What did it ever do to you?"

A sudden smile flashed across his face at her words, lighting it up. He let go of the book and glanced up at her shyly.

"I mean..." she stumbled over her words slightly, startled by the effect she appeared to have on him, "it's not like you have very many, is it?"

He laughed softly. "True."

"Then you shouldn't ruin the ones you have." She hesitated. "Especially if... they don't belong to you."

"It's Ruth's." He grinned. "She'd kill me."

"Ruth's?" She glanced at Ella.

"She and Ella are sisters. They live here together with–" he flushed, "they *did* live here together with their ma, Dawn."

"Did?"

"She was killed a few weeks ago. Bellator soldiers."

"Like Paulo's father?" He glanced up at her in surprise. "Anna mentioned it."

"Yeah. Used to happen a lot." He bit his lip. "Anyway, it's just the two of them now."

"You miss her."

"We all do."

Faith was aware that her hand was still entangled with Noah's, but found she didn't want to remove it. This moment was the most peaceful she'd had since arriving here. She felt safe, and calm, and, if not happy, at least comfortable. And her hand in Noah's was a large part of that.

"You spend a lot of time in here?" she enquired quietly.

"Yep." Noah dropped his gaze. "I grew up with Ruth. Dawn's like – was like – a second ma to me. She and my ma were good friends."

For a moment, they were silent, and then he stretched out his other hand to cover hers. Sandwiched between his, her own hand felt small. She could feel his skin, roughened from hard work, yet somehow his touch was tender. These were hands capable of healing, of caring for others.

He raised his eyes to meet hers and she sucked in a sudden breath. He shot a quick glance at Ella. When Faith followed his gaze, she found the other girl was still distracted, caring for Helen, paying them no attention. Noah's eyes returned to their hands, still entwined on the table. Faith felt him move, and for a second she thought he was going to withdraw, but then his thumb slid beneath the cuff of her sleeve, until it was touching the skin beneath.

He stopped for a second, as though waiting for her permission, and when she didn't object, he ran his thumb around her wrist, turning her hand over in his. When her palm was exposed, he traced a circle on it with his thumb, seeming fascinated by her skin. Perhaps he too was thinking of its softness in contrast to his own. Faith felt her heart start to race, and it was suddenly difficult to breathe. Growing bold, she moved her thumb so it crossed over his, echoing his movements. He shivered in response. When they stared at one another again, it was in confusion.

The spell was broken when Ella climbed to her feet, easing Helen up next to her. Noah jerked his hand away at the same time as Faith.

"I think she's a little better now." Ella said. "Ready to go?"

"Sure." Faith heard Noah say.

She could only nod, as they ducked back out into the tunnel and retraced their steps towards the other girls. Her heartrate had only just returned to normal when they reached the cave.

Chapter Thirteen: Noah

The next morning, Noah's first thoughts were of Faith. After making Ruth promise she'd wake him if anyone tried to disturb the girls during the night, he'd come home to find no sign of either Flynn or his ma. Grabbing some food from the small stash his ma kept in their makeshift larder, he'd gone to bed, hoping they were talking some sense into Jacob.

He emerged from his sleeping space relieved to see them both sitting at the table, their heads bent close together. They turned at his entrance.

"Tea?" Flynn offered, getting up to pour him one.

"Thanks." Noah took the empty chair and looked at his ma. "Any news?"

Flynn returned to the table, placing a steaming mug in front of Noah. When he had taken his seat again, he took a deep breath.

"So, it seems we're worryingly divided in our opinions about the Danforth girls." His ma ran a tired hand through her hair. "I'm afraid, whilst Jacob accepts that we shouldn't mistreat the Danforth girls, he doesn't consider them as a priority."

"The Eremus citizens, our community, our survival, are of paramount importance to Jacob," Flynn added. "Always have been. And he's always felt that Bellator owes us. That they deserve to suffer as a result of the suffering they've inflicted."

"It's hardly the Danforth girls' fault that–" Noah began, but his ma held up a hand to stop him.

"We know that. But the Bellator citizens don't come very high on his list," Anna finished. "He doesn't see what happened the other night as treating them badly. I know–" she held up a hand, anticipating Noah's interruption, "he didn't treat them *well*. But in his mind, he didn't hurt them, well, not intentionally, and what he and Paulo did was a necessary part of his plan to improve things for Eremus."

"And the other council members agree with him?" Noah felt his fists clenching once again, his positive mood disintegrating.

"Not all of them, but... enough." Anna shrugged. "We took a vote. It was pretty much fifty-fifty down the middle. Jan and Dane were on our side, but Jacob had a lot of the others convinced the girls were not to be trusted. Sarah, of course, but Denton as well, and Cora... more people than I anticipated."

"I don't think they're all quite as determined as Jacob though," Flynn turned to his partner. "Many of them seemed uncomfortable when you described Faith's injuries."

"But with Sarah stirring things up, you can see how they settled on his side of the argument." Anna swallowed the remainder of her tea in one gulp, replacing her mug on the table with some force. Noah shot her a questioning look. "Oh, you know she's been angling for a bigger say on the council for a while. Agreeing with everything Jacob says, arguing loudly with anyone who has a differing opinion."

"It's Harden I'm worried about." Flynn chimed in. "She has him at Jacob's beck and call constantly. And he doesn't know how to say no to her."

"Harden was—" Too late, Noah thought better of what he'd been about to say.

"What was that?" His ma turned to him, her eyes narrowed.

Taking a large gulp of the too-hot tea, Noah winced as it burned down his throat. His ma was pretty perceptive, and he was pretty certain she had her suspicions about Faith. A few weeks back, she wouldn't have listened to his side of the story, but lately she'd treated him differently, more like an adult. Perhaps he owed it to her.

He took a deep breath. "Last night, I didn't just come to the medcave by chance. I'd already been to the caves to see… Ruth." He paused, gauging his ma's expression. It told him nothing. "When I got there, she was just taking over from Harden. He told us some of the girls were at the medcave with you, but he was cagey about how many."

Flynn exchanged a look with his ma. "Interesting."

"He implied that anyone not in the cave was still being checked over by you. But you'd gone out so early, I knew you should have seen them all by that point. It seemed…"

"Suspicious?" His ma frowned. "Yes. I don't think he was put on duty by accident."

"You think Jacob was hoping to cover it up?"

"With a little help from Sarah." Anna tapped a restless finger on the tabletop. "They tried to treat Faith's wound before they brought her to me. If she hadn't needed stitches, they'd have just slung them both back in the cave and hope no one had noticed their absence."

"So Harden was involved with their little stunt last night." Flynn rubbed his stubbled chin with a hand. "Makes sense that Sarah would offer him to Jacob as support. It strengthens her position."

"So, she persuaded the council that dragging the girls out in the middle of the night, cuffed and blindfolded, was what…" Noah struggled to find the right word, "acceptable?"

"It wasn't as simple as that." Flynn sighed. "Jacob admitted they'd been a little heavy-handed with the girls. He agreed to consult the council with any future plans he had for them. That seemed to satisfy most of the members."

"But I wouldn't put it past him to keep things from us in the future, if he could get away with it." Anna shot Noah a pointed look. "Speaking of keeping things from us..."

"What?" Noah felt his heartrate pick up.

"You knew Faith before she came here, didn't you?" His ma sighed. "Want to tell us how you met her? I *suspect* it was the night you were trapped in the hospital."

"It was." Noah sighed. "And I'm sorry I didn't tell you." He shrugged. "I kind of figured I wouldn't ever need to. I didn't think I'd ever meet her again, but then Paulo–"

"What's Paulo got to do with this?" Flynn interrupted.

Noah turned to face him. "I told him about Faith... the academy... the testing."

Understanding dawned on Flynn's face. "That's why he decided they'd be useful, right?" He looked furious, and for a moment, Noah felt guilty for causing further trouble between them.

His ma slammed a hand on the table, making them both jump. "And *that's* why you hit him." Noah gave a reluctant nod. "I knew it wasn't like you."

There was an awkward silence, which Noah eventually felt the need to fill. "That's it, really. I feel guilty... I mean, the girls are here because of me. And now Faith's been injured... well..."

His ma reached out and took hold of his hand. "That's not your fault."

"But I..."

"No." Flynn's voice was stern. "You were naïve, and too trusting, but you didn't set out to hurt her."

"And Noah..." his ma tightened her grip on his hand, "we're not angry. Honestly. We understand, but... you have to understand any kind of relationship with this girl is... a bad idea."

"*Relationship?*" The word sounded strange.

"Faith must seem very *different*..." his ma said softly, "exciting... from the city... I can see how that would be attractive, but..."

Noah felt the heat of embarrassment flood his body. He stared at the ground, waiting for his ma to stop speaking. But it wasn't over.

"We really don't want to tell you what to do." Flynn laid a hand on his shoulder. "But with everything that's going on... these girls are stuck right in the middle of Jacob's plans for Bellator. Yes, we will try to keep them safe, but ultimately..."

"Ultimately what?" Noah bit out.

"We're saying things could go badly wrong, and we don't want you to get hurt." His ma stood, collecting the tea cups and returning them to the bowl to be washed. "Even in the best-case scenario, Faith will return safely to Bellator. Do you think you'll be permitted to see her after that?"

"What if she doesn't want to go back?" Noah knew he sounded like a spoilt child, but he found he couldn't help himself. "What if she stayed here?"

Returning to the table, Anna slid an arm around his shoulder. "Not many Bellator women could live happily in Eremus."

"You did."

She paused, searching for the right words. "I did, eventually. But I was desperate when I came here. And I mean, desperate. I wasn't actually *happy* here–" she shot a look at Flynn, "for years."

Noah struggled to his feet, shrugging off his ma's arm. He'd expected yelling, arguments, anger. But this calm, rational explanation of the facts was even more difficult to swallow. He couldn't storm out, claim that his ma was being unfair, not when she was being so reasonable.

He changed the subject. "What's Jacob planning, then?"

"He wants to make contact with Danforth." His ma glanced at Flynn. "Start some kind of negotiation with her. We think he's banking on showing Danforth we have the girls, and using them as leverage of some kind."

Grateful that they'd let the topic of Faith drop for now, he pressed on. "Leverage for what?"

Flynn frowned. "We're not sure. But he knows he went too far, dragging the girls out into the woods. And he plans to find ways to show those of us concerned for the girls' welfare that he does care."

"How?"

His ma hesitated before going on. "He's going to ask the girls to join the community for a meal, in the canteen."

Noah thought of Faith and her friends in the shared space which was so familiar to him. "He thinks it's a good idea, to parade them in front of the entire community? Really?"

"Really." His ma shrugged. "I'm not sure about it, either, but he seems determined. We couldn't say no. Not when we were the ones campaigning for better treatment."

"Jacob's main wish is for Eremus to have a better relation-ship with Bellator." Flynn sighed. "And, whilst your ma and I don't agree with the way he's gone about it, we have to admit opening talks with the city—real talks—could lead to far better things for our community."

"He's right," his ma looked at him searchingly. "If we can manage to come to some kind of a truce with Danforth and her government, we could negotiate all sorts of things... better access to resources, equipment, no more hiding... *think* how things might improve for us."

Noah's mind went immediately to Faith. If Eremus citizens were permitted in Bellator, then...

"But it's a big leap," Flynn added hastily. "At the moment, most of Bellator regards us as monsters. And Danforth won't be an easy woman to convince."

"But maybe..." his ma's face reflected a tentative hope, "just maybe the meal with the girls might be a start."

"When?" Noah burst out. Flynn looked at him questioningly. "When is this meal taking place?"

"Tonight."

Noah's heart leapt at the thought of seeing her again. Afraid his face might give him away, he stood up and grabbed a sweatshirt. "I'd better get off to my shift."

"We'll see you later, then." Anna peered at him closely. "But think about what we've said. We're not trying to be cruel. If it gets out you're close to one of the Bellator girls... well, the Eremus people might well start to look at you differently."

"Alright. See you later."

He headed out, knowing he would be early for his shift but desperate to escape the well-meaning advice of his parents. Taking his time, he wandered slowly along the tunnels, nodding at various people as he passed. As he rounded a bend close to the bathing caves, he heard a voice from behind.

"Noah, wait up!" Turning, he spotted Ella hurrying towards him. "Morning."

"Morning."

"Thought you might like to know I've just been down to see the girls."

He raised an eyebrow. "You did?"

"Well, after last night." She paused, leaning closer. "I mean... you and Faith seemed... close."

He dropped his gaze, wondering what she'd seen the previous evening. "Close?"

"Yeah, *close*." She rolled her eyes. "Don't try to deny it." Noah shifted awkwardly. "Anyway, they're both okay physically. Faith's face is still sore, but she was quite calm. Helen..." she trailed off.

Interested despite himself, Noah pressed her. "What?"

"She's still very withdrawn. Pale, quiet. I could barely get a word out of her."

"You're worried about her." Noah found it comforting that someone else seemed to care about the girls' welfare as much as he did.

"Yeah." She fixed him with a piercing gaze. "As you are about Faith."

"Well, I–"

Ignoring his discomfort, Ella went on. "They need us. These girls. They're alone in a hostile environment. And after the events of last night..." she dropped her gaze. "Well, we have to watch out for them."

"You hear that Jacob's planning some kind of dinner tonight? To *welcome* them. Show them they can trust us."

"I heard." Ella frowned. "You don't like the idea, either."

"I don't think the girls trust him the way they trust us. I mean... I'm not sure *I* trust him anymore."

Ella sighed. "Know what? Me neither. I keep wishing ma was here. She'd be on Anna and Flynn's side for sure."

Noah stared at the older girl. "So, we're taking sides now?"

"I think we might have to." Her face clouded with worry. "Jacob wants a fight with Bellator and the girls are right in the middle. And they're not all as strong as Faith seems to be." He knew she was thinking of Helen. "Noah," she grabbed hold of his arm with a strength that surprised him. "We have to be prepared to fight for these girls. Understand?"

He nodded. But as he headed away from Ella to his shift, his ma's words were ringing in his head. Already, his concern for Faith was making him take risks he wouldn't have dreamed of in the past. He trusted his ma more than most. Perhaps she was right. Any further involvement with Faith would lead to heartache. For both of them.

Chapter Fourteen: Faith

After they'd been delivered back to the caves the previous night, Faith had felt exhausted. The others had been awake, and desperate for answers to where they'd been. The good part of an hour had been spent retelling their story to the girls, whose reactions had ranged from terror that the same might happen to them, to fury over their mistreatment, which was worrying in a different way.

The only thing Faith had kept from the girls was the encounter with Noah. After she'd finished speaking, the day had been spent drowsing, on and off, broken only by the occasional whispered conversation with Sophia and a brief pause to eat. Used to the food now, the girls accepted it without complaint, but as Faith bit into the dry bread, she admitted she would welcome something different.

Her wish was granted when the cave door was rolled back later in the day. Ella's face appeared. "Hey." Her gaze sought out Helen first, then Faith. "You both look a little better."

Faith smiled, but Helen's only response was to nod. She hadn't said much since they'd returned to the cave, her body going rigid every time the cave barrier was removed.

Ella entered the cave, Ruth close behind her. They were both empty-handed. Once inside, they exchanged a glance which immediately set Faith on edge.

"What is it?" She clambered to her feet. "Why are you here?"

Ella held out a hand. "We're here... well, to bring you to the canteen."

The tension in the cave was palpable. "The canteen?" Diane said, her voice filled with questions.

"Yes." Ella crouched on the floor, her gaze levelling with Helen's. "Our leader, Jacob," Faith noticed Helen tremble at the name, "would like to invite you to eat with the community this evening."

"It's the first step," Ruth added quickly. "We hope that... if all goes well... he'll be willing to give you a few more privileges..." she gestured around the space, "maybe starting with better living quarters?"

"How do we know this isn't some... some kind of trick?" Though Avery's face blazed with her usual arrogance, her voice quivered slightly.

"You don't."

Less combative, Ella hastily followed Ruth's comment. "We're here to reassure you though. Look, as long as you behave... we're hoping Jacob will see the sense in treating you all better."

"What..." Avery pulled herself up to her full height. "No more middle of the night visits, when we're hauled outside against our will?"

"We hope not." Ella continued, ignoring Avery's sarcasm. "We think he might be coming around to seeing that, treated well, you might be of some help to us."

"He expects us to *cooperate* with him?" Avery muttered under her breath.

Catching her words, Ruth spun to face her. "Don't you get it? We're trying to help you here. That's the kind of attitude that will land you right back here with fewer privileges than you had to begin with."

Ella laid a warning hand on her arm. "But if you come with us now, eat your meal quietly..." she shot a sideways glance at Helen, "we really feel it'll be for the best."

Avery glowered, but fell silent, and within a few minutes the girls were hurrying along with Ella and Ruth to the canteen. As they approached the entrance, they hesitated, and Ella turned to face them.

"I get that you're nervous. But the majority of the community is just curious. You're different from them, that's all."

"Ready?" Ruth called ahead from the back of the line.

Seeing no objection, Ella turned and led them inside. Faith stared around as she walked in, remembering her first visit to this cave. Desperately frightened, she hadn't paid much attention to her surroundings then, but now, she found herself fascinated. The space was larger even than the bathing cave and filled with more people than she'd seen in several days. The scent of something cooking on the stoves at the far side of the space made her mouth water.

As the Danforth girls entered, a threatening silence descended over the room. Gone was the comfortable chatter which, for a moment, had reminded Faith of the Danforth dining hall back home. Instead, all eyes focused on the line of girls as it snaked across the space. Taking a deep breath, Faith put her head down and shadowed Ella to the tables at the front where people were lining up for food.

When she reached the front of the line, Faith looked up at the woman who was doling out what looked like stew. She was tall and thin, probably in her late thirties. Despite Faith's attempt to smile, her expression remained cool.

Thrusting a bowl at Faith, she jerked her head at some flatbreads piled in a dish at her side. "Take one."

Ruth leaned across from behind. "That doesn't look like an even portion, Cora."

"It's fine, honestly," Faith found herself saying, eager to escape the attention of the unfriendly woman. She tried to turn and follow Ella to a table, but Ruth placed a firm hand on her arm.

"Pass it back." She eyeballed the other woman. "I'm sure Cora just wasn't paying attention."

Scowling, the other woman held her hand out for Faith's dish. When it was returned, it contained a larger ration of stew.

Taking a flatbread, Faith smiled again. "Thank you."

Cora just nodded.

"Go with Ella." Ruth pointed to where the older girl was waiting. "I'm going to stay and supervise." She shot a dark look at Cora, and Faith decided she never wanted to be on Ruth's bad side.

"They'll come round," Ella whispered as she led Faith to a table. "They're not used to sharing rations. Food is scarce here, and some of them resent sharing it with you."

"I can understand that." Faith slid into place on the bench quickly. "It must be hard for them."

"Well, Paulo should've thought of that before he dragged you all here." Ella glared across the room at another table, where Faith assumed Noah's brother was seated. "It's not your fault."

After a few minutes, all of the Danforth girls were tucking into the surprisingly delicious stew. The only non-Danforth people at the table were Ella and Ruth. As other citizens entered, Faith watched them stare, then avoid the table, choosing to sit with other Eremus folk. Eventually, there was a noticeable ring of empty tables around the one where the interlopers sat.

Faith's thoughts went to Anna. She wondered if it had been difficult for her when she first arrived from Bellator, alone and pregnant. How long had it taken her to be accepted here? With growing admiration, Faith decided Anna must have had incredible strength to withstand the hostility she must have encountered. No wonder she understood their situation better than most.

The Danforth girls mostly kept their heads down as they ate, painfully aware of everyone's eyes on them. Eventually, the Eremus citizens went back to their meals, the noise of chatter between the citizens growing in volume again. Faith noticed how each table seemed to contain a mixed gender family group. Looking closely though, the families weren't traditional, like the ones in the Herstory books. She thought of Noah's own family: a female from Bellator, living happily with her biological son, a partner who was not his father, and her partner's nephew.

Hardly the nuclear family she'd read about.

Faith glanced around, wondering idly if Anna might be sitting somewhere close by with her son. She had yet to spot Noah, though she tried hard to convince herself she wasn't searching the room for him. Sophia, sitting beside her, had shoved a gentle elbow in her ribs a couple of times, and Faith knew she was warning her against attracting too much attention with her sweeping gaze.

Glancing over at Ruth, she frowned. Noah had been friends with her for years, he'd said. They'd grown up together. Unable to help herself, she wondered if Noah held Ruth's hand in the same way he'd held hers the night before.

"Room for another?" The familiar voice jolted Faith from her reverie, and she turned to see Anna bringing a tray over to their table. Sliding across the bench to make room for the older woman, Faith nodded hello, glad that no one could read her mind.

Anna sat down and tucked into her meal without paying much attention to the others in the room. As she did, Faith noticed curious glances being exchanged all around the room. Clearly, as the resident medic and an important member of the community, Anna's support meant something.

When her gaze fell on the table where the food was being served, she stiffened. Receiving a far warmer greeting from Cora than the Danforth girls had, Noah was collecting his meal. Nodding his thanks, he turned. Faith held her breath. Would he, too, make a statement by supporting them?

His eyes swept the room, coming to rest on their table. She waited for him to look directly at her, to smile, to acknowledge the moment between them the night before, but his gaze simply swept over her and moved on. Frowning slightly, Noah turned his back on her table, making instead for the other side of the canteen, and seating himself next to Flynn.

Faith looked down at the table, embarrassed at her disappointment. It wasn't like he owed her anything. Sensing that Sophia, ever attentive, had noticed her change of mood, she busied herself tidying her tray.

"Where do we take this?" She pointed down at her empty bowl.

"Just return it to the front," Ella pointed, "although you should wait 'til–"

But Faith was already on her feet. Hopping over the bench, she headed for the tables at the front, determined to prove she was more than a spoiled Bellator brat. Reaching her destination, she hesitated, unsure what to do next. Cora had disappeared and there was no one around to ask. But there was a large bowl of soapy water on another table. Eremus citizens, Faith decided, would wash up after themselves.

Moving towards it, Faith plunged her dish into the water. It was scalding hot, and she leapt back, gasping. The bowl slipped from her hands, shattering on the floor.

"What do you think you're doing all the way over here without supervision?"

Blushing furiously, Faith turned around. The voice was familiar, belonging to the older boy Ella had called Harden.

"I-I'm sorry." She cursed the stutter in her voice.

An older woman stepped uncomfortably close to Faith. "After more food, perhaps?"

"No!" Alarmed by how high-pitched the denial sounded, Faith tried to keep her voice calm. "No, I was trying to–"

"We were *assured* you'd stay with your supervisors." The volume of the woman's voice grew. Clearly, she wanted everyone to hear her. "We're told to trust you, yet your actions *already* suggest you don't wish to abide by our rules."

The small knot of people around Faith seemed to be closing in. "Look," she held out a hand, "I was just cleaning up after myself." She dropped to a crouch, picking up one of the larger pieces of the broken dish. Straightening, she held it out. "See? I'm sorry that I broke–"

Before she knew what was happening, Harden had leapt forward and clamped a hand down on her shoulder. His other hand tightened around her wrist, causing her to cry out and drop the piece of broken crockery.

"Arming yourself, huh?"

Too late, Faith understood. "No! I wasn't–"

"Let go of her." The crowd parted at Flynn's command. Stepping forward, he repeated his request. "I said, let go."

Reluctantly, Harden obeyed.

"She said she was cleaning up. That's all." Flynn waved a hand around at the people standing close by. "She was hardly trying to fight her way out. Look at her. How many of you would it take to overpower her, anyway?"

The citizens had begun to back away, most of their expressions reflecting their shame. Only Harden and the older woman remained.

"We have to be cautious, Flynn." The woman looked down her nose at Faith. "We can't just put our trust in these *strangers*."

"You may be right, Sarah," Faith didn't know how he was keeping a civil tone with her, "but we don't have to treat them like animals. You surrounded her. Threatened her."

"Acting like that is only confirming what they think of us already." As Noah appeared behind Flynn, Faith's heart gave a sudden jolt. He moved towards her. "Let me take you back to the others. You might feel *safer* over there."

Glaring at Harden and Sarah, he offered Faith his hand. Tentatively, Faith reached out and took it. As they turned and walked past the others, she could feel their gaze on her, but somehow Noah's support helped her to keep her head high.

Behind them, she heard Flynn's voice. "Show's over, folks."

Faith felt Noah uncurling her fingers and opening her palm out flat. For a second, she wondered if he was repeating his actions of the previous night. But instead, he brought her hand towards his face, studying it closely. She shot him a quizzical look.

"Just checking you didn't cut yourself."

"Thanks," she managed to whisper, but as they reached her table, he let go.

"No problem. Though maybe next time stay with your assigned supervisors. At least until people adjust to having you around."

She stared back over her shoulder at Flynn sweeping. "Guess it wasn't such a good idea. I was just trying to..."

"I know. But you have to understand... a lot of the people here have a healthy mistrust of anyone from Bellator." He motioned to her seat at the table. "Alright now?"

She nodded. A moment later, he had moved to the other side of the table, seating himself beside Ruth.

"You okay?" Sophia leaned close. "That was scary."

"Yeah." Faith tried to keep her gaze from Noah. "Bit of a stupid thing to do, I guess."

Farrah shuddered. "They really don't trust us, do they?"

"Do you trust them, though?" Anna's voice cut into their conversation. The girls looked at her, quizzically. "I mean... haven't you grown up thinking all Eremus men are beasts?"

They nodded. "And they've been brought up thinking Bellator is the enemy. It's a hard habit to break, that's all. Give it time."

She finished speaking, and her eyes clouded as they flicked to something over Faith's shoulder. A ripple of fear swept the table as, one by one, the girls' gaze followed. Curious, Faith turned, seeing Flynn approaching. Striding along beside him was Jacob.

"Good evening, ladies. Apologies that it's taken so long for us to properly welcome you to our community." He smiled broadly, as though he hadn't been the one to drag two of them out into the woods the previous night. Placing his bowlful of stew down on the table, he pulled up a stool and seated himself at the head of the table. "Shall we talk?"

Chapter Fifteen: Noah

Faith looked horrified, and after the events of the previous night, Noah couldn't blame her. From the moment the girls had spotted Jacob, a tension had cloaked the table. Wishing he'd ignored his ma's advice and taken a seat closer to Faith, Noah curled his hands into fists. The protective instinct which swept over him was becoming frustratingly familiar, and impossible to ignore.

He'd tried to listen to his ma. To be sensible and avoid her. He'd chosen a seat with Flynn, away from the girls' table, keeping his distance so he didn't reveal their connection. But when Harden had grabbed Faith, he'd leapt to her defence just as quickly as Flynn. He hadn't been able to help himself. Spotting his ma's warning look as they joined the others, he'd purposefully seated himself away from Faith, but still, he felt himself drawn to her.

And by trying to make nice, Jacob was only terrifying her. Noah could feel her fear radiating across the table. He knew their leader would have had more success speaking to the girls in their cave, when it didn't feel so public. After the incident between Faith and Harden, feelings ran high on both sides, but Jacob had never been one to attack a problem with subtlety. Smoothing his hands down the legs of his jeans, Noah tried to gauge the girls' reactions to Jacob's speech.

"...as you know," their leader was saying, after he had swallowed a few mouthfuls of the stew, "we didn't expect you to be here, and I'm sorry if our initial treatment of you has not been warm. We understand that you are..." he ran his gaze over the girls slowly, "*innocent victims* in all of this."

Around the table, the girls were silent. Some watched Jacob closely, a veiled hatred in their eyes, others weren't even able to meet his gaze. None of them seemed charmed by him, as the Eremus people so often were.

"I won't lie to you," Jacob continued. "We want things from Bellator." He rolled up his flatbread and took a large bite out of the end. There was a pause as he chewed, as though he were enjoying any ordinary meal with members of his own community. Noah had to admire his confidence. "We want to arrange talks with Danforth. Discuss her current position on males in the community. We're hoping she might consider amending or reversing some of the city's laws regarding men."

"I understand that my behaviour the other night was a little extreme." As Jacob bowed his head in what might have passed for remorse, Noah wondered if he even knew which two girls he had dragged into the forest handcuffed and blindfolded. "But it was a part of establishing Eremus in a position of strength. Now that I've done that, I'm hoping to contact Danforth to arrange these talks."

He took another spoonful of stew and looked around as he ate it, as if expecting one of the girls to interject. Noah knew they wouldn't. When Jacob had finished his mouthful he shrugged, as he'd given the girls a chance to speak and they hadn't taken it.

"I was wondering if you might have some ideas as to how I might... approach your governor." He smiled again. "I mean... we can make your lives here quite bearable, I think, and I'd be very happy to improve your living conditions if some of you were willing to… let's say… pass on information we might find useful."

"You want them to act as spies?" Anna sounded horrified.

"That's a harsh word for it." Jacob shrugged. "I just think they might be able to tell us things about the city… about the school, at least, which might help our cause." He turned to the girls. "Any thoughts?"

An uncomfortable silence settled over the table. Jacob continued with his meal, consuming the rest of his stew. None of the girls spoke.

As Jacob scooped the final morsels of stew into his mouth, he straightened. "Perhaps it will take a little longer for me to gain your trust. For now," he waved a hand at some other Eremus citizens who had just entered the canteen, "I've had some of my people set you all up in a much better living space. Call it a show of faith."

Pushing his stool back from the table, he stood. "I'll bid you goodnight, for now. Think about what I've said." He picked up his bowl from the table and, giving them a sharp nod, turned and strode away.

Even when he'd gone, the girls were silent. Anna shot a concerned glance at Flynn, but Ella was the first to speak.

"Maybe you'd all like to rest, now?" There were nods from most of the girls. "I'll find out where your new quarters are."

Pushing herself to her feet, she walked over to one of the citizens who had just entered. After a brief conversation, she returned, nodding at Ruth. "West tunnel."

Ruth stood, indicating to the rest of the girls to follow her example. They were desperate to leave the canteen, their eagerness to escape the perceived danger clear from the speed of their movements. As Faith turned to go, she shot Noah a final look of confusion. He felt like Paulo had punched him in the chest again.

"Thank you."

He turned to his ma. "For what?"

"For trying to steer clear of her. I can see it's not easy."

"I–" he struggled to find the words, "she needed–"

His ma squeezed his arm. "I know."

Shrugging her off, not unkindly, he stood up to leave. "I'm heading out."

His ma glanced over at Flynn. "Want me to walk back with you?" He shook his head. "Alright. See you later, then."

He could feel their pitying gaze as he walked away.

Shunning all company, he headed for the sky cave. With the working day over, it was deserted, and he finally felt like he could breathe. Once he had climbed to the top of the ridge, he sat, trying to calm the storm in his head. Everything was so complicated. He'd wanted to be a raider. Being one had led him to Bellator. To Faith. When he was with her, he felt different. Stronger. More capable. But, right now, he didn't know how to help her.

Fishing in his pocket, he took out Faith's necklace again. He still hadn't found the right moment to give it back. And now he'd seen the other Danforth pendants for himself. Every girl in the cave wore one. Except Faith. Every moment he kept it, he felt worse about it.

He turned the pendant over in his hand. Made from gold, it should have glinted in the light from the moon which streamed into the cave. The letter D was large and ornate, written in the academy's stylish, scrolling font. But the surface seemed tarnished somehow, and it had lost its sheen.

Probably from being crushed in his pocket. Amongst the dirt and grime of the tunnels. The pendant's value taunted him. He curled his hand into a fist. His ma was right. How could he imagine he had anything to offer Faith? A penniless Eremus boy, who'd lived his life underground like an animal.

Several times, he'd wondered if the missing necklace had played some part in the harsh punishment Faith had received on her return to the academy. He was also curious why she hadn't been issued a new one, fearing it was because Danforth's principal had planned to boot her out of the academy altogether.

Thrusting the item back into his pocket, he sighed. His people were currently in the midst of a war with her city. Any relationship with Faith would put both of them in danger. Jacob was determined to achieve his goal, to arrange talks with Danforth which would lead to freedom for Eremus, but he was kidding himself if he thought it would be easily achieved.

Perhaps, if Noah put his mind to it, he could assist Jacob in managing the talks with Danforth. After all, if they were successful, Eremus might gain the right to enter Bellator, to mix with its citizens. Again, his thoughts strayed to Faith and he cursed himself. He had no idea if she had even the vaguest interest in him.

He gazed down into the forest. Being here usually calmed his mind, but this time the trees weren't working their magic. And then, from the undergrowth below, something caught his eye. A rustling in the leaves which he might have dismissed as an animal, yet intuition told him it wasn't. He froze. If this was a Bellator guard, they were closer to discovering the Eremus complex than they'd ever been. The sky cave was not one which could be stumbled upon accidentally, yet the noises he heard indicated whoever was moving through the trees was not so far away.

Creeping to the edge of the ridge, he stared out. For a moment, there was nothing, and then, he saw it. A figure, moving through the trees in the distance. But not, he thought, a guard. The woman stepped into a clearing and was silhouetted by the moonlight and he could see she was missing the usual arsenal of weaponry. And instead of the close-fitting black guard cap, her hair was twisted upwards on the back of her head. Not a guard.

But not an Eremus citizen either.

Intrigued, he crawled over to one side of the ridge, and slipped over the edge. Years of experience clambering down the cliff side as a child worked in his favour, and he reached the ground in no time. Standing still, he listened closely for the sound of the woman's footsteps. Certainly, she wasn't used to moving around quietly. It took him no more than a minute to locate the direction she was travelling.

As he set off in pursuit, he realised he had no weapon other than the knife he always carried in his belt. He decided for now he would just shadow the woman, see where she went, and only try to intervene if she came too close to any of the tunnel entrances. For now, she appeared to be moving in the opposite direction, and he was fairly certain she didn't know where she was headed. His curiosity piqued, he moved a little faster, attempting to get closer to her, to see more of the mysterious woman who roamed the forest.

He hadn't yet managed to get a close look, but he was certain she wasn't a guard. What Bellator woman would consider hiking through dangerous territory, alone, in the middle of the night? He knew some of the more far-flung areas of Bellator, the fields and woods close to the city, were inhabited by citizens, and many of them took trips out into the forest on occasion. But only in daylight. Only in large groups, and usually accompanied by at least one guard.

He upped his pace, daring to get a little closer. The woman didn't seem to be travelling in any particular direction. Though she had been close to the sky cave, she hadn't discovered it, or she would have been trying to use it to enter Eremus. His heart pounding, he realised she had wandered close to one of the community's sentry posts. At present, those on guard had been instructed only to observe intruders to the forest, not to attack. But with feelings running high, mistakes could be made.

He was relieved when, ahead of him, the woman stopped. Startled by her abrupt change of pace, Noah was a little slow to halt his own progress, and stepped on a twig. It cracked beneath his foot, echoing through the woods like a gunshot.

Only a few spindly trees separated them now. The woman turned, slowly, looking up from a piece of paper which she held in her hand. She took a step in his direction. Stopped.

Noah took out his knife and held his breath.

"Who's there?" The woman folded what could have been a map and stowed it in a pocket. She raised her hands slowly in the air. "I'm not here to cause trouble."

Noah hesitated. The woman was brave. Wondering how to reply, he waited. Surely, she would say more? She had to know he was from Eremus: a threat.

"I'm looking for the girls." Did her voice shake slightly? "The ones taken from the hospital in Bellator recently. I know that they're here, somewhere."

Noah risked a reply. "What do you want with them?"

The woman seemed to relax. "I just want to know they're safe. I have... a message for them."

"What message?"

"I'd like," the woman straightened, "to deliver it in person."

Noah laughed. "And you think you'll be permitted to?"

The woman took another step towards the trees which concealed him. She looked to be the same age as his ma, but had an air of gentility about her which was absent from the Eremus citizens. Her hair was held back in a taut knot on her head, and she wore a pair of delicate, silver-rimmed glasses.

But the steely determination on her face was what made his decision for him. Without further thought, he stepped out from his hiding place. "What do you want with them?"

The woman started, but held her ground. "You're from Eremus." It wasn't a question.

"I am."

"The Danforth girls: Helen, Avery, Diane, Farrah, Sophia, Faith, Mary, Catherine." The list was reeled off without hesitation. "You have them?"

"I think you know that we do." Noah tried to stay casual, though the fact that she knew their names had to be significant.

She took another step towards him, oblivious to the knife in his hand. "Are they safe?"

"Who are you? Why aren't you frightened of me?"

Ignoring his first question, she nodded at his weapon. "You have a knife. But you haven't used it yet."

"Maybe I don't feel I need to at the moment." Noah glanced around at the trees which surrounded them. "You're alone. I've been following you."

"I am. A fact which I hope proves I come in peace. And not with Danforth's knowledge."

Noah scoffed. "And we're supposed to trust that? Believe that the Bellator governor *doesn't* know you're here?"

"It's the truth." She looked him up and down. "You're young."

"Yes. Many of my community are." He straightened, uncomfortable with her scrutiny. "Doesn't mean I'm helpless or weak. Or that I don't know the score."

"I'm sure it doesn't." The woman's calm continued to astound him. "Yet you haven't attacked me. In fact, none of the guards Danforth sent into the woods over the past few nights have been harmed. You kidnapped one... briefly... but only so your leader could send us a message."

This woman wasn't just an ordinary citizen. She knew far too much. But didn't that make her presence here doubly suspicious? For the first time, Noah cursed his decision to come out here alone.

"Are the girls safe?" The woman looked genuinely worried. "I mean... can you at least tell me that? Are you looking after them?" She frowned at his silence. "Are any of them ill?"

He frowned. "Why should they be ill?"

"I've reason to believe one of the girls in particular might be suffering from..." she paused, looking uncomfortable, "let's just say one of them might not be as... healthy as the rest."

Noah narrowed his eyes. "Which one?"

"From your expression, I think you know who I'm talking about." Her face creased into a frown. "And if that's true, then the girl in question *has* been suffering from some... symptoms."

Infuriated, Noah took a step towards the woman. "Who are you?"

She hesitated for a moment, as though considering how much to tell him. "My name is Charlotte. I know the girls well." Her gaze remained steady and calm. "I promise you, I only want to see that they're okay. Deliver a message to them." She proffered her hands in front of her. "Will you take me to your leader? I'll come quietly. I'd be happy to wear a blindfold."

A disturbance in the bushes to one side of the woman drew both their eyes. Before either of them could react, a figure stepped out from behind them. Noah didn't know whether he was annoyed or relieved to see Paulo striding towards them, a gun strapped to his back.

"I don't think that will be necessary." With no delay, he dosed the woman with a generous amount of Sleepsol, waiting a second before catching her in his arms. He turned to Noah with a wry grin. "Wondered where you'd wandered off to, little brother. Good thing I decided to follow."

Noah clenched his hands into fists. "Did you have to..." He gestured to the sleeping woman.

"Better than knocking her out with a punch, don't you think? I thought you'd approve of the humanitarian approach." Noah resisted the urge to argue. "Let's get her inside. Seems like she'll be a good addition to our hostages. Sounded to me like she had quite a bit of useful intel."

Paulo strode away, carrying the woman as though she weighed nothing. Noah hurried after him. Clearly, she had some insider knowledge of Bellator. She'd implied she had some understanding of Faith's condition. Once Jacob got his hands on her, who knew how she'd react? If he frightened her, she'd clam up, and he'd learn nothing.

"Where are you taking her?" He stumbled a little, envying his brother's grace and speed, despite his burden.

"To Jacob." Paulo paused as he reached the lower, more accessible entrance to the sky cave, waiting for Noah to push aside the fronds of greenery hiding it. "Find out where he wants me to put her until he can question her."

Determined not to let Paulo whisk her away, Noah re-hid the entrance from the outside world as fast as he could. The woman deserved a fair hearing, but would only be assured of one if people like his ma and Flynn knew she was here.

"But don't we need to–" He pursued his brother. "I mean, the whole council should–"

Paulo didn't slow down. Striding ahead, he ignored Noah.

"She's unarmed!" Noah called, hurrying after him. "You can see she's not a guard. She didn't attempt to attack me."

His brother ignored him. Rounding the corner, he disappeared up the tunnel towards Jacob's cave. Noah gave up the chase, knowing he wouldn't catch Paulo, even with such a heavy burden. If Noah wanted to find out more about the woman, he'd need others on his side. Quashing the urge to punch something, he headed home.

Chapter Sixteen: Faith

Whilst nowhere near as pleasant as the Danforth dorms, their new home was a definite improvement on the one they had known since they'd arrived in Eremus. Closer to the canteen, which Faith was learning was the hub of community life in the camp, it had eight thin bedrolls, additional blankets and, for the first time, some pillows, which made sleeping far more comfortable; several lanterns which their guards refilled on a daily basis; more space to walk around in and, best of all, was close to one of the Eremus bathrooms.

Hardly state of the art, the primitive system was nonetheless an improvement on the bucket they'd had to suffer previously. It allowed them some degree of privacy and they were allowed to access it several times a day. Their cave still had a sturdy wooden door, but they had been allowed out to bathe again, and had even been taken for a short period of exercise that morning. Better still, Ella had brought them some of the promised cards, and had spent an hour that morning teaching them some games.

Helen was still quiet and had only brightened up during Ella's visit. When the Eremus girl left, she lapsed into a worrying silence. Recognising her unhappiness, Sophia went to sit with her.

"It's fascinating how different things are here, isn't it?" she began.

Faith could see she was attempting to bring Helen out of her shell. Collecting three hunks of bread from the tray Ella had left, she joined them.

Sophia bit into the bread with enthusiasm, but Helen barely nibbled at it.

"Their family units are strange, right?" Faith added. "I mean the way they have mothers and fathers." She thought of Ella and Ruth. "Mostly, anyway." She leaned towards Helen. "Don't you think?"

"I guess so."

"It's so outdated," Avery's voice was scathing. "I mean… it's like going back to the way things were before the virus. When men ruled everything and women were nothing but babymakers and punching bags."

"That's not true." Diane spoke through a mouthful of bread. "The men here aren't all monsters."

"Not even when they forcibly drag us into the forest in the dead of night?"

Noting Helen's reaction, Sophia shot a dark look at Avery. "No. There are those who treat women with respect. And the women here… they have a say in the way things are run."

"Look at Anna," Faith added.

"I guess you're right," Farrah admitted, earning herself an elbow from her best friend. "Well, Anna's the medic, isn't she? Ella and Ruth aren't mistreated."

"It's a pretty small sample to base your assessment on." Avery sniffed. "I, for one, am not willing to just accept things are what they seem. Danforth says…"

"Yes, what *does* Danforth say?" Diane mocked. "I mean… since you seem to be her number one fan." Avery scowled.

"Well, you are! Why *are* you so willing to accept everything she says as gospel?"

"Maybe I'm just not so quick to abandon the teachings I've spent my whole life studying." Avery shot her a withering look. "I just think it makes sense to stay cautious around them... not to trust them too much."

"She's right." Farrah chimed in. "I mean, I think that Jacob... and maybe the other guy—Paulo, is it?—are the ones we need to be cautious around. The conversation with him at dinner was downright scary."

"Agreed." Diane muttered. "He knows how to turn on the charm when he needs to. I wouldn't trust him as far as I could throw him."

"Does anyone think we should help Jacob?" Farrah asked. "I mean... he asked us to think about it."

"No way!" Avery's retort was instant. "And make it easier for him to destroy our way of life?"

"What do you think will happen if we don't help him?" Mary's voice trembled. "I mean... would he...?" Her words hung in the air.

"I'm not sure." Diane shrugged. "But we know what he's capable of."

"Maybe we should consider giving him what he wants." Sophia said thoughtfully. "I mean, if it protects us."

"You've just *said* you don't trust him," Avery was breathing hard. "How can we know what he'll do with any information we give him?"

"He says he wants to talk with Danforth." Sophia shrugged, ignoring Avery's exasperated splutter. "What if we–"

"Do you think... if we helped them to set up these talks, we might get to go home?" Mary's face lit up.

"Maybe." Faith's heart went out to her. "But we'd have to be *careful* what we told them."

"Faith's right." Sophia looked directly at Avery. "As are you. Whatever we tell them, it can't be anything they could use to hurt people."

"Then what information are you suggesting we give him?" Farrah mused.

"Nothing about the city itself. No locations, no places we know people might be at specific times." Sophia's brow furrowed. "Jacob needs to arrange a neutral place to meet with Danforth."

Faith agreed. "Otherwise, both sides risk an attack."

"Where would be neutral though?" Catherine asked.

"Somewhere in the woods, but not too close to Eremus?" Faith offered.

"Jacob won't want Danforth anywhere near here." Sophia shook her head. "But what if we–"

She stopped abruptly. Hearing the distinctive sound of the door being unlocked, the girls tensed. Despite the improvement in their treatment, they still didn't trust all the Eremus citizens. Faith half-expected to see Jacob at the door, demanding a more satisfactory response to his question. She was surprised when Noah appeared. He was quickly joined by Ruth and Ella, who glanced around the cave with a smile.

"Are you guys ready for something new?" Ignoring the confusion on their faces, Ella forged ahead. "Jacob's decided that while you're here, being fed and receiving fairly decent treatment, you need to *earn your keep*, so to speak."

"Earn our keep?" Sophia queried. "What do you mean?"

"Just that you do some chores around the place."

"You're telling us we have to *work* for you now?" The expression on Avery's face was comical.

"Everyone works in Eremus," Ruth said.

"But in return for your efforts," Ella soothed, "you'll have a little more freedom to move around the caves."

Sophia was the first to stand. "What is it you want us to do?"

"Nothing too taxing to begin with," Ruth shot a pointed look at Avery, who narrowed her eyes.

"And *nothing*," Noah added from the doorway, with a sideways glance at Diane, "unsupervised."

"We suggested you might help in the canteen." Ruth walked around the cave, blowing out the light in each of the lanterns. "Somewhere we can keep an eye on you all."

"And don't worry, it's nothing that requires expertise," Ella reassured them, catching sight of the younger girls exchanging worried glances.

Avery scowled, but the others stood up and moved to the door. Bored as well as frightened, the offer to escape the confines of their cave for a few hours was a tempting one, even if it meant some hard work. When it was clear she'd be left behind in the darkness, Avery made a show of clambering to her feet, but eventually lined up next to Farrah.

"Ready to go?" Ella nodded at them before heading out.

In the tunnel, Faith made to join Sophia, who was standing with Ruth and Ella at the front of the line. As she hurried forward though, she felt a hand on her arm. She looked back to find herself staring into a pair of familiar green eyes.

"Walk with me?" Noah whispered, pulling her backwards.

Faith glanced at the other girls. Ahead of them, the group had set off in the direction of the canteen. Aside from Sophia, Ruth, and Ella, they were two by two: Helen and Diane, Mary and Catherine, Farrah and Avery. All paired up, just like they were going to the med centre for a blood test back in Bellator. Following orders, compliant as always.

Reassured, she fell into step beside Noah. His hand remained on her arm, surprisingly strong, encouraging her to slow her pace until the gap between them and the others had widened. Faith's heart was pounding so loudly she wondered if Noah could hear it. What could he have to say to her that the others couldn't hear? She would stay quiet and listen, she decided. Confiding in Noah had only led to disaster in the past.

When Farrah and Avery were out of earshot, Noah relinquished his hold on her arm and leaned closer. "I wanted to ask you about something... well, some*one*, really." He waited, as though giving her the chance to object. When she didn't, he continued. "We took another Bellator citizen captive last night."

All thought of remaining silent disintegrated. "You went into Bellator?"

"No. I found her here. In the woods."

"Wait, you mean *you* took her captive?"

"Not exactly, no." He paused, as though gathering his thoughts. "After dinner, I went outside to–" At his abrupt stop, Faith shot a sideways look at him, noting a faint blush on his cheek. He refused to meet her gaze. "I wanted some space to think. But while I was out there, I saw her."

"A guard?"

"No. An ordinary citizen."

"Wandering in the woods?"

"Not just wandering, as it turns out." Noah paused again, nodding as they passed some other Eremus citizens. Faith wondered if he was telling her things he shouldn't. The thought made her heart race even harder. When the others were gone, he continued. "This woman... said she was looking for the missing Danforth students. Seemed to have quite a bit of inside knowledge about you all. I tried to speak to her, get more information, but then Paulo turned up and–"

Stopping abruptly, Faith turned to him. "What did he do?"

Again, Noah took her arm. "Don't stop. It has to look like we're talking about nothing of importance... or not talking at all." Faith shook his arm off and started walking again. Beside her, she felt him relax. "Look... Paulo didn't hurt this woman. But he did knock her out and bring her inside. She's in– They're keeping her in your old cave."

"A prisoner?"

"Well, yes." He held up a hand at Faith's enraged expression. "Hey, she was stalking through the woods, very close to our camp. Surely, you can understand Jacob being suspicious. She could have been a threat."

They were approaching the canteen now, and Faith watched as, ahead of them, the girls disappeared inside. Ella stood at the door, ushering them through. Casting a backwards glance at Noah, she gave a small smile as she turned to follow the others.

Slowing his pace even further as they neared the entrance, Noah grasped Faith's arm once again. Abruptly, he changed direction, steering her away from the others.

"Hey!" Faith struggled, but he was stronger than she'd given him credit for. "What are you doing?"

"Trust me?" Not letting go, he moved closer. "Please?" His breath tickled against her ear. "I'm not going to hurt you."

Giving in, Faith allowed herself to be guided away from the others. It wasn't long before she realised they were heading for Ella's cave again. At the doorway, Noah paused to check that the tunnel was empty, then pulled aside the curtain.

He met her gaze briefly. "After you."

Faith felt her heart jolt in her chest. Hesitantly, she ducked into the living space beyond. Memories of their encounter the previous night came flooding back. Ignoring the table where they'd been sitting then, Noah took a seat on the bench at the side of the room, beckoning for her to follow suit.

She resisted, not trusting herself to be alone with him. "Why did you bring me here?"

"I just wanted to talk to you where no one would disturb us." He shifted awkwardly. "Would you sit down? You're making me nervous."

Aware of the close proximity the bench would bring, Faith lowered herself onto the far end of it, leaving as much distance between them as she could. When she looked up, Noah's face was unreadable.

"Won't you be in trouble for bringing me here?" She stared at him. "I mean, I get the feeling this little visit hasn't exactly been... approved by your superiors."

"You're right. It hasn't."

"But it must be important. For you to bring me here, alone with you, without Jacob," she fixed him with a piercing stare, "or *your mother* knowing?"

He didn't flinch at her accusing tone. Something about him radiated a confidence she hadn't seen in him before. She wondered if she should be afraid.

"Look, no one but Ruth and Ella know we're here. It's why we came to their place and not mine." He paused, eyeing her closely. "But I'll tell my ma about our conversation afterwards, and, actually, I don't think she'll mind that I spoke to you."

"You don't?"

"Well," he raised an eyebrow, "she'll mind in one way, but I hope, once I explain the reason for me speaking to you, she'll understand." He grinned wryly. "She might even thank me, if you're able to give me some useful information."

Stung by his words, Faith stiffened. "And what makes you think I'll just tell you what you want to know? Given our past history..." His grin disappeared and he shot her a frustrated look. "You know I'm right! I mean it's not like you have a great track record for keeping my secrets in the past, is it? And now you're *telling* me, outright, that whatever I say to you will be taken straight back to your mother. It's hardly a good way to gain my trust."

"You're right. I know." He held her gaze steadily. "But at least I'm being honest with you. I'm not lying to get you to trust me. Now, would you hear me out?" He paused. When she didn't argue, he shifted forward a little, narrowing the gap between them. "There's kind of a... division... in the Eremus council. We *all* want to gain acceptance from Bellator... reduce our community's suffering, stop hiding... but let's say there's a slight difference of opinion in the way we plan to achieve this."

His gaze was steady and his eyes earnest. Faith had suspected he was going out on a limb bringing her here, but she hadn't expected him to confide things, private things, about the Eremus council to her. In doing so, surely, he was risking his entire community.

Seeming to anticipate her question, he hurried on. "So, I'm trusting you with information about me. About Eremus. Because last time I wasn't worthy of your trust. And I felt like I owed you something before I asked you to trust me again." Shifting forward again, he closed the gap between them. "I'm hoping you won't make me regret it."

He shot her a rueful smile and she looked away. He was trying, she could see that. But past experience held her back. His closeness confused her, and when she opened her mouth, she wasn't sure what would come out of it. Perhaps it was better, safer, to remain silent.

When she glanced up again, he was still watching her. The expression in the green eyes was intense, urging her to speak. She closed her eyes and shook her head, sensing his disappointment. Pushing herself to her feet, she moved to the opposite side of the cave. When the table stood between them, she felt able to speak again.

"Who was this woman you found in the woods, then?"

"I was hoping you might tell *me* that."

"What did she *look* like? And you said you spoke to her. Didn't you ask her name? I mean," she qualified, "*before* Paulo went all caveman on her?"

He grinned, and she felt absurdly pleased at his reaction to her attempted joke. "I don't know... she was slight, in her forties, maybe? With brown hair and these tiny little glasses." Faith felt her heartrate increase at the description. "She only gave me her first name though. Charlotte."

"Charlotte..." she ran the name over in her head, "it's Kemp!" The name came out louder than Faith had planned. Noah jumped at her sudden outburst, then cocked his head to one side. Taking a breath to calm herself, Faith lowered her voice to answer his unspoken question. "She's a professor. At Danforth."

Chapter Seventeen: Noah

"One of your *teachers*?" Noah looked thoughtful. "Interesting."

From her position on the other side of the cave, he could feel Faith's curiosity. He still wasn't certain that separating her from the others had been the right thing to do, but when he'd described his encounter with the mysterious woman to Ella, she had insisted that speaking to Faith was the fastest way to discover more about her.

On his return home the previous night, the only one there had been Flynn. His ma had been called away to the medcave to care for a sick child. After Noah had told him about the woman in the forest, Flynn had gone straight over to Jacob's to speak to him. By the time he got there, though, the woman had already been locked away in the girls' original cell. Their leader was not keen on allowing others to question her.

Since Noah had no way of getting close to the woman, asking Faith a few questions had seemed like a good idea. But now, alone in his friend's home with her, he was less sure. She'd seemed uncomfortable since they'd got here, and her sudden leap away from him did not suggest trust. He couldn't blame her. His behaviour towards her must have been confusing. But now, more than ever, he wanted her to trust him. If Faith knew things about Kemp, things which even Jacob couldn't discover, it could help them figure out why she was here. And he had to admit, spending time alone with her was enjoyable, if a little confusing.

She regarded him from behind the table, her eyes narrowed. "Why would Kemp come all the way out here?"

"Don't you know why?"

Faith was silent, her brow furrowed.

"Jacob's concerned she's been sent by Danforth... as some kind of spy." He hesitated. "But I got the sense that she was..." he sighed. "I've been wrong before, though."

"You think she's here trying to help us?" Noah glanced up, surprised by how well Faith read him. She sighed. "I mean... she's one of the nicer teachers at Danforth. Strict, of course, but fair. But she..." she broke off, frustrated.

Fighting the urge to move towards her, Noah curled his fingers into his palms. "She what?"

"I don't know. When I got in trouble for being out of school without permission that night, she..." Noah felt a twisting in his stomach at Faith's mention of their encounter in the hospital, "I had a detention..." noting his look of confusion, she explained, "like a punishment? I had to sit with her after school for a couple of hours, complete an extra assignment to make up for what I did. And she seemed different."

"Different?"

"I don't know... she set me an assignment... that was standard... but then she messaged me with some information to help me complete it." Her eyes lighting up, Faith began pacing across the cave. "Stuff I'd never seen before. News reports from years ago... about the origins of the academy and Chancellor Danforth's background."

Noah watched her, fascinated. Her wariness had disappeared as she tried to work out her teacher's behaviour. She came closer to him, then moved further away as she paced the length of the cave, sharp gestures of her hands punctuating her speech as she spoke.

"I wish I could remember more of... it said something about a group of citizens objecting to the academy before it opened... they thought its purpose might be less than ethical." She grimaced. "They were probably right." She rubbed her forehead tiredly. "I don't know, a lot's happened since then. It was odd, though, because Kemp didn't speak to me about it. She didn't even tell me she'd sent it, really. But when Anderson, that's our principal, came in to haul me out," she paused her pacing and glanced at Noah briefly, "she had the tech professor search my wristclip—they found the photos I'd taken in the hospital and figured out where I'd *really* been. Anyway, when Anderson looked through my mailbox, the message had disappeared."

"What do you mean?"

"I think Kemp deleted it."

"You mean she didn't want your principal to know she'd given it to you?"

"Exactly." Faith stopped in front of the bench where Noah was seated. "Like she'd be in trouble for drawing my attention to the information. For showing me something which might give away the academy's true purpose."

"There's a chance she's on your side?" Noah mused.

"Maybe." A frown creased her face and she lowered herself back onto the bench next to him. "I can't be certain, though."

"There's something else." Noah waited a second, until she looked at him. "Kemp was *specifically* concerned about one of you being sick." He leaned closer. "Faith, you're the only one of the girls who's suffered any kind of illness. Do you think she's looking for you? Checking to see how you've been affected...?"

As he watched, her face clouded over. She bit her lip, and looked down at her lap. When she spoke, her voice was a whisper.

"You mean because of the drug they gave me?"

"Maybe." Taking a chance, he took hold of her hand. "It's probably nothing. I mean... you were a little dizzy and feverish at first, but... I mean you haven't been feeling sick more recently, have you?"

She shook her head. "But if they gave me the same stuff they gave to Serene... I mean..." she swallowed hard, and when she looked up at him, her eyes were filled with tears. "Noah, it *killed* her."

Shifting forwards, he slid an arm around her, moving her towards him until her head rested on his shoulder. For a moment, she resisted, but then he felt her relax against him as though all the fight had gone out of her. Encircling her with his other arm, he held her close, sensing her drawing strength from him. For a moment, they were silent. When she drew back, her face was pale, but resolute.

"I have to be rational. Serene had an immediate reaction to the drug, and she died a few days later. I was given it well over a week ago, and I survived the initial bad reaction. Since then, any symptoms I've had have been quite mild, considering. And there's no way they can have given me the exact same specification of drug they gave Serene. They had to have learned from their mistake. Whatever the academy's purpose is, they don't want us to *die*."

Unable to help himself, Noah smiled. Immediately suspicious, her eyes narrowed. "What?"

"I was just admiring your resilience. Here's me racking my brain for ways to talk you down from the ledge, but you did it yourself." He shrugged. "You didn't need me at all." She blushed, and it was his turn to ask. "What?"

"The hug might have helped. A little."

His smile broadened and he found himself leaning closer. "Glad I could be of service."

The moment hung between them, and Noah thought about the necklace. It was in his pocket. This was the perfect opportunity to return it to her. Yet something held him back. Things were good between them. *Really* good. If he gave it back now, she might feel betrayed. He wasn't sure he could bear the thought of her turning against him again.

He was still thinking about the pendant when Faith changed the subject. "You said the council are divided over how to deal with Bellator?"

"That's right."

"And you want me to believe that you... that your mother, and Flynn... don't want to hurt its citizens."

He nodded solemnly. "Very much so."

She cocked her head to one side. "You know, against my better judgement, I do. I mean... if it was just you, then I might not feel so confident." Noah tried to keep the hurt from his face, knowing his prior betrayal deserved her mistrust. "But your mother insisted we were looked over in the medcave, Ella and Ruth have been nothing but kind to us... and in the canteen the other day, Flynn rescued us without a–"

"So did I."

She frowned at him. "What?"

"In the canteen. I rescued you too." He flushed and looked away. "Well, I tried."

"You did." She poked a finger in his arm, almost playfully. "And you're about as different from our expectations of men as anyone could be."

"And that's..." he narrowed his eyes, "a good thing?"

"Yes!" She stared more closely at him, seeming to sense his uncertainty. "Yes, it is."

"Good." He cleared his throat. "I'm glad."

They were silent for a moment. Noah wondered what she was thinking. He reached into his pocket, his fingers closing around the necklace. Surely, he owed it to her to return it. He had just made his mind up to hand it back when she spoke again.

"I wonder..." she hesitated, "I wonder if there are things I... we... could suggest which might... make it easier for Eremus to contact Danforth. To bring about some kind of... peaceful communication."

He let go of the pendant. "You'd do that?"

"I'm not sure." She frowned. "Maybe. If I trusted that what we told you wasn't going to be used in a... a violent way... you know, to hurt people."

"I would never–" He took his hand out of his pocket and grasped hers, more tightly than he'd intended to.

She winced, and he released her. She massaged the hand, shooting him a look of amusement. "I know *you* wouldn't, obviously, but... others, well..."

He stared at her. "What?"

"I said, others–"

"Not that. About me."

She smiled gently. "I said, I know you wouldn't."

"Wouldn't what?"

"Intend to hurt people."

"You do?"

She nodded slowly, as though considering her words. "Yes. I hadn't realised it, not til right now, but... actually... I do. I know you wouldn't hurt me... not deliberately anyway. You're just a little too... trusting. But that's sort of what I like about you."

She stared at him, and suddenly he felt his mouth go dry. The smile died, and the atmosphere in the cave changed. Noah felt his breath catch in his throat, and couldn't look away from her. Slowly, fearful that she might bolt, he leaned towards her, stopping only inches from her lips.

She gazed at him, her eyes wide. Gently, he placed a hand on her cheek. They were both trembling, which somehow made him feel better. Emboldened by her response, he ran his thumb over her lips, slow, and featherlight.

"Noah?" His name was barely a whisper.

He could see the uncertainty in her eyes. This was unfamiliar territory for him, but for her it was totally foreign. The first move would have to be his. Taking a deep breath, he closed the gap between them, leaning forward until his lips touched hers.

It only lasted a second, but when he drew back, he knew things had changed. His heart was racing, and the expression in her eyes suggested she felt the same. Her lips had been soft, warm, and uncertain, yet the fleeting contact had set off sparks in his chest. He held his breath, waiting to see how Faith would react.

For a second, she drew back, but only to shift her weight slightly, so her body was aligned even more closely with his. He heard her draw a breath, and this time they both leaned forwards, their second kiss initiated on both sides. But just as he felt her exhaled breath tickle over his lips, a movement from behind brought him back down to earth.

"What *are* you doing, little brother?" He jumped to his feet, staring at the man who loomed in the entrance to the cave. Paulo. His brother was not smiling. "Who gave you permission to separate this girl from the others?"

Aware that Faith had also struggled to her feet beside him, he took a step away from her. "I- I–"

"Wanted to have a bit of fun, did you?" Paulo's gaze swept over Faith in a way which made Noah's blood boil. "Guess I can understand that... but you have to know we can't trust these girls. I mean," again he stared at Faith, "she's probably just looking for an easy way back to Bellator..."

"I'm not–"

"She wouldn't–"

Noah heard Faith's protest as loudly as his own, yet doubted it. Was Paulo right? Was he being naïve? Hating that his brother could knock his confidence so quickly, he stiffened, refusing to look at Faith. "It's none of your business what we were doing."

"Alright. I'll let it slide for now. But let's get her back with the others. You haven't forgotten, have you, that she's a prisoner." Stepping forward, Paulo took hold of Faith's arm and guided her out of the cave. Noah could feel her eyes on him, but refused to return the gaze. Seething, he followed them through the tunnels and into the canteen. As they stepped inside, Paulo stopped.

"Wait for me here, Noah." Paulo began guiding Faith towards the others. "I want to make sure you get to your assigned shift, this time."

Fuming, Noah waited. He was scheduled to help his ma in the medcave all morning. Paulo didn't need to walk him there, like a child. But he knew not to push his brother any further.

The Danforth girls were assisting Ella and Ruth with the preparation of the evening's meal. Once Faith had joined them, she didn't look back. Paulo leaned down and spoke to Ella, gesturing to Faith as he did so. A look of concern shadowed Ella's face, and Noah prayed he hadn't gotten the sisters into trouble as well as himself.

Eventually, Paulo headed back towards him, jerking his head in the direction of the tunnel. "Let's go."

Noah followed, bracing himself for a lecture. But when he fell into step beside his brother, Paulo's expression was filled with concern. "Look, I admire your courage," he began. "I mean... Faith's pretty, and I know you and she have a history, but..." his expression grew serious, "you should know she could get you into a lot of trouble."

Noah felt his fists curling into his palms at his brother's words. "It's got nothing to do with you."

Paulo shrugged. "Maybe not, but if she's taking you for a ride... trying to use you to get out of here, well... it'll be bad for you in the end."

"She's not." Noah tried to speed up, but his brother only matched his pace. Eventually, he stopped and turned to face him. "If you're finished, I'm quite capable of finding the med-cave on my own."

"But I'm not. Finished, I mean." Paulo leaned closer. "Can't you see? I'm trying to protect you. Stop you from getting yourself into trouble."

"I can take care of myself, thanks."

"If you say so." Paulo masked a smirk and began walking again. "But I think I'll walk you to your shift all the same."

Giving up, Noah plodded after him. It was clear his brother wouldn't leave until Noah was safely delivered to his ma.

They walked in awkward silence for a few minutes, until Noah couldn't bear it any longer. "You find anything else out from the woman in the woods?" Paulo frowned. "We searched her. She had nothing on her but a backpack with a flashlight, a few snacks, and some water. No weapons."

Noah whistled softly. "She's brave."

"Or stupid." Paulo shook his head. "Jacob's been question-ing her, but she's not saying much. Insists she's here for the girls' protection."

"Maybe she is."

Paulo's head snapped to attention. "And what would you know about it?"

Noah gestured in the direction of Ella's cave. "I asked Faith."

Paulo's step faltered, but Noah kept going, enjoying the feeling of superiority. "Her full name's Charlotte Kemp. She's a teacher at Danforth."

Now Paulo was the one playing catch up. He raised an eyebrow. "So you weren't just trying to get her alone to–"

"No." Noah cut him off. "I wasn't."

"Clever." Paulo sounded impressed. "Well, Jacob's trying to work out what she's doing here. He's concerned that she's some kind of spy." Paulo shrugged. "But she won't talk. Says she wants to speak to the girls."

"Will Jacob let her?"

Paulo shrugged. "He's thinking about it." They reached the tunnel which led to the medcave. "Here you are. Don't go taking any other... detours."

"I won't."

As Noah went to move past him, Paulo shot out an arm. "I'm serious. You need to be careful." He frowned. "Jacob's changed lately. Since we kidnapped the girls. He seems... I don't know... different. More determined."

"Determined to what?"

"To get back at Danforth. I don't know if it's destroying the seed bank, or the power he thinks having these captives gives him," Paulo relinquished his hold on Noah, "but he's on a mission." He turned to go. "You'd be wise to watch your step around him."

Shaken by the warning, Noah moved towards the medcave, hoping his ma wasn't about to start on him too. When he entered, she was busy scrubbing medical equipment in a tub of scalding water, a task she often chose to complete when she was feeling agitated.

She turned at his footsteps. "It's about time you got here."

"Sorry." He joined her, picking up the utensils she had already cleaned. He walked to the cupboard to put them away. "I got held up."

His ma tutted. "I wanted to speak to you about what happened last night. Flynn filled me in on what you told him, but he wasn't able to get anything out of Jacob."

"I know." Noah returned to her side. "That's why I volunteered to help Ella take the Danforth girls to their shift this morning. She seemed to know so much about them..." He shrugged. "I wanted to see whether they could tell me who she was."

His ma narrowed her eyes. "Go on."

"Faith recognised her from my description." He made sure he kept his ma's eye contact. "She's a professor at the school."

"Really?"

"Yeah, her name's Charlotte Kemp. She teaches..."

But he stopped. His ma was staring at him, her face white with shock.

"Ma? What is it?"

"Charlotte... *Kemp?*" Her voice shook as he nodded. "Then... then I know her."

CHAPTER EIGHTEEN: FAITH

After a less eventful dinner than the previous one they had shared with the community, the girls were allowed to return to their cave. Preparing the meal had given most of them a new sense of purpose, and none of them had found it taxing. Flynn, Ella, and Ruth had circulated after they'd eaten, spreading the message that the Bellator captives had worked hard all afternoon cooking the food, and many of the citizens seemed to have warmed to the Danforth girls. There had been no new confrontations, and even a few tentative smiles as people passed the table where Faith sat with her friends.

When Ella had escorted them back to the cave, she had promised them another shift the following day, this time working on a different task in a new location where they would come across a different group of Eremus citizens. She was hoping if they showed they were prepared to work hard, people would begin to accept them, stop seeing them as the enemy. The mood once Ella left had been much more positive.

Faith thought back to her conversation with Noah, knowing she should fill the girls in on Kemp's arrival. She hadn't dared to mention it during dinner. She was also wondering if the other girls might be more receptive to the idea of helping Eremus, now that they had been treated a little better by its people. The idea of both communities living alongside one another still seemed an impossibility, but she could see how much better things might be if the two could somehow negotiate living side by side more peacefully. Having said that, she had no idea how the girls would react.

As they settled down for the night, Diane reached for the pack of cards. "Anyone up for a game before bed?"

"No, thanks." Avery had been strangely quiet for most of the day, and now chose to sit away from the others. She seemed to expect Farrah to follow her, but when the other girl made a move to join the game, her face fell. Grabbing the hairbrush they had been provided with as part of their improved living quarters, she turned her back on them all and began running it through her long, blond hair.

Happy to have something to occupy them, the rest of the girls shuffled forward into a rough circle. Only Helen, sitting at the side of the cave quietly, shook her head. Since the midnight incident, she had remained withdrawn, and Faith was worried about her. But they could hardly force her to join in.

Diane began to deal. "So, Faith," her tone was casual, and she didn't look up from the neat piles of cards, "you going to tell us where you disappeared to earlier?"

Feeling the heat rise in her face, Faith cleared her throat. "Um... I was..." She decided to opt for the truth, and now seemed like a good time to tell them about Kemp. "Noah wanted to speak to me." She felt all the eyes in the cave turn towards her but continued, despite her discomfort. "They found a Bellator citizen wandering in the woods today."

Diane's hands stilled. "A guard?"

"No." Faith could see hope rising in some of the girls' expressions, dread in others. "It was Professor Kemp."

"What was she–" "Why on earth–" "Kemp?"

Faith held up a hand to calm the others. "I don't know what she's doing here, before you ask. But I wouldn't hold out too much hope of a heroic rescue mission. They brought her into the community and locked her in the cave they used to keep *us* in." She felt bad as she watched Mary and Catherine's faces fall. The youngest students had been the most frightened by their experience, and were the most naïve in wishing to be saved. "Noah wanted to know if we knew her."

"And what did you tell him?" Now Diane's shrewd eyes bored into hers.

"The truth. That she was one of our teachers and that I had no idea why she'd be in the forest looking for us." Noticing Avery's eyes boring into her, Faith defended herself. "What would have been the point of lying?"

"Possibly no point at all." Avery placed the brush on the ground beside her. "But I think we need to be careful what we say to these people. Who knows what he'd do with any information you fed him."

"I know what you think of Noah, but I happen to think he wants to help us." Faith tried to keep an even tone, knowing it would do no good to get angry. "Just like Ella and Ruth, and Anna."

"Are you *sure* that asking you about Kemp was the *only* reason he wanted to get you alone?" Avery raised an eyebrow. "I mean, we all know what men can be like. And you two have prior... *history*."

"Yes. I'm certain." Refusing to be cowed, Faith straightened and met Avery's eye. "Whatever your prejudices about males, Noah doesn't fit into them. He's so far from what we were taught to believe, he's—" Blushing, she took a breath and got back on track. "He just wanted to talk." She glanced around at the eyes which regarded her, some mistrustful, some concerned, others merely curious. "Look, he isn't so bad. He says all Eremus wants is the chance to talk with Danforth. To have her *consider* accepting males again... grant them some rights, rather than hunting them down every chance she gets."

"And you believe him?" Farrah's gaze was doubtful.

"They want us to grant men *rights*?" Avery laughed, but the sound was hollow. She seemed almost frightened. "When we fought so hard to gain independence from them?"

"How can they think that we'd accept them?" Catherine's eyes were saucers. "Look what they did to us in the past!"

"According to Danforth, you mean." Faith turned to her. "Haven't you started to question what they teach us, yet?"

"Question it?" Mary's expression matched that of her friend.

"Have you seen the males who live here?" Faith picked up her cards, reminding herself to be patient. "Are they *all* like that? Like the vicious, violent beasts we learn about?"

Catherine bit her lip. "Some of them–"

"*Some* of them, perhaps." Faith interrupted, knowing she was thinking about Jacob. "But not all.

"Faith's right. Look at Flynn. He helped us." Faith was grateful for Sophia's interjection. "Think about Noah. Even Ella and Ruth! They *choose* to live alongside men. They're happy to trust them."

"And look at how Bellator behaves towards the people here." Diane chimed in. "Seems to me, women are *just* as capable of violence."

"But not all of them." Faith repeated her earlier comment, hoping the truth would start to hit home.

"Bellator only acts violently to protect us." Farrah was picking at the edge of one of her cards.

"That's what they tell us." Faith shrugged. "But does that make it right?"

"Think about all the children who live down here." Sophia gestured to the door. "They don't deserve the treatment they get from Bellator. They've never even set foot in the city. And I suspect we've been responsible for the deaths of just as many women and children as we have violent men."

"Sophia's right." Diane jabbed a finger at them. "All humans are capable of violence Especially when backed into a corner. The gender doesn't matter. And in the same way, there are citizens of *both* genders in *both* communities who choose to act peacefully."

Sophia was nodding. "We just have to decide on the type of people we want to be."

"Exactly." Glad to have Diane and Sophia on her side, Faith continued. "So what if... what if, we decided we wanted to help build two calm, positive communities which could live alongside one another without resorting to violence?"

Mary still looked confused. "What do you mean?"

"What if we chose to..." again, Faith took a deep breath, "to help Eremus?"

"Help them?" Farrah sounded doubtful. "But why?"

"To avoid further violence in either community?" Faith met Farrah's gaze. "I mean, let's think about this. Jacob already set off a bomb in the city. That's a serious attempt to get Danforth's attention. What if we talked to him, like he asked us to? What if we were able to help him gain an audience with Danforth... with no more bloodshed?" Noting the doubtful faces around her, Faith pushed on. "I mean... if what Noah says is true, most of the Eremus citizens just want to stop living in fear of Bellator. If we can help them achieve that peacefully, then we'd be doing a good thing."

"Are you *serious?*" Faith turned back to Avery, whose response had bordered on a shriek. "You want us to help these people? This man... who ripped us from our home without a second thought. Who held a gun to your head the other night?"

Put like that, Faith had to admit she could see Avery's point. "I know what you're saying. But if helping him means no one else has to suffer violence, surely that's a better option?"

"I guess if we help him," Diane added, "he'll be more inclined to let us go. Once he has what he wants, at least."

"Can you hear yourselves?" Avery had drawn herself up to her full height. "Can't you see that giving a man what he wants sets Bellator society back about thirty years?"

"Can't you see that there's something seriously wrong with Bellator society as it stands?" Faith retorted. "Compromising with Eremus... meeting them halfway might be the only way to resolve all this peacefully."

"And a peaceful resolution means Eremus will set us free," Sophia said.

Avery seemed to deflate a little. Taking advantage of her momentary silence, Faith pressed her point. "Look, what Jacob needs is the ability to bring Danforth to a location where she can't plan an attack in advance. Surely, helping him to achieve that will avoid any violence on either side?"

"If you could pull it off," Avery muttered, but offered no further objection.

"We need somewhere neutral," Diane mused, "where they can talk calmly."

Cheered by Diane's support, Faith voiced the idea she'd been considering ever since her conversation with Noah earlier in the day. "What if they used our wristclips?"

Sophia understood immediately. "Clever."

"Our wristclips?" Mary looked confused.

"They could turn them on..." Sophia looked thoughtful, "use the navigation system... bring Danforth to a location of their choice."

"Yes!" Faith had to bite back a smile at the positive reaction to her suggestion. "It would mean that Jacob could have control over the location, be there in advance... check it out..."

Diane was nodding. "There'd be no chance of Danforth finding the caves, which is his biggest fear."

"But Danforth wouldn't be on the defensive either," Farrah mused, "as she might be if the Eremus men tried to enter the city."

"There's one thing you haven't thought about," Avery rejoined the conversation.

"What's that?" Diane asked.

"The clips'll be well out of battery by now."

"You're right." Faith sighed, realising the error in her plan. "That's going to be an issue."

"It's worth a thought though... I mean, if we could somehow manage to charge them," Sophia was more encouraged, "Jacob would only need to turn them on and it would draw Danforth right to him."

"Do you really think this could work?" The voice was a whisper, coming from the far side of the cave. Faith turned to see Helen, her pale face almost hopeful. "You think we might be able to get out of here? If we help him?"

Faith's heart went out to her. The episode in the woods with Jacob and Paulo had clearly shaken her.

Sophia stood up and moved across to her, sitting beside her and placing an arm round her shoulder. "It's worth a try, isn't it?"

"Well, don't come crying to me when it all goes horribly wrong and all we end up stuck down here for good." Avery turned away sulkily. Stretching her arms widely, she pulled her blanket towards her and lay down. "Keep it quiet, would you? Some of us are trying to sleep."

"Alright everyone," Diane stage-whispered with a sideways glance at Avery, "we have a plan which *most* of us are happy with. Shall we get on with the game?"

As they settled down to play a couple of hands of cards, Faith found herself hoping desperately that her idea would work, and that Avery's pessimistic prediction would never come to pass.

Later that night, something woke Faith. Coming to, she blinked, her tired eyes struggling to adjust to the dim light from the lantern. Sitting up, she glanced around, mentally checking each of the Danforth girls was still there. She was relieved to count seven other bodies in the room. Her gaze came to rest on Avery. She was sitting up against the cave wall, her blanket wrapped tightly around her body. Her eyes were wide open and she looked stricken.

"Are you alright?" The other girl's gaze was fixed on the cave entrance. Faith shuffled closer to her, keeping her voice low. "Avery! Are you okay?" Faith glanced at the door. "Did you hear something?"

Slowly, Avery's head rotated until she was facing Faith. "I... I was..." She shook herself. "No. I didn't hear anything. Why do you ask?"

"Have you forgotten Jacob's midnight visit, already?" Faith still shuddered when she remembered being dragged out of the cave with Helen while all the others slept. "I thought maybe..."

"Oh yeah." Avery had the decency to blush. "Must've been scary."

"It was." Faith narrowed her eyes, suspicious of the unusual empathy. "I mean... looks like they didn't intend to hurt us, but still..."

"I guess everyone has an agenda, don't they?" The older girl studied her nails. "And it's hard to know who to trust."

Faith searched for the right thing to say. Avery had never been a friend, but there were so few of them here in Eremus, it made sense to stick together. "Surely, we can trust each other, at least?"

A shadow crossed Avery's face. "You'd think so, wouldn't you?"

"What does that mean?"

"Nothing." Avery shook her head. "Can I ask you something?"

"Sure."

"You disappearing with the skinny boy today... was it some kind of strategy?"

"Strategy?" Faith blinked. "What do you mean?"

"Like, getting friendly with him might... offer you some kind of protection." Avery stared at Faith, her eyes narrowing. "It's not, is it? You really like him."

Avery sighed and lay back down. There was a silence, so long that Faith wondered if the other girl had gone back to sleep. Eventually, the other girl propped herself up on one elbow and stared at Faith, her expression unreadable.

"You know, I've never had a very high opinion of you,"

"No kidding." Faith rolled her eyes.

"Back at the academy... it seemed to me that everything you did went against Bellator's principles. Against what Danforth would have wanted." She paused, cocking her head to one side. "But now we're here, I figure you might actually have our best interests at heart. For the most part, anyway."

"Um... thanks?"

"And I'd hate to see you get yourself into... trouble before we manage to get out of here." A brief pause, where Avery closed her eyes, as though she couldn't believe what she was about to do. "Can I give you a word of warning?"

Faith gritted her teeth. "Sure."

"Don't leave yourself alone with that boy for too long, will you? There are things you could do together which would land you in a very difficult situation... once we're back in Bellator." Avery raised one eyebrow. "Remember our Biology lessons about the old ways, when men and women lived side-by-side? The consequences of such unregulated... liaisons?"

Remembering Noah's kiss, Faith felt herself blushing. She'd had no real idea what he was about to do, but instinct had taken over. She'd read about relationships between males and females in the past, but nothing had prepared her for the sensations which had washed over her at his touch. But to suggest that they had gone further...

She dropped her gaze, blushing furiously. Ignoring her discomfort, Avery pressed on.

"You'd find yourself in a lot of trouble if you ended up back in Bellator expecting an Eremus child. In fact, I think perhaps you should be grateful that you were, um... interrupted today, don't you?"

Faith sat bolt upright. "It was *you* who told Paulo where I was?"

"Not where you were, Faith." Avery examined one of her nails, "I didn't know *where* you were."

Faith shook her head in disbelief. "But you *told* him about us?"

"I merely pointed out that you'd disappeared." Avery picked at a stray piece of polish on her thumbnail. "Paulo found you all by himself."

"So much for us trusting one another."

"I was *worried*. Like I said, I didn't want you to get yourself into any... trouble." A shadow crossed her face. "You don't believe me."

"No. I don't."

Ignoring the flash of hurt on Avery's face, Faith turned her back on the other girl, relieved when she fell silent. But as Faith pulled her blanket around her, questions whirled around in her head, refusing to let her sleep.

Avery had suggested she was using Noah, for protection. What if *Noah* thought that was her reason for kissing him too? Worse still, what if his purpose in kissing *her* had been similar?

Why was Professor Kemp here? Was it too much to hope that she was on the girls' side? And was helping Eremus the right way to go? Or was she being manipulated again?

And finally, Faith was hopeful that using the wristclips could lead to peaceful talks between the two communities. But was

Avery right? With so many different agendas, would it lead to even more bloodshed?

Chapter Nineteen: Noah

"Jacob said he wanted me with you?" Noah pulled a sweater over his head as he followed his ma through the tunnels the following morning.

"Apparently." His ma didn't stop walking to answer, and he was forced to pick up the pace to catch up. "Sarah showed up earlier this morning, said Jacob spent most of yesterday trying to get Charlotte to talk to him without much success. He's getting frustrated. And now he knows we have history, he wants me to try speaking to her." She shrugged. "Obviously he thinks I might have more luck."

"But why bring me along?" Whilst Noah was happy he'd get access to Kemp without a struggle, Jacob's motives puzzled him.

"I'm guessing it's because if I have any chance of her trusting me after all these years, I'll need to fill her in on what's happened to me since I left Bellator." This time, she did glance over her shoulder at him. "Jacob wants her to know you're my son. That you were born here. Brought up safely."

Suddenly, Noah understood. "So I'm proof that Eremus isn't such a terrible place?"

"You got it!" His ma hurried on. "You're his poster boy for how nice we all are."

After his ma's revelation the previous day, they had spent the rest of their shift discussing her relationship with the Danforth professor. At the end of the day, his ma had gone to Jacob to ask if she might be allowed to see her old friend. At first, he had been reluctant, but after acknowledging he'd had limited success speaking to her himself, he had changed his mind. Anna had talked at length about the mysterious woman, and even Jacob could see the benefit of gaining their new prisoner's trust by revealing Anna's presence in Eremus.

Charlotte Kemp was around Anna's age. Back in Bellator they'd known one another from childhood. Assigned to the same district, they'd grown up together and, both being intelligent, they'd stayed on in school for longer than many of their peers. Both had admitted they were very glad that the academy had not been up and running when they were still in education. In their late teens, they'd selected different specialities, Kemp choosing to train as a teacher and Anna as a medic. This had meant they'd spent less time together, but they'd remained close. Kemp had been one of the people his ma had missed the most when she left Bellator, and she confessed that she'd always thought Kemp would be the one who would have tried to discover what had happened to her.

As his ma had talked, Noah had gotten a real glimpse into her previous life. Her relationship with Charlotte sounded a lot like his friendship with Ruth, and, once again, he was struck by how much his ma had given up for him. By the time she'd run out of stories, he'd felt closer to her than he had in a long time.

They reached the tunnel which led to the cell where the girls had originally been kept. Memories of Faith's first night in Eremus came flooding back as Noah passed the guard post. It still made him shudder to remember her horror at discovering his betrayal. He was glad things were better now. Much better, in fact. Sucking in a deep breath, he forced his mind away from the kiss of the previous day.

As they approached the cave entrance, they could hear Jacob's voice echoing out into the tunnel, his tone sharp. "You haven't changed your mind, then?"

There was an indistinguishable murmur in reply. Exchanging glances, Anna and Noah hurried forward. Hearing their footsteps, Jacob emerged from the cave to greet them.

"She's still not talking?" Anna said.

He shook his head. "Anna, you have to gain her trust. Get her to tell you what she's doing here."

"I'll do my best. I still think you could be treating her with a little more respect." His ma looked flushed, and Noah wondered if she was angry with Jacob or nervous about seeing Kemp again. She had yet to step into the cave, almost as though she were putting off the moment. She dropped her voice to a whisper. "You still think she's here on Danforth's orders?"

"Not sure." Jacob shrugged. "All I know is, I issued a threat. Danforth has never responded well to threats. With the girls here, she won't just blanket-attack the woods where she suspects we're hiding. She'd risk her own people." He frowned. "But sending a spy into the midst of our camp is just her style. I need to know if that's what Kemp is."

"Alright." Anna nodded. "I'll talk to her. But it's been a long time. I can't promise anything."

Noah watched her inhale and step towards the cave, but Jacob held up a hand to stop her. Nodding, he ducked inside first, leaving them to follow.

With a grimace, Anna gestured to Noah to follow Jacob. Seconds later, he was standing inside the cave. It seemed a little larger now that there was only one prisoner inside, but it was still only dimly lit, and there was little evidence that Kemp was being housed in better conditions than the girls had been on their arrival. At the rear of the cave, their prisoner stood in the shadows.

Hearing them enter, she turned to them. Her face was stony, and Noah wondered what had been said to her to cause this alteration. When he'd come across her in the forest, she'd been pleasant, open to discussion with them, willing to come peacefully into their community. Now she bristled with hostility.

"Haven't you given up yet?" She scowled openly at Jacob, but then her eyes met Noah's. She relaxed slightly. "Oh, it's you."

"Yes." Behind him, he felt his ma move into the cave. "How are you?"

"I'm tired. Tired of all the questions, and of this man's refusal to–" She stopped, her eyes fixing on Anna, who had stepped around Noah so the light from the lantern spilled across her face. She took an uncertain step forward.

"Hello, Charlotte." His ma's voice was choked with emotion.

"Anna? Anna, is that you? What are– I-I mean..." She trailed off.

"It's me." Anna stepped forward, holding out a shaking hand.

Ignoring it, Charlotte stumbled on. "You mean," she glanced at Jacob, "...all this time, y-you..."

"I've been here." Anna nodded. "All this time."

A range of emotions raced across Charlotte's face. Gone was the cool, hard exterior. In its place were confusion, joy, alarm, anger, and fear. "I thought you were dead. They, they searched... for *weeks*. In the end they told us you'd been captured by a stray group of males in the forest and killed." Charlotte's already-pale face drained of colour, and she swayed on her feet.

"Why don't we sit down." Anna stepped forward, taking Charlotte's arm and easing her onto the ground. She frowned at Jacob. "We'd be better off if you'd provided her with a stool or a chair."

Jacob merely glared. Anna took a seat beside Charlotte, giving her a moment to process the shock. Shifting from foot to foot, Noah watched his ma. She looked different. Younger, somehow, and wistful, as though the sight of her old friend reminded her of what she'd left behind. After a few moments, she took Charlotte's hand gently.

"I know this is a shock. But I'd like to fill you in on what happened to me that day all those years ago. Alright?" Kemp managed to nod. "I ran away from Bellator. Do you remember I had the Gentest? I spoke to you about it the night before." Another nod, as though Kemp didn't trust herself to speak. "Well, it told me the baby I was expecting was a boy."

Something in Charlotte's face changed. A look of understanding dawned, and she pulled her hand away from Anna's. "You mean...?"

Anna nodded. "I can't explain it. But I already felt like his mother. I didn't want to lose him. So I ran. In the woods, I found some people from Eremus... they helped me." She lowered her gaze. "I've been here ever since."

"And, and the child?" Charlotte's voice was so quiet, Noah had to strain to hear her. "What happened to the baby?"

Anna paused for a moment, seeming almost afraid to reveal the full truth. Eventually, Jacob shifted impatiently, jolting them all back to reality. Slowly, Anna turned to Noah. She nodded at him, and he took a small step forward.

"I believe you've already met him." Anna smiled proudly. "Charlotte, this is Noah."

For several moments, Kemp just stared at him. Eventually, she pushed herself to her feet and came forward, staring into his face. "You have a *son*. And he must be..."

"He turned sixteen a few weeks ago."

Kemp glanced at his ma and then turned back to him. "You grew up here?"

Noah nodded. "I did."

"And they accept you?" She shot a pointed look at Jacob. "Treat you well?

He glanced at his ma. "Mostly, yes."

"Mostly? It was difficult for some people to live with you here?"

He shrugged, blushing under the close scrutiny. "I guess... for some."

Charlotte turned back to Anna. "I-I don't know what to say."

Anna came to join her. "Don't say anything, for now. It's been a long time since... well, let's just say many things have happened since we last saw one another. You and I can't claim to know one another well any more. But there will be plenty of time for us to catch up later. For now..." she glanced at Jacob, who had cleared his throat, "will you trust me? Can you tell me why you came here?"

Charlotte's face closed up again. "I'll tell you what I told him. I came here for the girls. To check they were alright. To speak to them. I played by your rules. I was willing to be brought here blindfolded, so I couldn't bring anyone in the city back here." She glared at Jacob. "Instead, one of you knocked me out and carried me inside. And you wonder why the women of Bellator think you're all brutes."

Jacob stepped forward, his fists clenched. Noah cut him off, deliberately keeping his voice low and calm. "We're not all brutes."

His ma stepped next to him. "They're not. Not by a long way. But they've been treated poorly by Bellator for years, and they're extremely frustrated by it." Her voice hardened. "Truth be told, we all are. Not just the men."

"That may be true." Charlotte straightened. "But your poor treatment is not down to me. Nor is it down to those girls you have here. And I assure you, once I've actually been *allowed* to see them, I have some information that you'll find very helpful." She folded her arms. "Until I'm assured of their safety though, I'm not saying anything else."

"Fine." Jacob looked as though he was about to explode, but he gave a tight nod. "I'll have one of them brought here."

"One?" Kemp frowned. "One doesn't tell me they're all safe."

"Two then. But that's your lot. You can ask them about the rest. Once they're here, and you've seen they're unharmed, you talk. Right?"

Kemp nodded.

Jacob raised the walkie talkie to his lips. "Paulo. Come in."

A second later, there was an answering crackle. "Paulo here."

"Bring a couple of the Danforth girls to the cave where we're holding the teacher."

"Got it. Be there in a minute."

Jacob hooked the walkie talkie to his belt and glared at Kemp. "Happy now?"

"Happier than I've been since I woke up in the darkness down here."

Jacob scowled and strode out of the cave. Left alone with the two women, Noah felt awkward. They were both silent, and simply stared at one another as though they didn't believe the other was real.

"You're really okay?" Charlotte said finally.

His ma shrugged. "It's not been easy, I won't lie." She nudged Noah with her shoulder. "But I'd never have given him up."

Charlotte nodded, her eyes never leaving his. "You know, when I came across him in the forest, he was so pleasant. Decent. I'd hoped that when I came across an Eremus citizen they'd be... well, kinder than the Bellator rumours of Eremus folk suggest."

"And was he?"

"He was." A grin spread across Kemp's face. Noah got the impression she didn't smile often, but it made her look almost mischievous. "We were doing alright until that other oaf turned up."

Anna rolled her eyes. "That other oaf is a member of my family too."

"But he was older than Noah." Charlotte's eyes shot to Anna's. "Much older."

Anna shrugged. "It's a long story. Flynn... I guess you'd call him my partner... well Paulo is Flynn's nephew. A lot of the families here are mixed like that. In some ways, it's a bit like Bellator... the communal aspect of life here. We support one another as a whole. But our family units are very close-knit, even when the bonds are not biological. Anyway, Paulo lives with us." A shadow crossed her face. "Well, he did, until recently."

Paulo's absence was still very much felt in their cave, and Noah knew his ma felt responsible.

"Sounds like you have a very full life here." Charlotte looked wistful. "I'm glad you found somewhere where you could be happy."

"Are *you* happy, Charlotte?"

"It's Kemp." The woman looked wistful. "No one calls me Charlotte these days. And I'm not as happy as I used to be. Things in Bellator..." she trailed off. "In truth, they're not so good. Danforth is extremely powerful, and many citizens don't agree with some of the things she's doing."

"Things like what?"

Kemp looked uncomfortable. "We're not certain yet."

"We?" Anna raised an eyebrow.

"I will say I belong to a group that's trying to change things. Investigate. Protect those who Danforth endangers."

Noah's thoughts went to Madeleine, but his ma was one step ahead. "We know of a resistance. You're saying you're–"

"I'm part of it, yes."

"And they sent you here?"

Kemp blushed. "No. They were against me coming, but–"

Anna frowned. "You want us to believe that you're not Danforth's spy, that you belong to the resistance, but came here without their support?"

Kemp stiffened. "It's the truth."

"Well, it might be. But we haven't seen one another for sixteen years. A lot could have happened during that time."

"You have connections with the resistance?" Noah watched his ma hesitate, then give a small nod. "Check with them. They'll confirm it."

"Even if *I* believe you, Jacob won't take my word for it." Noah's ma sighed. "I'm happy to see you, truly I am." She jerked her head at the cave entrance. "But if he decides you're the enemy, I won't be able to protect you."

"I understand."

An awkward silence fell over the cave until they heard the sound of footsteps in the tunnel outside.

"Brace yourselves. The oaf is here." Noah's joke fell flat as Jacob ducked into the cave again, his face stern. Caught up in his ma's reunion, Noah hadn't thought about which girls Paulo might bring until they were standing in the doorway of the cave. First, the rebellious girl who had tried so hard to escape when the Danforth students had first arrived. She walked in slowly, her expression cautious.

"Professor Kemp." She nodded at her teacher. "Good to know they're extending the same hospitality to you as they did us when we first arrived."

"Hello, Diane. It's good to see you safe and well." Charlotte's eye travelled to the door, where a second figure had just entered. "Faith!"

Noah felt like his heart had stopped. As he turned to look at Faith, he felt his ma's eyes on him and tried to keep his expression blank. But Faith wasn't looking at him. Her gaze rested on Charlotte Kemp, and her lips were twisted into a genuine smile. This was a person from her own world. A person she knew and trusted.

"Professor." She nodded slightly. "It's good to see you."

The pleasantries over with, Jacob cleared his throat. "Perfectly safe and healthy, as you can see. Now if you could–"

Ignoring him, Kemp stepped forward, stretching out a hand to both girls. "Are they treating you okay?" She placed a hand on Faith's forehead. "Are you well?"

Noah felt himself blush as Faith's gaze circled the cave, coming to rest on him. After a second's pause, she looked away. "Mostly they are, yes." Noah winced inwardly at her use of the same word he'd spoken only minutes ago. "We're all alive, all safe." She paused, her eyes flicking to Jacob and Paulo's. "For the moment, at least," she added.

"I don't like the sound of that." Kemp peered into Faith's face. "Have you been sick at all?"

"A little. When we first arrived." Faith confessed. "Some dizziness, a little sickness. But I've improved lately."

"I'm so glad." Letting go of Faith, Kemp stepped away. Turning to face the rest of them, she took a breath. "Alright. I'm satisfied the girls are alive, at least. And Faith's health is one of the things I came to talk to you about."

CHAPTER TWENTY: FAITH

Alarmed by the mention of her name, Faith froze. Any news about her health had to be linked to the drugs she'd been given. Every eye in the cave was fixed on Kemp, waiting for her to speak again. Aside from Noah's.

The Eremus boy's eyes rested on Faith. She wasn't looking at him, but she could feel his gaze. No one else seemed to notice, but even as Kemp continued to speak, Noah's focus did not waver. And when she glanced over, he smiled. After their conversation the previous day, he had to know how Kemp's words had affected her. The smile was his attempt at soothing her.

Right now though, she couldn't return it. Turning back to Kemp, she tuned into her speech.

"... given an experimental drug." Kemp was saying, her face serious. "Faith was given a blood test just before the kidnapping." She looked at Faith, her eyes clouded with worry. "The results went straight to Danforth herself."

Beside her, Faith felt Diane stiffen. Others were staring at her now, mostly with pity. Straightening her spine, Faith kept her own gaze on Kemp, who was hurrying to continue.

"Let me explain a little of the history. The academy was set up to allow certain girls a more... advanced education. They get to be the first to use the newest tech, some of the most cutting-edge inventions. Students at the school are very much envied. But the excellent curriculum and facilities come with a price, which few people in Bellator are fully aware of." Faith glanced at Diane, both of them well aware of the price some students had to pay.

"Citizens believe students are selected because they show exceptional promise. In reality, they're chosen because their medical records suggest they're strong and healthy, and will respond well to certain... drugs the government wants to trial." Kemp hesitated. "For a long time, Danforth has wanted to fortify our community against *any* male influence. Despite public claims to the contrary, she's well aware of rebel groups like Eremus which could threaten the status quo."

Faith thought back to the time when she'd believed that Eremus did not exist. Glancing at their surroundings, she wondered how she could have been so naïve.

"Like those before her," Kemp continued, "she is concerned that men could somehow regain power, and all her efforts have gone into securing Bellator against this. To this end, she's had her best scientists trying to create innovative new drugs for all sorts of purposes: strengthening our bodies, developing our reaction speeds, revolutionising our procreation process-es..." She glanced at Faith in concern. "I fear the most recent one takes things a step too far."

Seeing Jacob about to interrupt, Kemp held up her hand. "That's where we come back to Faith. Let's just say that one of the drugs Danforth's been testing recently has yielded... interesting results. Prior to Faith, the drug had been given to another girl. It..." she paused, her face clouding over, "did not have the desired effect."

"You mean it killed her." Diane burst out. "Serene *died* because of that drug. And then you gave it to Faith."

For the first time, Kemp's face hardened. "*I* didn't give it to her. But, yes, she was given an improved version of the drug which was also given to Serene."

"Which is why you're asking if I'm sick?"

Kemp nodded at Faith. "Are you?"

"Well, I was to begin with. As I'm sure you already know." Faith shuddered as she remembered the pain. "I was left in that room to live or die."

"You were. And I'm sorry for that." Kemp admitted. "But you didn't die. And since the severe initial reaction, you've showed relatively few aftereffects. And the results of your recent blood test have Principal Anderson and Danforth very excited." Kemp's face softened. "It's one of the reasons I came here."

Jacob moved forward. "She's important, then?"

"Extremely." Kemp turned to face him. "And with the damage you managed to do to our seed banks, Danforth is more concerned than ever that we... that she can get Faith back."

Faith took a step towards the door. "You've come to take me back?"

"And you think we're going to let you?" Noah's voice had an undertone of steel that Faith hadn't heard before. "For her to be experimented on?"

"No." Kemp kept her eyes on Faith. "I've come to tell you to stay away."

There was a silence as the group took in the professor's words. After a pause, she continued. "I was just telling Anna and Noah that I belong to a group who object to many of Danforth's practices. We try to fight against what she's doing, but it's extremely difficult."

"Wait." Jacob had taken a step forward. "Are you saying you're part of the resistance movement?" Kemp nodded. "Why didn't you just come here through the tunnels? Madeleine could have given you access."

"Not if she doesn't know I'm here." Catching Jacob's look of confusion, Kemp tutted. "The resistance has many disparate sections. Members know what they need to know to complete their specific mission. We don't have access to everything." Kemp shrugged. "While I was aware the tunnels existed, I didn't know any of their specific locations. And Madeleine–"

"You expect us to believe you're resistance, but offer no proof?" Jacob interrupted, smirking. "I'm guessing, as our *prisoner*, you'd be willing to say anything to protect yourself."

"Check with them." Kemp turned to face Jacob full on. "When I saw Danforth's reaction to Faith's test result, I asked them if I could come here. They were against it."

"So you came without their permission?" Paulo sounded impressed.

"I did. The girls' lives were at stake, and the knowledge I had about Faith's importance to the chancellor was too vital to ignore. Now, I'm not certain what Faith's tests results prove." For a moment, Kemp looked almost frightened. "But I'm certain experimenting with this drug is dangerous. We *have* to prevent Danforth from getting Faith back."

"Clearly, the resistance is not as concerned about this news as you." Jacob's tone was sarcastic.

Kemp flushed. "Not as yet, no. But I was worried enough to defy them and come here without their knowledge. Doesn't that tell you something?"

"It tells me you're something of a loose cannon. One who I can't afford to underestimate." Jacob cocked his head to one side. "You're *certain* you can't tell us what this drug might do?"

Kemp's face hardened at Jacob's mistrustful tone. "Like I said, I've been trying to find out. Without success. I have my suspicions, but it's extremely difficult to... to gain *any* information on this particular project, even as a professor at the academy. Which tells me it's important. And more than likely, that others would disapprove of it." She sighed. "Whatever it is, I fear it will give Danforth more power than any single person should have."

"I'll need to check your story." Jacob eyeballed the professor. "You can't expect us to just believe you're resistance without evidence."

"As I said," Kemp held Jacob's gaze. "you're welcome to contact them."

Out of the corner of her eye, Faith noticed Noah stiffen. The older man's attitude towards Kemp obviously infuriated him. Faith had just become Jacob's most valuable pawn, and Noah clearly didn't trust him. The idea that Noah was on her side was comforting.

There was a silent standoff for a few seconds. Eventually, Jacob shrugged. "Can I ask you a question?"

"You can ask." Kemp shrugged. "I'm not guaranteeing I'll answer."

"You mentioned damage to the seed banks. Would I be right in assuming our explosives destroyed your entire stock?"

Kemp nodded. "Whilst some of the pods remained undamaged, the power to the freezer system was cut off. The back-up generator was also destroyed. The seed was lost before the engineers got the system up and running again."

"Alright!" Jacob turned to Paulo with a wry smile. "I'm *certain* Danforth sees the long-term problem of having no male seed and no new babies. She'll—"

"Of course she does. She's not stupid." Kemp cut in. "But that's what makes her all the more dangerous."

"So *you* say." Rolling his eyes, Jacob turned away. "I'll contact Madeleine. For now, you'll stay here." He led the group outside the cave. "Paulo, the door."

As Noah's brother bent to lift the barricade, Professor Kemp shot Faith and Diane a smile. "Take care, girls. I'll see you soon."

"We'll see about that." Jacob turned to Faith and Diane. "Let's get you back to the others."

"I can take them if you need to–" Noah began, but Jacob cut him off.

"I hear you've gotten a little too... *close* to some of our prisoners." Noah flushed. "Paulo and I will see them safely back to the cave."

Faith stiffened. Being brought here by Noah's brother was one thing. But the memory of what had happened the last time she'd been alone with Jacob and Paulo was still fresh. Beside her, she felt Diane open her mouth to object, but Anna beat her to it.

"You'll make sure they go *straight* back to the rest of their friends, won't you? No detours, this time?" Her meaning was clear. She would be keeping a much closer eye on what happened to the girls from now on. Noting Anna's glare, Faith felt a rush of gratitude at her attempt to protect them. "I'll check on you later, girls."

She jerked her head at Noah, and they headed up the tunnel together, Noah shooting anxious looks over his shoulder. Clearly, he had similar concerns about leaving them alone with their leader.

When they had disappeared, Jacob gestured to Paulo, who was just securing the door over Kemp's prison. "Come on then."

Faith glanced nervously at Diane as they trailed behind the two men. Everything she had learned about Jacob so far made her uneasy in his presence. Noah didn't trust him. And despite all their previous dealings with one another, Faith trusted Noah's judgement.

For now, though, Jacob ignored them, turning to Paulo instead. "I'll need to speak to Madeleine. As soon as possible."

Paulo dropped his voice and Faith only just caught his reply. "Do you believe her?"

"Not sure." Jacob's volume matched Paulo's now. Beside her, Diane sped up, attempting to hear more of the men's conversation. "...a potential asset... keep her here until... plans should continue..."

Giving up, Diane leaned closer to Faith. "Think Kemp's really a spy?"

Glancing ahead, Faith made sure that the men were deep in conversation. "Maybe."

"Did you know anything about this *resistance* movement?"

Faith shook her head. She'd known that there were people in the city who disagreed with Danforth. The idea that there were enough of them to form a group to fight against the chancellor was a revelation.

"Me neither." Diane nodded at the men in front. "It doesn't seem like they trust Kemp though. Not yet, anyway."

"Jacob definitely doesn't."

"She's brave, coming here. I wouldn't want to be in her shoes right now." Catching Faith's confused expression, Diane clarified. "What do you think he'll do if he discovers she's lying?"

Faith shuddered. "I hope we don't find out."

"Me too. And after she came out here to help us. To tell us..." Diane stared at Faith. "Looks like you're more valuable than even Jacob thought."

"Maybe."

"What do you think he's planning?" Diane paused. "He has to be thinking about a trade with Danforth, surely. Otherwise, what's he keeping us here for?" Faith went cold at the suggestion, but her friend ploughed on, unaware of the effect her words were having. "We'd better hope she *is* part of this resistance. Might stop Jacob from doing something totally rash if his allies in Bellator are against it."

The thought was comforting. Surely Jacob wouldn't want to sever his connection with people inside the city who supported Eremus. But if Kemp was lying, who knew what Jacob would do with the information?

"Let's keep this to ourselves, for now." Faith turned to Diane. "The stuff about the resistance, anyway. Don't want to frighten the others."

"Agreed."

"And perhaps we should think more about ways we can help Eremus..." Faith held up a hand at Diane's expression. "I mean, if we cooperate, surely Jacob will appreciate it."

Diane looked doubtful. "I suppose he might treat us better."

"And it might take the heat off Kemp." Faith pressed on. "I mean, if he has something else to occupy him, he won't–"

"Hurry up, girls." Jacob and Paulo had noticed the girls were lagging behind. "We have things to do. And I don't want to be accused of treating you poorly. Let's get you safely back where you belong."

Before she lost her nerve, Faith hurried to catch the two men. "You asked us recently... if we might have any ideas... of ways that you might contact Chancellor Danforth."

Jacob stopped abruptly. "I did."

Faith took a deep breath, hoping she'd said enough to convince Diane that this was a good idea. "I have a suggestion... a way that you could... arrange to speak with her, *without* putting your people at risk."

Jacob turned to face her. "I'm listening."

"Use our clips."

The older man frowned. "I'm sorry?"

"Our wristclips," Faith explained. "The devices we were wearing on our wrists when we were kidnapped."

"Ah, yes. I remember." Jacob smiled. "I believe Noah gave us the tip off to make sure they were dealt with before we gave away the Eremus position. Smart boy."

Forcing herself not to react, Faith pushed on. "So you're aware they work as location sensors. That's why Noah had you deactivate them." She glanced at Diane, who nodded encouragement. Relieved, Faith continued. "We thought perhaps they could be used to get Danforth where you wanted her, without giving her all the power."

Paulo looked faintly suspicious. "And how would that work?"

"You could tell Danforth to meet you at a specific time and date, but in a secret location," Diane explained. "One that would only be revealed when you activated the locator."

Jacob looked intrigued. "I see... you're suggesting Danforth wouldn't know where she was going in advance. Alright, I'm starting to see the potential benefits."

"We could be there *first*." Paulo was already planning. "Scope it out. Have our people in place."

Jacob shot him a warning look. "How about we discuss this *elsewhere*?" He nodded at the girls. "Let's get you back now, girls." He started walking again. "You've given me a lot to think about." He threw back over his shoulder. "Thanks for that."

Faith hurried to keep up. "There's one more thing you need to know."

Jacob didn't slow his pace. "What's that?"

"The clips will be out of power. I mean... you don't appear to have any kind of generator down here. You'll have to find a way to charge them... if you're going to use them."

"We'll find a way." Jacob turned once again to Paulo. "Madeleine, perhaps?"

They reached the cave and Paulo stepped forward to re-move the barrier. Faith was the first to step inside, her eyes immediately seeking Sophia's. Relief flooded her friend's face as their eyes met.

"Well?" Avery stood up and strode forward. Faith had the distinct impression that she'd been angling to be taken to Kemp, and was incensed that she'd been left behind. "What happened?"

"I'm sure the girls will fill you in once we've gone." Jacob gave Faith a stiff nod. "Thanks. I'll make sure you're sent a little extra dinner in, to show our appreciation."

"You mean we're not eating in the canteen tonight?" Farrah asked. The disappointment in her tone was evident.

"You enjoy the communal meals?" Jacob smiled. *"That's good to know."*

"So... we can join the others?" Catherine's tone was hopeful.

"Not tonight."

As Paulo pulled the wooden slab over the door, Jacob's face was the last thing they saw.

"Another time," he paused, and Faith knew it was deliberate, "maybe."

CHAPTER TWENTY-ONE:
NOAH

As he filled his backpack, Noah couldn't stop his hands from trembling. Ever since the meeting with Danforth had been arranged, he'd felt uneasy. So many things could go wrong with the mission. And this time, he wasn't only worried about his fellow Eremus citizens. Now he feared for Faith and her friends, the innocent pawns stuck in the middle.

He didn't fully trust his own side anymore. Not all of them, at least. His ma, Flynn, Ruth, and Ella, a few others in their close circle. But he knew Jacob's determination to get the better of Danforth would let little stand in the way. Paulo seemed to have aligned himself with their leader. And then there was Harden's ma, who had made no secret of her indifference towards the Bellator prisoners.

It had been a week since Professor Kemp had arrived in Eremus. A week since Faith had suggested the girls' wristclips be used to bring Danforth into a position of Eremus' choosing, allowing them to have control over the meeting. Following these twin revelations, Jacob had made quick work of speaking to Madeleine, who had confirmed that Kemp was indeed a member of the resistance.

Posted undercover at the academy, she was of great importance to them, so her refusal to follow orders when she had charged off after the students had not gone down well. The news that she was safe had come as a relief, however, and Madeleine had asked Jacob to take good care of her. As a result, she had been moved into the same cave as the rest of the girls.

Jacob had also enlisted Madeleine's help to charge the wristclips, and to deliver the anonymous message which stated when the meeting was to take place, and gave their demands.

Danforth was to attend in person.

Danforth was not to bring more than twenty guards.

Danforth would not know the location of the meeting until an hour before.

The meeting was to be peaceful.

Bellator would give Eremus a chance to state its concerns and be listened to.

In return, Jacob guaranteed he would bring along two of the academy students, as proof that they were healthy and being kept safe. If all went well, he would use the same method to arrange a second meeting, where agreements could be finalised and the girls' safe return arranged. Both parties had things to offer now, and Jacob seemed certain they could come to an agreement which suited them all.

Noah wasn't so sure.

He hadn't seen Faith since the day in Kemp's cave. Now that Jacob was suspicious of their relationship, he had not been allowed anywhere near her. The prisoners had only been permitted to join the rest of the community once for a meal in recent days, and Jacob had insisted on them sitting with the council.

He hadn't even dared to ask his ma how Faith had seemed. He wasn't sure if she knew about the kiss that Paulo had witnessed, but he didn't want to give her any more indication of how strong his feelings for Faith were. Not when things were so strained in the community. But he hadn't been able to prevent himself from glancing over at Faith several times during the meal.

She'd been quiet, from what he could tell. Most of the girls had. They had responded to Jacob only when he had directly asked them a question, and the rest of the time had kept their heads down, busying themselves with their food. His ma and Flynn had managed to engage Kemp, and a couple of the older girls in conversation, but the two youngest had looked like frightened rabbits for the entire meal. Helen's eyes hadn't left her plate. Her dinner remained unfinished, much to Ella's dismay.

Faith had only looked over at him once. As he finished his meal and stood up to clear his plate, he chanced one final glance over at the council table and caught her eye. She hadn't smiled, but had nodded, ever so slightly, and held his gaze for what felt like an age. When Ruth had sent a sharp elbow into his side, he'd jumped.

"Earth to Noah."

His friend had poked fun at him, but there was also a look of concern in her eyes. When he'd met her later in the den, their secret cave, she'd confided her worries.

"Don't get me wrong. I like Faith." She'd said, her head bent over her latest drawing. "I just... I can see how important she is to you, that's all."

"And that's a bad thing?"

She had looked up at him at last. "It is if she's right in the middle of all this. The great plan to meet with Danforth. To even the score."

"You think that's what this is about?"

She shrugged. "It is for some people."

Everyone had been involved in the arrangements for the mission. Led by Jacob and Flynn, the community had fortified all entrances to the tunnels, just in case something went wrong and Danforth's forces came looking for them. All the usual raiders and many other citizens had been asked to come along to the meeting, either to be part of the delegation which faced Danforth, or to remain hidden in the trees around the meeting point. Ready to leap out in defence of Eremus, should it be necessary.

Noah had begged to be allowed in the main party, but Flynn had point blank refused. Instead, along with Ruth and a couple of other younger raiders, his role was to conceal himself in a position between the tunnel settlement and the meeting, with a clear view of the proceedings. If anything went wrong, they were assigned to warn the folks back in the caves to batten down the hatches or, if the worst happened, evacuate. It was not a job for a warrior, and, whilst Noah knew he wasn't warrior material, he did feel he could have been placed in a more frontline position.

The only piece of good news was that Faith was not to be taken to the meeting. Deemed too important, she was to remain behind in the caves. The only students deemed appropriate to accompany the mission were the younger girls and Sophia.

Noah couldn't help but think that Jacob had purposefully chosen them because, unlike some of the more outspoken girls, they wouldn't cause any trouble. A second nagging voice said they were also, horrifically, expendable. Noah had promised himself he would do what he could to guarantee their safety. But his assigned position wasn't going to make it easy to help them.

The prisoners were to be kept at a distance, and only brought forward when Danforth required proof of life. Noah could imagine Faith's fear and frustration when she discovered her best friend would be put directly in the line of fire.

He could only hope she wouldn't take any drastic action when she found out who'd been chosen.

From the cave beyond his sleeping quarters, he heard noises. Hurriedly, he pushed the final few items into the pack. Flynn must have returned. One of the citizens who'd be on the frontline facing Danforth, he'd been called to a last-minute meeting about the arrangements. Fastening the pack, Noah was about to move into their communal space when Flynn spoke. Something about his tone made Noah stop and listen.

"News from Madeleine."

"Jacob spoke to her?" His ma sounded surprised.

"Just over the walkie talkie." Noah heard him moving further inside the cave. "She thinks she's being watched... is worried the guards might have made a connection between her and the meeting demands."

"She delivered them as discussed?" His ma's tone matched Flynn's.

"Yep. During the night, mailbox on Elliott Street, on the north side of the city." Noah heard the familiar sound of Flynn easing himself into a chair. "She's pretty sure they're watching the house, though."

"The extra security measures?"

Noah imagined Flynn nodding as he listed the precautions. "She's covered the tunnel entrance with furniture, she isn't making contact with any other resistance members, she's going about her business as normal, but..." he trailed off.

"We've had scares before." Anna's voice dropped lower, and Noah had to lean closer to the curtain. "It'll mean us severing contact with her for a while, that's all. The interest will die down eventually, as long as she doesn't give them any more reason to suspect her."

"I hope so." Flynn yawned loudly.

"Look, they'll be busy today with the meeting." Noah heard a false note of cheer in his ma's voice and knew she was putting on a brave face. "I'm sure they'll decide they've more important things to do and stop their scrutiny soon."

"And if they don't?"

There was a long pause. "I guess..." Anna's voice was a whisper now, "there's always the emergency option." She made a strangled noise in her throat. "...not ideal... there for a reason... we agreed..."

"But if Madeleine doesn't..."

"...aware of the consequences... won't do it... absolutely necessary."

Burning with curiosity, Noah pulled aside the curtain. "Won't do what?"

Flynn looked alarmed at his sudden appearance. Glancing at Anna, he shook his head. Then he turned back to Noah. "Never mind. Nothing you need to worry about."

"But I–"

"Flynn's right." His ma bustled over, bending down to fasten his backpack. "We've got enough to worry about today without additional pressure. Madeleine's very experienced. She'll be fine." She pointed at his pack. "Are you ready to go?"

Noah hoisted it on to his back, trying not to scowl. "Yes."

"You have everything? The meds, some snacks, water... we might be there a long time."

"Yes." Noah hated the childish tone of his voice. "I have everything."

"Alright." His ma turned to Flynn, who was already clambering to his feet and pulling on his own pack. "Then let's go."

As he followed his ma and Flynn through the tunnels, he ran over the plan in his head, a thrill of excitement accompanying the nerves. Could they really pull it off? Negotiate terms with Danforth for Eremus to have rights, to be left alone rather than attacked, to be allowed to enter Bellator without the threat of execution? If so, all sorts of possibilities would open up for them.

The initial requests they were going to make of the Bellator leader were simple. They wanted Danforth to acknowledge their existence, and announce to her citizens that Bellator would start the process of negotiating peaceful associations between the two communities. Flynn and Anna just wanted to come out of hiding, be able to live their lives with some sense of security. Jacob, Noah suspected, wanted more.

They could only hope he wouldn't push too hard.

They exited the tunnels via their assigned route and began making their way to the agreed meeting point. A clearing on the east side of the forest, it was a good two miles from the caves. It had excellent vantage points which would help them to see Danforth coming, and many places where they could conceal themselves from her guards. They knew the spot well, which gave them the advantage.

The location wasn't far from Swallow Lake, one of Noah's favourite places. He'd been taken there occasionally as a young boy, when the Bellator patrols had lessened and Flynn had felt it safe to venture further from the caves. The days they'd spent there were among the happiest in his memory. The sense of peace he'd felt there, even as a young boy, had never been equalled. Swimming in the cool waters on a hot day, lying under the whispering trees, looking up at the great expanse of sky, were his idea of heaven.

He'd always appreciated Flynn including him on the outings he took there with Paulo, and, eventually, when Paulo had longer shifts and wanted to spend more time with his friends, just the two of them. He'd never told his ma about their visits. Far more cautious than Flynn, Anna would never have allowed it. But the trips to the lake had given him a sense of freedom from the darkness of the caves which he'd sorely needed. It remained their secret, something he cherished dearly.

As they passed the lake, Noah and Flynn exchanged smiles. It had taken them almost an hour to reach their destination. Along the way, they were aware of other Eremus citizens moving along the various paths under the trees around them. As part of the plan, they had all left at different times, via different exits, to confuse anyone who Danforth might have watching the woods. They walked in silence, keeping to the less well-trodden paths, and though Noah could hear his heart pounding in his ears, they did not encounter any trouble.

When they reached the clearing, Jacob was already there, directing people to their positions. He nodded curtly. "You know your places, right?"

"We do." Flynn turned to Noah. "Stay out of trouble, okay?" He winked.

"I'll do my best."

Flynn grinned, and turned to Noah's ma. "You too." He pulled her into a fierce hug, whispering something in her ear.

When they parted, Anna was blinking hard. "Be careful."

"Aren't I always?" Flynn took a step back. "Take care, both of you. I'll see you later." And he was gone, moving to join the other citizens who'd been selected to support Jacob on the other side of the space.

His ma turned to Jacob, gesturing to her backpack. "I've some basic medical supplies, but they won't be much use if we have any serious injuries."

"Hopefully it won't come to that." Jacob soothed, but his eyes were already elsewhere, taking account of the citizens as they arrived and, Noah thought, calculating the strength of the Eremus force. "The idea's to talk peacefully, right?" Jacob raised an eyebrow. "That's what you want?"

"That's what *we* want." Anna frowned. "Isn't it?"

Jacob nodded. "Of course." His eyes drifted to another group which was just arriving. "You know your station, right Noah?"

Noah nodded. "But are you sure I can't–" he began, taking one last stab at gaining a more important role in the morning's proceedings.

His ma shot him a dark look. "You *know* the plan."

Perhaps surprised by the sharpness in her tone, Jacob returned his attention to them. "Let's not criticise the boy for wanting to play his part. After all, we're making history here." He turned to Noah. "Your role is just as important as any of the others. If things go wrong," he glanced around the clearing, "we *must* warn the rest of the community. I can't imagine a more important job."

Noah thought differently, but knew better than to argue. As he and his ma walked away from their leader, he was fuming. As they made their way towards his ma's position, a dense thicket of bushes to the far side of the space, she turned to him.

"You'll follow orders, right?"

He turned to her. "What?"

"I mean," for once, she sounded vulnerable, "you won't try to do anything... rash?"

He sighed. "I'll do what I've been told to." They reached the spot and he bent to unload the top layer of his pack, medical supplies which his ma was desperately hoping they wouldn't need. Placing them on the ground under the bushes, he straightened. "Same applies to you, though, right?"

She smiled, and extended her hand. "Be careful."

"I will." He returned her comforting squeeze. "You too."

"I'll see you later." She echoed Flynn's words and turned back to organise her resources. Noah knew it wouldn't take her long.

Reluctantly, Noah shouldered his pack again and made his way to some trees a little further from the meeting point. Reaching it, he glanced around. The woods were quiet. The other Eremus citizens in the vicinity knew how to conceal themselves: to a casual passerby it would appear as though the woods were deserted but for the animal life.

Noah knew better.

There would only be twenty Eremus citizens standing in the clearing with Jacob, fulfilling the demands stated in the message sent to Danforth. But hidden up in the branches of the surrounding trees, crouched in dense thickets and bushes, lying on their bellies underneath hedges in a mile radius around the meeting point were large numbers of Eremus citizens, armed with the numerous guns and knives Jacob had spent years accumulating.

Despite this, Noah had never felt more alone.

He settled into as comfortable a position as he could manage, leaning back against the trunk and looping the straps of his pack around a nearby branch. Closing his eyes, he tried to relax. A cool wind rustled the leaves around him. Small animals scuttled about beneath him, and several birds were singing in the trees above his head.

And less than five hundred metres from where he sat, a group of Eremus citizens waited for the Chancellor of Bellator and her guards to arrive. What would happen at that point was anyone's guess.

All they could do now was wait.

Chapter Twenty-Two:
Faith

I t had been a lonely, stressful week. The girls had been kept in their cave for the majority of their meals, and allowed out only for bathroom breaks and to complete short shifts in various locations around the settlement. When Professor Kemp had been brought to join them, the mood had brightened briefly, but their happiness hadn't lasted long.

Whilst still keeping his promise to provide for them, Jacob had become far more controlling. He had begun splitting them into pairs, sending two of them to work in the canteen, two out foraging with the guidance of an older citizen, two of them on cleaning duty in the communal areas. Some of the older girls had even been assigned to the tunnel excavation crew.

Something was going on. Taking them at their word, Jacob had started to put a plan into place involving their wristclips. Faith was certain of it. Frustratingly, they'd been left in the dark about the details. They hadn't even seen much of Ruth or Ella, who might have confided some useful information. Whenever either of them had come to bring food or other supplies, they'd always been accompanied by other citizens whom the girls didn't know.

During their visits, they'd not had much to say, other than a polite exchange of 'How are you?' and 'Is this finished with?' Faith suspected that this was purposeful. Knowing that Ella and Ruth had become close to the girls, Jacob seemed to be keeping them at arm's length, withdrawing some of the support they'd come to depend on, now that he understood how vital they were.

How vital *she*, in particular, was. Faith hated that Danforth needed her. And even more, she hated that Jacob and the other girls now knew this. They had reacted in different ways: Sophia and Diane were sympathetic, but Farrah and Helen had regarded her with suspicion since she'd told them Kemp's news, and the younger girls didn't seem to know who to trust.

Though she hadn't said as much, Avery appeared jealous of Faith's value to Bellator, despite the threat it might carry. Since their conversation in the middle of the night, the older girl had treated Faith even more coolly than usual, and she was grateful that she hadn't been assigned to any shifts alongside Avery.

Instead, Faith had spent the last few days working in the canteen alongside Mary, Catherine, and Helen in rotation. The younger girls were quiet at the best of times, but in the presence of Eremus citizens, they were virtually mute. Faith didn't blame them. And since the traumatic night when the two of them had been forced out into the woods and used as bait for Danforth, Helen barely looked at anyone.

Sophia had become quite worried about her. Aside from Ella, who she'd grown quite close to, Helen wouldn't open up to anyone. When Ella had any spare time, she spent it with Helen, but even that had happened less since Kemp's arrival and the tightening restrictions placed on them. So being placed on a shift with her was less than comfortable.

Faith would have far preferred the company of Sophia or Diane. Placed together, they might even have managed to get some useful information out of the Eremus citizens they'd been scheduled to work with. But the pairings seemed to purposefully divide friendships. As a result, Faith found herself enduring hours of nervous silence, or having to try and comfort the younger girls, who were frightened about what the upcoming meeting with Danforth might mean for them.

She was convinced they were being separated on purpose. Jacob wanted to make sure none of them had the chance to run, now that they were becoming more aware of the tunnel layout. By keeping them apart, never letting them know in advance where the rest of the group would be working, he prevented them from staging any kind of escape.

Of course, he was banking on none of them being prepared to leave the others behind. And, for the most part, it was a good call. Avery was the only one Faith felt might attempt to do this. But even she was unlikely to set off through the forest alone. Farrah remained friendly with the others, and Faith doubted she would be prepared to abandon them just because Avery asked her to. The rest of the girls, Faith was sure, would stick together as best they could.

Every night when they were brought back to the cave, they discussed where they'd been stationed that day, trying to build up a mental map of the underground settlement. It was tricky, though. Kemp was new to the settlement, and being mostly stationed in the medcave with Anna, she didn't have a good sense of the route to any of the other key locations. The senior girls tried to recall as much as they could, but since they were mostly assigned to a single sector, it was hard to make connections between the different areas within the tunnel system. And the younger girls seemed unable to describe the location of their shifts with any accuracy at all. This, Faith was sure, was why they'd been the only Danforth girls so far permitted to go outside the caves.

Assigned to one of the older citizens on several occasions, they'd been allowed out into the woods to collect wild plants and herbs. It seemed the Eremus diet was heavily supplemented by what they could find growing freely under the trees. Their resilience in the face of almost overwhelming odds fascinated Sophia. But Faith was more interested in building up a picture of key routes through the tunnels. She found it particularly difficult to remain patient with Mary and Catherine's vague descriptions of their route to the exits.

Jacob also appeared to be limiting their access to other Eremus citizens at mealtimes. The only dinner they'd been permitted to eat in the canteen with the others, despite Faith spending most days preparing the food for it, had been incredibly frustrating. Announcing that the meal was a thank you for their cooperation with Eremus, Jacob insisted they sit with the council. He'd even had their food served up to the table, instead of the usual self-service system.

Most of the girls had appreciated the special treatment. Kemp had certainly enjoyed her conversation with Anna, who it seemed she knew from Bellator. But afterwards, Diane had pointed out that, if they were seated with the council, their conversation could be monitored. And since they hadn't left the table during the meal, they hadn't had the chance to communicate with any of the other citizens either. Jacob was clever, Faith had to admit. By presenting the meal as a celebration, he'd managed to gag them without seeming like the enemy.

It had been more than a week since Faith had seen Noah, and she suspected he was purposefully being kept away from her. Jacob knew about their prior connection, and now he'd been made aware of how important she was to Danforth, he wasn't about to allow them to get too close. He couldn't afford anyone within Eremus to develop a relationship with her. It would threaten his power, if he couldn't guarantee all citizens were totally on his side.

So she'd seen nothing of him. During the meal, she hadn't dared to look at him, frightened to stoke the suspicions she was sure were already swirling in Jacob's head. Not to mention Anna's. She had no wish to get Noah into any more trouble. But she hadn't been able to stop thinking about their kiss. As he'd gotten up to leave, she'd risked a glance at his table.

Their eyes had met, and the expression in Noah's implied he'd been waiting to meet her gaze, perhaps glancing over at her often throughout the meal. Later, Sophia had confirmed she'd noticed him looking their way many times since he'd arrived. Trying to convey her thoughts, Faith had held his gaze for as long as she'd dared. Only when Sophia had grasped hold of her sleeve and yanked at it, had she torn her eyes from his.

She'd thought of him often since. Hoped that he'd wander into the canteen while she was working there, or pass her as she moved to and from the bathing cave. But she had not caught even a glimpse of him since.

"Penny for your thoughts?"

Faith realised Sophia was speaking to her. "Sorry?"

Her friend nudged her with affection. "You were miles away."

Not wishing to worry her friend, Faith sidestepped the question. "I was just wishing we knew more about what they're planning."

"Liar." Sophia's tone was gentle, but there was concern in her eyes.

"Huh?"

"You were thinking about Noah."

"Maybe." Faith looked away.

Sophia let it go. Stealing a glance at Professor Kemp, who appeared to be sleeping, she kept her voice low. "When do you think the meeting will happen?"

Their teacher hadn't approved of them helping Jacob. She didn't trust him, even now that he had relented and allowed her to move into the cave with the girls. They had learned it was better to keep conversations about the Eremus leader's actions for moments when she wasn't listening.

"I don't know. Soon?" Faith sat up and leaned closer to her friend. "How long do you think it'll take Danforth to respond to a request to meet with Jacob?"

"Not long, I shouldn't think. And now that he's managed to charge the wristclips..."

Her friend was right. Aside from the awkward meal, the only time Jacob had been near them was earlier today, when he had brought them a single wristclip, powered up and ready to go. Ignoring Avery's permanent scowl, he'd spent over an hour in the cave, asking Faith and Sophia to demonstrate its different functions. They'd had little choice but to show him how it worked, both of them praying they weren't making a mistake by helping him. When the Eremus leader had left, he'd had a wide smile on his face.

Faith found herself hating him. "You're right. Now that he has the locator chips working, he can guide Danforth to any place of his choosing. He won't waste time."

"What do you think he'll say when he has her in front of him?"

"Hopefully, *I come in peace.*" Sophia grinned, but then the smile died. "It won't be very funny if he doesn't though, will it?"

Hearing the conversation, Diane shuffled closer. "I overheard a conversation in the tunnels which was quite interesting."

Diane had been one of the students tasked with joining the tunnel crew. It was the hardest role they'd been assigned so far, consisting mostly of loading wheelbarrows with piles of rock and stones. When they were full, some of the Eremus men took them away and returned with them, empty, for the process to begin again.

The debris was created by the group of citizens assigned to extending the tunnel system. Diane and Sophia had spent lots of time discussing the ingenuity of the scheme, which was Eremus' way of creating space for their growing community. Even Faith had to admit the existence of such a large number of people, living almost out of sight underground, was to be admired.

Diane and Farrah, and on one occasion, Helen, had spent several hours loading up the wheelbarrows. When they'd returned, they'd been exhausted, their skin coated with a thick layer of dust and sweat, and their hands covered in cuts and grazes. So far, however, it appeared to be the only place citizens had been overheard referencing the approaching interaction with Danforth.

Checking that Kemp was still sleeping, Diane leaned even closer and dropped her voice. "They mentioned the weapons store being accessed. And I heard one of them say something about an unexpected surprise."

Sophia's eyes widened. "What kind of surprise?"

Diane shrugged. "I don't know. The guy... Harden, I think he's called... was laughing about it. But then one of the others... a girl around our age... I think he called her Sid or Sil or something... spotted me and gave him a nudge." She clenched her fists in frustration. "He shut up after that."

"I'm starving." From across the cave, Farrah paced to the door. "Isn't it breakfast time yet?"

"I should think so... soon at least." Sophia soothed. "I think they might be late, to be honest."

"How would we even *know*, though?" Avery gestured at the cave around them, dark, aside from the two lanterns at either end.

"You don't think..." Mary's voice was timid, "that they've forgotten, do you?"

"I'm sure they haven't." Sophia moved across to her. "Perhaps they're just busy with something else today."

"Sure. They've got bigger things on their minds." Avery turned to face them. "Their plans with the wristclips, for example. Who knows what they have in store for Danforth now that you've armed them with knowledge they were never meant to have."

"Oh, give it a rest, Avery." Diane sighed.

"You know why we did it." Faith forced Avery to meet her gaze. "We have to hope that whatever he's planning has a positive outcome."

"I never thought I'd say this," Avery sighed, "but I hope you're right."

"It doesn't resolve the issue with the lack of food," Farrah repeated.

"Do you think they were doubling up last night?" Diane gestured to the trays which the previous night's dinner had been brought on. "Perhaps they *anticipated* not being able to get to us early this morning?"

Faith chewed her lip. "Maybe."

The tray they had been brought the previous evening had contained a larger ration than usual. Not exactly double their normal meal, but there had been extra bread, an additional pitcher of water, and several cereal bars, which they hadn't known existed in Eremus.

"Stolen from the city, no doubt," Farrah had commented with a frown.

Faith suspected Farrah was right, but having seen how the Eremus people were forced to live, she could well understand that the risk of getting caught by Bellator guards was worth it if they ensured their citizens didn't starve. She had to admit, her sympathy with the people here was growing.

Faith believed the words she'd spoken to Avery. She really was hoping that the meeting with Danforth would go well. If Eremus managed to secure some kind of peaceful agreement between the two communities, perhaps its people would be allowed to live and work alongside the women of Bellator, find legitimate ways to earn a living, pay for food, and ensure their children never went hungry. And, selfishly, perhaps she might be allowed to stay here, but not risk starvation herself.

Diane was examining the contents of the tray. Unused to any kind of rationing, despite the time they'd spent as prisoners here, the girls had taken advantage of the extra food and gobbled most of it down the previous night. There were three cereal bars remaining, and two hunks of slightly dry bread.

"We can split what's here." She began breaking the bread apart and dividing it into pieces. "And I'm sure they'll appear at some point. We know they need to keep us safe and healthy."

They passed the food around, each eating their assigned portion in silence. As Faith was finishing her food, a noise at the door drew everyone's attention.

"You see?" Sophia told Mary. "I told you they hadn't forgotten us."

Mary began to smile, but the happy expression died as her eyes fell on the newcomer. At the door stood Paulo, Noah's brother. Professor Kemp jerked awake, stiffening as he strode inside, his eyes roaming the cave. Behind him came two other male citizens, both tall and broad-shouldered. Neither of them spoke.

Faith found herself shivering as Paulo looked from face to face. She tried to read his expression as his eyes alighted on each girl. Diane was greeted with a definite shudder, Helen, a slight shake of the head, Avery and Farrah, the same. As she tried to work it out, he glanced at Faith herself, his eyes indicating a definitive dismissal. He moved on to Sophia, giving a worrying nod. Then his eyes flicked between the two youngest girls, as though he were tossing a coin over which one to choose. Finally, his eyes came to rest on Catherine, who was sitting a little way from her friend, frozen mid-chew.

"Her." Paulo pointed a finger at Catherine, who let out a small squeal. "And her."

Faith's breath caught in her throat as he pointed at Sophia. Before she could react, the two males at the entrance came forward and took Sophia and Catherine by the arm.

Kemp was on her feet. "Where are you taking them?"

Paulo turned to the teacher. "Jacob has arranged a meeting with Danforth. He needs proof that the girls are still alive. Being treated well."

"That's a matter of opinion," Diane shot at him.

Knowing it wouldn't make a difference, Faith stood up and stepped forward. "Can't you take me instead?" She looked from Sophia to Catherine. "Instead of..." she hesitated for a second, but catching her friend's eye, turned towards the younger girl, "her? She's so young."

"Sorry. No." His tone was not unkind. "I have my orders."

"I don't think you should be–" Kemp took hold of Catherine's arm.

"I'm afraid you don't have a say in this." Paulo gestured to the men, who began leading the two girls out. "Don't worry. We won't hurt you." He turned to those left inside. "You must know how important you all are to Eremus." His tone was respectful, gentle, almost. "Especially now. Your friends will be kept safe."

Faith could only watch as Sophia and Catherine were hustled towards the cave entrance. Catherine had started to cry quietly, and, witnessing her friend disappearing out of the cave, Mary joined in. As Sophia moved into the tunnel, she glanced back at Faith.

"It's not for long. I'll be fine."

"Listen to her," Paulo said. "She's right."

"See you soon." Sophia managed a small smile. Beside her, the man tugged on her arm. A second later, she disappeared.

"They'll be back later today." As he turned to leave, Paulo collected the empty tray. "I'll have someone bring you some more food soon."

Following the others, he slid the door back into place. As they heard the lock being slid across the cave mouth, Faith massaged her fingers on her temples, wondering how she'd stop herself from going mad over the next few hours.

In the end, she didn't have long to wait. The door was reopened what seemed like only minutes later. Glancing up, the girls smiled, expecting to see Ella or Ruth with a tray of food and water.

Instead, the older woman who'd harangued Faith in the canteen during their first meal appeared. Sarah, Faith remembered. She did the same as Paulo had done not half an hour previously, only this time, when her eyes came to rest on Faith, they lit up. Something in them made her shiver.

"You." She beckoned with a finger. "Come with me."

Chapter Twenty-Three:
Noah

Noah's back ached. Around him, the woods continued to whisper their secrets quietly, undisturbed by the marching feet of twenty Bellator guards. He'd been sitting in the tree for what felt like hours, but had heard nothing, other than the usual forest rustlings, since the moment he'd climbed up there.

His branch gave him a clear view of the path beneath, yet allowed him to remain hidden. Knowing he'd be there for a while, he'd tried to settle in a comfortable position, but he found he could neither remain still nor keep his mind from racing. The situation reminded him of the night of the girls' kidnapping, where nothing had gone as planned.

Again, he was an observer. Again, he didn't know what to expect. Again, he was at the mercy of another person's scheme.

If Noah crawled towards the end of the branch he was lying on, he had an undisturbed view of the clearing. He'd already done it several times. Everyone was in their agreed position:

Jacob in the centre, flanked by Flynn and Jan. Twenty of Eremus' best raiders fanned out behind them.

They'd decided to include a woman in the frontline, if only to demonstrate the equality of the Eremus society. Noah's ma had lobbied to be in the lineup, but Jacob had said no. He felt she'd be better used as medical support, should they need it. Selfishly, Noah was glad. He was finding it hard enough to have Flynn in the enemy firing line.

Further from the centre, a second ring of citizens was concealed in the bushes. These were more difficult to see, but Noah could pick them out here and there: the muzzle of a rifle sticking out from a hawthorn thicket; a flash of darker green which he knew was the peak of Dane's cap; a slight rustling of bushes here and there which might have been dismissed as the wind, had Noah not known otherwise.

The last time he'd checked, the clearing had looked exactly the same. The only thing that had altered was the slightly slumped shoulders of the surrounding raiders. They were tired of waiting. Tired of the constant tension which would not ease until Danforth had been and gone.

Noah hated to admit it, but he was beginning to think Danforth wasn't coming.

Ruth was close by. She'd passed beneath him on her way to her position, whistling and giving him the thumbs up as she pointed to her chosen tree. Once she'd shimmied up it, however, he'd lost sight of her, and even though he knew he could reach her side in seconds if she needed him, it wasn't comforting. He'd have felt far better if they were together.

But since the soft whistling sound which had indicated their readiness, the instructions were to remain in place, alone. Separating themselves meant they minimised the number of citizens who were caught, should the worst happen. And, once Jacob gave the signal for radio silence, all talking had been forbidden.

His thoughts went to Faith. Was she pacing the cave, fretting about Sophia? Might she even be concerned about him, just a little? Shifting position again, he sighed. She probably didn't even know he was here. The girls were hardly privy to Jacob's plans. And why would she worry about him anyway?

He stretched widely, curving his spine one way and then the other in a vain attempt to ease his discomfort. He was just considering digging into his food supply when something changed. Freezing, he listened. There were no new sounds. No stamping of boots, no commands being delivered, no rustling of leaves as guards brushed past.

But something was different.

Creeping along the branch again, Noah checked that the path below him was empty and craned his head to survey the clearing. It didn't take long to spot what was different. While Flynn and Jan still stood in the centre of the space, Jacob was absent.

Noah ran his eye over the semi-circle of raiders who were backing those at the front. Were there fewer of them now? A rapid count confirmed his fears. But where had they gone?

Noah thought back to the early morning meeting. He'd never asked Flynn what it was about, but perhaps the plan had changed. He tried to relax. If Flynn wasn't worried, he shouldn't be either. Yet the reduced number of Eremus citizens in the space had him on edge. There were few enough of them as it was, without limiting the number prepared to face Danforth. And what about the citizens hidden further out? Noah couldn't even see them properly. If they were gone too, it left them vulnerable.

He couldn't leave Flynn down there with minimal back up. Heart pounding, Noah retreated along the branch. Checking the ground below once again, he slid down from the tree as silently as he could and began to pick his way closer to the meeting site, skirting the edges of the path.

He'd only taken a few steps when he heard footsteps. Crouching low, he turned towards the sound, one hand on the knife at his belt. A faint rustling emanated from somewhere nearby. For a second, Noah imagined Danforth herself appearing at his side, eyes dark and piercing, a fearsome-looking machine gun clenched in her hands.

Shaking, he retreated into the bushes at the side of the path and waited. The rustling noise stopped for a second, then started up again, closer this time. Wiping sweat from his forehead with his sleeve, he eased the knife out from its holster and raised it. But which direction to point it in? He listened again. The noise was coming from behind him.

But before he could turn, an arm grasped his. He tensed, then relaxed, as a familiar figure appeared between the leaves.

"Your face!" Ruth chuckled.

Noah jabbed an elbow into his friend's side. "Thanks for the heart attack, pal."

"Anytime." Her face turned serious. "Guess you couldn't stand not knowing what was happening either."

"It's not that." He leaned close to his friend, keeping his voice low. "Jacob's gone."

His friend's eyebrows shot up. "What?"

"So has some of the back-up."

"But why?"

"No idea." Noah shrugged. "But Flynn's vulnerable. We can't leave him out there with reduced protection."

"Okay." Ruth jerked her head in the direction of the meeting. "Come on then."

They crept through the bushes together, slowing their pace as they neared the clearing's edge, looking for a suitable place to hide. Ruth gestured to a dense clump of bushes, large enough to conceal them both, yet with soft leaves which cascaded to ground level. Noah assessed her choice. The bush would make less noise when disturbed, and provide good cover, yet allow them to see and hear what was going on in the clearing. Nodding his agreement, he slid between the leaves.

Ruth followed. Once they were well-concealed, they crept forward, both holding their breath. The bushes stood close to one side of the clearing, allowing them a partial view of Flynn and Jan. Jacob was missing. Yet the remaining people in the space did not seem alarmed, nor were they taking any action. Noah had to admit the leaders exit must have been part of the new plan, but despite the others' calm, something about the situation didn't feel right.

At a sharp elbow in his side, he turned to Ruth. "Well?" she hissed. "What do we do?"

"I'm not sure."

Noah leaned forward so he had a better view of the main entrance to the space. The meeting location had been chosen well, allowing the Eremus citizens good cover on three sides. This meant there were plenty of places for their back up to remain concealed, and left the more open fourth side of the area as Danforth's most likely entrance.

There was no sign of her though. And while Jan and Flynn appeared calm, Noah couldn't properly see their faces. He was about to suggest they return to their original positions when Flynn turned to say something to Jan. His expression, whilst not fearful, was apprehensive.

"He looks worried." Noah turned to his friend. "And maybe.... confused?"

"About what?"

Noah shrugged. "Not sure. They had a last-minute meeting this morning. He never told me what it was about. But maybe..." he squinted at the raiders, "maybe they changed something."

"You think Jacob went to check if Danforth was close?"

"Maybe." Noah frowned. "But Flynn... his expression... I'm wondering if... maybe he doesn't know the full story."

"Danforth's supposed to be here by now, right? She's had enough time... from when Jacob turned the locators on?"

"I think so?"

"Then... maybe she's just not coming?" Ruth's eyes skimmed the woods around them. "Where's your ma stationed? She might know more. We could ask her."

"No," Noah retorted. "I promised I'd follow orders. She'll kill me if she finds out I'm not in position."

Again, he glanced at the guards standing around Flynn and Jan. The majority of them stood to attention, their eyes fixed on the entrance to the clearing. Off to one side though, one raider caught his eye. Sil, a close friend of Harden's, who'd been with them on the trip to the hospital in Bellator. When the raid had gone wrong, she'd been amongst those who wanted to cut-and-run.

Noah didn't trust her. Right now, her stance indicated a tension he couldn't see in any of the others. Every now and again, she darted a glance into the forest to her left. The eyes of every other raider remained focused on the entrance to the clearing, yet her gaze kept roaming to the same spot. As Noah watched, the glances seemed to get more regular, as though she was expecting someone to appear.

Beside him, Ruth shifted. "Well, we can't just sit here doing nothing, I mean–"

But the rest of her sentence was obliterated as the sound of multiple explosions filled the air. Clapping their hands over their ears, they threw themselves to the ground next to one another, as the very air around them seemed to shatter. The blasts echoed around the clearing, rolling on and on until it seemed they would never stop.

Beside him, Ruth moved closer, blindly groping for his hand. Shunting sideways so their bodies lay side by side, he grasped her hand in his and held it tightly against his chest. Her eyes were wild with terror which he was certain reflected his own. Throwing his other arm around her shoulder, he huddled closer to her as the bellowing roar dominated the clearing.

When it was over, Noah tentatively raised his head. In the clearing, the neat formation of raiders had broken up. Citizens who had previously been standing to attention in a near-perfect semi-circle were now scattered far and wide, having raced for cover when the first bombs had exploded.

Flynn and Jan lay prostrate on the ground, only metres away from the bush where they hid. It looked like Flynn had flung himself over Jan's body. For a moment, Noah thought his heart would stop. He was on his feet, readying himself to run to Flynn's side when he felt Ruth's hand close around his ankle.

"Careful," she warned, struggling to her feet beside him. "Wait."

"Why?" He strained to loosen her hold on him as she transferred her hand to his arm.

"Where's the damage?"

"What?"

"It *sounded* bad." His friend pointed into the clearing. "But it was further away than we thought."

Breathing more slowly now, Noah ran an eye over the clearing. Aside from the scattered raiders, there was no visible impact. Trees remained standing, bushes rustled in a slight breeze, no injuries caused anyone to cry out. He glanced back to Flynn and Jan. To his relief, neither looked hurt. They had struggled to sit up and seemed to be trying to work out the source of the explosions. He followed their gaze.

From the far side of the forest, a dense plume of smoke rose into the air, coming from the very direction that, only minutes ago, Sil's eyes had been focused. He scanned the area for Harden's friend, but she was nowhere to be seen.

"D'you think that Danforth…?" Ruth began.

"Maybe." Noah frowned. "Not sure."

"Is it safe to…" Ruth gestured towards Flynn.

Together, they crept out of the bushes, keeping a sharp eye out for any flashes of the blue Bellator guard uniform. It only took them seconds to reach Flynn, who was already on his feet. His eyes lit up as he saw them approaching.

"Thank goodness." He paused, and his face changed. "Though you shouldn't be away from your posts." He turned to Noah. "Are you both alright?"

Noah shook off his concern. "What just happened?"

All around them, raiders were getting to their feet. Checking that no one was hurt, they began making their way towards Flynn. He leaned close to Noah, lowering his voice, trying to get the words out before the rest of the citizens reached them.

"I'm not sure." He frowned. "At first we thought Danforth, but–"

"This is our fearless leader's work." Beside Flynn, Jan's face was like thunder. "I'm not sure what he's up to, but it's no coincidence that this happened right after he left."

"What?" Ruth's face was white. "You mean... the explosion wasn't–"

"Don't think so." Flynn shook his head. "Jacob went to check the perimeter. Least, that's what he said." He waved a hand at the remaining guards in the clearing. "Took some of the others with him."

"Some of his closest allies." Jan jabbed a finger in the direction Jacob had disappeared. "Clearly, there's a large part of the plan *some* of us weren't told about."

"What do you think..." Noah sucked in a breath. "I mean, what's going to happen now?"

"That's anybody's guess." Jan's gaze darted around the field, agitated. "We'll have to be ready for anything."

Flynn looked thoughtful. "I did wonder where Sarah was."

"Me too," Jan spat out. "Didn't think she'd want to miss being in the thick of this."

"Nope. She wouldn't." Flynn's eyes roamed the edges of the clearing. "But I'd be willing to bet she's elsewhere right now, tasked with a totally different mission."

Chapter Twenty-Four:
Faith

"Time to go."

As she hauled Faith into a standing position, the smile on Sarah's face was sly. Whatever the cause of the explosion which had rocked the forest around them, it had pleased her.

Since she had removed Faith from the cave, ignoring Professor Kemp's fierce protests, the older woman had said little to her. They had seen no one on their journey through the tunnels, and Faith suspected only a select few knew about her removal from the cave. She had been taken in a direction she'd never been before, and their cautious progress had suggested Sarah was trying to avoid others.

At first, Faith had been as awkward as possible, questioning Sarah regularly about where they were going and demanding to know why. Her quizzing had been mostly ignored, until they had reached one of the tunnel exits and Faith could see the woods ahead. As she continued to protest, Sarah had spun round to face her.

"Enough!" Her face had been scarlet. "No more of your stupid questions. We're going outside, and if you continue to chatter like a demented monkey, you put us both in danger."

"But what if I–"

"What if nothing." Sarah had grasped her by the arm and shaken her. "You don't speak, unless I ask you a direct question. You walk alongside me silently. When I say stop, you stop. When I say move, you move." She had leaned so close that Faith had been able to feel the heat of her breath in her face. "And quickly. Got it?"

"Got it."

With that, Faith had been hustled out of the entrance and into the woods. From that point on, Sarah hadn't spoken. Frightened, Faith had concentrated on putting one foot in front of the other as the older woman had led her through the forest on a route she was certain meant they were trying to stay out of sight.

Sure enough, they'd encountered no one. After walking for well over an hour, they had come to a small, hidden cottage. With no preamble, Sarah had taken Faith inside the small outbuilding next to it and thrust her into a rickety wooden chair. Using a length of rope, she'd secured Faith's arm to a set of shelving, instructed her to remain silent, and left.

For what seemed like hours, Faith had sat still, listening to the sounds of the woods as she pondered what might be about to happen to her. Clearly, Jacob had a plan other than that of simply talking to Danforth. A plan of which Faith was very much a part. Her only comfort had rested in the fact that she was valuable to the Bellator leader, so it was unlikely that Jacob wanted her dead.

What he did want remained to be seen.

She had no doubt that Jacob was behind Sarah's actions. And no doubt people like Flynn, Anna, and Noah knew nothing about her abduction. Why else would they remove her from the cave, alone, after Paulo had collected Sophia and Catherine?

She had wished, desperately, that she was with the other girls. At least they might have offered some comfort to one another. And, who knows, they might have managed to come up with a way to escape their fate. But alone, Faith had felt so vulnerable.

Determined not to give in, she had studied her small wooden prison. It was clearly used for storage: the shelving units which stood around the edges were filled with boxes of various sizes, though the one she'd been tethered to simply contained a few stray papers which, on closer inspection, appeared to be maps of Bellator and the surrounding area.

Sarah wasn't stupid. She had positioned Faith in such a way as to prevent her from reaching most of the containers. But there was one on the neighbouring shelf which had almost been within her reach. Straining away from her shackles, Faith had managed to get to it.

Lifting the lid with the tip of her finger, she'd stood on her tiptoes to look inside. It appeared to be filled with packets of dried soup and noodles, presumably stolen from Bellator. Lying on top of the food, however, was a box cutter. Faith's heart had leapt as she'd spotted it.

Ignoring the fact that the rope was cutting into her wrist, she had managed to hook it with her index finger and pull it towards her. That was the moment the woods around her had exploded. The wooden walls of the shed had rattled as though they might collapse.

Faith had been gripped by a fear so intense she had almost blacked out. Dizziness threatened to overwhelm her, and for several minutes after the blasts had stopped, she had fought the light-headedness, breathing in and out of her nose slowly until her balance returned to normal.

When it did, she had just enough time to retract the blade of the box cutter and slip it into her pocket before the door burst open. Sarah had appeared, smiling slyly. She'd made quick work of untying Faith, and pulling her to her feet again, laughing at her unsteadiness.

"Buck up, girl. There's more in store for you yet."

As she was dragged towards the door, Faith noticed Sarah was wearing a wristclip. It hadn't been there earlier, she was sure of it. Reluctantly, she followed the older woman, concerned by its sudden appearance.

Outside, the sky was glowing. Ignoring it, Sarah pulled Faith along through the trees, keeping a vice-like grip on her arm at all times. The bombs had to be Jacob's doing. The fact that Sarah was unfazed by the explosions which had ripped through the forest told Faith she'd known about them beforehand. A catalyst, Faith was certain. And they marked the start of something which couldn't end well.

Not for her, anyway.

She tried again to steady her breathing as they moved through the forest. Nervous glances to her right showed a significant blast had ripped through the area, destroying foliage, wildlife, and presumably, people. Faith thought she heard cries, carried on the wind, and the occasional shout suggesting that some of the bomb's intended targets were still alive.

They had to be Bellator guards. Shaken as she was, Faith felt a fury surge through her at this second betrayal. She'd suggested the wristclips be used to protect the Eremus people from Danforth's considerable force. She'd asked that they be used to set up a peaceful meeting, and not be instrumental in any loss of life.

Instead, they had been used to draw Danforth's people into a trap. She watched Sarah closely, noting how many times she glanced down at the device on her wrist. Faith wasn't close enough to read the information on the tiny screen, but she could see from the illumination that it had been activated. Were they, even now, drawing more guards to their deaths?

A glance at the backpack Sarah carried set her heart racing. She wondered if it was filled with explosives. Had she inadvertently become part of a plot to exterminate large numbers of Bellator guards? Sweat broke out on her forehead and her knees almost gave way beneath her as she was hauled along in Sarah's wake. Was this a suicide mission?

Her thoughts went to Noah, but this time she felt certain he wasn't involved. She knew him better now. This had Jacob's fingerprints all over it. And the group of Eremus citizens who genuinely wanted to negotiate a peaceful treaty with Bellator would never have sanctioned this kind of violence.

She wondered where Noah was. Somewhere in the trees, surely. Was he thinking of her, worrying about her whereabouts? Or did he assume she was safely back in the caves, as Jacob had led everyone to believe? She imagined his fury at the explosions, the innocent loss of life. This was not his way.

For a while, they appeared to be travelling closer to the site of the bombs. Faith could feel the heat of the fires, which still raged among the dry brush of the forest. Surely, they couldn't be heading right into the danger zone? But she could do little about it at the moment. Sarah was an impatient captor, urging Faith onwards. Wherever they were headed, time was of the essence.

As they passed a dense thicket of hawthorn, they heard a cracking of twigs underfoot. A Bellator guard stumbled out of the foliage. The woman's uniform was singed, her face blackened, both hands clutching her side. Faith recoiled, only to feel Sarah's baton at her back.

"Help me!" She stretched a hand towards Faith, its palm bloody.

"I- I—"

The woman's face was not threatening. She was wounded, and badly. Faith took a deep breath and steeled herself to step forward, to offer help. Her hand had just closed around the guard's arm, when she felt herself being jerked backwards.

The woman's eyes widened in surprise as she was caught off balance by the sudden movement. She staggered sideways and crashed to the forest floor, crying out in pain.

"She's hurt!" Faith spun to face Sarah.

"So?" The Eremus woman's face was stone. "She's supposed to be *dead*. We can't–"

But another set of footsteps sounded in the bushes. More certain than the first woman's had been, the approaching newcomer did not sound like they were impeded by injury. Sarah raised a hand which, to Faith's horror, contained a small pistol. But as a tall figure emerged from the greenery, she relaxed.

"Ma!" The young man stepped onto the path. Faith searched for his name. "What are you doing here?"

Sarah jerked her head at Faith. "Taking care of our insurance policy. And..." She broke off, shaking the wristclip at the young man, who nodded.

"Got it." The young man's eyes swept over Faith briefly. "She behaving?"

"So far." Sarah jerked her head at the smoke. "It went well, then?"

An uncertain smile crossed her son's face. "Better than we imagined. There are a lot of dead guards back there. Sections of trees are still burning... we might need to go and..."

"Never mind that, for now. Harden!" Sarah's tone was sharp as her glance moved to the guard who was struggling into a sitting position. "We have a more pressing issue to deal with."

Harden's eyes moved to the woman, whose hands were groping at her belt for a weapon which wasn't there. As tears of frustration began to fall, she reapplied pressure to her wound.

"Can you take care of this for me?" Sarah nodded to Harden's gun.

He glanced at the gun, then at the woman on the ground. "I- Well, I–"

Impatiently, Sarah shook her head. "Never mind." She raised her weapon.

Faith watched the woman's eyes fill with terror. "No... I- you can't–"

"I think you'll find that I can." There was a sharp crack and the woman crumpled.

"No!" Faith cried out, but Sarah had already holstered the pistol.

"Let's go." She checked the wristclip again. Jerking her head at her son, she began pushing Faith forward again. "We can't afford any more delays."

With tears streaming down her cheeks, Faith walked on. Their small group skirted the edge of the bombsite, heading into a greener area where the acrid, burning stench was less potent. Harden strode ahead of them, his weapon ready. He didn't seem afraid to use it. Faith wondered what had made him hesitate with the guard.

"Almost there." Sarah jabbed a finger into Faith's side. "Pull yourself together, girl."

Faith wiped a hand across her cheek, hiccupping several times as she tried to regain control. They reached a thicket of bushes and Sarah pulled her backwards, stopping her progress.

"Here's where we wait." She tapped a button on the wristclip to deactivate it, then turned to Harden. "You know where you need to be?" He nodded and turned to leave. "I'll see you later then. And Harden?" He stopped and glanced back at his mother. "Well done today."

"Thanks."

It struck Faith that Harden's answering smile was not genuine, but he had disappeared before she had the chance to study his expression further.

When he had gone, Sarah turned to Faith. "Look at the state of you. Can't have Danforth seeing you like this, can we? She'll think we're treating you badly."

She removed her pack and rummaged in it until she found a clean cloth and her water bottle. Splashing some liquid on to the cloth, she handed it to Faith. "Clean yourself up, girl."

Faith did her best to wash away the grime on her face. When she removed the cloth, it was smeared with soot from the fire and even, to her horror, a reddish mark which she feared was the guard's blood.

"Better?" She handed the rag back to Sarah, her voice brittle.

"Nope." Sarah leaned closer. "You missed a spot."

Grasping the back of Faith's head, she scrubbed her forehead hard. Faith flinched at the harsh treatment. In response, Sarah tightened her hold on Faith's hair, hauling her head backwards and scraping the rough cloth against her skin. Unable to help it, Faith cried out.

Abruptly, Sarah released her hold on Faith, eyes darting to the space beyond the bushes. For a second, she looked panicked. Her hand shot out and slapped Faith, the pain reverberating through her head. Spinning her around, she pulled her close, one arm snaking around Faith's shoulders to hold her still, the other clamped down over her mouth.

"Shut up and keep still."

Her cheek stinging, Faith focused on breathing through her nose and keeping her body limp. If she had to fight Sarah off, the best weapons she'd have were the element of surprise, and speed. For now, she'd play along until she could figure out what was going on.

Sophia and Catherine were somewhere in the forest. The rest of the girls were back at the cave. She couldn't just cut and run, leaving them here. But she had a better idea of the caves' location now, and a clearer sense of how to make her way through the tunnels. She could get back there alone, if she had to.

Apparently satisfied that she wasn't going to struggle, Sarah eased backwards, removing her hand from Faith's mouth.

"We need to move." She pressed a hand at Faith's back again, directing her around the side of the bushes. "Quietly."

Faith obeyed, stepping as silently as possible. When the trees ahead of them thinned out into a large clearing, Sarah guided her into some dense bushes where they could stand with a good view of the space ahead. It was filled with various Eremus citizens, standing in some kind of formation: two in the centre, a ring of others around the outside. All held a weapon of some description.

Despite the organised appearance of the force, there was an air of confusion surrounding them, as though they weren't entirely sure what was happening. Faith squinted at the two figures in the centre, looking for Jacob. But one of them was female, a woman she didn't recognise, and she was certain that the male figure was Flynn.

Their heads were bent close together, their expressions intense. Flynn gestured towards the bushes where Faith and Sarah were standing, and, for a second, she thought he was pointing at her. When the woman turned to look, Faith realised they were probably discussing bombs which had exploded in the forest behind her.

The woman jabbed a finger at her arm, and Faith was relieved to see that they weren't wearing wristclips. Flynn was not part of the betrayal, then. Perhaps some of the council had not been in on Jacob's plan. Faith's eyes roamed the field, searching for the Eremus leader. Where was he?

Her eyes swept the edges of the space, expanding the search. She began to make out additional figures, standing partly concealed in the greenery. Jacob had prepared a substantial force to face the Bellator guards. Yet not all of them were out in the open. Faith wondered how many more were hidden in the bushes. The Eremus people knew these woods so well, it would be easy for large numbers of them to conceal themselves in the shadows.

A sudden sound in the forest behind them made Faith's captor tense, and Sarah abruptly swung Faith round to face the approaching threat. She raised the pistol once again, this time resting her arm on Faith's shoulder. As the footsteps grew closer, Faith steeled herself for a second shot.

But Sarah's arm relaxed as Jacob emerged from the trees. His face was similarly smeared with soot which told Faith where he'd been, but he was smiling.

"Going well so far."

"Indeed." Sarah nodded at the clearing ahead. "All the important people in place?" Jacob nodded. "And everyone else is right here, as planned, despite the lack of prior information. Told you there was no need to worry."

Prior information? Faith wondered how much of his plan Jacob had shared with the Eremus citizens. She thought about Flynn's expression. He'd definitely been in the dark about the bombs.

"You were right." Jacob followed Sarah's gaze. "Just a matter of time before they get here. The people I had in the rear with the clips should be driving them in this direction." He glanced at Sarah's wrist. "You turned yours off?"

"Of course. Soon as we got here." Sarah smirked, and Faith felt a surge of hatred for her. "There must be quite a number of confused guards wandering the woods right now."

"Not too many, I hope." Jacob grimaced. "That was the whole idea."

Sarah glanced back at the woods behind them, where a film of smoke still hung in the air. "How many do you think survived?"

"Not sure." Jacob wiped the sweat from his forehead. "But we should be facing a seriously reduced force."

Sarah raised her eyebrows. "Think she's here in the forest?"

"Danforth? No chance. I knew she wouldn't risk it. Same way I knew she'd send more guards than agreed. It's not in her nature to act peacefully. That's why we needed..." he gestured behind him, "this."

Faith closed her eyes and fought to keep her face neutral. So the explosions had been a deliberate act on Jacob's part, aimed at getting rid of a large number of Danforth's guards. She wondered how many had died in the blasts. How many were lying injured in the woods?

And, more importantly, how many had escaped unscathed? From what he'd said, Jacob was still using the other wristclips to manipulate Danforth's remaining forces. If they feared further explosions, the guards would be doing everything they could to avoid the locations suggested by the chips. How many were being herded here right now into yet another trap?

"I'd better go and brief Flynn," Jacob nodded at the clearing ahead of him. "Guess it's time to let him in on the plan, now he can't try to stop it." He gestured to Faith, the first time he'd acknowledged her presence. "Have her ready in case we need her."

"Will do." Sarah tightened her hold on Faith once more, pulling her into a vice-like grip.

Jacob nodded in satisfaction. "Good. Keep her quiet. And make sure you stay hidden, unless I give the signal. Don't want to show our hand *too* early."

As Jacob strode away, Faith's heart began to hammer. The sound it made was so loud she felt sure it would summon Danforth's forces more successfully than the transmitters in the wristclips.

CHAPTER TWENTY-FIVE:
NOAH

Jacob's reappearance caused a murmur to spread around the clearing. Striding out of the forest, he'd headed straight for Flynn and Jan. Since then, their heads had been bent close together, their hushed conversation marked by abrupt gestures and dark expressions.

Beside him, Ruth shifted to get a better look. "Flynn doesn't look happy."

"Not happy? He looks furious." Noah grimaced. "Not much he can do now, though."

Soon after the explosion, Jacob had been in touch on the walkie-talkie. Flynn and Jan had been instructed to keep everyone in position and await his return, where he would give further orders. Everything, Jacob had reassured them, was going to plan.

Just not the plan they'd been made aware of. "He used one of the wristclips as a decoy," Flynn had told them before he sent them back to their hiding place. "To draw Danforth's forces to a second location."

"Why?" Ruth had asked, puzzled.

Jan had shaken her head. "So he could detonate the bombs. Reduce enemy numbers."

"Did you two *know* about this?" The words had been out before Noah could stop them.

Flynn had shot him a horrified look. "Of course not!"

"I'm sorry." Noah had stammered. "I know that. It's just—"

"It's alright." Flynn had been quick to forgive. "Jacob wouldn't have told us about this. He'd know we'd never have agreed to it." Turning to Jan, he had thrust a hand at the smoke-filled sky. "Does he really expect Danforth to talk peacefully now?"

"It's not a likely outcome, is it?" Jan's reply had been bitter. "Not when we've just blown up large numbers of her guard." Turning to Ruth and Noah, she had hustled them back the way they'd come. "Off you go. Whatever he's planning, you don't want to be out in the open when this goes down."

Noah and Ruth had reluctantly returned to the bushes which edged the clearing. Flynn and Jan had instructed the rest of the Eremus citizens to resume their initial positions, though a few had been instructed to move a little closer. No one knew what was going to happen next, so Flynn's defensive strategy seemed wise.

If Jacob's face when he returned was anything to go by, his plan had worked. Now, they waited. Presumably their leader was still expecting to face off against Danforth, though Noah wasn't sure how he could guarantee this happening now that her forces were scattered.

His thoughts returned to the girls. Now that he knew of the changes to Jacob's plan, he was questioning everything. Were Sophia and Catherine here somewhere, hidden in the bushes to be brought out if Danforth requested proof of life? Or had Jacob brought none of the girls, relying on the bombs to frighten Danforth into surrender?

It had even crossed Noah's mind that Jacob had brought along *all* of the girls, perhaps in pairs with a guard assigned to each. The thought of Faith, hiding somewhere close by, directly in the line of fire, made him feel sick.

Beside him, Ruth tensed. Creeping a little closer to the clearing, she cocked her head to listen. Noah strained forward. And then, he heard it. Multiple, panicked footsteps heading in the direction of the clearing. It had to be what remained of Danforth's forces.

With total calm, Jacob gave an order and the raiders shifted into a circle, protecting the three council members in the centre. At a second command, they raised their weapons. When the group had first stood in the clearing, they had appeared organised yet unthreatening, ready to talk calmly with Danforth. Now, the picture was very different.

Noah exchanged glances with Ruth. They'd hoped for a peaceful discussion between the two communities, but there seemed little chance of that now.

The sound of footsteps halted. For a moment, there was silence. And then, from behind the treeline, a voice.

"People of Eremus, hold your fire." There was a pause. "We are heavily armed and ready to use *extreme* force the moment it becomes necessary. Do we have your assurance that we can proceed in safety?"

"You do." Jacob nodded. "Please move into the clearing. We only want to talk."

There was a muttered command, and a group of Bellator guards edged out of the trees on the other side of the clearing. Machine guns raised, they advanced towards the Eremus raiders.

Noah held his breath as Ruth counted. "Twenty-no, twenty-four."

"How many do you think they had to start with?"

"A fair few more, I'd say." She shrugged. "But a lot of these could still put up a good fight."

She was right. A few of the guards had hastily-bound wounds and one was limping, supported by a fellow citizen. But aside from sooty faces and torn uniforms, the rest looked unharmed. They took their time entering the space, their eyes wary. Directed by a tall woman with cropped dark hair, they circled the enemy. Eventually they stood in pairs, back-to-back, one facing the Eremus raiders in the centre, the other facing the trees at the edge of the clearing.

"Clever," Ruth whispered. "They're well trained, even under pressure."

Once they were in place, Jacob took a step forward. "I count twenty-four of you. My message requested only twenty people at this meeting."

The short-haired woman, clearly their leader, stepped forward. She gestured at the bushes surrounding the clearing. "You didn't obey that command yourself."

Jacob gave a wry smile. "But I think you had a larger force than this when you set off on your mission."

"We did." Noah had to admire the woman's resilience. The ability to remain calm when a great number of her fellow guards had just been blown to pieces was admirable. She continued, keeping her tone even. "You seem to have been more... *prepared* than we had anticipated."

"We were." Bowing his head, Jacob took the guard's words as a compliment. "Over the years, I've learned not to underestimate Abigail Danforth."

Now the woman's face flashed with fury. "*Chancellor* Danforth is indeed a formidable foe. One you'd be wise not to toy with."

Jacob gestured with one hand and the circle of raiders parted. Weapon in hand, the Eremus leader strode forward until he was standing in front of the guard.

"Your name?"

"Lieutenant Hammond."

"I'm Jacob Williams. Head of the Eremus council. Can I ask why I'm not dealing with Danforth herself? I did ask that she be present at the meeting."

"She knew better than to trust you." Hammond frowned. "Did you think she'd attend in person? When you're capable of pulling a stunt like this?"

"Not really." Jacob glanced down at his gun. "Just as I knew she'd send a larger force than I requested." He waved a hand at the treeline behind the Bellator guards, where the dark smoke still rose into the air. "My defensive action means we can actually meet on more equal terms, don't you think?"

Hammond's face darkened. "It means the death of numerous Bellator citizens, which I can assure you won't please the chancellor."

"She could have just followed my instructions. Then no one would have had to die."

"Really?" Hammond's sarcasm was biting. "You'd have broken the rules, whatever the chancellor did."

"Maybe that's true." Jacob shrugged and swung his arms wide. "It seems we're at a stalemate, however."

"How so?"

"I'm not happy speaking to *you* about the situation. Danforth was supposed to be here."

Hammond scowled. "She will be. Not that you deserve the chance to speak with her." She hesitated, as though struggling with something. "Hold on a second."

Like most of the raiders who surrounded Jacob and Flynn, Noah and Ruth tensed. A multitude of eyes swept the clearing searching for any sign of an approach. Hammond laughed mirthlessly and Jacob's face darkened, hating to be the source of anyone's amusement.

Ignoring his expression, Hammond gestured to the guard beside her. The woman removed her pack and bent to retrieve something from it. Desperate to see what it was, Ruth and Noah strained forward.

Carefully, the second guard placed a small, black device on the ground. As she straightened, Hammond began to tap commands into the clip on her wrist. Slowly, a flickering light appeared above the object, growing in size and brightness until a large, two-dimensional image hovered in the air in front of Jacob.

A woman's face, pale and hawk-like, stared out at the Eremus leader.

"Danforth." He spat the word like it was poison.

"Jacob Williams." The woman's tone was calm, considering the situation. "I hear your explosives just decimated my forces."

"You broke our agreement." Jacob's words were not loud, but uttered through clenched teeth.

"*Our* agreement?" Danforth hissed. "I don't recall agreeing to anything."

"You were supposed to be here. In person."

"Did you *really* believe I'd show up in your territory with just twenty guards to defend me?" The image flickered, as though Danforth's fury was attempting to leap through the screen. "I don't think so."

"We said the talks would be peaceful."

"And do you consider what has happened today to have been..." Danforth paused deliberately, *"peaceful?"* Jacob held her gaze but didn't respond. "And there's that little word *we* again, Jacob." She clicked her tongue against her teeth. *"You* were the one who requested the meeting."

Jacob was fuming. "And I *specifically* requested–"

"You did *not* request. You made *demands*. In fact, your actions today have..." she paused, as though the words caused her physical pain, "made it very difficult for me to listen to you."

"Get off your high horse, Abigail. I think we know each other well enough to understand how the other one's mind works. I knew you wouldn't just send a small force into the woods... into, as you say, *my* territory. You couldn't. Your paranoia wouldn't let you." Jacob paused, his fists clenched by his sides. "Can you blame me for taking defensive action?"

There was another long pause before Danforth responded. "Perhaps not."

"You always did need to be in control. If I hadn't sent this message of our strength, of Eremus' power, then..."

Ruth jabbed an elbow into Noah's side. "Does Jacob *know* Danforth? I mean—"

"Sounds like they've past experience of one another, doesn't it?" Noah frowned. "But why wouldn't we know that?"

Ruth shrugged and turned back to the clearing, where Jacob was still speaking.

"...mean you have to listen to what Eremus has to say."

"Go on, then." Despite the horrendous losses she'd suffered, Danforth still seemed very much in charge. Her expression reminded Noah of a fox toying with its prey. "I'm listening."

Jacob glanced sideways at Flynn. "I'll leave it to someone you have less... hostility towards."

Flynn stepped forward, his face calm. "Chancellor, my name is Flynn. I've been a member of the Eremus council for many years."

"You have a council?" Danforth sounded surprised.

"We do. It consists of a number of people chosen from throughout Eremus. We come together to make important decisions about how our community is run. We wanted to talk to you..." he shot a look at Jacob, "...peacefully, about the possibility of our people living safely in the woods, without fear of attack from your guards."

"You want guaranteed protection from my protectors?" Danforth laughed, the harsh sound echoing around the clearing. "After what just happened to them?" She scrutinised Flynn closely. "Did the council know about the attack? I mean..." the screen wavered in the air, giving the chancellor a ghostly appearance, "large numbers of my guards were just murdered. When you talked about setting this meeting... this *peaceful* meeting... up, did you all decide the best way to get what you wanted was to blow my people sky-high?"

Noah looked at Ruth, knowing they were both thinking the same thing. In the cold light of day, it was clear that this had been exactly what Jacob had been thinking. But the word *all* grated on him. That Jacob would make these decisions without discussion with the whole community was unforgiveable.

Flynn flushed and Noah knew he took the same view. But how could he object to what had happened? Eremus had to appear united, or any power they had over Danforth would disintegrate. Flynn dropped his gaze for a second. When he looked up again, his eyes were cold. "It seems, Chancellor, that these actions, though extreme, may have been justified. I mean, given that you did not comply with Jacob's requests for this meeting."

Noah knew Flynn had purposely avoided using the words *our* and *we*. It was his diplomatic way of sounding like he agreed with Jacob, without including himself in the actions he despised.

When Danforth raised an eyebrow, Noah wondered if she had noticed. "Go on."

"Thank you." Flynn stepped closer to the screen, as though he were appealing to Danforth in person. "The people of Eremus have lived in hiding for too long now. We barely scrape a living from the forest, we're forced to steal from Bellator to supplement our food stores, we share what little we have amongst ourselves. But there's never enough. In many cases, our citizens starve." He paused, staring at Danforth, his eyes earnest. "You're aware of our existence. You hunt us down because of some archaic belief that all men are monsters.

"What you're not aware of, perhaps, is our true numbers. You're certainly not aware of the size and power of our weapon stores, which we have demonstrated to you twice now." Noah noticed a shadow cross Danforth's face. Flynn's words were hitting home. "However, I assure you, our chief concern is the safety and survival of our community. We don't want to use force. We don't wish to dwell on the past. We'd like to look to the future."

"And exactly how do you imagine that future being different?" Danforth's tone was so cold it sent shivers down Noah's spine.

"We're prepared to start small." Flynn gestured to the forest around him. "We ask only that you permit us to live here safely, without being hunted down and killed. To ensure we have enough to eat, so we're not forced to resort to stealing simply to feed our children. Perhaps, in the future, we could work towards living peacefully alongside the women of Bellator."

"You ask a lot." Danforth sneered.

"For the future, perhaps," Flynn continued. "Today, we only ask that we open discussions. *Peaceful* discussions. That you consider our plea."

"And if I'm not prepared to?" Danforth countered. "I mean, you cost me a lot, today. To ask me to consider you as *peaceful* is a bit of a stretch."

"For years... *years*..." Jacob butted in, "you have hunted down and killed my people. As many of them as you could find. You've proved yourself a worthy enemy, and one which I've always known would be difficult to beat." He shot a glance at Flynn. "Some of the council believed you might entertain peaceful discussions. I, however, knew better. Hence," he jabbed a finger at the smoky air behind him, "the display of strength. And, now, you need to listen to us." He jerked his head at Flynn once again.

"Chancellor, you know that we could..." Flynn looked uncomfortable, "well, that we hold certain, shall we say... advantages over you. We have things you want. Things which we will consider handing over to you, if you agree to our requests."

"They're *requests* now, are they?" Danforth was openly sarcastic.

"Or we could just keep those things from you, if you're not prepared to cooperate with us." Jacob ground out.

Noah shifted, uncomfortable with the reference to the Danforth students as objects which might be traded. But the chancellor was considering Jacob's words.

"You seem..." Danforth turned to Flynn, her expression shrewd, "somewhat uncomfortable discussing your bargaining powers."

Flynn met her gaze steadily. "I don't relish holding anyone hostage. If there had been another way you might have engaged with us, we'd have taken it."

"Do you *all* feel this way?" Danforth turned back to Jacob. "This is simply about your community gaining some rights?" Danforth continued. "And not about... revenge?"

"Of course." Jacob's tone was calm, but his fists were still clenched at his sides. Noah wondered if Danforth could see them. "What else would it be about?"

"I see." Danforth's face loomed larger as she leaned closer to the camera which projected her image into the clearing.

"What do you *see*?" Jacob snapped.

"They don't know." An unpleasant smile spread across Danforth's face as she watched Jacob attempt to respond. "Not all of them, at least."

Noah and Ruth exchanged glances as a murmur crawled around the clearing. Every eye was fixed on Danforth.

"The people you claim are so important to you?" She smiled, as though she knew she was about to drop a bombshell as powerful as the explosives Jacob had detonated earlier in the day. "They don't know you originate from Bellator, do they?"

Chapter Twenty-Six: Faith

Faith watched the Eremus leader's face flash with fury. All around him, the citizens he claimed to champion reacted to Danforth's revelation. The sense of shock was tangible. Faith had to admit, she was as confused as the Eremus people. How could Jacob be from Bellator? The city had been female-only, aside from the drudges, for as long as she could remember.

It took her a couple of seconds to realise the revelation was not new to Sarah Porter. Behind her, the woman stood unmoved. Clearly, she was one of Jacob's closer confidantes. Faith wondered if other members of the council knew. She could not see Flynn's face from where she stood, but physically he seemed unmoved by the news, and was not reeling, the way the other citizens in Jacob's protective circle seemed to be.

Faith refocused on her captor. As the conversation in the clearing had gone on, Sarah's hold on Faith had loosened as she strained to listen to what was going on. Taking advantage of the reprieve, Faith attempted to creep forward a little, so she could hear the rest of Danforth's words clearly.

The hand on her arm tightened. "Oh no you don't," Sarah breathed, her mouth close to Faith's ear. "If you're spotted before Jacob wants, I won't be popular. Be still."

Jerking Faith closer to her, Sarah secured a vice-like grip on her arm. Faith suspected it would leave a bruise. Giving up, Faith complied with Sarah's wishes, letting her body go loose. Let Sarah think she had learned her lesson. It would give her a better chance of escape later, should she need it. Fingering the box cutter concealed in her sleeve, she bided her time and refocused on Danforth's words.

"They really don't know, do they?" Danforth's eyes danced with delight. "Well, perhaps the knowledge will convince them of your main motive here: revenge. But you don't want your people to know that, do you? Because, maybe, you'd lose their support." She paused, glancing out at the raiders she could see behind Jacob with satisfaction. "That's it, isn't it?"

When Jacob raised his eyes to Danforth's image on the screen, they were filled with fire. "My people trust me. They know I want the best for them. They don't–"

But Danforth cut him off. "When I received your message, I found it *extremely* difficult to believe you'd be able to let the past go. I mean, to forgive and forget what happened all those years ago? I'm not sure *I'd* be able to do that. And you... you're a man. How you'd be able to control your violent impulses remembering the day you fled from Bellator, I don't know."

Jacob began to splutter a reply, but was cut off once again.

"I mean..." Danforth's words took on a mocking tone, "you were *furious* at the time. I can't believe the years have... softened you so much that you could simply... let it all go."

Faith could see what Danforth was doing. If she made Jacob angry enough, he'd lash out. It would give her all the proof she needed to maintain the image of the vicious beasts that men were. Of course, she would be recording the exchange via the datadev, so she could use it later to further prove all men were monsters. She was clever.

The news that Jacob had *lived* in Bellator was shocking. But he wasn't old enough to have lived there when men and women had coexisted. And the fact that he had *run away* from the city, that he'd been furious about the treatment he had suffered there, implied something different. Had he been some kind of prisoner, held against his will?

The air in the clearing had changed. Instead of focusing on Danforth, the Eremus citizens were staring at their leader. Jacob's face had turned puce. Events were not turning out as he'd expected. He was losing control of the situation. And he didn't like it.

Behind Faith, Sarah had loosened her hold once more. A backwards glance told Faith she was distracted by the two leaders' exchange, though her expression seemed to will Jacob to retain control rather than question him. As Danforth let her words hang in the air, Faith felt Sarah draw in a deep breath. In the clearing, Jacob dropped his gaze to the ground, his entire body rigid.

Danforth let the silence stretch out for a while before continuing the onslaught. "From their reaction, it's clear your people don't know the truth about your past. I wonder if they'll be quite so... responsive to a leader who hasn't been straight with them."

"No." Jacob jerked his gaze up to meet Danforth's. "I think you'll find my people trust me enough to follow my orders."

"Do they, though?" Again, a deliberate pause. Faith was reminded of a cat playing with its prey. It didn't seem to matter that Danforth wasn't here in person, she was having no problem gaining the upper hand. "If I were you, Jacob, I'd be getting nervous."

Jacob straightened and took a deliberate step forward. "I think perhaps you're forgetting the cards we hold. Perhaps you need to be *shown* what's at stake. Then you'll see. My people are as loyal as yours. And I don't even have to *pay* them to protect me."

Before Danforth could retort, Jacob snapped his fingers. Behind her, Sarah tensed, and Faith steeled herself for whatever came next. Evidently, Jacob was about to show his hand. She found her entire body was shaking as she considered how Danforth might react at the sight of her. But to her surprise, they remained where they were.

Instead, from the trees at the far side of the space, Paulo appeared. With horror, Faith spotted Sophia at his side. Her face was pale and her eyes wide, but otherwise she seemed calm. Behind her came Catherine, guided by Harden. His grip on the younger girl's arm reminded Faith of his mother. Catherine was crying brokenly, and she stumbled as she attempted to keep up with her captor's rapid pace.

"Recognise them?" Jacob took a step towards Danforth, jabbing his finger so close to the image that the Bellator leader's face was disrupted for a second. "These girls, as I'm sure you know, are only two of the eight we are holding here in Eremus. I hear that they're very... valuable to you."

Danforth was scowling now, and she seemed to be weighing her response. Her eyes flickered to Hammond's and she nodded slightly. A movement beside Jacob drew Faith's gaze to Flynn as he turned slightly to watch the girls' approach. His face had paled, as though directly threatening the Danforth girls was not something he was comfortable with.

On the screen, the chancellor had recovered her composure. When she spoke, it was to the two Danforth students. "Sophia..." her eyes glanced down and up again swiftly, and Faith wondered if she was consulting a list with the girls' names on it, "and Catherine, is it?"

The two girls nodded.

"I'm sorry you find yourselves in this most... difficult and dangerous position." She paused for a second, steepling her fingers at her mouth, as though she was considering what to say next. "You must be terrified. The men who have kidnapped you are indeed living up to the characteristics of the males you've been taught about at the academy. I'm sorry you've had to experience this sort of treatment." Her face adopted a look of concern which Faith was certain was fake. "Are you safe and healthy?"

Catherine was wide-eyed and silent, but Sophia found her voice. "We are."

"And the rest of the girls?" Danforth frowned. "Faith, Farrah, Helen, Mary, Diane and..." she paused for a second, "Avery?"

Faith wondered why Avery was at the end of Danforth's list. The final name seemed to ring with significance for the chancellor. But then, Avery had always been the golden girl of the academy. Perhaps the chancellor's attitude shouldn't have been surprising.

"They're all safe too."

"Rest assured, ladies, your safety is of the utmost importance to us. We will do everything in our power to make sure you are returned safely to Bellator, to the school which I know is your haven..." Faith swallowed a bitter retort at the words, "...unharmed and able to resume your former lives." She turned her attention to Jacob once again. "Alright. Allow the girls to return to Bellator safely. Then we can discuss your demands."

Jacob laughed. "No chance. You think I'll give these girls up with nothing but empty assurances?"

"I won't bargain with you."

"I think you will. I mean," he paused, "you've got quite a lot to lose." Jacob gestured at Sophia and Catherine. "More than just these girls. I hear you're having some issues with your fertility stock. How do you intend to continue breeding without male seed?"

Danforth's eyes widened, but she regained control quickly. "We have... contingency plans in place."

"Really?" Jacob sneered. "If you think you'll get away with going back to the old ways, you're in for a shock."

"The *old* ways?" Now it was Danforth's turn to sneer. "Of course, you'd think *that* was my plan. You don't know any better. But things have changed since you... shall we say since you were a *guest* of Bellator's. No. When you caused us all that trouble, I decided I'd never leave the city having to depend on men again. For anything." She shook her head. "Such primitive methods will *not* be necessary. I have... other, more... sophisticated plans in place."

"I don't believe you. I have, and I'm quoting your words here, *Abigail*, more power than I've ever had before. *Eight* of your precious Danforth students currently reside with us, including one who I think you'd be *particularly* keen to get your hands on." Faith recoiled at his words, earning herself another shove from her captor. "Not to mention that our community is filled with strong and healthy men, all with the potential to help Bellator reproduce for decades to come. That is, as long as you're prepared to grant us the right to live equally alongside your *precious* women."

Danforth's face twisted. "You don't have as much power as you think."

"Oh really," Jacob raised an eyebrow. "Our bombs decimated your force today. And there are more of us here than you might think," he gestured at the woods around him, "*surrounding* what remains of your guards. We could, in fact, finish these people off right now."

"I don't doubt that you'd try," Danforth retorted. "But who do you think would survive the longest in a hand-to-hand battle? My highly trained, super-fit soldiers, with their powerful weapons, or your ragtag band of outlaws fighting with whatever meagre arms' supply you've managed to gather?"

"We've done a pretty decent job of hurting your *highly trained* soldiers so far."

Danforth scowled. "And to think, this was supposed to be a peaceful discussion. What a shame you had to ruin it."

"Don't lay all this at my door, Abigail," Jacob snapped. "You never had any intention of discussing things peacefully, nor were you prepared to seriously consider granting us any rights. No. You won't do that unless you're forced to. Which is why I did what I did today. And I'd do it again."

"Really showing your true colours now, aren't you Jacob?" Danforth gave an exaggerated sigh. "But men will always be men, I suppose." She raised an eyebrow, challenging her enemy. "It seems we're at a stalemate, then. Whatever shall we do?"

"I have an idea." Striding forward, Jacob grasped hold of Sophia's arm and thrust her towards the screen. "Don't think that I won't consider..." he thrust a gun at the young girl's temple and she cried out, "*eliminating* your precious students, if you don't start taking me seriously."

"You wouldn't." Faith marvelled at Danforth's face, which remained calm, despite Jacob's blistering rage. "These girls are your bargaining chips. If you kill them, what power do you have left?"

"Do. Not. Test. Me." A malicious expression had settled on Jacob's face. "This girl is one of *eight*." He forced Sophia to her knees. "If I have to end her life to prove I'm serious, so be it." Sophia started to cry, softly, desperately. Jacob ignored her. "I'll give you to the count of five."

Horrified, Faith's eyes circled the clearing. The expressions on the faces of the Eremus citizens were mixed, but it was clear that many of them were uncertain about their leader's intentions. Flynn had taken a step forward, his face ashen. Even Paulo looked appalled.

On the far side of the clearing, Faith could see Noah and Ruth. They had emerged from their hiding place, disturbed expressions on their faces. But could she rely on any of them to save Sophia? She wasn't sure.

In the centre of the clearing, Jacob had started to count. Faith was running out of time.

She'd been very careful to remain still and compliant since Sarah's last attack. The woman behind her was less attentive now. She seemed excited, perhaps anticipating a victory on Jacob's part. No doubt looking forward to being rewarded for her part in it.

Slowly, Faith inched her right sleeve upwards, her fingers groping for the box cutter. Once she had it within her grasp, she inhaled deeply, and twisted her body sharply to the side, the way she'd been taught in her Danforth self-defence classes. Praying the element of surprise would give her the advantage she needed, she dropped to the ground and darted away from Sarah.

For a second, the older woman stared at her in surprise. Her gun was still tucked in her belt. Before Sarah could reach for it, Faith raced towards the clearing, her improvised weapon clutched in her hand. If she was as valuable as Kemp had claimed, Sarah wouldn't shoot her. Especially not from behind, with so many witnesses present.

As she burst into the clearing, several things happened at once.

Danforth shouted an order to Hammond, who primed her weapon and aimed it at Jacob. Flynn sprang forward and grasped Jacob's arm, attempting to pull the gun from Sophia's temple. As several Eremus citizens surged forward, the crack of a gunshot echoed through the clearing.

Racing towards Sophia, Faith couldn't work out where the shot had come from. A short silence followed the sound. Time seemed to stand still. And then, all hell broke loose.

The raiders began shooting at the Bellator guards. More Eremus citizens exploded from the bushes, their own weapons primed. The air was filled with cries and the sound of gunshots.

Hammond screamed an order. Faith couldn't make out the exact words, but the hand she flung out towards Sophia and herself seemed to indicate the guards should protect them.

Thankful it probably meant a minimal use of the machine guns, Faith plunged ahead.

The crowd seethed and foamed, people fighting, yelling, falling. Faith couldn't see her friend any more. The scent of blood filled the air, as knives flashed and bullets zipped past. Faith caught a glimpse of Catherine struggling to escape the mob, her face stained with tears; Anna pulling a wounded raider away from the fight; Flynn on the ground, grappling with one of the Bellator guards, but there was no sign of Sophia.

Pausing at the edge of the melee, she screamed for Sophia. Somewhere close by, Sarah Porter's strident voice was coming closer, calling her name. To one side, more Eremus citizens burst from the bushes, weapons in hand, to join the fight. Finally, she saw Sophia stumbling forward from the midst of the battle. As her eyes came to rest on Faith, they filled with fear.

"Run!" she screamed, jabbing a finger towards the forest.

Behind Sophia, Hammond appeared. Grasping her by the arm, she attempted to haul Sophia out of harm's way. And then, the Bellator guard spotted Faith. Her eyes widened and, without missing a step, she changed direction, heading for her new prey.

Faith was trapped, surrounded, the prize that both sides wanted. As Hammond bore down on her from in front, her stride eating up the distance between them, Sarah advanced from behind.

"Go!" Her friend was still urging her to escape. "Get out of here!"

Faith's eyes flicked between her advancing enemies. For a second, she was paralysed. And then, a hand grasped hers. She turned to see Noah, his face creased with concern. Behind him stood Ruth, her gun raised, its target alternating between Hammond and Sarah.

"Let's go." Noah tugged at her hand.

"But Sophia–" Faith gestured helplessly at her friend.

"They won't hurt her." Noah hauled on her arm, pulling her close to his chest. "We have to get you out of here."

With tears streaming down her cheeks, Faith gave in. As they hurried out of the clearing, she wondered what would happen to all those left behind.

CHAPTER TWENTY-SEVEN:
NOAH

H e wasn't sure where they were running to, but knew they'd have to slow down soon. Noah had to admit he was impressed with Faith's ability to match his pace and, on occasion, even overtake him. But they were both tiring, and the need to rest, even briefly, was pressing.

When he and Ruth had rushed forward, their intention had been to help. Help Faith, help Sophia, help Catherine. Help Flynn, who Noah had lost sight of once he was in the thick of the fight. But they hadn't had any kind of plan. It had all been impulse, sudden and panic-driven. From the second he'd seen Faith racing out of the woods towards Sophia, some kind of improvised weapon in hand, Noah had been terrified.

The fact that they'd had to leave behind the friend Faith had been trying to save cut him like a knife. They said nothing as they ran, but Faith's reluctance to leave Sophia had been clear. Was she angry with him now? He wasn't sure. And he wasn't sure what comfort he could offer her if she questioned him about Sophia's safety.

At the moment, they were on their own. Ruth had stayed behind to hold off those trying to reach Faith, and to support the rest of the Eremus force. In his desperation to get Faith away from what had turned into a full-scale battle, they hadn't even discussed a time or place they might meet later. And as they raced through the woods, he was racking his brain for a safe haven.

Thinking back, he was grateful for one thing. The Bellator guards had not let rip with their machine guns. He presumed they'd been instructed not to, so as to protect the academy students. This only confirmed their importance to Danforth. It was the reason he felt they were fairly safe leaving Sophia behind: neither side was likely to harm her.

He only hoped Faith would agree.

They broke out of the treeline and came into the open, slowing as shafts of bright sunlight pierced their eyes. Swallow Lake lay ahead, its waters gleaming. Noticing it, Faith stopped dead.

"You alright?"

She turned to him, her expression guarded. "Can we stop for a minute?"

Glancing back over his shoulder, he scanned the forest. So far, it seemed like they'd evaded anyone following them. He strained his ears but could hear nothing other than the sound of the wind in the trees.

"Maybe just a quick water break."

He removed his pack, leaning it up against the rocks for a moment. Thankful for the brief respite, he flexed his aching muscles before rummaging in his pack for his water bottle. When he located it, he unscrewed the top and offered it to Faith. For a moment, she looked as though she was going to refuse, but good sense prevailed. Slipping the box cutter into her pocket, she took the bottle. Swallowing a good amount of water.

He nodded at the weapon. "Where'd you get that?"

"Long story." She wiped her mouth and passed the bottle back. "Involving Sarah kidnapping me as part of Jacob's master plan."

Noah grimaced. "Some master plan."

As he lifted the bottle to his lips, Faith regarded him steadily. "Do we need to conserve that?"

"No." He gestured at the lake. "We can refill. I have some purifying tablets in my pack." He glanced almost apologetically at her. "Another item we take from the city." He sighed. "It's food I'd be more concerned about. I mean... if we were staying out here."

"*Are* we staying out here?"

He sighed, thrusting the bottle back in his pack. "Honestly, I don't know."

Her face clouded over. "You don't know where we're going?"

Noah dropped his gaze for a moment, feeling a stab of panic pierce his gut. Taking a breath, he met her gaze as steadily as he could. "Not really."

She stared at him, her eyes narrowed. "Not *really*?"

"I'm sorry." He sighed. "It all happened so fast. I just knew I wanted to... I mean you were..."

She held up a hand. "What about Sophia? I mean Jacob had her. And his gun, it was..."

"I know. I'm so sorry." Noah hung his head. "I have to believe that it was just a threat. You're all too important to both sides for him to just–"

"But what if it's not *just a threat*?" Her voice was shrill. "What if he's already killed her?"

"Sshh!" He glanced at the trees again. "They'll be searching for us. We need to stay quiet."

She glared at him, but fell silent.

"I hope you don't think–" he hesitated. "I had no idea about the bombs."

"I know you didn't." She shook her head. "How many guards do you think died though? I mean... there had to be—"

The cracking of a twig in the distance startled them, and Noah shouldered his pack again. "Let's keep moving."

"Where to?"

Noah scanned their surroundings. Behind them, the woods. To one side, the large expanse of water. To the other, the forest smoked, sections of the tree line still consumed by fires from Jacob's bombs. That was another worry. They'd have to be careful to extinguish it later. Who knew how much of their foraging ground had already been destroyed?

He pointed along the side of the lake. "This way. Let's hope the fire hasn't spread too far." He sighed. "We definitely shouldn't stay still right now." Grasping her hand, he found it was shaking. He smiled in what he hoped was an encouraging way. "Come on."

"Shouldn't we still be running?" Faith asked.

"Not unless we have to." He shook his head. "We won't be able to maintain that pace for much longer."

They hurried onwards, heading towards the lake. At its edge, Noah directed them onto a path which ran alongside it, snaking in and out of the trees which lined its edges. The air was thick with smoke.

"We should stay low." Faith waved a hand in front of her face. "Smoke rises. They taught us about that at the academy, when—"

Her sharp intake of breath made him look at her. She had glanced back over her shoulder, and her face was a mask of horror.

He froze. "What's—?" He followed her gaze, and spotted the two Bellator guards emerging from the treeline. "Dammit!"

As they broke into an all-out sprint, Noah cursed himself for allowing them to rest. His free hand went to his belt, where he had a small knife. His original assignment had required him only to warn the community if necessary, so he hadn't been issued with a gun. He grimaced. It wasn't much protection, but if he had to use it, he would.

"Think there's... only the two..." Faith's breath came in gasps.

That was good news, at least. But two guards meant at least two guns. A single knife was no match for that, and Noah knew it. He urged her forward. If they kept a rapid pace, perhaps the guards wouldn't fire. Moving targets were far more difficult to hit, and they wouldn't want to risk shooting Faith.

He tried not to think about the fact that he was dispensable.

They raced onwards. So far, the guards hadn't gained any ground, but they were tired. If either of them tripped and fell, it would spell disaster. Noah's mind sifted through the possibilities. They couldn't head for the caves, leading the guards right to the rest of the community. But they couldn't hide either, unless they managed to outstrip their pursuers.

To their right, the smoke was thicker, the bushes were showing more signs of damage. Clearly their path was taking them closer to the site of the fire. It was difficult to stay low and manage to run at any kind of pace, and their lungs were struggling to cope with the thickening smoke. In desperation, Noah guided Faith closer to the lake. It meant they were wading through dense reeds, which made the terrain more challenging, but at least there wasn't as much smoke.

Glancing towards the forest, he could see actual flames, mocking them from the trees. Behind them, he could hear the sound of the guards' footsteps growing in volume and the odd shout as the two women communicated with one another.

Straightening up, he studied the path ahead. There was a sharp bend coming up. Impossible to see around. If they turned the corner in enough time, perhaps they could divert their course, find a safe place to conceal themselves until the guards passed by. But his usual hiding spots were all extremely flammable. There was no way they could take shelter in trees or bushes which lay directly in the path of the fire.

Still, Noah took Faith's hand. "Faster!"

With a burst of energy fuelled by fear, they sped ahead. As they rounded the bend, he risked a backwards glance, heartened that the guards were still some distance behind them. If they could only take shelter somewhere. Anywhere.

Hearing Faith's sharp intake of breath, he spun to face the direction they were headed and stopped dead.

To their left lay the lake, to their right, sections of burning bushes which would roast them alive. And the path ahead was completely blocked by a fallen tree.

"No!" he choked out, his mind racing, "A bomb must've..."

The natural barricade formed by the tree and its surrounding foliage stood several metres high. It would take precious minutes to climb. Minutes they didn't have.

Faith clutched his arm. "What do we do?"

Approaching the trunk, he peered upwards. "We could climb... but it would slow us down." He slammed a hand against the wood. "There's no time!"

"Leave me." Faith stepped away, gesturing to the pile of debris. "Start climbing. You can get away. I'm their priority."

"No!"

"They won't hurt me. You know that."

"No. I *won't* just leave you here."

Suddenly, Faith launched herself at him, grasping hold of his face with both hands and pressing her lips to his. The contact was so sudden and unexpected he hardly had time to react. A second later, her lips were gone, leaving his feeling somewhat bruised. She turned to face the opposite direction.

"Go!" she hissed, over her shoulder. "Before it's too late."

Noah's eyes travelled in the only direction he hadn't considered. It was risky, but the only other choice. Taking her hand, he spun her around to face him.

"I said *no*." He pushed her towards the lake. "You can swim, right?"

Her eyes widened, but she nodded her head as they headed for the water. Ignoring its frosty temperature, Noah waded in. Faith followed, gasping sharply.

"Where are we going?" She was breathing hard. "They'll still follow."

"Not if this works." Noah clutched her hand. "Do you trust me?"

"Yes." There was no hesitation.

"Alright then. Stay behind me. Move as quietly as you can."

Together, they waded deeper. Noah could tell from Faith's expression she was frightened, and appreciated the trust it must have taken to follow him into the water. Her gaze clung to the shore on the opposite side of the lake, and he knew she thought he intended for them to swim across.

Shaking his head, he put a finger to his lips and bent his knees until his body was mostly submerged. He hadn't let go of her hand, and pulled her under with him, hearing her sharp intake of breath as the water enveloped her. When she was crouching next to him, he guided her along.

Further round, there were places where the water was far more difficult to access. They didn't have to go very far until they reached a section where Noah was hoping they could hide. Here, the bank was higher, clogged with reeds and tangled plants, which hung right over the water. As they moved closer, they had to force their way through the dense greenery, but eventually they reached the lake's edge once again.

It was much deeper here, the water reaching their waists. Anchoring himself in a stable position, Noah circled an arm around Faith to steady her, pulling her body close to his own. He rearranged the curtain of fronds until it cascaded over their heads, concealing them from the guards. For now, at least, they were safe.

They waited, hearing the thumping of the guards' boots growing in volume. At the same time, a thick pall of smoke drifted over the lake. The fire was spreading. Noah's throat was clogging up and even taking shallow breaths was a challenge. He looked at Faith. She was shivering, and her face was pale, but she met his gaze with determination.

"Okay?" He mouthed.

She nodded in response, her teeth chattering. Would bringing her into the lake make her ill again? For a moment, he felt a stab of guilt. But they'd run out of options. Even now, he wasn't confident they'd escape.

Above them, the guards' boots had stilled. Instead, the leaves of the bushes close to them rustled as they began to search.

"No." More rustling. "...can't have headed that way. The fire... suicide."

"But where did they...?"

A pause. The air was still, even the creatures of the forest seemed to hold their breath.

"Must've climbed over."

"Really?" The tone was doubtful. "Surely they didn't have time."

"... better explanation?" the guard sounded exasperated. "Unless..." she paused, then her footsteps came closer, "the lake?"

Noah pulled Faith even closer. If they made themselves as small as possible, perhaps the guards wouldn't spot them. The clump of reeds was not enormous, but Noah was hoping that went in their favour. That, glancing at it, the guards would assume it wasn't large enough to hide two people.

Despite the danger, he was aware of Faith's body pressing against his. They were aligned from shoulder to ankle, closer than they'd ever been. The intensity of her gaze was so fierce that he couldn't catch his breath. His lips were still bruised from her sudden kiss. He was still astounded by her readiness to be captured so he could escape.

"We'd see them if they'd tried to swim for it." The guard sounded doubtful. "No way could they have made it all the way across already. Lake's huge."

"But..." the second guard was less certain. "Couldn't they...?"

Noah felt the plants surrounding them move, as though a hand was rifling through them. He glanced at Faith. Her body had tensed suddenly; her face was filled with alarm. She brought a hand up from under the water and clamped it over her mouth. Too late, he realised what was about to happen as she lost her battle against the smoke.

Her body convulsed twice as she coughed, the sound only slightly muffled by her palm. Panicking, Noah swept a hand through the water, hoping it would disguise the very human sound.

Above them, he heard the guard grunt. "D'you hear that?"

"What?" The other woman was further away.

"That noise." More frantic rustling above them. "And the water..."

Noah held his breath. Beside him, Faith was doing the same. The coughing fit had subsided but the regular rise and fall of her chest had not resumed. They waited, Noah clutching the knife in one shaking hand. The leaves around them continued to whisper.

And then there was a new sound. At first, a light pattering on the waters around them, then a hiss, as the intensity of the shower increased. Finally, the heavens opened, and Noah found his cheeks stinging from the torrent which sliced through the fronds. The only upside of the attack was the thunderous sound of the rain pelting down.

"Come on." One guard shouted from a distance. "They *must've* gone this way."

"I thought I heard something." The voice close by was puzzled. "Down here somewhere."

"An animal or some kind of water bird." The first guard sounded frustrated. "Listen, if they made it over this, then they're further ahead of us than ever."

"Alright." Finally, they heard the guard closest to them move. "Let's get after them. Hopefully the storm will slow them down."

The two voices began to recede, as the cracking of branches indicated their retreat. "Think Danforth... reward..."

The other guard snorted. "More like she'll punish us for not..."

The sound faded. As Faith sagged against Noah, he became aware of how tense their bodies had been. He dropped his head, allowing it to rest on top of hers. They stood still for several minutes, leaning into one another as the rain continued to pour.

Chapter Twenty-Eight: Faith

E ventually, Noah stirred. "Y'okay?"

Faith raised her head. "You think they're gone?"

"Pretty sure."

"T-that was a close one."

"Too close." He brought a hand to her cheek. "When you started coughing, I–"

She shuddered. "Best not to think about it."

Now that the interlopers were gone, the air filled with the sound of insects and woodland creatures stirring. Noah shifted away from her, his body shivering. "S'pose we'd better move. Get dry. Figure out where we're going."

"Wait." She refused to relinquish her hold on his waist. As his eyes met hers, the intensity was back.

"What is it?" His face creased with concern.

"Thanks."

"What for?"

"For not leaving me."

He raised an eyebrow. "You thought I would?"

"No."

Suddenly, they weren't close enough. Closing the gap between them, she pressed her lips to his again. This time, the kiss wasn't rushed. This time, she gave him the chance to respond. As the kiss deepened, he pulled her body flush alongside his. Her pulse was racing and she was out of breath when they parted.

She stared at him. The boy—the almost-man—whom she had been so afraid of when they first met. His eyelashes were spiked with water, and rivulets of water were dripping from his hair and cascading down his face. He was one of the least threatening people she'd ever met.

She bit her lip and braved the question. "You done this a lot?"

"What?"

She ran a finger down his cheek and over his lips. He shivered. "This."

"No. Have you?"

She laughed. "Hardly."

He pulled her closer, kissing her again. "I like your laugh."

"What?"

"Your laugh. It's just..." he shrugged. "I don't think I've heard it very often."

"Well, there hasn't been a lot to laugh at since we met." She rolled her eyes. "Speaking of which..." she shuddered, "I'm not sure why I'm laughing right now. It's freezing. Think we're safe to leave the water?"

"You're right. We could catch our deaths." He eased away from her, pushing his head out between the reeds. "I think we're okay."

"Good." She ducked out from their hiding place. Turning, she took his hand and began to wade back in the direction they'd come, towing him behind her.

As they approached the bank, Noah peered in both directions. "Looks like we're safe, for now at least." He glanced at the sky. "We should keep moving. This rain doesn't seem to be stopping and we're already cold."

"Too right." She wrapped both arms around her, stamping her feet a little. "What's the plan, then? Are we running away? Just the two of us?"

"No!" Noah flushed at her words. "I mean, that wasn't the plan... Like I said, there was no plan." He shrugged. "Other than to get you away."

He smiled faintly, and Faith wondered if he was having similar thoughts to her own. Currently, her mind was filled with images of the two of them alone in a cave on the far side of the woods, with a roaring fire to warm them as the rain poured down outside. She shook her head. There were definitely more important things to focus on right now.

He raised an eyebrow. "You okay to keep moving?"

"Think so."

"Should warm us up a little." He gestured at the path which led along the other side of the lake. "Hopefully it will take the guards a while to work out that we didn't climb over the tree. Means we shouldn't risk leading them back to the caves."

"Is that where we're going then?" She took a breath, unsure what she wanted his response to be. "Back to the caves?"

As he walked, Noah attempted to wring the water out of his sweatshirt. "I don't think we have a lot of choice. I mean, we *have* to get warm and dry. The guards aren't the only danger. I mean the storm should put the fire out, but if we stay wet for too long, we risk getting sick."

"You really think we'll be safe there?" Faith rubbed her hands up and down her arms. "I mean with Jacob and Sarah, and–"

"We have to hope so." He sounded pained. "I mean, there are enough people on our side... Flynn, my ma, Ella... There'll be a meeting to discuss things. Decisions will have to be made. People won't be happy with what Jacob did today." He paused, reaching for her hand. "I'd love to tell you that we could survive out here alone in the forest, together, but I'd be lying."

"Thanks for your honesty." She shot him a brief smile. "It's a nice idea, but I have to agree, it doesn't seem very practical." She closed the gap between them. "I'm glad you cared enough to come for me. Even *without* a plan."

He put his arm around her shoulder. "Your knight in shining armour!"

"Oh no!" She rolled her eyes in mock horror. "We don't believe in those in Bellator. We women rescue ourselves." Feeling bold, she winked at him. "Though I do believe we've rescued each other today."

He laughed, then peered more closely at her. "You sure you're alright?"

"I'm fine."

"You're shaking." He tightened his hold on her. "Stay close, as much as you can. It should help us both keep warm."

The downpour had lessened somewhat, but as they hurried along, Faith found her whole body was aching with the cold. She tried to ignore it and keep up a decent pace, despite the constant dripping of water from the trees they walked beneath. Beside her, Noah was quiet. Faith wondered if his thoughts had returned to the battle as hers had.

"Think Soph'll be alright?" Her voice was a whisper.

"I hope so." He glanced at her. "I'm so sorry we couldn't bring her with us. But that guard... she was so desperate to get her hands on you."

"I know..." Faith stepped over a branch which lay across the path. "You should've seen that Hammond's face... when she realised who I was."

"Proves Kemp was telling the truth, I guess. About you being important."

"Yeah." Beside him, Faith shuddered. "I mean, I believed her... when she first told us. But it really hit home today."

Noah paused for a moment. "Listen, there were lots of people back there who would've tried to help Sophia. Ruth, Flynn, my ma..." He trailed off.

"You worried about them too?"

He shrugged. "Yeah. I mean... we've no idea how it... how it ended. Danforth's forces might've annihilated us."

"She didn't have too many guards left." Faith grimaced. "Not once Jacob detonated his bombs. Eremus definitely outnumbered them."

"But their weapons are much more powerful."

"I'll bet Bellator backed off in the end." Faith tried to sound convincing. "Let's just hope there weren't too many casualties."

Noah walked ahead to clear some branches out of their way. "Danforth won't give up, will she?"

"No." As she followed him, Faith sighed. "And I get the feeling Jacob won't either."

She thought back to the morning, to her optimism at how the communities of Bellator and Eremus might actually come together. How naïve that seemed now. She glanced at the boy who walked a few steps ahead of her. What hope was there for them now? How could the two of them even begin to get to know one another better, when both sides would brand them traitors for even trying?

As though he knew she was thinking of him, Noah turned. She hurried to catch up, slipping her hand into his. His answering squeeze made her feel a little better. She didn't let go of it until they came within view of the tunnel entrance.

By the time they reached the caves, the rain had stopped. As with Sarah earlier, they moved along the less-travelled routes, which hid them better. Once again, Faith marvelled at the

Eremus citizens' knowledge of the forest, knowing she'd have gotten hopelessly lost by herself.

This time though, her companion was far more thoughtful. Noah had kept a keen eye out behind them all the way back. He'd continued to lead them along the quiet paths, between sections of damp foliage, always guiding her over obstacles he suspected would be slippery.

Finally, they reached one of the entrances to the tunnel complex. As they crouched in some bushes a few metres away, Noah paused to scout the area. So far, they had seen no one and heard nothing. Faith didn't know if that made her feel comforted or more on edge. They sat for several minutes, shooting nervous glances at one another.

"You any warmer?" Noah said finally.

She shrugged. "Not much."

"Guess we'd better get you inside." He shot a final nervous glance at the entrance. "Suppose we have to go in there sometime."

They crept forward, darting into the bushes which hid the entrance to the Eremus community. Pausing to listen, Noah gave a quick nod before disappearing between the leaves. Faith took a deep breath and followed, wondering what she was plunging back into.

On the other side, Noah had come to an abrupt halt. Faith almost crashed into him, managing to place a hand on his back to stop herself just in time. There was the click of a rifle being primed. Faith felt Noah tense. He reached back as though making sure she was shielded by him.

And then a voice spoke from the shadows. "Noah? That you?"

"Paulo?"

There was a click, and a flashlight beam illuminated the tunnel. "You're alright!"

At this point, Faith had no idea which side of the Eremus disagreement Noah's brother was on. She knew he was fairly close to Jacob, which didn't bode well. Noah knew him better though. Remaining still, she decided she'd take her cue on whether to trust him from Noah.

"Yeah, it's me." A pause. Noah took a step forward. "What are you doing... all the way out here?"

"Council wanted security on all the entrances, in case any stray guards were still wandering the woods." Paulo's eyes travelled to Faith. "Where did you two get to? You're soaked."

"The other side of the forest. Was trying to keep Faith clear of Danforth's guards."

"Good plan." Paulo sounded impressed. "You managed to avoid them?"

"Yeah. It was a close one though. Two of them followed us, but we managed to sidestep them. Then we got caught in the storm."

"Glad to see you're back safely." Paulo clapped a hand on Noah's shoulder. "Well done."

Noah shrugged off the touch. "What happened after we left?"

"More of the same." Paulo shook his head. "Both sides had casualties, but we managed to hold our own. In the end, Bellator accepted they were beaten and retreated." He gestured over his shoulder vaguely. "Jacob's on the warpath though." He turned to Faith. "You'd better get her back to the cave with the others, and quickly."

Noah's eyes narrowed. "Why?"

"Jacob's orders. He's more determined than ever that the girls are... kept safe... especially..." he glanced at Faith. "Given that Danforth is *clearly* desperate to get them back." Faith was just wondering how safe she actually felt under Jacob's protection, when Paulo stepped towards them. "I can take her, if you'll cover me here for a while?"

Noah stared hard at his brother. "You don't trust me?"

"It's not that." Paulo looked torn. "Let's just say Jacob's not certain where your loyalties lie. And you *don't* want to be on the wrong side of him at the moment." As Noah waited, his brother ran a hand across his forehead frustratedly. He seemed to be battling with something, though Noah wasn't sure what. It wasn't like Paulo to be uncertain.

Eventually, he sighed. "Just make sure she gets there, okay? For your own sake."

Faith felt Noah take hold of her arm again. Glad of the protection, she edged closer to him. "I'll take care of her, don't you worry."

Ushering her ahead of him, he hurried them away from his brother. Instead of heading for the girls' cave, he took a different turning. After a few more turns, Faith knew where he was going. Impressed with his resistance to Paulo's instructions, she followed him towards the canteen.

They didn't come across anyone else, but as they approached the entrance, a low hum of voices emanated from within. Noah tightened his hold on her, but for the first time, Faith pulled away.

He turned to her in surprise. "What's wrong?"

"Nothing. It's just–"

"Just what?"

"I don't think we should..." she gestured between them. "We've no idea what's waiting for us on the other side of this wall. Who made it back... who didn't... who might be injured... how your community feels about us."

"So?"

"So, I'm not sure it's a good idea that you align yourself with me so openly."

Hurt flashed across his face. "You don't think I already did that when I helped you escape back there?"

"Maybe." She shrugged. "But I don't think we should make it any worse." Pulling the box cutter from her pocket, she held it out. "And I guess you'd better take this. Don't want them thinking you armed me."

Sighing, he accepted the improvised weapon and pocketed it. "Alright. For now, we'll keep... *this*..." he paused, and Faith wondered if he was also wondering what *this* might be, "to ourselves."

They stopped in the doorway to the canteen. Inside, there was a kind of organised chaos. Some citizens were hurrying about, attending to the injured, who had been laid out on tables not unlike the Danforth girls when they had first been brought here. Others huddled together in small groups, their heads bent close together, muttering in hushed voices. An air of shock shrouded the place, as though no one could quite get their head around the day's events.

Faith spotted Anna and elbowed her companion. Following her gaze, Noah wasted no time in heading to see his mother, who was bending over one of the raiders, her face creased with worry.

"Ma?"

For a second, she didn't respond. Then, without warning, she straightened and thrust her arms around her son. "Thank goodness you're back." She pulled away. "You're wet." Reaching across, she pulled a blanket from a pile close by and handed it to him. "What happened?"

"We ran." He passed it to Faith before reaching over to collect a second one for himself. "We were followed by some guards, so we had to hide for a while." Glad of the warmth, he wrapped the blanket around his shoulders. "We're fine. You don't have to worry."

Anna's eyes moved to Faith. Instantly, they widened in alarm. "You'd better take her back to the cave, and fast. Jacob's not here at the moment, but we have a lot of talking to do when he gets back. The further away the girls are from this, the better."

"What do you mean?"

"I mean..." Anna leaned closer. "That Jacob seems more determined than ever to make sure that Danforth doesn't get her hands on the girls. And now..." her face clouded over, "now that there are fewer of them..."

Faith's heart began to hammer against her ribcage. "Fewer?"

"Ma? What happened?"

Anna grimaced. "You'd better come with me."

As she led them across the canteen, Faith was aware of the stares of those around her. Clearly, news travelled fast. Every single citizen here was fully aware of her importance to Bellator, and of Noah's actions to save her today. He was right. It was useless trying to separate herself from him. In the minds of the Eremus people, for better or worse, they were linked.

Shrinking as far down in the blanket as she could, she followed Anna to the opposite side of the space. Here, only a few tables had patients on them. As she passed the first few, she noticed they were covered from head to toe with ragged blankets. She felt her heartbeat stutter as her gaze darted from table to table. These citizens weren't merely injured.

Biting her lip, she looked for Anna. Just ahead of her, the medic had halted at the final table. The body on it was slight, and Faith knew instinctively that it was a child. She held her breath as Anna pulled back the sheet.

"I'm so sorry," she whispered. "She was caught in the crossfire."

Faith lowered her gaze to the figure on the table. Catherine. The young girl lay motionless, a vivid red streak staining the front of her shirt.

"No," she choked, her head starting to spin.

Noah was at her side. Placing an arm around her, he tried to steer her into a seat on one of the benches, but as a thought hit her, she fought him off.

"No!" She struggled against his hold. "Where's..." Her eyes roamed the other covered bodies for a moment and she had to fight the urge to start tearing the sheets from them all. "Where's Sophia?"

"She's not here." Anna's expression was unreadable.

For a second, hope flared in Faith's chest. "Then she's..."

Anna's face darkened. "I mean... she's not dead."

As quickly as it was ignited, the hope died. Reaching for the table to hold herself steady, Faith braced herself for Anna's next words. "Where is she?"

"There was so much confusion..." The older woman shook her head. "we're still trying to piece it all together. But we think..." she straightened and looked Faith in the eye. "I'm so sorry. But we think, when the guards retreated... they took her."

The room started spinning and a rush of heat threatened to overwhelm Faith as she fought to hear Anna's final words.

"I'm afraid she's back in Bellator."

Chapter Twenty-Nine:
Noah

After his ma had pressed them to dry off properly and change their clothes, Faith allowed Noah to accompany her back to the cave. When they got there, Sil was on guard outside.

"Hey, Noah." She straightened as she greeted him, narrowing her eyes when she spotted Faith.

"Sil." He managed to nod, remembering the strange expression on her face in the clearing earlier in the day. Sil had known about the bombs. Had she been in on it too? How many other trusted members of the Eremus community had been aware of Jacob's plan?

"I'm just bringing Faith back. Okay if I..." He gestured to the cave entrance.

"Go ahead." Sil settled herself back against the wall.

Noah removed the wood from over the door with a heavy heart. Despite the panic of the afternoon, he'd enjoyed the time he'd spent with Faith. Being alone with her in the woods had felt right, somehow. And now, when he could feel her distress at the losses she'd suffered today, he didn't want to abandon her. He hated the fact that, when she needed his support, he had to lock her away.

Faith had barely spoken since she'd heard the news about Sophia. Noah suspected she was blaming herself, blaming him. He'd also questioned whether, if they'd stayed in the clearing for another couple of minutes, they might have been able to rescue Sophia and Catherine too. But there was little he could do about it now.

Professor Kemp was the first person he saw when the cave entrance was opened. Climbing to her feet, she came forward immediately.

"Faith!" There was relief in her voice. "Thank goodness!"

Ushering her student inside, Kemp pressed her to sit down, then hurried to pour her a cup of water from the pitcher.

"Give her a minute, ladies." She shooed some of the other girls away as she handed the cup to Faith. "She'll talk when she's ready."

Returning to Noah, she glanced pointedly at the empty space behind him. "And the other two? Where are they?"

Jerking his head into the tunnel, Noah had ignored Sil's stare and brought the teacher a little way away from the cave mouth. The older woman looked pale, but there was a steely glint in her eye as she joined him.

"I'm sorry. It's just Faith." He hesitated. "We... we think Sophia was taken back to Bellator by the guards."

"And Catherine?"

"She was caught up in the raid. I'm afraid that..."

"She's dead then?"

Noah winced at her bluntness. "Yes. I'm sorry."

Kemp closed her eyes, pain clouding her face. "This is what I was most afraid of." Her fists clenched at her sides. It was the first time Noah had seen her lose control. "How can he risk the lives of innocents so casually?" Opening her eyes, she peered closely at him. "You *do* seem like you're sorry." Kemp had cast a glance at Sil, who was still regarding them curiously. "I'm not sure your sentiment is shared by everyone around here."

"Maybe not. But I am. Truly sorry." He'd dropped his voice, feeling like a traitor. "And you're right not to trust everyone here. We don't all..."

"Want the same thing?" Kemp's expression was bitter. "No. I got that." She paused for a second, as though she was weighing her words carefully. "Look, we heard the explosions from here. The bombs... was that Danforth? What happened?"

Noah glanced at Sil, who appeared to have relaxed. Instead of watching them, she had closed her eyes and leaned her head back against the wall. Taking Kemp's arm, he moved them both a few steps further away and dropped his voice low.

"It wasn't Danforth."

"Then... Jacob?" Kemp didn't look surprised.

Noah nodded. "The explosives were meant to take out a large number of Danforth's guards. But..." he made sure he met her gaze as he continued, "the majority of the community were *not* aware of them... until they went off."

Kemp sighed deeply. "How many guards were killed?"

"I'm not sure." Noah grimaced. "Quite a lot, I think. Jacob seemed–" he suppressed a shudder, "*pleased*. He drove what was left of them right to our original position. The group we eventually faced numbered fewer than thirty. They were angry, though." He reflected. "I'm guessing they'd lost a good number of colleagues."

"An effective move on Jacob's part, then." Kemp held out a hand to stop Noah's protest. "Obviously, the murder of so many Bellator women is appalling and tragic. But our leaders are alike in many ways. If Jacob wants to make Danforth sit up and take notice, he's gone the right way about it."

"I suppose so." Noah shook himself, trying to take in everything that had happened. "There's something else, though. Whilst Jacob and Danforth were talking it became very clear that he... well, he knew her."

Kemp's head snapped up, her razor-like focus back. "Knew her?"

"Yeah. We were pretty shocked too. "It seems like... originally... he was from Bellator."

"He admitted to this?"

"No. Danforth accused him of it. But he didn't deny it."

"Interesting." Kemp rubbed a hand against her chin thoughtfully. "But you don't have any more details?"

"Sorry." Noah shook his head. "He didn't seem very keen to discuss it with so many people listening."

"I'll bet he didn't." Kemp frowned. "Where's your mother right now?"

"Tending to the injured. There were quite a few on our side too."

"Thought she might be." Kemp gave a faint smile. "Think there's any chance she might come down here at some point? *Without* one of Jacob's goons? I'd like to speak to her."

"I'm sure she would. I'll ask her."

"Thanks." Kemp cocked her head, staring hard at Noah. "She's happy here? Your mother?"

Startled by the sudden question, Noah was lost for words.

"I mean... we used to be friends..." Kemp continued, as though she wanted to clarify the bond they had shared, "we were close... always wanted to be a medic. Clearly, she's managed to do that here, to some extent at least. But... it must have been difficult."

"I think it was. Her values have always been... very different."

"And that's made it hard for you, right?" Kemp's gaze was piercing.

"I guess so."

"You're so like her." Kemp stretched a hand towards his face, then thought better of it and dropped her hand to her side. "Compassionate. Fair." She grinned, suddenly. "Pretty stubborn, I suspect..."

"Maybe." He cleared his throat, embarrassed. "Anyway, I'd better..." he jerked his head away. "Things I have to do, before I..."

"Of course. I'll take care of her for you." She shot him a look which suggested she knew Faith was more than just a prisoner.

He fought off a blush. "Thanks."

"Just..." she paused, chewing her lip in the first sign of nerves Noah had seen from her, "keep an eye on us, would you? I don't trust that leader of yours one little bit."

"I will. In fact," he glanced at Sil again, "I might make sure we have a guard we trust on this door at all times, for the time being anyway."

Kemp's face was somber. "That might be wise."

After escorting Kemp back to the cave, Noah moved past Sil and headed straight for Ruth and Ella's. When he arrived, Ella was sitting alone on one of the chairs, looking a little shellshocked.

"You alright?"

"Not really. Ruth's just finished filling me in on what happened." She pushed her hair away from her face. "It's terrible."

Noah sat down opposite her. She looked drained, but he wondered if they were all that way. "I know. It is." He glanced at the inner cave, concealed by the ragged curtain. "Ruth asleep already?"

"Asleep? Not likely. She feels worse than anyone about not managing to rescue the other girls." Ella's face clouded over. "No. She's gone to see if she can help your ma."

It made sense that she would want to support those tending to the injured. He'd left his friend trying to get the other two Bellator girls out, and she'd been unable to help either of them. Keeping busy would be her way of coping with the guilt.

"How's Faith?" Ella's eyes had filled with tears. "I was sorry to hear about her friends."

Noah turned to face Ella. "Faith's... well, she's not good. As you'd expect. Losing Catherine is... unthinkable. And Sophia's her best friend."

"It's just terrible." Ella dropped her gaze. "And I can't believe I was stuck down here. Totally helpless." She massaged her temples and sighed. "We were so frightened when the bombs went off. And to find out that *Jacob* was the one behind them—"

Ella had been tasked with staying behind, partly to keep the canteen running but also to guard the girls' cell. Up until now, Noah hadn't really considered how those left in the settlement might feel. But Ella's face suggested she had suffered just as much as those close to the battle.

"I'm so sorry. It must have been awful." He leaned a little closer. "For you, and for them. It's kind of why I came down here." He paused, waiting until Ella's gaze met his. "I'm worried about them. And I know you're as tired as the rest of us, but... could I ask a favour?"

Ella straightened. "Sure."

"I'm concerned that... since we seem to have some kind of... division... down here, the girls need to be guarded by someone we trust."

Ella frowned. "Who's down there now?"

"Sil." He made a face. "And she's too close to Harden, in my opinion."

"Agreed." Ella was already on her feet. "I'll get straight down there."

Noah stood alongside her. "Thanks. I really appreciate that."

Ella was already gathering her things together. "No problem," she called over her shoulder. "Can you stay here and let Ruth know where I am before you head off to bed, please? She won't be long."

"Of course."

"Thanks." She threw her pack over her shoulder and headed for the door. "See you later."

Noah found himself intensely grateful for Ella's selflessness, her willingness to go out on a limb to support girls who were not from her own community. There was definitely more than one way to be brave. He closed his eyes resting his head in his hands on the table as he listened to his friend's footsteps recede down the tunnel. What seemed like only seconds later, he heard footsteps approaching.

He sat up. "What'd'you forget?"

But it was Ruth in the doorway instead of Ella. She looked puzzled for a second. "Where's El?"

"She went to guard the girls. Sil's with them tonight, and after the day's events, I think we should have–"

"–someone we trust down there?" Ruth nodded. "Totally agree. Anyway, I'm glad you're here. Save me coming to get you."

"Get me? Why?"

"I've just finished up helping your ma in the canteen. When she left, she said she was off to a council meeting. I'm guessing there'll be a *very* interesting discussion about what happened today." She leaned forward and grabbed his hand. "How about we go down there and see what they're saying?"

"What? Demand entrance to the meeting?"

"No. They wouldn't let us in. But they're not holding it in the canteen, as usual. It's in the raider training space."

The raiders' training cave was further from the central community than the canteen. The space was large, and had many adjoining caves, which were used for storing the raiders' weapons and kit. Ruth knew them well.

"I'm wondering if..." she paused, her eyes glinting, "what if we could sneak into one of the side caves? If they are where I think they are, I'm pretty sure I know of a place we can hide and be close enough to listen in. You in?"

"Sure." Noah didn't hesitate. Since the encounter with Danforth, his follow-orders-without-question attitude seemed naive. Perhaps bending the rules was the only way to stay ahead of the enemy. Though he wasn't entirely sure who the enemy was right now.

Ten minutes later, he and Ruth slipped into the kit room on one side of the main training cave. It was empty, and contained a number of boxes, stacked high across the rear of the space. They could already hear the sound of raised voices from the far side.

Ruth crept towards a second exit, which led into the cave where the meeting was being held. Beckoning to Noah, she disappeared between a couple of the stacks of boxes. He joined her, finding the position shielded them from view, yet allowed them to overhear the voices of the council surprisingly well.

"It was a sensitive operation." Jacob sounded defensive. "It made sense not to include everyone. I didn't want to risk–"

"You didn't want anyone to stop you, no doubt." His ma sounded like she was speaking through clenched teeth.

"Alright, Anna. I won't insult you by lying." Jacob huffed. "I *did* feel like there were those among you who would object to my plan."

"The whole idea was that we would try to communicate *peacefully* with Bellator." Flynn sounded more reasonable. "That we'd make them see we weren't savages, that we wouldn't–"

"Jacob was convinced we couldn't trust Danforth not to bring an army with her," Sarah Porter's strident tones cut across Flynn's. "And he was *right*."

"That's not the point. We *agreed*–"

"I know what we agreed, Anna." Jacob's tone was cold. "But if we'd have stood in that clearing and blindly turned on a single locator chip, Danforth would've been on us in minutes with a huge contingent of guards. We'd have been overwhelmed, unable to defend ourselves."

"Instead of only four dead, we'd have lost most of our best raiders." Sarah added. "You can't deny it. By using multiple wristclips in an intelligent way, we were able to gain control of the situation."

In the adjoining cave, there was a growing muttering in response to Sarah's words. Ruth and Noah exchanged glances. It was difficult to tell whether people were siding with Jacob or objecting to his latest actions.

"Sarah's right. How would we have come back from that?" Noah imagined Jacob's piercing stare directed at his ma. "Yes, what I did was violent, but it was *necessary*. Now that Danforth has lost a good portion of her guard, she'll be more prepared to negotiate. We're still holding six girls captive, *and* we have their teacher, too. We didn't give away our location, nor did we lose any weapons. We are a little low on explosives now, but otherwise, I'd say we're in a position of great strength."

"If you say so." Noah didn't know how Flynn was managing to remain calm. "But there are other issues we need to discuss."

"Like what?"

"The large section of forest you damaged with the bombs, for one." Noah thought this was Jan.

"The location for the explosives was chosen carefully to minimise damage to our foraging grounds." Jacob said smoothly. "It was felt that sustaining the damage was worth it, if it meant we reduced the Bellator force."

"Felt by who?"

Sarah hurried on, again quick to back Jacob up. "The storm put out the fires, so they weren't able to spread further and damage other areas of the forest."

"That was more luck than good management, though." Jan sounded scathing.

"Either way, we didn't lose a lot. So, if we can focus on the important things, I'd like to—"

But Jacob was cut off. "Hold on a minute." This was a new voice, and one Noah couldn't identify. "I'd like an explanation for Danforth's little *revelation* this afternoon."

Even from the next cave, Noah could feel the atmosphere change. A momentary silence fell over the meeting and the air was charged with energy. Straining forward, Noah and Ruth listened intently, not wanting to miss a word of the Eremus leader's explanation.

After a lengthy pause, they heard footsteps in the cave next door, as though Jacob had stood and begun pacing.

"Well?" The same voice, mistrustful, determined. "Is it true?"

"It's true, I was born in Bellator." Jacob still sounded un-flustered. "Thirty years ago, their fertility system was very different. Instead of having the frozen seed storage banks, they had living subjects who provided them with the male seed necessary to procreate."

Beside him, Noah felt Ruth draw a sharp breath. The only explanation for Jacob living in Bellator was that *he* was one of these subjects.

In the next room, Jacob's footsteps had stilled. "I can see from your faces that you are jumping to the correct conclusion. I was one of those men, whose birth was permitted for the sole reason of continuing the Bellator population. To begin with, I didn't know there was a different kind of life. We were kept separate from the female community, but we weren't mistreated. We were just very limited in our activities: we ate, we exercised, we had a decent education and access to an unlimited number of books. We saw no one, save for a limited number of medics and, of course, the other subjects."

"Eventually, we became tired of the way we were treated. A number of us plotted to break out and escape from Bellator. I had befriended one of the medics. Marie was a younger woman, who didn't entirely agree with the system, the way we were kept for our seed alone." He paused for a moment. There was a murmur, as though someone had asked a question, but Noah couldn't hear it. "Oh yes. You'd be surprised how many Bellator citizens disagree with the way the city is run."

"He's right." This was Flynn. "Look at Madeleine and her resistance colleagues... people like Kemp, for example. These people exist. They just don't feel like they have the ability to publicly object. Not yet, anyway."

"Thanks." Jacob sounded faintly surprised that Flynn had agreed with him. "As I said, Marie and I became... close. I gained her trust." As he continued, the sound of footsteps returned and his voice changed in volume as he paced closer to the cave where they crouched, then retreated from it. "Eventually, she let her guard down with me. Said she'd support us with our escape. She was going to accompany me. She was the one who provided us with keycodes, accessible routes out of the facility we were kept in, the guard schedules."

Noah's leg started to thrum with pins and needles. As slowly as he could, he altered his position to a new, more comfortable one. As he did, his foot knocked a box. He flinched as it began to wobble, but Ruth leaned over him and caught hold of it. Together, they eased it back into place, listening to see whether the noise had alerted anyone to their presence.

Jacob was still talking, as though nothing had happened. He sounded like he was further away now, and they had to strain to hear him. "...night of our escape... everything covered. We drugged the guards... keycodes... get out of our cells, followed the map... outside." As he returned to their side of the cave, his voice grew louder and they could hear him better. "I was meant to meet Marie in the alley which ran along the back of the facility. She was going to open the outer door for us. When we got there, it was already standing ajar. I eased it open and checked the alley myself." His voice took on a desperate tone. "I swear to this day, it was clear."

"But there was someone out there?"

"No one I could see. But, yes." Jacob sighed. "When we stepped outside, Marie appeared on the opposite side of the alley. Waiting for us. But then I saw something move, in the shadows, and I knew we'd been betrayed. I tried to get to her in time, I really did. But the guards started firing, fast and hard." He stumbled over his words. "By the time I… she was already gone. I turned back and the alley was filled with guards. The men behind me were being picked off as they ran. I knew I couldn't help them. So I fled."

"You got out without being hit?" Flynn asked.

"Yes. I've no idea how. I didn't stop running until I reached the woods. Then I walked. I wandered the forest for days, until I came across Eremus. The community lived in the woods back then, and there were far fewer of them. No one really looked too hard at where I'd come from. I said something about being from another male community in the north. There were more, back then, before Bellator managed to eradicate them. I guess people here were just grateful to swell their numbers. They didn't ask too many questions."

"And you've been here ever since." Noah thought his ma sounded calmer, though he recognised an undertone in her voice which suggested she was working hard to keep control.

"I have."

There was a short silence. Noah tried to take in Jacob's words. What must it have been like for him, for any man, to be a prisoner of Bellator, useful for a single purpose? For once, he could see Jacob's side of things, comprehend his anger.

But Anna wasn't finished. "What does Danforth have to do with all this?"

Jacob choked out a strangled laugh. "She was a lower-level member of the Bellator government at the time. Visited the facility regularly. It was her idea to replace the remaining male prisoners with the frozen seed banks over time. It *simpli-*

fied things, she said. It's what made her. After that, she rose through the ranks without issue."

"How do you know that?" Flynn sounded a little suspicious.

"I returned to the city a few times, at night. Stole a few newspapers, listened to conversations where I could. Once the resistance became more established, I spoke to Madeleine and Evelyn, another of our resistance contacts, about it. They told me the rest."

"What happened to the other men?" Trust his ma to be concerned for the other prisoners' welfare.

"They were either shot or recaptured." Jacob sighed. "And then, when Danforth had collected all the seed that Bellator needed to keep it going for thousands of years to come, she had no issue with having them all executed. Probably regarded it as getting rid of the vermin."

An audible shudder ran round the room.

"So you see, I have *extremely* unpleasant memories of Bellator." Jacob finished. "But it doesn't mean my aim is selfish, that all I want to do is avenge the deaths of Marie and my fellow prisoners. I haven't waited this long and worked this hard simply to see Danforth dead. Please know you can trust me. I want the *best* for Eremus. But I also know Danforth. She's ruthless. We have no choice but to think like her if we hope to stand any chance of getting her to change her policies about men. Hence my decision to set off the bombs today."

"Alright, I take your point." Anna didn't sound comforted by Jacob's words. "Your story's quite moving. But why didn't you tell us about it earlier?"

"When I arrived here, I didn't want to be pitied or mistrusted. I wanted a fresh start. So I buried the past and focused on building something of value here. Is that so difficult to understand?"

"I suppose not."

"I'm glad you agree." Noah wasn't convinced his ma did, but she knew better than to push Jacob further, for now at least. "And with that out of the way, we have another pressing issue."

"What's that?" Jan sounded weary.

"We were aware that Madeleine feared she was being watched. When she has concerns like these, we know she puts certain measures in place to protect herself and to protect us here in Eremus." Noah could hear murmurs in the cave, as though the council members were interested. "When we returned from the meeting, I went through the tunnels towards Bellator."

"You did?" This was Flynn, who sounded exasperated. "Again, *why* didn't you tell anyone you were going?"

"Things were chaotic. People were upset. I didn't want to add to everyone's worries unless I had to." He paused, allowing people the chance to object. When no one did, he continued. "I assure you, I didn't go near Madeleine's house. I merely went as far as the safety point. I approached in darkness, with great caution. When I reached the hole in the tunnel wall, I was confident there was no one around. I turned on a flashlight for a few seconds to check the pebble. It was white."

Noah's mind went back to his first journey to Bellator, where Paulo had explained the pebble system to him. White, he remembered, was a warning to take care.

"You think she's in trouble?" Paulo asked.

"Perhaps." Jacob sounded like he had begun pacing again. "But the stone wasn't black, so I don't think we should panic." Noah remembered the colour which signified extreme danger with a shudder. "Last time we spoke, she felt she was being watched. Maybe this is just a reflection of that."

"We should still take additional precautions." Jan sounded concerned.

"How about we station a citizen at the safety point? Cautiously, of course." Flynn suggested. "At least until we know what's going on. They can alert us if anything happens there. Warn us if there's any kind of threat."

"Good idea." It sounded like Jacob had moved further away again. "...thinking a similar thing."

"I'll take the first shift." Noah recognised his brother's voice for the first time.

"Thanks, Paulo. We'll send someone to replace you in a couple of hours."

"But–"

"No arguments. You can't do a whole shift, You're as exhausted as the rest of us."

"On that note, can I suggest we all get to bed?" Jacob suddenly sounded weary. "I mean... if I've answered all your questions?"

A hum of conversation grew in the neighbouring room, and there was a shuffling of feet, as though the council were preparing to leave. Noah and Ruth stared at one another in alarm. With no time to exit without being seen, they were stuck.

Ruth leaned closer. "We'll wait 'til they've all gone, then head back. We'll tell your ma you came over to keep me company."

Accepting it was their only option, Noah shifted position again. His limbs were aching from spending so long crouched in the small space. The training cave emptied and the noises receded, until the silence surrounded them. Noah was about to stand when Ruth grasped his arm hard, her fingers digging into his skin. He started to object, then froze.

"We managed to get away without discussing the Danforth girls, then."

Sarah Porter's voice. Clearly the adjoining cave was not quite empty.

"For now." Noah wasn't surprised to find Jacob was still there. "And there were plenty of other things to occupy us."

"Your Bellator story went down well." It sounded as though Sarah was preparing to leave. Shuffling footsteps reached Noah's ears as her voice began to fade. "I think a fair number of them were on your side."

"I'm not so sure," Jacob sounded frustrated. "Jan isn't happy. She carries a lot of weight with the older citizens. And I don't think that Flynn and Anna will let this go. They'll be back, asking about what we plan to do with their precious little innocents."

"And what will you say when they do?"

The volume of the pair's voices continued to reduce as they made their way out of the cave and down the tunnel. Noah and Ruth strained to hear their last words.

"Whatever I have to." Despite the distance, Jacob's voice was loud and hard. "Those girls are the key. We've already lost two of them. We can't afford to lose any more. From now on, I won't have anyone—*especially* not Flynn and Anna with their bleeding hearts—stand in my way."

Chapter Thirty: Faith

"I have to go back."

"Are you mad?" Diane had been pacing the cave as she listened to Faith's story. "That's what Danforth wants!"

"But Sophia–"

"Sophia *nothing*." Diane spun to face her. "I know you feel guilty. And yes, I wish things were different too. But if what the professor says is true, you marching straight back into the academy will give Danforth more power than she already has."

"She's right." Kemp nodded. "Sophia's a sensible girl. She'll cope."

Faith was exhausted, yet she couldn't even think about sleeping yet. Since Noah had left, she'd been recounting the events of the past few hours. At first, it hadn't been difficult. She'd explained the cottage in the woods where she'd been taken by Sarah, the brief sojourn in the shed while her captor waited for the signal, and the shock of the explosion ripping through the woods.

No one had interrupted her. Not even Avery, though she had fumed all the time Faith had spoken, her eyes blazing. But as Faith recounted the damage caused by the bombs, the injured guard in the forest, and Sarah's cold-blooded execution, there had been muffled gasps and horrified murmurs all around.

"We heard it. In the distance." Helen had whispered when Faith paused for a moment. "The explosion, I mean." She'd shuddered. "We thought it was Danforth. Thought we'd be blown to bits, buried alive down here."

"I told you she'd never risk our lives that way." Avery spoke for the first time, her tone bitter. "Didn't believe me though, did you?"

Helen lapsed into silence, and Faith considered the uncertainty experienced by those trapped down here, with no idea what was going on. Though Ella had come down to see them after the explosion, she had not been able to offer any real comfort. The citizens left behind had been as much in the dark as the Danforth girls. Not for the first time, Faith wondered if both societies were broken. There were just as many secrets and lies swirling through the air in the caves as there were back home. And just as much mistrust and suspicion.

Her story had become harder to recount once she began describing what happened in the clearing. When Faith described how Jacob held a gun to Sophia's head, her voice caught in her throat. And by the time she got to Catherine, Faith had to pause and breathe deeply to stop herself from putting her head in her hands and sobbing.

She'd left out the part where she'd fled through the woods with Noah, partly concerned the others would feel she abandoned their friends. The intensity of the fear she'd felt, hiding in the waters of the lake with the scent of smoke filling the air, the sound of the guards' boots and the rustling of leaves threatening to overwhelm her was too disturbing to relive right now. And she certainly wasn't willing to admit to the kisses she and Noah had shared. Instead, she mentioned being separated from the others during the fight, letting them believe that Noah had come across her later and guided her back through the forest.

When she'd finished talking, she glanced around, trying to make sure the others had taken in everything she'd told them and fully understood their position. The one thing that was clear to her was how determined Jacob was to hold their presence in Eremus over Bellator. Danforth wanted them back. But Jacob wasn't giving them up without a fight.

It seemed like a stalemate, but Faith had no doubts: Jacob wouldn't hesitate to use them to get what he wanted. The news that he had an old score to settle with the chancellor had been even more disturbing. Now that he'd taken out a good portion of Danforth's guard, he stood a better chance than ever. And he wouldn't want to wait. She hated to admit it, but Avery had been right.

What Faith hated more than anything was the power both leaders had. Being stuck in the middle, the most vital pawn in their game, was terrifying. But Faith saw it came with power of its own. Danforth was fascinated by Faith's test results. If she wanted her back so much, perhaps Faith held some of the cards, at least. By returning to Bellator, Faith could change the situation for the better, perhaps. At least she might be able to save Sophia from whatever Danforth was putting her through. She had to try.

The girls had reacted to her story in very different ways. Most obviously affected was Mary, who had thrown herself against Helen's chest the moment she heard the news about Catherine. Helen, as usual, had said little, but comforting the younger girl seemed to help her to calm her own feelings. Farrah had simply sat in silence, her face growing paler with every word Faith spoke. Avery had listened patiently, showing more restraint than Faith thought her capable of. Aside from her comment defending Danforth to Helen, she had not interrupted. Ever since her return to the cave, Faith had been waiting for the *I told you so*, but so far, it had not materialised.

Kemp's face was pale and etched with concern. Diane was the only one who didn't seem able to sit still and focus. Her agitation put Faith on edge. As the older girl strode towards her again, her expression fierce, Faith stretched out and grasped her hand. Diane glanced down at her in surprise, but noting the look on Faith's face, gave in and slid to the ground beside her.

It felt odd to have someone else sitting in Sophia's usual place. Faith felt her friend's absence keenly. Aside from her captivity at the academy, there hadn't been a day in the past six years where they'd been apart. And when she considered where Sophia was now, and what might be happening to her, she couldn't bear it.

"Listen to me," she pleaded with Diane. "I don't mean I'm just going to head into Bellator and give myself up. But I can't just let Sophia go back and... and be..." She broke off.

"Alright, I get it." Diane's expression softened slightly. "I do. I just don't think you should be so desperate to race back there and give Danforth exactly what she wants."

"She's right."

Faith turned to face her professor. "Why *is* she so desperate to get her hands on me?"

Kemp hesitated. "Look, all I know is that I don't fully trust Danforth. I've worked at the school for years. At first, I only had my suspicions. But lately..." she paused, biting her lip. "Let's just say I've been watching Anderson closely. Danforth too. They're obsessed with revolutionising Bellator's procreation methods. Since Danforth started working for the government, years ago, it's been her main focus. It's what got her the position of chancellor."

"Really?"

"Oh, yes. She's had a real impact on the Bellator reproductive processes over the years. Built her election campaigns around it. The establishment of the academy was one of the first things she did as a senior member of government. I worry about…" she cast a glance around the cave, "its true purpose."

"You think she wants to hurt us?" Helen's voice quivered.

"I think she wants to use you." Kemp shrugged. "And if you get hurt in the process, well…" she trailed off.

"You're wrong."

Kemp swung round at the sound of Avery's voice. "I'm sorry you think so." Her voice was not unsympathetic.

Avery turned to Faith. "You say when Jacob spoke to her, Danforth asked about us?" Faith nodded, wondering where the conversation was going. "She said our names… as though she was making sure we were alright? *All* of us?"

"Yes." Faith frowned. "Why do you ask?"

"Surely, that's proof she cares about us. More than…" Avery's face twisted, "*that man* out there. She isn't the one who set off explosives to kill people today."

"That's true." Kemp said. "And no one's condoning Jacob's actions, but just because he's proving Danforth's theory about men, it doesn't mean she's blameless. I assure you, the things she is doing with the students at the academy are—"

A sound at the cave entrance diverted her attention. The girls followed her gaze, bracing themselves for what might come through the gap once the barrier was removed. Experience, Faith thought, had taught them all to be cautious.

But when the light from a lantern spilled into the room, the faces behind it were friendly. "Hey," Ella's voice was warm and soothing. "How are we all doing in here?"

Ruth carried a tray in from the tunnel. On it was a jug with steam rising from it, several cups, and a plate filled with something Faith couldn't identify. "We thought after the day you'd had, you might like something a little comforting."

"Tea and biscuits, everyone?" Ella said brightly. "Well, they're oatcakes, but they should do the trick. Help yourselves."

Ella gave the plate of oatcakes to Kemp as Ruth began pouring the hot liquid. Adding a spoonful of honey to each one, Ella passed the cups out carefully.

"We took this from Cora's stores." She brandished the jar. "She'd kill us if she found out."

"Then why...?" Helen asked. Her eyes had brightened since Ella's entrance.

"Anna's orders." Ruth shrugged. "You've been through a lot. Sweet tea's good for shock."

"Thank you," Faith murmured, accepting a cup.

Though it burned her tongue, the drink tasted better than any she'd had in a while. And while the oatcake was plain, she had never appreciated an offering of food quite so much. Memories of the delicious food and drink she'd been used to at the academy flooded back; she knew she'd never take such luxuries for granted again. But she also knew that she could do without them if she needed to.

"How are you all feeling?" Ella took a seat on the ground beside Helen, her face serious. "I mean... it's been a terrible experience for all of us, but..." she cast a glance at Mary, "you lost two friends today."

There was silence for a few moments. Faith felt Ruth's gaze on her, but when she looked up to meet the other girls' eyes, they were filled with concern.

"You're right." Kemp's voice cut through the quiet. "We're all in shock. What happened today was terrible." She frowned. "What I can't quite get over is how similar our two leaders are."

Ruth's eyes flicked to the professor. "Similar?"

"Yes." Kemp took a breath. "I knew that Danforth was ruthless and capable of putting her goals above the safety of her people. I just didn't think the Eremus leader would be the same way."

"I guess you're right." Ruth nodded thoughtfully.

"I was just telling the girls they can't trust our esteemed chancellor. Her plans for the Danforth students are not clear, but as a teacher at the school I know enough to doubt that she has the girls' best interests at heart."

"What do you mean?" Ella looked horrified.

"Danforth has always been obsessed with Bellator's reproductive processes." Kemp warmed to her theme. "The drug Faith was given before the kidnapping? I'm convinced it has something to do with procreation. She was testing it... on small numbers of students." She shot a look at Diane. "With disturbing results."

"Like Serene's death," Diane muttered.

"Yes." Kemp looked sideways at Avery. "But since the kidnapping. Since Eremus set off the explosives at the fertility unit, Danforth has stepped up her efforts. She has Anderson giving it to half the school population."

"What?" Faith's heart lurched in her chest. "You mean she's authorised its use, even though it–"

"Hold on." Avery interrupted. "What happened to the fertility unit?"

"The male seed supply was destroyed." Kemp said.

"So..." Faith could see the wheels turning in the older girl's head, "Bellator is unable to reproduce? At all?"

Kemp shrugged. "At the moment, yes."

Avery's face blanched. "But that means..."

"It means that Danforth is panicking. The drug she gave to Serene, and Faith, and now many other students, is part of her plan. A plan she's determined to make work."

There was another silence as the girls took in what Kemp was saying. Avery had stopped arguing, but her face was white. Mary whimpered slightly, and Helen gathered her close again. Faith wondered how much of the information the younger girl had taken in. The trauma of losing her friend was bad enough. Now discovering that returning to the place she had considered her home, a place of safety, was also threatened, was a hard pill to swallow.

For Faith, though, the most disturbing part of it was knowing Danforth was subjecting the other students to femgazipane. She shuddered at the thought.

Ruth shuffled forward a little. "Can I ask you something?"

Kemp turned to her. "Of course."

"We discovered something... disturbing... today." Faith watched her closely. She seemed ruffled, upset about something. "I'm not sure if Faith told you, but our community learned today that Jacob, our leader, used to live in Bellator."

There were gasps from many of the girls. Faith had left out that piece of information when retelling her story earlier, feeling they'd had enough shocks for one day.

"But how...?" Farrah exclaimed. "I mean... he's *a man*. He couldn't–"

Faith caught sight of Avery. For once, she was silent. But her eyes were wild and she looked almost pained.

"I'm sorry," Ruth pressed on. "I know this must be upsetting. But it is for us too." She turned back to Kemp. "He told us he used to be part of the fertility programme... in the old days?"

Kemp's eyebrows had raised, but at Ruth's words, an understanding dawned. "Really? Well, that explains a lot."

"I wondered..." Ruth went on, "could he be lying? Or might it be the truth?" She glanced across at her sister, whose eyes were also glued to Kemp. "We're not sure how much we can trust him anymore."

"What does she mean?" Avery bit out. "How could he be from Bellator?"

Kemp turned to her. "You should know from your Herstory lessons that Bellator reproductive systems used to be very different."

"Instead of seed banks," Helen parroted the facts, "the government kept live male specimens in a specially-designed laboratory."

"That's right." Kemp said. "The men there did not *live* in the city but were kept solely for the purposes of procreation..." she paused, glancing at Mary, who looked confused, "baby-making."

"So, Jacob *could* have been one of these... specimens?" Ella's nose wrinkled at the offensive term.

Kemp thought for a moment. "He could. He's around the right age, I think."

"Current Bellator protocol for reproduction involves women being impregnated by a sample from the seed bank, right?" Farrah asked.

"Yes."

"Then... when they didn't have the frozen seed..." her nose wrinkled in distaste, "they..."

"They used fresh samples from the male specimens," Kemp said, matter-of-factly, "until the Barbarian Revolt."

"That's when some of those *beasts* escaped, right?" Avery said, her eyes narrowed. Faith saw Ruth and Ella wince at her insulting reference. She wondered how Avery could still use the term after spending so much time with the people in the caves. "They ran riot through the city."

"Until they were caught and executed," Diane added.

"Thank goodness." Avery's fists were clenched by her sides.

Ruth opened her mouth to argue with her but stopped as Kemp sat bolt upright. "Wait! Jacob was *part* of the revolt?" Kemp's eyes swung to Ruth's. "He managed to escape?"

Ruth nodded. "That's what he said. He ran from the city... ended up here, in Eremus."

"How long ago?" Avery's voice was strident, panicked.

"I don't know." Ruth cast her a disdainful glance. "He's been here forever."

"Why does it even matter?" Farrah stared at her friend, perplexed. "The government got rid of them. To protect us. They've been gone from the city for years, now."

"But don't you see?" Avery clutched on to Farrah's arm so hard her friend cried out. "It means that... that Jacob could... his seed might have been..."

"You mean we could have been conceived from his seed, don't you?" Helen caught on before anyone else. "That Jacob could be our... father."

The shock was so great that no one spoke for several minutes. Faith watched the faces around her as they reeled from yet another mental blow. Bellator children didn't have fathers. Fatherhood wasn't even a concept in the city. To think it might be possible to *meet* the man whose DNA was rooted in your body, well... it was a disturbing thought.

Eventually, Ruth broke the silence. "Is it *so* repulsive for you all to think of the men who might have fathered you?"

Avery shot her a poisonous glance.

"I mean it." Ruth's voice hardened. "Here in Eremus, men and women bring up their children *together*."

Noting the shudder which went through some of the girls, Ella tried to soothe them. "To have two caring parents is a wonderful thing."

"Do *you* have two caring parents?" Avery said.

Ella flushed. "Well, no. But that's mostly down to the Bellator guards who killed them. Not a fault in our system."

Avery had the grace to look ashamed.

"I'm sorry to hear about your parents, Ella." Kemp sighed. "Clearly, neither system is perfect. And we seem to do all we can to destroy one another." She frowned. "Jacob's vendetta makes a lot more sense now. If he fled during the revolt... and heard later what happened to the other male specimens, well, I can see him holding a real grudge against Danforth."

"What did happen to them?"

"As Avery said, they were all executed... eventually." Kemp chewed her lip, lost in thought. "Any fresh samples they had in the lab were preserved immediately. These were the first to be frozen. They gave Danforth the idea for using seed banks permanently. She forged ahead with large scale freezing soon after the revolt, and once they were fully stocked, she signed the remaining men's death warrants."

"Wait... the revolt was in 2094, right?" Diane asked. When Kemp nodded confirmation, she turned her gaze to Avery and Farrah. "We're all nineteen, right? There's no way Jacob could be our father. He left way before we were born."

For a moment, Avery's face flooded with relief. But the sensation was fleeting. Faith knew she was thinking that her father had been one of the other specimens. That he had been a living, breathing human. It was a concept none of them had ever considered, and one which Faith suspected would take them a long time to adjust to.

Ella glanced around, sensing the shock hanging in the air. Squeezing Helen's arm affectionately, she took her empty cup and stood up to begin collecting the rest.

"I think perhaps we've had enough revelations for today..." she raised her eyebrows, "on both sides." She shot a sideways glance at Ruth, who hurriedly helped her. "It's very late. We'll leave you to rest now. Let's hope things look... better in the morning."

"Thank you for the tea." Kemp smiled at the two young women. "It's good to know there are people here who are on our side."

Ella smiled. "Of course. It was the least we could do."

Picking up the tray, she nodded at her sister to collect the extra lantern and they retreated towards the door. "I hope we haven't... upset people further." She sighed. "It wasn't our intention."

Faith attempted a smile as the pair left. Most of the others were still in a state of shock and didn't seem capable of forming a response. As she pulled the wooden barrier back into position, Ruth returned the smile. Faith thought she looked as shellshocked as the girls inside the cave.

Once the sound of their footsteps retreated down the tunnel, Faith turned to Kemp. "That was a lot to deal with. It does sound like Jacob and Danforth have some kind of history. And neither of them cares who gets caught in the crossfire."

Kemp rubbed a tired hand across her forehead. "It does seem that way."

Faith eyed her teacher. "You admit that neither Jacob nor Danforth can be trusted to do the right thing, then?" Kemp nodded. "Then I'm back where I started." Faith sat back. "I have to go back. For Sophia." She held up a hand to stop Kemp's protest. "No. Danforth *needs* me. That gives me some leverage, surely? I can't just leave Sophia to—"

"There's no way you can go back." Kemp's chin jutted out stubbornly. "I can't believe you're even considering it."

Sighing, Faith changed tack. "Why did you come here?"

Kemp narrowed her eyes. "You know why. Once I realised how important you were to Danforth, I came here to find you. To make sure you were safe. And, most of all, to make sure you *didn't* return to Bellator."

"Where do they think *you* are, then?" Diane asked. "I mean... did you *tell* Anderson or Danforth you were going to look for Faith? Do they think you're coming back?

"I didn't actually tell anyone I was going." Kemp flushed. "But yes, I hoped that I could go back... with a story about how I'd gone searching for Faith, but not been able to locate her. Or, better still, found evidence she was dead."

An idea struck Faith. "What if *you* took me back? What if we made my arrival back in Bellator very public... so people knew I'd returned from Eremus, unharmed."

"The media would love it," Diane chimed in. "*Miracle of Danforth student returned from the dead.*"

Encouraged, Faith warmed to her subject. "I mean... I wouldn't go back without a reason. Maybe I could do some good. Ask for certain assurances... that Eremus would be given immunity... that the other girls at the school would be protected... that Danforth would have to give reports on the drug testing to the general public... on a regular basis. Surely, if I was under that kind of scrutiny, Danforth wouldn't be able to hide what she was doing any more?"

"We could force her to go public with it..." Diane was up and pacing again, "her work would *have* to be more regulated. She couldn't experiment on you with the whole of Bellator watching."

"You're being naïve." Kemp turned away. "Danforth *controls* most of the media. Those who *have* attempted to write and publish information she didn't want in the public eye have suffered, believe me."

"But it's got to be worth trying, surely?" Faith shifted closer to her professor. "I can't just sit here. I can't leave Sophia and the others to–"

"You don't have a choice," Kemp snapped. "Going back would be suicide. Even if I came with you, I couldn't offer you any kind of protection."

"And you seem to be forgetting one very important detail." Avery spoke for the first time since Ella and Ruth's exit. "It's hardly likely that Jacob will let you both waltz out of here. He knows how important you are to Danforth." Once again, the pained look crossed her face fleetingly. Meeting Faith's gaze, she scowled. "As if *you* could make it safely back to Bellator alone anyway."

"Concerned about her safety, are you?" Diane raised an eyebrow.

"Hardly." Avery dropped her gaze abruptly. "I just don't have much confidence in her abilities."

"Avery's right. Trying to get back to the city alone would be extremely dangerous. So let that be an end to it." Kemp nodded. "Now, I think we all need to get some rest."

Recognising that Kemp would not change her mind, Faith let it go. But as those around her settled down to sleep, she couldn't stop thinking about going back. Not rashly, as Kemp had suggested. But with a sensible plan, which allowed her to prevent Danforth from experimenting on innocents with no one to stop her.

As Diane settled down to sleep next to Faith, the same determined expression was reflected in her eyes.

"Talk tomorrow?" the older girl mouthed.

With an imperceptible nod, Faith closed her eyes, feeling better than she had since she had re-entered the cave. She wasn't alone. The comforting thought meant she was asleep within seconds, with drifting smoke and a confusion of voices haunting her dreams.

CHAPTER THIRTY-ONE: NOAH

After a three-hour shift sitting at the safety point close to Madeleine's house, Noah was grateful to see his replacement approaching, even if it was Harden. It had been four days since the raid, and there was still no sign of the woman who had helped them for so long.

His ma was worried. Whilst Madeleine had gone AWOL before, it had never been for this long, and the timing of her disappearance and the raid seemed too coincidental. It also meant they'd had very little in the way of news from the city. Under normal circumstances, the resistance member followed up with the council after every raid or attack, making sure they knew whether or not their presence in Bellator had been detected, if members of the resistance had heard any worrying rumours, or whether the raiders should avoid using certain entry points to the city on their next visit.

To have no news whatsoever after Jacob's devastating attack on the city's forces was terrifying. Though their leader was thrilled that the explosion had killed or injured large numbers of the Bellator guards, others were appalled at the level of violence which had been used. Jacob was desperate for confirmation that the city's defences were compromised and was rumoured to be already considering his next move.

Flynn, Jan, and Noah's ma were far more cautious, insisting the council had to get some kind of a handle on Danforth's reaction to the attack before taking further action. Even some of those who had been staunch supporters of their leader in the past seemed bewildered by his actions. There had been many whispered conversations in the tunnels since the attack on the Bellator guards. The atmosphere was strained and no one was sure who to trust.

Noah was restless. While he didn't want to blast into Bellator all guns blazing, there was no doubt the raid had caused a change in the way Danforth regarded Eremus. Surely, she would want to take further action against them, to prove her power to her own citizens, if nothing else? If his community did nothing, they left themselves open to an attack from the city which could completely destroy them. But in truth, he wasn't sure what they could do without risking revealing their position.

"Any sign of her?" Harden jerked his head towards the tunnel which led to Madeleine's home.

"Nothing." Noah climbed to his feet and stretched his aching limbs.

Harden leaned down and peered into the narrow entrance, shining his flashlight along the passageway. "Think she's dead?"

Startled, Noah turned to his old enemy. "No. Why'd'you say that?"

Slinging his pack on the ground, Harden shrugged. "She's never been gone this long before."

"Doesn't mean we have to think the worst." Noah thought back to the white pebble. "It's not like she left the danger signal."

"S'pose not. Being dead would be better than her being captured by Danforth though." Harden took a seat, leaning his back against the wall and closing his eyes. "Imagine what she could tell them. We wouldn't stand a chance if they knew our location. It'd only take one stealth attack and..." He mimed a large explosion.

"What, like the one you helped Jacob with?" Noah stared at Harden, wondering if he cared about the large numbers of female guards he'd helped to assassinate.

Harden opened one eye. "You got something to say, Madden?"

Noah fought the urge to take a large step back. "Only that Jacob's little explosion killed a lot of Bellator women."

There was a flash of something Noah couldn't identify in Harden's eyes. "They were threatening us. Our community. If we'd have given away our true location... if that number of guards had arrived at the meeting point, we wouldn't have stood a chance."

Noah had to admit Harden was right. Although he didn't agree with Jacob's methods, the chancellor was not a woman to underestimate.

"Okay. I take your point. But don't you feel... I mean..."

"What?" Suddenly Harden was on his feet again. "Guilty?"

This time, Noah did step back. Harden was not much taller than him, but his bulk was more than double Noah's.

"I guess so. I mean. All those women are dead now... because of what we did."

Harden's eyebrows shot up. "*We*? It had nothing to do with you."

"No. But that's not the way Danforth will see it."

Harden looked as though he were fighting some kind of internal battle. For a moment, Noah thought he was going to lash out, but after a moment, he sucked in a breath through his teeth and stepped away. As he slumped back to the ground, Noah prepared to take his leave, but then the other boy spoke again.

"At least I'm not a coward."

Noah almost laughed. Harden definitely didn't know him well if he thought Noah could be provoked by that kind of taunt any more. But he turned back all the same.

"Coward? How?"

"Seems to me your only contribution to the raid was to run away with your little lady friend."

"She's not–" Noah stopped himself. Taking a breath, he parroted the same explanation he'd been giving for days. "The remaining guards were a threat to our hostages. I merely protected the most precious of them by removing her from the danger zone."

Harden snorted. "And that was your *only* concern? Unlikely. I've seen the way you look at her, Madden. It would be cute if it wasn't such a betrayal."

"Betrayal? How?"

"Because she's from Bellator. Those women are brought up to hate us. They'd sooner see us dead than respect us as equals. Danforth is pure evil and does her best to make sure every woman in that city follows her example."

Noah couldn't help but reflect on how Harden's words about the women of the city sounded similar to those he'd heard from Faith and the other girls about the men of Eremus.

"Do you honestly think they're *all* like that?"

Harden glared at him. "How could they not be, with Danforth in charge?"

"Then what's the point of us trying to gain our equality? Why would we bother, if they're all so hateful?"

Harden didn't seem to have a response to that one. Snarling, he closed his eyes again.

"Have you actually spoken to any of them? I mean... properly?" Noah took a step closer again, noting that whilst Harden's eyes stayed closed, his expression had altered. "They're all quite different. I mean, I know Faith best, but she's quite different from Sophia, and Avery is another kettle of fish altogether. They're like *us*. Every one of them different in terms of personality. I mean it's not like you could argue that you and I are the same, is it?"

Harden sat up. "Not likely."

"Well then. There you go." Noah stretched his back once again. "Alright then, I'll be getting back."

He turned to go, hoping his words had gotten through. But he hadn't travelled more than a few steps before Harden's taunt followed him.

"You're so naïve, Madden. You're being *used*." He laughed, cruelly. "You actually think... once she gets back to Bellator... your little lady'll want to have anything more to do with you?"

Noah kept walking, ignoring the jibe. But as he headed for the hub of the community, his mind was on Faith. He knew she wasn't using him. Same way as he wasn't using her. But as for there being any kind of future for them, as friends, or whatever else might be happening between them, Harden was right. If they continued down this road, there was no way the two communities would ever be able to exist peacefully alongside one another.

He hastened his steps, eager to get back. He hadn't been able to see Faith since he'd delivered her back to the girls' cave after the raid. There'd been too much to do, what with caring for the injured and dealing with the dead, plus keeping an eye out for Madeleine. And there were too many people watching him. He'd had Ruth and Ella keeping an eye on the girls for him, though. So far, at least, there'd been no change in their treatment.

Jacob was very aware there were those in the community who objected to his actions, and one way he had attempted to mend people's opinion of him was by ensuring the Danforth students were taken care of. He had barely allowed them out of their cave since the raid though. It had to be hard on them. His ma had promised to speak to Jacob about allowing them some limited exercise and time to bathe, today, and he was hoping, if she were successful, he might actually be able to have at least a brief conversation with Faith.

He headed to the medcave first, knowing his ma was more likely to be there than anywhere else. On the way, he noticed how quiet the tunnels were. Under normal circumstances, he would have expected to pass numerous citizens standing around chatting or exchanging smiles and greetings as they moved between shifts. But recent events had everyone running scared. Those people he did see nodded at him stiffly or hurried past with their heads down.

As Noah approached the medcave, he heard voices. At first, he didn't immediately recognise one of them.

"If they were watching her, she might well have gone underground." It was female, but not one he knew.

"Wouldn't she have let us know though?" This was his ma.

There was a pause. "Maybe she couldn't. If she really thought they were on to her, perhaps she couldn't risk it."

His ma was with Kemp, Faith's professor. Moving closer, Noah made sure his footsteps could be heard so they didn't think he was sneaking around listening to their conversation.

"Ma?" he called ahead.

"In here."

He drew the curtain back and entered the cave. Inside, it was more cramped than usual, due to several extra cots which had been hastily set up to accommodate the citizens injured in the attack. The majority of the beds were empty now. Three of the Eremus citizens hadn't survived their injuries, two bullet wounds and one man who'd been stabbed with a vicious-looking knife. They had joined the other four citizens who had been taken to the bomb site and burnt on a pyre, so as not to alert the Bellator authorities to their presence.

Most of the other patients had quickly recovered from what were just minor injuries, and had resumed their normal duties. At the moment, there was only one person remaining in the medcave, a friend of Ella's called Jack who had been shot in the shoulder. His ma had managed to remove the bullet and they were hoping he would recover, as long as the injury didn't become infected.

He was sleeping on the cot closest to the door. His ma and Kemp were on the far side of the space, packing up the extra cots for removal. Noah shot a quizzical glance at the newcomer, surprised to find the professor had been allowed out when the girls were not.

"I asked for extra assistance." His ma shrugged. "Told Jacob that Kemp here was medically trained. He allowed her to come and help me."

Noah turned his head to the professor. "I thought you taught history."

"It's *her*story actually," Kemp shot back. "And I do."

"And your medical training?"

She shrugged. "I have a little. All the Danforth teachers are first aid trained."

His ma tossed a blanket at her. "So she's not an expert. Jacob isn't to know that."

Kemp shook out the blanket and folded it, laying it neatly on the pile which lay on the cot in front of her. "See? I'm being very useful."

Noah smiled. He wasn't used to seeing this more lighthearted side to his ma. He liked it.

"Any sign of Madeleine?"

He shook his head, moving to strip the blankets from another of the cots. "Nope. Been down there for three hours. There's no sign of her."

His ma raised her eyebrows at Kemp. "Think the guards might still be watching the house?"

Kemp shrugged. "Perhaps. If Danforth thinks there's some kind of link between the attack and Madeleine, she won't give up."

"Would we know if there were guards in her place?" Noah shuddered. "I spent the last few hours imagining I could hear noises echoing down the tunnel to where I was sitting."

Kemp shook her head. "Not likely. Madeleine's a real expert with the Bellator tech. Her entire apartment is soundproofed, and she has it set up with some kind of buffer so Wi-Fi communication is only possible when she needs it to be."

"Huh?"

"What I mean is, whenever she leaves the house, she activates a kind of shield which scrambles all communication. It means location chips are useless, no one can be tracked inside the house, and no one can send any kind of electronic message from within her walls."

"I see." Noah wasn't sure he fully understood the set-up, but he could see how rendering all the Bellator guards' sophisticated tech useless would be a good thing. "But walkie talkies work, right?"

Kemp nodded. "Yeah. They use radio waves. Bellator stopped using that kind of communication device years ago. But it works in our favour."

"Along with the safety system." Anna added. "Those pebbles are pretty basic, but they do the trick."

Noah finished folding the blanket and placed it on the pile Kemp was creating. "How's Jack?" He jerked his head at Ella's friend. "I said I'd let Ella know."

"He's okay. No sign of infection yet." His ma shot her final patient a worried glance. "We're hoping a little rest will help him fight it off."

"That's good." Noah managed a smile. "Listen Ma, Harden took over from me this morning. He suggested Madeleine might've been captured by Danforth." The two women exchanged worried glances. "You think so too, right?"

"We don't know." Kemp shook her head. "It's possible."

"Harden said we'd be better off if she was dead." Noah shuddered. "You don't think she is, do you?"

"We hope not." Anna nodded at her friend. "Charlotte here thinks she might have gone underground."

"Down here? Wouldn't we know if she was in Eremus?"

His ma laughed. "Not literally underground. But... deeper undercover. She's always managed to maintain a more public profile in the past, but if Danforth's guards have suspicions about her, she may well have to hide herself away, leave the public stuff to someone else."

Kemp stepped forward. "The resistance has different levels of involvement. Some of the women live and work quite publicly within the city. Like me. We're the eyes and ears of the movement. But there are others who barely ever show their faces. People whose cover has been blown, or who have other skills, which are more suited to working at night, out of sight, let's just say."

"You think Madeleine's with them?"

"Perhaps. There are a few concealed hideouts. The main one is located beneath the Bellator Central Library. It's a museum now... filled with old books which most of the city's citizens access digitally. But the building is one of the oldest in the city. It has huge cellars which stretch the entire length of the structure, and it's run by members of the resistance who keep the underground area very private. Danforth is all about modernity. She doesn't concern herself with the city's history much, unless it fills the coffers or helps her to control the population." Kemp shrugged. "So it's the perfect place."

"Will she be angry with you?" Kemp stopped folding and looked at Noah, her eyes narrowed. "I mean... you left without her knowledge, right?"

"I did. But I think she has bigger things to worry about now than a single rogue member." Kemp picked up the pile of blankets and carried them towards the chest at the rear of the space. "Look, as I said, Madeleine is very experienced. We have to hope that... if she knew there was a risk... she got somewhere safe. And I think the library is the most logical place."

"Well, I hope she made it there then." Noah found himself suddenly desperate to get out of the medcave. "I'll get on and speak to Ella. If you don't need any more help?"

"We're good thanks." His ma nodded at Charlotte, who was closing the lid of the blanket box. "We can manage for now."

"Great." He waved a hand as he headed out the door. "I'll see you later then."

He headed for the canteen, finding it almost empty. Harriet gave him a small wave from a table in the corner, but on the opposite side of the space, a small group of citizens had abruptly stopped talking at his arrival. Moments later, they got up and hurried out of the communal room. Noah sighed. The recent mistrust which had invaded the usually solid community was difficult to deal with. Jacob certainly had a lot to answer for.

He was just helping himself to a slice of bread and some cheese when Ruth poked her head in.

"You're back." She was out of breath. "Best come now if you want to actually speak to Faith."

He was already walking towards the door. "They're coming out?"

"Jacob said we could take them down to bathe. But they won't be there for long. Ella's with them, and we managed to send Jacob's guard off on an errand, but they're almost done and he wants them straight back to the cave after that. If you're quick, you can help us walk them back."

It only took them a few minutes to reach the bathing cave. At the entrance, Noah halted. "I'd better wait here." He shot an awkward glance at the curtain across the opening. "Oh... would you let Ella know that I checked on Jack? Ma says he's doing okay." Ruth nodded and disappeared inside. The area was quiet at this time of day, a fact he was grateful for, feeling desperately awkward standing outside the entrance to the women's bathing area for no good reason. The silence in the tunnel meant he could catch odd noises coming from inside the cave itself. The sound of splashing water, occasional chattering, and bursts of laughter, but no individual words.

He imagined what a relief it must be for them to escape from their prison cell. To be able to get clean, after several days of sitting in a confined space, with only brief bathroom breaks and no way of washing other than the couple of bowls of water Ella had provided. He pictured Faith as she'd been in the lake alongside him, soaked to the skin and shivering. He'd circled his arms around her to keep her warm, enjoying the feeling of her body so close to his own.

Shaking his head to clear it, he straightened and moved a little further from the entrance, backing into a small alcove in the tunnel wall. The voices were louder now, and there was no more splashing water, so he assumed the girls were drying off before returning to their cave. They would be out soon.

Pressing his fingers to his forehead, he tried to clear his mind, decide on what he wanted to say to Faith in the limited time they would have. He knew he wanted to convey something to her. A sense of how important she was to him. How he longed to spend more time in her company. But also, how other members of his community were making that difficult at the moment.

Most of all, how she could trust him, no matter what.

Behind him, someone cleared their throat softly. "Noah?"

He turned. Faith stood in the cave entrance, a tentative smile on her face. She had dressed hurriedly, not taking the time to dry off, and her t-shirt clung to her skin. Her hair was still damp, and hung in tendrils around her face. She looked so vulnerable. For a moment, he was still, but then he closed the gap between them and grasped her hands.

"Hey. How are you?"

"I'm alright. We're alright. Better for," she gestured to her wet hair, "this."

"Yeah. Ma's been lobbying Jacob to let you out properly for days. I'm only sorry you can't get some exercise or join in with some of the shifts as well. But he…"

"I know. This is better than nothing, I guess." She glanced around, then met his gaze. "Everyone's been so jittery since the attack, what with Sophia gone, and Cath-rine…" her voice broke on the name and his heart went out to her. "Then, with everything Kemp told us, and finding out about Jacob's origins, well…" She looked up at him. "It's been a difficult few days."

"I'm glad that being let out, even for a while, is helping."

"It is." She managed a small smile. "And if it means I can see you again, well… that's an added bonus."

He blushed, and leaned closer. "For me too."

"Listen." She took a deep breath. "I wanted to tell you… Kemp told us that Danforth's testing the drug—the one she gave me—on the other girls at the academy."

"That's terrible." He squeezed her hands, knowing the gesture was useless. "I'm so sorry."

"B-but I can't–"

Noah heard the catch in her voice. "It's not your fault."

"But they're suffering…" she stammered, "that horrible reaction I had… they'll all be…"

Glancing both ways, Noah checked the tunnel was empty, then tugged at her hands, drawing her into the privacy of the recess in the stone wall. Once they were partly hidden from view, he pulled her to him, marvelling at how it seemed like the most natural thing in the world.

She gave in to the embrace, putting her arms around him and resting her head on his shoulder. "And now Sophia's there, too. Who knows what they're putting her through?" She tensed, and he could feel her hands close into fists behind his back. "What if they think she can tell them things?" Her voice was a whisper. "Things about me. Things about Eremus. What if they *hurt* her?"

He had no idea what to say. Tightening his hold on her, he hoped the embrace could somehow convey his regret. After a moment, he pressed his lips gently to the top of her head. She only grasped hold of him more tightly.

"Noah..." she was breathless, "I can't bear it. I can't bear to think of her... of all of them... back there... with no one to stand up for them..."

Holding on in the vain hope he could somehow soothe her, comfort her, he stroked a hand down her back. When she straightened, she was shaking. Tipping her head back, she met his gaze for a second. Her eyes were haunted, agonised.

"Noah, I–" She opened her mouth, then closed it, seeming to give up on words. Instead, she came up on to her tiptoes and pressed her urgent lips against his own.

CHAPTER THIRTY-TWO: FAITH

T he world was spinning. In reality, Faith was aware that, not three feet from where she and Noah stood, the other girls were dressing and preparing to leave the bathing cave and return to their cell. But for the moment, in the empty tunnel, she and Noah seemed miles away from the rest of them.

It had begun instinctively. A way to staunch the pain and panic which had threatened to overwhelm her ever since she'd realised Sophia was gone. She knew kissing Noah was pleasant. But the embrace they shared in the lake had gone beyond anything she had encountered before. Now she knew the strength of the sensation, something inside urged her to kiss him again, as though the action might numb the sick dread which consumed her.

Part of her thought Noah would stop it. That he would be the sensible one, aware of how it would look to a passing Eremus citizen, or to the girls in her own group, even, if the two of them were seen together. But he hadn't. After an initial pause which she thought came from surprise, he had responded with equal fervour. She wondered if he was trying to chase away demons too.

And as they stood, their bodies aligned, their lips locked together, their breath coming in gasps, it seemed like nothing could stop them. She was vaguely aware of Noah's hands tangled in her hair, smoothing it back from her face, stroking her cheek. She knew her own hands were fixed, one on his back, the other at his waist, as though she could meld his body to hers, make it impossible to tear them apart.

Because this might be the last time they saw one another.

The thought came to her suddenly, but she knew it was true. She'd spoken to Diane. They'd agreed. They both wanted to go back to the city, knew they couldn't simply stay in Eremus and await their fate. Not when Sophia and all the other girls' lives were at risk. If Kemp wouldn't help them, they'd find some other way.

On reflection, their determination to march right back to the academy seemed rash and immature. But it didn't mean their instinct was wrong. They just had to be more sensible about their return. Ask around, talk to those in Eremus whom they trusted. See what they could discover about secretive routes back into the city.

Knowing there was a resistance movement working against Danforth had given Faith hope. Surely, if she and Diane could find them, they could be persuaded to help. Without Kemp's guidance though, Faith wasn't sure how they were going to locate Madeleine and her associates.

But they were going back. No matter what.

She knew it was the right thing to do. But as the kiss deepened, she felt a little part of her begin to shatter. The idea of betraying the boy who'd been so kind, who'd rescued her on more than one occasion, cut deep. She pulled back suddenly.

His eyes flew open and he gazed at her in alarm. "What?" He glanced left and right. "It's alright. There's nobody here."

"No. I- I–" she broke off, sighing. "I don't know."

"I'm sorry..." he looked confused. "I didn't mean to–"

"It's not you." Faith sighed. "I just–"

"Are you worried about us being caught together?" Noah frowned. "Because you're right. I don't think it would go down well on either side." He took a step back, his face sad. "In fact, I can't think of a time when it would ever go down well."

"Me neither." She stepped in close to him again, clasping his hands in hers. "Don't you see? Unless things change, we can never be... together."

"Do you want to be together?" He was whispering.

"I don't know." She saw the flash of hurt in his eyes. "I don't mean I don't want to. I just mean I can't ever imagine a time when we could even... explore the possibility. Can you?" He shook his head. Feeling an overwhelming sense of sadness, she leaned her forehead against his. "I wish I could. But until things change..."

His eyes grew earnest. "Listen, I've been talking to my ma and Flynn. They still want to try and work towards a non-violent resolution to this. They're hoping we can somehow show Danforth that despite recent events, Eremus does want to come to a peaceful agreement. Now that Jacob's made his point, they're hoping to persuade him to be less provocative."

Faith raised her head to look at him. "You think he'll listen?"

"I don't know." He clasped her hands closer. But it's worth a try, don't you think?"

"Maybe." They fell silent for a moment. "You know Kemp's part of the resistance, right?"

He cocked his head. "Yeah. Jacob checked her story out with Madeleine... our contact. She's helped us a lot, in the past. With the raids and so on. Getting us access to places where we might source food or meds, that kind of thing. She confirmed that Kemp's part of the wider network. Some kind of plant at the academy. A spy, I suppose."

"Do you know what the resistance *does*?" Faith worked to keep her tone casual.

"I guess they disagree with the way Danforth runs things. And try to... protect people who fall foul of her?" Noah frowned. "Why are you so interested?"

Faith considered how much to tell him. Diane had made her promise not to give away their intention to leave, to anyone, but especially not to Noah. She knew he'd be against it. His protectiveness sent another wave of sadness through her. And guilt. If she left without telling him, he'd be devastated. If she tried to explain it to him, he would do everything in his power to stop her.

But leaving Sophia and the others to fend for themselves was not something she could live with. If she was the key to Danforth's plan, she had to do what she could to stop it. Here in the woods, she was powerless. In the city, Faith hoped she could gain a better understanding of what was going on. She didn't want Danforth to have control over her. Yet she didn't want Jacob to have that power either.

She decided on a version of the truth. "I just wondered... if the resistance is so determined to bring Danforth down, and that's what Eremus ultimately wants as well, then..." She trailed off, allowing Noah to come to his own conclusion.

"You mean the two groups might... help each other? If we have a common goal?"

"Maybe." Faith shrugged. "I don't know enough about it. But the resistance already helps you to gather resources... they're on your side, I mean. Wouldn't it be worth seeing if they'd be willing to help in your fight for equality too?"

"I guess it wouldn't hurt to ask." Noah looked thoughtful. "But we're having trouble communicating with Madeleine at the moment. She's... well, last thing we heard, she was worried that she was being watched. My ma was just saying how it's happened before. She usually just lays low for a while. But if her cover's been broken, well... she might be forced to go into hiding."

"Hiding?" Faith leaned forward. In the distance, the girls sounded like they were ready to leave. She had to keep Noah talking, and quickly, if she wanted to learn more about the resistance's hiding place. Her heart beat faster as she waited for him to continue.

"Apparently there's some kind of central underground base... beneath the library in Bellator. Do you know it?"

"The library?" Faith tried not to look too interested. "You mean the museum?"

"Yeah. She said it was some kind of exhibition now... guess you don't read physical books so much these days."

"No. Mostly things are digital." She risked another glance at the bathing cave entrance. So far, it remained empty. *"Beneath* it, you said?"

Noah nodded. "It has cellars. I guess the building is pretty old. And it's overseen by resistance folks. They do their best to keep Danforth in the dark. Seems like she's not too interested in an old building filled with dusty books."

"Nope. She's all about modern tech." Faith rolled her eyes. "And you think Madeleine, might have gone there?"

"It seems as likely a place as any. But she might have to stay there, permanently, which leaves our connection with the city fairly weak. For now, at least."

Faith tried to look sympathetic. "I guess so."

"So, if we were thinking of speaking to the resistance about our efforts to gain equality and rights..." he trailed off momentarily, "...well, it might take some time to set up our connection again."

"It's worth a thought though, right?" She hated herself for giving him false hope, but couldn't stand the look of desolation on his face.

He smiled. "Definitely."

From further down the tunnel, Ruth's voice echoed. "Ready, ladies?"

"That's a warning for our benefit." Noah gestured towards the sound. "I'm sorry we don't have longer."

"It's fine." Shaking her head, Faith leaned forward once again. This time, she grasped Noah's face with both hands and pulled him towards her. Planting a light kiss on his lips, she closed her eyes and told herself it would not be the last one they shared. When she backed away and met his serious gaze, though, her heart ached. "You'd better go, hadn't you? Can't let them see you."

"S'pose so." Reluctantly, he took a step back. "Before I do..." he trailed off awkwardly.

"What is it?"

His hand went to his pocket, drawing something out of it. He stared at the ground for a moment, then raised his gaze to hers. "Look, I need to apologise."

He held out his hand, the palm open. On it, lay a Danforth Academy pendant.

"This is mine." She reached for it, turning it over with a smile. "See this scratch, here? It got stuck down the side of my bed once. As I pulled it out, it scraped against the leg." She looked up at him. "I lost it when I was..."

"In the medical storage room." Noah blushed, but kept his gaze on hers. "You dropped it. I picked it up. I should've given it back straight away, but..."

Faith found herself smiling. "You took it? Why?"

He shuffled his feet. "I'm not sure. I guess, out of curiosity, at first. Then, because it reminded me of you. I've thought about giving it back so many times, but..."

"...you thought I'd be angry?"

He nodded. "So I'm sorry. I didn't want to keep this from you. Not anymore. I wanted to be honest."

At his words, Faith felt a stab of guilt. Taking his clenched fists into her hands, she replaced the necklace in his palm. "You keep it."

She thought he shivered slightly at her touch. "You're sure?"

Words deserted her, so she just nodded.

"Thanks!" Her heart almost broke at his appreciative smile. "You know, I'll come and see you, whenever I can. Ruth will help us. I'm past caring about what people think."

"I'm glad. Hopefully it won't be so long between visits, next time." She had to force out the words.

"It'd better not be." He winked, and she felt like a tiny sliver of glass was slicing into her heart. "Now I'd better go, before they come out here looking for you."

He jogged away down the tunnel. Attempting to banish the guilt, she edged back to the bathing cave entrance. Inside, Ruth and Ella were calling out to the others to make sure they had everything with them before they left. Avery was fussing about her hair still being wet, so slipping back in without being noticed wasn't too tricky.

On the journey back to the cave, she fell into step beside Diane, making sure she slowed her pace. Diane picked up on the cue, and soon they were several feet behind most of the others. The only people behind them were Ella and Helen, who were bringing up the rear of the group and were deep in conversation.

Since Helen's frightening midnight experience in the woods with Jacob and Paulo, she had been extremely withdrawn. These days, Ella seemed to be the only one who could make her smile. Noticing that they were holding hands as they walked along, Faith shot Diane a questioning glance.

"They've been inseparable all morning." Diane kept her eyes forward and her voice low. "I don't think we need to be concerned about them listening. They're too wrapped up in spending every moment they can with one another."

Faith looked at them more closely, her eyes widening. "Are they–?"

"Together?" Diane looked amused. "I think they would be, given the chance. Not that Eremus would encourage any kind of relationship between our two communities. But you know all about that, don't you?"

Faith jerked her gaze forwards once again, feeling like she was intruding on a private moment.

Diane leaned closer. "Everything alright? You manage to see Noah alone?"

Faith felt a blush rise up her cheek. "Yeah. Thanks."

The older girl rolled her eyes. "He have anything interesting to say?"

"Actually, yes." Pushing away the sense of betrayal, she filled her friend in. "He told me their contact in the resistance movement... she's gone missing."

Diane turned to her. "That doesn't sound like *good* news."

"No, listen. It *is*. Noah said, if she hasn't been captured by Danforth..." she held up a hand at Diane's horrified expression, "... which they don't think she has... that she might well have joined some others who have an underground base in the city."

"That's more like it. Where?"

"In the cellars under the old library."

Diane tensed, but kept walking. "So, we have somewhere to head for now."

"Yes. The problem will be getting out of here. Between Jacob's paranoia over losing his prize assets, and Noah and Ella's concern for us–"

Diane snorted. "Concern for you and Helen, you mean."

"Whatever." Faith narrowed her eyes at her friend. "Anyway, they're watching us like hawks."

"One thing at a time, though." Diane looked thoughtful. "They let us out to bathe, at least. If it becomes more regular, we can try and time an escape... look at when they're guarding us less... know our way out. It's possible."

"Noah said..." Faith swallowed hard, feeling like she was betraying him, "Anna and Flynn are trying to get us more freedom... to bathe, to exercise, and so on."

"That's great. So we just have to bide our time. Be sensible about it."

Faith thought of Sophia and pulled in a deep breath. "Diane... what if we don't *have* time?"

Her friend's expression was grim. "We'll just have to hope Danforth's not in too much of a hurry. It'll take some time to test the drugs properly." In a rare show of understanding, she patted Faith's shoulder awkwardly. "At least we know it's not killing them anymore. That's something."

"I suppose." Faith thought of Serene and felt a stab of guilt. Diane had already lost her best friend. "Okay. So, we wait. We watch and learn. And when they let their guard down... when we can see that they're allowing us more freedom... we take our chance?"

"That's right. In the meantime... we gather even more information about the layout of the tunnels, their exits, the routes back into the city. It won't be time wasted, I promise." Diane shot a look over her shoulder. "I think we should start with Ella. She's older. More in tune with the council. And definitely," she jerked her head towards Helen, "on our side. Let's see what we can find out about–"

"Find out about what?" Faith looked up to find Avery hovering just a little way ahead of them. Her face was unreadable.

"We were just talking about whether Jacob might allow us to be assigned to some shifts again." Faith had to admire Diane's quick thinking.

"That's hardly likely."

Avery's tone was scathing, but Faith thought she looked a little disappointed that she hadn't caught them plotting something scandalous. They would certainly have to be careful where they discussed their escape plans over the next few days.

As Diane dropped back to start a conversation with Ella and Helen, Faith marvelled at her calm. Within seconds, she'd engaged the other girls in what appeared to be a casual conversation about the potential for future shifts. Ella responded with her usual friendliness, and Faith could see how quickly Diane put her at ease. Avery stomped along beside Faith, but said no more.

She'd been right. Their plan was a good one, considered, and cautious. But she couldn't stop her heart from hammering against her chest as she thought about them racing through the forest in the darkness in the dead of night. Heading for Bellator, the very place she'd wanted to flee in the first place, with no more than a vague destination in mind.

Heading away from Eremus. And Noah.

CHAPTER THIRTY-THREE: NOAH

At dinner that night, Noah found he couldn't follow the conversation. Something had unsettled him, ever since his conversation with Faith, and he couldn't shake it off. Her kisses, while very welcome, had been unpredictable, more fervent, desperate, even. And something about their conversation had seemed off.

There had been an undertone of something... an air of urgency about Faith's questions which had set him on edge. He'd been on the verge of asking her about it when Ruth had given the signal and he'd had to go. But he hadn't been able to focus on anything else since.

"...and I'm so tired of–" Ruth broke off and jabbed a sharp finger into his arm. "Hey! What's with you tonight?"

Noah turned to his friend. "Huh?"

"You're miles away. You haven't listened to a word I've said."

"Sorry." He turned to give Ruth his full attention. "What were you saying?"

"I was *saying* I'm sick of the uncomfortable atmosphere down here."

"Me too." Ella spoke from across the table. "On shift in the canteen this morning I barely exchanged ten words with Cora. We've known these people all our lives and suddenly it's like–" she broke off, her voice pained.

"Things'll get better." Ruth reached over and squeezed her sister's hand. "They have to."

"I hope so."

"It's just–" Noah strained to hear his friend as she lowered her voice. "No one knows what's going to happen next. People are frightened to express an opinion in case it gets back to the wrong person."

"Well, I hope something changes soon." Ella stood up, sighing as she picked up her empty plate. "Be ready to leave in a minute, okay?"

"Leave?" Noah asked, as Ella walked away.

Ruth glanced around, checking no one was listening before she responded. "Your ma managed to talk Jacob into letting the Danforth girls out for some exercise tonight."

"Really?" Noah perked up. "That's great."

Ruth rolled her eyes. "Thought you'd be more interested in that topic." Her face sobered. "Be careful won't you, Noah?"

His eyes narrowed at her tone. "Careful?"

"I'm sorry, but I can't see any situation where you and Faith could–"

He cut her off. "You don't think I know that? We were having the same conversation in the tunnel today."

Ruth's eyes widened. "You were?"

"Yeah. We were." He sighed. "I'd like to think that someday we might... but unless Ma and Flynn can change Jacob's attitude, it's useless."

"Well getting him to agree to let them out more is... a start, at least."

"Maybe." Noah gazed around the canteen gloomily. "But allowing them short periods of time each day to bathe and exercise is a far cry from allowing them to have proper control over their lives… or letting them go free."

"Would you want her to have that choice?"

"Of course." His gaze jerked back to Ruth's. "Why wouldn't I?"

His friend's tone was gentle. "Because she might choose to return to Bellator."

He stiffened. "I doubt it."

"What do you imagine would happen?" Ruth shifted closer, dropping her voice lower. "Jacob would give her the choice to remain here as an Eremus citizen and she'd just… decide to stay?"

"Why not?" Noah had to fight to keep his tone even. "Look at how they treated her."

"You're right. She probably wouldn't want to go back to that." His friend placed a hand on his arm. "But she's used to a *very* different kind of life. How do you know she'd be willing to give all that up to stay here with you?" Though he knew she meant well, Noah found his best friend's words hard to listen to. "You hardly know her."

"I know her well enough. I know that…" He sucked in a deep breath, not wanting to show how much this mattered to him, even to the person who knew him best. "I know she's not shallow. She doesn't need all that luxury. That's not what matters to her."

"True." Ruth nodded, her eyes kind. "And I know that's what you… like about her. But her goodness is what will take her back to Bellator." She held up a finger to stop his protest. "Her best friend has been taken back there against her will. Would you stand by and do nothing if *I* was in the same situation?" She held his gaze for a moment, watching the emotions flood across his face. "I thought not."

"You really think she wants to go *back*?"

Ruth shrugged. "I don't know. Maybe not yet. But I know I couldn't live with myself if something bad happened to you and I hadn't done everything I could to stop it." She picked up her plate and stood. Ella was gesturing to her from the other side of the canteen. "Sorry, I gotta go. Your ma's agreement with Jacob was tentative at best, so we'd better get down there. If he changes his mind..." She threw her hands up in frustration.

Noah nodded. At the moment, there was no predicting what their leader might do. He stood up to follow his friend, but she held out a hand to stop him. "Look, I'm happy to help you see her, but don't get greedy. If we do this more than once a day, people will get suspicious. We can try to arrange for you to see her again tomorrow."

Nodding reluctantly, Noah settled back down and watched the sisters leave. Ruth was right, he risked being watched even more closely if he tried to see Faith so often. Better to play it safe. But the nagging feeling that something was wrong refused to leave him.

Unable to settle, he finished his meal quickly. He would go home and speak to Flynn. Perhaps he would have more recent news from Bellator. Anything to shake off his agitation. Threading his way through the tables in the canteen, he cleared away his dishes and headed for home.

Flynn had made quick work of eating that evening and headed home for some much-needed rest after a long shift in the tunnels. If Noah was quick, he could catch him before he went to bed.

But when he reached the cave, it was empty. His ma was probably still at the medcave, but Flynn's absence was more puzzling. He was about to head out again to look for him when he heard footsteps coming up the tunnel. Seconds later, Paulo poked his head in, a look of alarm on his face.

"Need Flynn." He was out of breath. "He here?"

Noah shook his head. "Said he was coming back here to go to bed after dinner, but there's no sign of him. No idea where he is."

"Dammit!"

"What's up?"

Ignoring him, Paulo picked up his walkie talkie. "He's not here."

After a brief crackling, Jacob's voice emanated from the small black box. "Don't panic. Keep trying to contact Dane. Head for the Bellator tunnel. We'll meet you there."

"Got it. Over and out." Without another word, Paulo turned to leave.

"Paulo!" Alarmed, Noah hurried out into the tunnel after him. "Hey Paulo, wait up!"

His brother barely slowed his step. "Emergency, Noah. Can't stop."

"What's going on?"

"Walk with me, if you have to."

Racing to catch up, Noah tried to match his brother's pace. As they delved deeper into the tunnel complex, Paulo brought the walkie talkie to his lips once again.

"Dane! Come in, Dane! Dane?" His face twisted in panic.

"What's the matter?"

Paulo turned to him. "He reported a possible breach not long ago."

"A breach!" Noah's heart began to race. A breach meant there were intruders *inside* the cave system. In all the years they'd been living down here, there had never been a breach. "Where?"

But the walkie talkie had buzzed to life again. "Found Flynn." Jacob barked. "He's heading for training and storage... will grab some extra weapons. We've activated lockdown. The raiders are being mobilised as we speak."

Paulo raised the device to his lips again. "I'm heading for the Bellator tunnel entrance right now. Should get there fairly fast."

"On the way, but..." Jacob's voice crackled in reply, "...probably get there first... converge at the entrance... set up a defensive barrier. Don't go ahead alone, alright?"

"Roger that."

"Over and out."

Paulo repeated the words, then hooked the walkie talkie onto his belt. Not slowing his pace, he continued his explanation. "Dane was on duty at the tunnel leading to Madeleine's. Reported some kind of disturbance around fifteen minutes ago. He was going to investigate. Now none of us can get hold of him."

Noah took in his brother's words. If the disturbance was from Madeleine's end, it meant they hadn't been breached from the woods. But it also suggested Madeleine had been right—the guards *had* been watching her. And if they'd found their way into the tunnels from her house, the entire Eremus population was at risk.

"We have to hurry." Paulo picked up the pace, beginning to run. "Do you have a weapon?"

Noah's heart sank. "A knife. That's all."

Paulo paused momentarily, slipping the pack from his back. Lowering it to the ground, he made quick work of opening it. Inside, Noah could see a number of smaller handguns.

"Why do you–?"

"A few of us have been carrying extra since the attack. Flynn's idea. And just people he trusts." Noah doubted that included Jacob anymore. "It was just a precaution." Paulo shrugged. "But right now, it's looking like it was a sensible move." He slid one of the guns out and handed it to Noah. "You know how to use this. Remember I showed you?"

Taking it from him, Noah nodded.

"Bullets." Paulo pressed them into his hand. "Load it as we move, okay?" Paulo reshouldered the pack, squinting at Noah closely. "Are you sure you want to come? You could be useful up here... help with the evacuation."

"No. I'm a raider."

"Alright." Paulo shook his head. "Stay behind me then. I only hope Anna forgives me for bringing you along."

Remembering the last time his brother had sneaked him out to Bellator, Noah shuddered. "A lot's changed since then. This time, you might really need me."

"Won't argue with that." Paulo called over his shoulder as he started running again. "We need every raider we can muster."

With shaking hands, Noah loaded the gun and followed his brother, slipping the remaining bullets into his pocket. Now they were armed and knew their destination, there was no hesitation.

Paulo was fitter and faster, but adrenaline lent Noah speed, and they reached the point where the tunnel forked in record time. Ahead of them was the tunnel leading to Bellator. So far, they were the only ones there. Paulo shot a nervous glance up the tunnel, listening intently. They could hear nothing.

He raised the walkie talkie once more. "Dane. Come in, Dane. What's your status?"

But aside from a hissing sound, there was no response. After a few moments, Paulo took a deep breath. "Better get this barricade set up while we wait."

One of their defensive manoeuvres was to erect barriers using large sections of wood which they stored at key junctions in the tunnels. Noah had been involved in practice runs of this many times, so he knew where the barriers were located, but he'd never had to do it under such stressful conditions with only two people.

Together, he and Paulo dragged out the wooden slabs and wedged them in place across the tunnel entrance. They had almost finished when support began to arrive. Jan hurried from one direction, backed by three of the other older raiders, Noah's neighbour, Dan, Denton, and Beth, who set immediately to helping them.

Moments later, Harden, Sil, and two others, Mick and Harriet, arrived, from the direction of the canteen. Together, they made short work of completing the barrier. When they were done, the entire tunnel was blocked off aside from a small gap which allowed a single raider to slip through at a time.

Noah watched Paulo do a head count. There were ten of them. A decent number, but if there were thirty well-armed guards in the tunnel, they'd be quickly overcome. Noah knew they should wait for back up, but the closer the threat got to Eremus, the more at risk their entire community was.

Paulo conferred with Jan, the only other council member present. Their voices were low and urgent. When they were done, Jan raised her walkie talkie.

"Come in, Jacob." When the leader had replied, she went on. "We have ten raiders at the Bellator tunnel junction and feel we shouldn't wait to investigate the threat further. We'll leave four citizens at the barricade to protect Eremus. The rest of us will proceed towards Madeleine's with caution. Please send more raiders ahead as back up when they arrive."

"Will do." Jacob's reply was instant. "We're only a few minutes away now."

Noah was shaking as Jan and Paulo talked again, their eyes ranging over the group. There was a heated debate for a few seconds, but eventually, Paulo turned to them.

"Okay. Denton, Beth, Sil, Harden: stay here and maintain the barricade."

Harden opened his mouth to argue, but seeing Paulo's face, thought better of it. Positioning himself behind the wooden barrier alongside the others, he readied his gun.

It was clear to Noah that Paulo and Jan had only selected people they trusted to proceed along the tunnel. People with no affiliation to Jacob. And he was willing to bet that his ma's friend Beth had been left behind to keep an eye on the others. Noah swallowed hard. He was grateful his brother had faith in him, but wondered what might lie ahead for those leading the frontline of the mission.

"The rest of us will head onwards down the tunnel. We'll use stealth, try not to alert anyone to our presence. Turn off your walkie talkies." Paulo demonstrated with his own. "Don't want them to give us away." He looked back at the group who were staying behind. "As long as it's safe to do so, we'll radio back more details on our position."

"Any questions?" Jan paused for a second. When there was no reply, she continued. "Alright then. We'll be off. See you on the other side."

The remaining raiders slipped through the gap in the barrier and continued towards Madeleine's. Without discussion, they knew to move silently, hugging the edges of the passageway. Their advantage lay in their awareness of the tunnel system's layout and their experience with the darkness and the rough ground beneath their feet. It was what set them apart from the Bellator guards, who would be unfamiliar with the underground terrain. Noah hoped it would give them the upper hand.

He remembered another journey along this section, after the kidnapping of the Eremus girls. Half-carrying Faith, he and Ruth had staggered towards home, terrified by what had happened and relieved they'd escaped. Right now, he was heading back into the dragon's lair, his stomach churning, his legs trembling. But if Eremus was at risk, he would go.

The tunnel seemed to go on forever. A flashlight was too much of a risk, so they felt their way along slowly in the darkness. As they got closer there was no sign of disruption, and Noah found himself daring to hope that Dane's walkie talkie had simply run out of batteries, or that he'd dropped and broken it. That they would find themselves at Madeleine's door without encountering a threat.

But as they approached the bend in the tunnel that led to the final stretch before Madeleine's house, Jan held out a hand to stop them. Faintly, somewhere ahead of them, was the sound of multiple footsteps. Multiple voices.

From out of the darkness, Noah felt a hand clutch his arm. He almost cried out, but when he felt Paulo's hand over his mouth, he closed it and listened.

"We'll hide." His brother's voice was no more than a breath against his ear. "Just before the pass. You know it?"

Noah nodded, knowing his brother would feel the movement. A little further along the tunnel, there was a narrow section where rocks jutted in from either side, making it difficult for more than two people to walk abreast. From this position, as long as there weren't too many of them, the raiders would be able to deal with the guards a couple at a time.

"Duck behind the rocks. Three left, three right." Paulo continued to murmur orders. "Wait for them to come to us. Have your gun loaded and ready. Got it?"

"Got it." Noah whispered. He was about to ask a clarifying question when he realised his brother was gone. All around him, he heard the same whispered instructions, until a low hiss signified they were moving ahead.

He followed the others, his steps unsteady as they crept forward. It wasn't far, but the closer they got, the more aware of the approaching footsteps they became. Finally, they reached the pass without issue, following Paulo's instructions and concealing themselves behind the rocky outcroppings on either side of the tunnel.

Noah found himself crouching against the wall, with Mick in front of him, and Jan taking the lead and closest to the enemy. On the other side, Paulo headed the group, Dan and Harriet at his back. They'd easily go unnoticed until the intruders were close enough to attack.

They were ready. Noah leaned back against the wall and checked once again that his gun was loaded. Holding it ready at his side, he fingered the additional ammunition in his pocket. It was a good plan. Let the enemy come to them. Surprise them at the final moment.

But how many guards were there? Would six raiders be enough to hold them off? Would his shaking hands even be able to pull the trigger when he was close enough to look his enemy in the eye? If there were large numbers of guards, he could only pray that Jacob arrived with back up before it was too late.

Wiping his sweat-soaked hands on his t-shirt, he tried to remember to breathe in and out as they awaited the arrival of the enemy.

Chapter Thirty-Four: Faith

The girls had been taken to one of the lower caves in the Eremus settlement. Faith wondered if it was where the raiders trained. It was deserted, and spacious enough to allow the girls to exercise. While it wasn't much, Faith was hopeful it was the start of a more lenient routine. Only when Jacob permitted them more freedom could she and Diane work out a way to escape.

Diane had been right: the conversation with Ella had been useful. Without much encouragement, the older girl had confided the locations of various key places in the settlement. Faith had discovered the way she and Noah had re-entered the caves on the day of the attack was to the north of Eremus. Of all the well-concealed entrances, this one would be easiest, as it would lead them in the direction of Bellator. If they could find it again.

Their other option was the route underground through the tunnels, where they'd originally been brought in. But since they'd been unconscious, and had no memory of the route, neither of them felt that was sensible. They'd be more likely to get lost, trip, or injure themselves. And if no one knew their location, it was a dangerous prospect.

She envied Kemp, who was permitted to help Anna most days and seemed, on the surface at least, to be allowed far more freedom than the girls. It was the reason she wasn't with them now. Faith knew the trust was linked to her role in the resistance. If she was an associate of Madeleine's, then Jacob counted her as being on his side. She and Diane hadn't shared this information with the rest of the group. With Sophia and Catherine gone, the girls had been extremely shaken up, and neither Faith nor Diane fully trusted Avery.

Tonight, they were guarded by three Eremus citizens. Ella and Ruth, who were welcome companions, and Carl, a man who Faith presumed was Jacob's ally, since both sides seemed to be keeping a close eye on their whereabouts. Carl had agreed to stand guard outside the door, while Ruth and Ella remained inside the cave with the girls.

After several minutes of yoga stretches, which, to Faith's alarm, she'd struggled to remember, she had begun jogging in a small circuit around the cave. She had just stopped for a water break when Carl entered. His eyes went to Ella first, and he scowled. She was sitting where she had been since their arrival, chatting with Helen at the far end of the space.

Spotting his expression, Ruth hurried over and intercepted. Though Faith couldn't hear their exchange, she saw Ruth's face drain of colour.

"Ella!" Though her voice wasn't loud, its tone was shrill.

The entire room went silent. Ella was on her feet in seconds, crossing the cave to join her sister. There was a terse exchange between the three Eremus citizens, their heads bent close, their expressions grim.

"What's going on there?" Diane's voice startled Faith.

"Something's wrong." With a feeling of foreboding, Faith offered the bottle of water to her friend.

Diane took a swig and passed it back. "I wonder if it's something we might take advantage of."

"What?"

"Trouble for them might be good for us." She gave a deliberate nod. "They might be less... attentive."

Not knowing whether to feel hopeful or terrified, Faith continued to watch the trio as they talked. When they broke apart, she waited anxiously to see what they would do next. Nodding at Ella, Ruth headed out the door. With a grim expression, Ella turned to speak to the Danforth girls. Behind her, Carl was stone-faced.

"Listen... sorry to cut this short, but something's come up." She shot a nervous glance over her shoulder at Jacob's guard, and Faith wondered if she felt less secure now that her sister was gone. "We need to take you back to the cave. In fact," she frowned, "we may need to take you elsewhere."

"Elsewhere?" Helen chewed her lip. "Why?"

"There's a... a situation." Ella was considering her words carefully. Faith had never seen her so tense. "We have them, from time to time. It just means we need to go into a kind of stealth mode."

"What do you mean a *stealth* mode?" Avery hissed, her tone accusatory.

"Kind of... like a lock down?" Ella tried. "If we think there's a risk of intrusion or... attack, we have places where we conceal ourselves. To ensure we're not found."

"We're under *attack*?" Mary looked horrified.

"We might well be." Carl spoke over his shoulder as he crossed the cave to one of the large wooden chests which were arranged around the edge of the cave.

"Well, we're not sure what's happening yet." Glaring at him, Ella laid a hand on Mary's arm. "This is just a precaution."

Faith thought of Noah. "You mean the entire community hides?"

"Most of us." Ella hurried around, collecting up odd belongings from the benches. "The raiders go elsewhere, to protect us. Same way the Bellator guards would protect you back home."

"That's where Ruth's gone, right?" Diane surmised.

"Yes." Ella glanced at the door again. "So, I'd appreciate it if you guys could follow us, and..." she glanced at Carl, who had hauled open the lid of the chest, "...trust that we'll take you somewhere safe." She glanced around at them, one by one. "Alright?"

They nodded and hurried to line up at the entrance to the cave. Faith watched, as Ella joined Carl. She leaned down to grasp something from inside. When her hand emerged, it was holding a gun.

Diane walked across to her. "Want me to take one of those, too?"

Scowling, Carl lifted out a second weapon, larger than the one Ella held. "Not likely."

"No, thanks." Ella was more polite. "Jacob would kill us if we armed you."

Reaching back inside the chest, she took out a second gun. Fastening one to her belt, she held the other in her hand and reached inside the chest once more. This time, she brought out a canister Faith recognised as the spray the raiders had used on them during their kidnapping. Noting their horrified expressions, Ella shook her head.

"It's just a precaution. For defensive purposes, that's all." After Carl had armed himself with a second gun and a knife, he closed the lid of the trunk. As he straightened, the walkie talkie on Ella's belt blared.

"Ella? Carl? Come in!"

Holstering her second weapon, Ella raised the device. "Jacob?"

"Are you within earshot of the captives?"

"Yes."

"...you and Carl... outside for a moment?... Need to speak with you."

Ella glanced at the cave's single exit. "Just a second." She turned to them. "Stay here. We'll be just outside the door. Won't be long."

"Go ahead, Jacob." Jerking her head at Carl, she stepped outside, holding the device to her lips again. "We're outside now..."

With a glare at the girls, Carl followed her, a gun still grasped in his hand. As her voice faded into the background, the girls stared at one another.

"Well, this is... interesting," Avery muttered.

Mary was shivering. "What's happening?"

Again, it was Helen who stepped across to comfort her. "I'm not sure. But we're with Ella, and we trust her, don't we?"

Avery let out a hollow laugh. "Well, we all know *you* do."

Helen ignored the jibe, focusing on the younger girl at her side. "Let's give her a minute. She'll work out what's happening and come back for us."

"What if it's a rescue?" Avery let the thought hang in the air. "What if Danforth's sending her guards to get us out of here?"

"After what we've learned over the past few days, are you still so desperate to go back?" For once, Farrah sounded annoyed with her friend.

"Well, I don't much want to stay *here*." Avery frowned. "If it's a rescue, then we should..." she cast a desperate glance around the cave, "I don't know, try to get to the guards. Let them know where we are."

"That's far too risky." Helen seemed to have found some courage. "How would the guards *know* we're from Bellator? We're not in uniform anymore."

"She's right." Diane added. "They might just shoot first, ask questions later."

Mary's eyes widened and began to fill with tears. Instantly, Helen pulled her into a hug. "Don't worry. That's what Ella's gone to work out. She won't let them hurt us."

"Danforth wouldn't risk our lives like that," Avery said, but her voice was hollow. Sensing she had no support, she lapsed into silence.

"I hate to admit it," Diane whispered to Faith as the others continued to speculate. "But Avery might have something."

"What?" Faith fought to keep her expression neutral. "You think we should try and find the Bellator guards and let them march us right back to Danforth?"

"No." Diane rolled her eyes. "But this might be a good chance to get back to Bellator. If we're only being guarded by a couple of Eremus citizens, and we're on the move..." she let the thought dangle, "... if they take us somewhere we're even a little familiar with, perhaps we could get away from them, get out of the tunnels and into the woods? Then we could hide... 'til we're sure it's safe. Head for the city once we're sure there's no threat."

"Right now?" Faith stared at her. Perhaps if it had just been Ella, they might have managed to dupe her somehow, but Carl was definitely Jacob's man. He'd be much harder to fool. "You want us to go *tonight*?"

"Maybe." The older girl shrugged. "I mean, we said we'd watch and wait... take the opportunity when it came along. This might be it."

Faith was still considering her reply when Ella returned. If anything, she looked even more concerned.

"Alright." She waved her hand towards the door. "Let's go. Carl's waiting outside."

"But where are we going?" Mary whimpered.

"Don't worry." Ella hushed her. "I'm taking you somewhere safe."

Obediently, the girls hurried towards the door. Carl took the lead, and Ella brought up the rear of the line. At first, the tunnels they walked through were empty, but as they got closer to the centre of the cave complex, they passed several Eremus citizens. They were all in a hurry, gathering belongings and supplies, arming themselves with weapons, shushing younger children.

"Are they all going to hide somewhere?" Diane asked, staring at a small group which, like all the others they'd seen, scuttled past in the opposite direction. "Shouldn't we be going with them?"

Ella looked uncomfortable. "Jacob has somewhere else in mind for you."

"What about Professor Kemp?" Diane asked.

"She'll stay with Anna." Ella caught Faith's look of concern. "Don't worry – she'll be kept safe."

Faith leaned close to Diane, dropping her voice to a whisper. "We're his prisoners. He wants to keep us isolated. He won't want us sheltering with the rest of his community."

Diane clicked her tongue in disgust. "Not even in an emergency?"

They had hung back on purpose, ensuring they remained at the rear of the group with Ella, who would definitely be the easier guard to escape. Faith felt a stab of guilt at taking advantage of her trusting nature.

She wasn't sure what Diane's plan was. They didn't know the tunnel system well enough to simply break off and make a run for it, especially not when there was a potential enemy lurking somewhere in the darkness. For now, it made sense to stay with the group and keep their eyes open for an opportunity.

Faith's thoughts turned to Noah. He was a raider, like Ruth, so he'd be positioned closer to the threat, and not racing to hide. But that didn't stop her from looking for him. Was he in danger? Might he be concerned about her? Shaking her head, she tried to clear it. It was pointless to worry about Noah. She could do nothing to help him. But her thoughts kept straying to him, no matter how hard she tried to focus on their own situation.

The air around them grew cooler as they travelled, and Faith thought she recognised a few of the twists in the tunnel. When she'd first come down here, she'd thought one rock wall looked much like another. But more recently, she had been paying attention to her surroundings, and certain areas of the tunnels had begun to be more familiar.

As they rounded a bend, Faith heard noises ahead. Not gunfire, as she'd feared, nor explosions, but more subtle sounds. The wind in the trees, birdcalls, perhaps a rustling of creatures on the woodland floor. Suddenly, it hit her. They were heading *out* of the caves.

But why? Ella was clearly following instructions to take them somewhere away from the rest of the Eremus community. Faith had assumed it was for their own protection, or at least to keep Jacob's prized prisoners away from the Bellator guards. But what if he was actually taking them straight to Danforth? What if they were an *offering*? Part of some kind of exchange?

She grasped Diane's arm, stopping her in her tracks. The other girl stared at her in alarm and behind them, Ella gasped. Before Faith could voice her fears, Carl stopped the group from the front. He nodded to Ella, more comfortable with her doing the talking.

"Alright." Ella walked a little further forward down the line. "We're heading *outside*. Don't be frightened. We're trying to protect you. If the guards manage to break in, Jacob wants you all as far away from here as possible. There's no way he wants Danforth getting her hands on you."

The group was silent, all eyes fixed on Ella. Some were trusting, others suspicious. But no one argued.

"We're taking you to a cottage we sometimes use for shelter and storage during Bellator raids." Faith tensed at her words. "We're going to move through the forest together. Slowly and safely, making as little noise as possible. It's quite a long walk, but there's no reason to think the threat is out here. As long as we take it steady, we should be there in an hour or so. The cottage has sufficient provisions for us all, and we can stay there, out of sight, until the danger has passed. Okay?"

The group nodded. At the front, Carl moved off again. As he disappeared through the foliage at the exit, Diane shot a curious glance at Faith. For a moment, Ella stayed further forward, speaking to Helen and Mary. Taking advantage of the lack of guard, Faith leaned close to her friend.

"This cottage. I think I've been there before. It's where Sarah took me during Jacob's meeting with Danforth."

Understanding dawned on Diane's face. "You know where it is?"

Faith shrugged. "Kind of. I never went inside the cottage itself. Sarah shut me in the outbuilding. But I know it's closer to Bellator than here."

A hopeful expression dawned on Diane's face. "So you think...?"

"This might be our opportunity. Two guards. An outdoor location, closer to the city than the caves." Faith dropped her voice even lower. "And best of all... I think the building I was locked in had some maps."

Diane's eyes widened. "Of the woods? Of the routes to Bellator"

"Yep."

"Alright!" Diane looked elated. "For now, then, let's just follow along like the others... don't give anyone a reason to think we'll cause trouble. With any luck, when we get to the cottage, they'll drop their guard or fall asleep..."

"Then we can slip into the woods..." Faith couldn't believe she was saying it, "and head back to the city."

Diane sucked in a deep breath. "Bellator resistance, here we come."

Chapter Thirty-Five: Noah

As they waited for the approaching enemy to reach them, Noah wondered what had happened to Dane. Was the raider lying dead somewhere close to Madeleine's apartment? Or had he been taken prisoner? He remembered the jovial man who had been a part of his team the last time he had ventured into Bellator. He didn't deserve to die at the hands of the Bellator guards.

None of them did. And yet, it was a realistic possibility. Running through the various potential outcomes of the upcoming confrontation, Noah's hands were shaking so hard he could barely hold the gun still. What use was it anyway, right now? The rational part of him knew if he fired, he'd have no idea whether he was hitting a friend or a foe. But he was ashamed that he found the cold metal in his grasp comforting.

Being at the back of their formation was also comforting, but it meant he couldn't see what was coming. By sound alone, though, he knew the enemy was closer. Both the voices and the footsteps had grown in volume since they had been crouching here. He strained his ears, trying to work out how many guards were in the approaching group. But the false echoes created by the tunnel were confusing. One moment, it seemed as though there were only a couple, the next, his ears conjured up fifty.

His legs were beginning to betray him, pins and needles tingling their way upwards from his ankles. He tried to shift his body into a more comfortable position, but was rewarded by a hiss from Jan at the sound he made. Eventually, he settled for leaning back against the wall slightly, which allowed his legs some degree of relief.

A few moments later, a powerful beam of light swept across the narrow space between the tunnel sides. Noah tensed. This flashlight was nothing like the cheap ones they had in Eremus. Guard-issue, these were capable of flooding a space with illumination, ensuring total visibility. Noah was extremely glad they'd made it to the rocks which concealed them before the enemy arrived.

As the light passed over them, he caught sight of his brother's face. Pale and tense, he nevertheless looked determined. Noah was painfully aware that Paulo had placed himself at the forefront of the assault. For once, he was grateful for his brother's overprotectiveness. Glancing over, Paulo caught his eye and a strange expression crossed his face. Noah tried to smile, but the light was gone before he could see his brother's response.

Hushed voices drifted from beyond the rocks. "Halt." The flashlight swept the tunnel again. "Rhian, anything on the datadev, yet?"

There was a tapping sound, followed by a series of bleeps, then a sigh of frustration. "Nothing. The communicator isn't functioning down here. I haven't been able to get a signal since we went inside the house back there."

"Dammit." Whoever was in charge sounded annoyed. "We should've let Hammond know where we were headed."

"Sorry. I s'pose we're pretty deep underground. Or maybe it's being blocked."

Another voice. "Should we go back?"

"Not yet." The leader sounded frustrated. "We've come this far. And I'd like to be certain we're actually on to something before we get her all excited." There was the sound of shuffling feet. "It's a little narrow up ahead. Let me check it out before we proceed."

There was almost complete silence for a few seconds. Noah was suddenly very aware of how loud his breathing was. He inhaled slowly, then held his breath. A single set of heavy boots approached from the other side of the rock-wall. The beam of light grew in intensity.

From what they'd said, it seemed like the team had stumbled across the tunnel on some kind of patrol. Noah found himself daring to hope it wasn't a pre-planned and purposeful attack. Perhaps that even meant there weren't many of them. As the volume of the footsteps increased, he wondered how close the guard would have to be before she spotted Paulo and Jan.

He didn't have to wait long to find out. A single gunshot reverberated off the walls with vicious effect. Noah winced and slammed his free hand over one of his ears, pressing the other ear to his shoulder to muffle the noise. He felt, rather than heard the thud, as the guard's body collapsed forward into the gap between the two sides of the tunnel. The flashlight she carried now cast an eerie light on the roof of the tunnel.

For a moment, an eerie silence filled the space. A moment later, panicked shouts pierced the air.

"Get back!" "How many–?" "Defensive positions!"

The voices did not belong to his fellow citizens. A stealth attack required silence. Let the guards on the other side believe there were a hundred of them crouching out of sight further up the tunnel. Eremus had always survived on their cunning. They had little else in their favour.

Their first move had been successful. But the fallen guard was now blocking the tunnel. As the guards on the other side attempted to regroup, Paulo reached out and extinguished the woman's flashlight. In the darkness, Noah felt Jan and Mick move forward.

There were muted noises as they grasped hold of the body and began to drag it through to their side of the pass. The woman made no sound. Paulo had always been an accurate shot, and Noah was glad she wasn't suffering.

Realising he was the only one on his side of the tunnel, for a moment Noah felt vulnerable. But he wasn't alone for long. Taking advantage of the confusion on the opposite side of the wall, Paulo shifted across to whisper additional instructions.

"Going to turn the light on them," he hissed. "See the size of the threat."

Noah knew his brother was right. But the thought of the beam illuminating an entire battalion of Bellator guards on the other side of the wall was terrifying.

"Buck up, brother." Paulo nudged Noah with his shoulder. "I don't think there are that many."

He waited until Jan and Mick were crouching behind them once again. "Ready?"

Noah felt his brother position the lantern to the side of the rocks. A second later, there was a loud click, and the tunnel ahead was flooded with light. The Bellator guards gasped, reaching hands up to shade their eyes.

Taking advantage of their temporary blindness, the raiders ran their gaze over the group of guards. Noah began to count. Two, three... One of the guards turned on a second lantern, its beam just as bright. Noah found himself squinting. From behind him, he heard the crack of a gun again. There was a cry and a shattering of glass as Jan's shot hit its mark and the enemy light went out.

Able to see again, Noah continued to assess. Four, five...

Their own light went out, leaving the entire tunnel in darkness once more.

"I counted six, maybe seven," Paulo whispered. "And we have the advantage. We can take 'em out in pairs or singles as they approach."

As the rest of the group muttered their approval, a thought occurred to Noah. He leaned close to his brother. "What if they retreat?"

He almost felt Paulo's frown. "What?"

"What if they decide to go back? Return with a larger force?"

There was a pause. Noah could feel his brother working through the idea. "You're right," Paulo said finally. "We have to stop them. Otherwise, we risk them discovering the entire settlement."

"So we'll have to..."

"...get behind them."

As Paulo leaned forward to fill Jan in, Noah fought to keep control. Much as he balked at the thought of moving out from behind the solid wall of rock which protected them, he knew it was necessary. As things stood, they faced a minor threat which they could potentially neutralise. With these guards dead, there would be no one to report back on their location.

But moving out from behind the wall meant leaving themselves vulnerable.

A second later, Paulo was back. "Jan reckons the other team can't be far behind. But we can't wait. How many bullets do you have?"

Noah fumbled in his pocket. "Around ten, plus those already in the gun."

"Alright. You take the flashlight. Aim it in their direction. When I give the signal, switch it on. While they're blinded, Jan, Mick, Dan, and I will rush them. The others will cover me, taking out the guards at the front, while I try and get past them. Once I'm behind them, they can't get back. Harriet has more ammo than you. She'll provide you with back up from here. Alright?"

"But what if you–?"

"No time for buts." Paulo cut him off. "Get into position."

Ashamed at how grateful he was for the less dangerous assignment, Noah closed his mouth and accepted the flashlight. It was heavier than he'd expected, but he straightened and wedged it in place on a flatter section of rock. Placing his finger on the switch, he ducked behind it.

Ahead of them, he could hear scuffling feet and whispered orders which mirrored their own. Paulo was right. If they wanted the element of surprise, they needed to act now.

Noah felt Paulo's hand on his shoulder. "Ready?"

He took a deep breath. "Ready."

"Don't let me down, little brother." Paulo nudged the others. "Now!"

Noah jammed his finger on the switch. Immediately, the tunnel ahead blazed with light. As Jan led the raiders out around the rocky wall which had shielded them, Noah realised he had no idea what he'd do if those who'd gone ahead of him were killed. But there was nothing he could do now.

As light bearer, he was forced to watch the attack unfold. The lantern he held was as vital to the manouevre as the weapons brandished by those who had charged ahead. But as he continued to crouch behind the rocks, he didn't feel very brave.

It all happened very quickly.

At first, Paulo stayed behind the others, dropping low to avoid attention. The others raced forward, firing rapidly. The two central Bellator guards fell quickly, thanks to Jan's excellent aim and the shock which paralysed the enemy for a few seconds. But after their initial hesitation, the remaining guards dropped into defensive positions either side of the tunnel and began to return fire.

Noah ducked, attempting to keep the light in place whilst avoiding any stray bullets. The noise was deafening, but this time he could do nothing to shield his ears. At a short gap in the volley, he raised his head and risked a glance at the chaos ahead. He couldn't immediately see Paulo, but watched Mick and Dan take out a third guard to the left. Beginning to feel more optimistic, he swept his gaze across the space once again.

His heart stopped. On the right of the tunnel, Jan lay on the ground. Her body was ominously still. Paulo was crouching at her side, attempting to shield her. Raising his arm, he began firing repeatedly at two guards who were close by. The first of them collapsed, screaming and clutching at her chest. With a flash of fear, her partner retreated a couple of steps down the tunnel. Noah saw the panic on Paulo's face. If even one guard made it back to Bellator, they were finished.

His heart racing, Noah looked for the other raiders. Mick was leaning heavily against the tunnel wall to the left, putting pressure on a wound in his leg whilst attempting to fire at the remaining guards. For a moment, Noah couldn't see Dan at all, but then he spotted his neighbour crouching a few yards further down the tunnel. His face was creased with pain and he was nursing his shoulder.

Noah's heart sank. They'd managed to defeat half of their enemy. But with three raiders down, they were in real trouble. Taking a deep breath, he slipped his gun into the holster on his belt. Attracting Harriet's attention, he pointed deliberately at the lantern, then at himself, then over the top of the rocks.

Understanding, her eyes widened. She nodded.

And then there was nothing else for it.

With one final glance at the scene ahead, Noah attempt-ed to memorise everyone's position. Then, he pressed the switch, plunging the tunnel into total darkness.

Grasping the flashlight in one hand and keeping his other one thrust out in front of him, he stepped out into the dark-ness. After taking four steps forward, he stopped. Using his toes, he managed to navigate his way around the bodies of the Bellator guards who had fallen first. He took another three steps forward, then side stepped to his left, praying that the guards who were still on their feet had not moved far.

On his next step forward, his foot hit something. He thrust out a hand, trying to steady himself. When it collided with flesh, he recoiled. The body beneath him groaned, and he felt a hand close around his arm.

"Help me," an unfamiliar voice whispered.

But he couldn't stop. Resisting the urge to flee, he yanked his arm away and set off again, realigning his course. This time, his progress was unhindered. When he'd taken fifteen steps, he knew he was clear. Spinning to face the opposite direction, he held the flashlight high and snapped it back on.

As he'd hoped, most of the guards and raiders were still facing Eremus. With their backs to him, he had the advantage. The guard who'd been attempting to retreat was only a foot or so in front of him, her gun pointing in the opposite direction. Without thinking, Noah placed the light on the ground and leapt forward. Circling his arms around her, he grasped her wrists firmly. The woman cried out, but loosened her hold and he was able to wrestle the weapon out of her hands.

She spun round, her face a mask of shock. Noah faced her, barring her path back to Bellator with her own weapon. Without a word, she raised her hands in surrender. Glancing back at the others, Noah wondered what to do next. Whilst the woman closest to him was not endangering them, there were two other guards still standing. As they slowly turned to face him, he readied himself to fire, wondering if he had the courage.

A sudden commotion from the direction of Eremus startled them all. The beams of several flashlights winked from behind the rocks, and seconds later a much larger group of raiders burst through the gap between the rocks. Those at the front held up panels of wood as shields.

From behind the barrier came a familiar voice. "If you want to live, surrender your guns."

Flynn. As calm and steady as ever. Noah sagged with relief. As the two remaining guards exchanged glances, there was a tense silence. The two women began slowly lowering their guns. For a moment, Noah thought they were obeying Flynn's order. But then, as one, they leapt towards the threat, all guns blazing.

It was a final, desperate attempt. Most of the bullets slammed into the wooden panels with a dull thunk. As the raiders behind the barrier returned fire, Noah leapt forward and grabbed hold of the surrendering guard with his free arm. Pulling her to the ground, he pushed her to the side of the tunnel, thankful when she didn't resist. Noah could feel her shuddering beside him long after the shooting had stopped, though he felt oddly calm.

When Noah dared to glance up, the remaining guards lay crumpled on the tunnel floor. Flynn had ordered a cease fire and the raiders had obeyed, immediately lowering their guns and the wooden shields. Releasing his hold on the guard, Noah checked his body for wounds. There were none. A cursory glance at the woman next to him told him his actions had protected them both.

An air of shock pervaded the tunnel as Flynn took charge, surveying his surroundings and barking orders to his team. Within a few minutes, the remaining guard had been checked for additional weapons and taken prisoner, the injured were being given first aid, and citizens were beginning to use the sections of wood as stretchers to evacuate the wounded and the dead.

Noah remained where he was, knowing the illumination from the flashlight was still vital to the citizens who were moving the bodies. Now the danger had passed, he felt like he was about to collapse.

Eventually, Flynn approached. "You alright?"

He opened his mouth to speak, but found words had deserted him. As Flynn waited patiently, Paulo approached, his face unreadable. "That was a risky move."

Flynn raised an eyebrow at his nephew. "What happened here?"

Paulo turned to face his uncle. "As you can see, this was only a small group."

Flynn frowned. "Bigger than yours though."

Paulo waved his concern away. "From what they said, they'd stumbled upon us by mistake. Our main aim was to stop them from getting back to the city and giving away our location. I was trying to get behind them, bar the tunnel so they couldn't retreat." His gaze shifted to further down the tunnel, where Ruth was helping Mick to his feet. "But we'd only taken a couple of them out when Jan was hit, then Mick and Dan went down too. I was trapped." He took a deep breath and glanced at Noah. "I thought we'd had it."

Flynn nodded. "What changed?"

"Noah was at the back with the light." Paulo returned his gaze to his uncle. "He just... switched it off. Then... somehow... in the *darkness*... he made his way behind the guards, turned the light back on and..." he hesitated, as though he didn't believe it, "...disarmed the woman who was trying to run."

Flynn's eyebrows shot up. "Quick thinking."

Noah flushed. Paulo gave his uncle a tired smile. "It was."

"And you're certain this was all of them? No one knew they were down here?"

"We think so." Paulo nodded. "They said their location equipment wasn't functioning properly."

"That makes sense." Flynn shot a concerned glance at Jan, who was being loaded onto one of the makeshift stretchers. "A close call, though."

"Too close." Paulo leaned forward and eased the flashlight out of Noah's hand. "Relax, brother. Danger's over. You did good."

"Thanks," Noah managed, an unfamiliar feeling of pride mingling with his fear and grief.

"No time to sit around and celebrate though." Flynn was already on the move again. "We need to get back. There's work to do."

CHAPTER THIRTY-SIX: FAITH

It was dark, and the flashlights at the front and rear of the line did little to light the way, so the trek to the cottage seemed to take forever. The night was not cold though, and the forest had dried out after the recent storm. Faith and Diane had lingered at the rear of the group. For a while, they'd attempted to memorise the route, should they need to return to the cave settlement without their guards, but in the shadowy light of the moon, one tree looked very much like another.

They walked silently, for the most part. Carl remained at the front, forging ahead, but Ella kept a regular check on the entire group, working her way up and down the line to ensure everyone was safe. Even Avery was quiet. At one point, Mary fell over a stray tree root and cut her knee, but the injury wasn't serious and her fear kept her from crying out. Helen helpfully provided her with a torn section of her oversized shirt to bind it, and she continued on without much fuss.

The woods were different at night. Louder, somehow. Numerous creatures, too shy to appear by daylight, clearly felt emboldened by the darkness. Small animals on the forest floor scuttled out of their way as they passed, and Faith heard what she knew to be the hunting calls of several predatory birds in the trees above their heads. The moon was almost full and cast a silvery glow through the woods in some places, but in others the thickets and trees were so densely packed together that there was almost no light at all.

Both their guides knew the forest well. Faith suspected they'd have been moving much faster were they not held back by their inexperienced companions. Ella regularly hurried to the head of the line to ask Carl to slow down for them. As always, she was attentive to their needs, making sure Carl stopped to allow them to rest and drink water at several streams along the way.

In terms of food, she was unable to help them. Their abrupt exit from the caves had not allowed her time to gather provisions. But she had reassured them several times that there was a small store of food at the cottage.

Faith wondered if there were larger creatures lurking in the forest. Ones which they should be afraid of. At one point they came to a clearing where a majestic stag stood, his antlers gleaming in the moonlight. For a moment, the Danforth girls glanced at one another, alarmed, but Carl merely paused to reroute them, circumnavigating the regal creature so he did not react to their presence.

"Isn't he dangerous?" Mary had stage-whispered into the night air.

"Not unless you startle him." Ella smiled at her. "He's not really a hunter. He could gore you badly with those antlers if he needed to, but he'd only do that if he thought you were dangerous."

The stag remained still as they passed him. Only his head tracked their progress around the edge of the clearing. Faith met the creature's gaze, turning to watch him even as they walked away. His eyes were gentle, his manner calm and dignified. Something about him made her think of Noah.

She felt a stabbing pain in her chest as she thought of the boy she was leaving behind. Somehow, she'd thought she'd have more time with him. She tried to tell herself this way was better. If they'd had more opportunities to talk, she might have been tempted to confess what they were planning. And he would have tried to stop her.

Still, disappearing without a word seemed a cruel betrayal of his trust. She felt guilty about deceiving Ella and Ruth too. The sisters had been good to them, and to sneak away without a word felt wrong.

What choice did she have, though? Sophia had already been back at Danforth for several days. Long enough to be questioned, tortured, given multiple doses of femgazipane. Faith couldn't live with the idea that her friend was hurting and she wasn't doing anything. Only with the support of the resistance could she and Diane try to change things. But Jacob would never voluntarily free them. The current situation might be their only opportunity to escape.

It was extremely late when the cottage finally came into view. Faith was happy to discover it was the same one Sarah had brought her to. She could see the outbuilding round the side, but Ella ushered them into the cottage itself, leaving Carl outside to scout for firewood. A basic but surprisingly homely dwelling, it had a couple of bedrooms with real beds, and a sofa and chairs which, though old, were very comfortable.

"This place will shelter us well enough, until we get the signal to go back," Ella smiled around the group.

"When might that be?" Avery complained, but Faith thought she detected a note of fear in her tone.

"Not 'til the morning, at the earliest. When the coast is clear, they'll let us know. For now, we should fix ourselves something to eat and then get some rest."

She busied herself opening a couple of chests at the back of the main living area, pulling out several blankets and handing them out. When Carl returned, he set to work lighting a fire to warm them. An investigation of the cupboards in the small kitchen appeared to reveal very little, so Ella headed for the door.

"Just need to grab some provisions from the shed," she called.

"Can I help?" Faith offered, quickly, shooting a look at Carl, who was still occupied with the fire.

"Sure. Thank you."

Carl offered no objection as Ella headed for the door. Faith followed, ignoring Diane's curious gaze. Once they were outside, the older girl hesitated, peering at the trees which surrounded the cottage.

"Are you worried someone might find us?" Faith murmured.

Ella shrugged. "It's unlikely. Eremus used to visit this cottage all the time, but there was an incident several years ago... around the time that Anna came to us. I was only a child... some Bellator guards stormed the place. One of our older citizens, Robert, was killed."

"I'm sorry."

"It wasn't unusual for us to lose people back then." Ella shrugged. "I didn't know Robert really, but he and my ma were close. He was very well-respected in the community, so it hit us hard. We pretty much abandoned the place after that, but lately Jacob has felt enough time has passed for us to use the place occasionally."

Faith followed her across the overgrown garden to the outbuilding, her heart pounding. She watched as Ella unfastened the padlock and slid the key back inside the front pocket of her backpack. Easing the door open, she walked in, beckoning Faith to follow.

Once inside, memories came flooding back. Faith closed her eyes for a second, the musty scent transporting her back to her imprisonment, the sound of the explosions ripping through the woods, the satisfied grin on Sarah's face as she flung the door open, ready to bring Faith to Jacob.

"Are you alright?"

Faith's eyes flew open. Ella stood looking at her, a concerned expression on her face. "You're not feeling ill again, are you? Do you need me to take you back across to the cottage?"

"N-no, I'm fine." Guilt lanced through Faith as she tried to smile. "Sorry – I think the walk just tired me out, that's all."

"Alright. If you're sure. Maybe some food will help to restore you." Ella moved across the space and pulled one of the boxes down. "Let's see... there should definitely be some..."

She muttered to herself as she rifled through the boxes. Taking advantage of her distraction, Faith sidled over to the shelf Sarah had tied her to. Glancing over at Ella to check that she was occupied, she slid a finger underneath the papers and rifled through them. As she had thought, a couple of them were maps of the woods and the surrounding area. One of them definitely had Bellator marked on it, with various locations she felt sure were targets for the Eremus raids.

"Here we are." Faith turned back quickly, letting go of the papers as Ella brandished a packet of instant noodles triumphantly. "Easy to prepare. And they don't go bad. There are eight of us, right?" Faith nodded. Ella counted out four of the noodles, grabbing a packet of biscuits as well. "This should do us for now. If we're here for longer, Carl or I will have to forage some fresh food."

It struck Faith again how thoughtful Ella was. As they made their way back inside together, Faith tried to quell the guilt which gnawed at her.

Within the hour they had warm noodles in their bellies and felt much better.

"Sleeping arrangements," Ella announced, when Carl had gone outside to replenish the firewood. He'd refused Diane's offer to help him, clearly not trusting her. Faith was far more concerned about escaping him than Ella. "There are two bedrooms, with beds for two people in each. Carl and I will stay out here on guard in rotation. Would you all like to take turns sleeping in the beds?"

Diane was quick to volunteer to stay in the main living area. "I'm just as happy out here on the sofa, if other people want to take one."

"Me too," Faith agreed.

"We'll take a room with a bed," Farrah called out, "...if no one minds?"

She and Avery were already on their feet. They had shut the door behind them before anyone had a chance to argue.

"Selfless as ever," Diane joked.

"I'll join the little one in the other room, if that's okay with you all?" Helen cast a curious eye over the room. "I'd like to keep an eye on her."

Mary had been asleep in one of the bedrooms for the past hour. She had dropped off on the sofa well before the food was ready. Ella had carried her to one of the beds, and they'd saved her some food for when she woke.

"That's fine by me." Diane waved a tired hand.

"Sure thing," Faith agreed.

Ella climbed up from her place on the rug. "No problem. I'll just come in and check you have everything you need."

The two of them disappeared into the second bedroom and closed the door behind them.

"Do you think she'll be in there long?" Diane asked, raising an eyebrow. "I mean... with the two of them being so..." she flushed, "close and all?"

Faith smiled. "I'm guessing not, if Mary's asleep in there too. But we might have a few minutes before she and Carl get back."

Diane leaned closer. "What's the plan, then?"

"Well, I was right. There are maps outside. Ones which I'm pretty sure will guide us back to Bellator. Ella has a key to the shed in the front of her pack." Faith glanced at the door where Ella and Helen had disappeared. "I wonder if..."

But Diane was already on her feet. She hopped off the sofa and hurried over to the kitchen bench where Ella's pack lay. Unzipping the front pocket, she eased out the keys as quietly as she could and slipped them into her pocket. But instead of returning to the sofa immediately, she opened the main body of the pack and began rooting through it.

"What are you doing?" Faith hissed. "Carl could be back any minute!"

Ignoring her, Diane continued to search. Faith shot another worried look at the front door. When she looked back, Diane was holding something in her hand.

"Gotcha!" Fastening the pack again, she hastened back to the sofa, flinging herself down next to Faith, whose heart was pounding.

Diane grinned. "Now we have access to the shed with the maps, and a way of sneaking out without our guards knowing." She brandished the can of sleeping spray at Faith. "Remember this?"

"We're going to *drug* them both?" Faith shuddered.

"Well, if you'd rather steal their weapons and kill them, be my guest." Diane shook her head at Faith's horrified expression. "How else do you suggest we get out of here without them noticing?"

Faith had to admit Diane was right. "Okay. But Ella's so kind. I'd feel terrible. Can't we just wait til they're asleep or something?"

"Don't you get it?" Diane frowned. "I'm trying to protect her. We go missing when Ella's on duty... in charge... and Jacob will blame her for our disappearance."

Understanding dawned. "He might even think she was involved. That she... helped us."

"That's it." Diane slid the can underneath her sweatshirt out of sight. "But if we knock her out, hopefully they'll assume she had nothing to do with it."

"I guess you're right. I mean, she couldn't have helped us if she's unconscious, right?"

"Exactly." Diane cocked her head at Faith. "Now, you're absolutely sure about this? Because... once we do it, there's no going back. Jacob will be furious when he finds out you're gone."

Faith grimaced. "That's why I have to leave. Can't stand the thought of him having so much control over me. At least this way, it's my decision."

"Well said." Diane applauded silently. "So we wait until we're sure the other girls are asleep? Hit our guards with the spray, wait 'til they're out, then grab the map and get out of here?"

"Yeah." Faith chewed on her lip. "We'll need to work out how we can use one can on both of them without the second one reacting. Might be difficult."

"Hopefully one of them will sleep. Then we can do them in turn."

"Hopefully." Faith rearranged the blanket over her knees and slumped down, trying to get comfortable. "Better look like we're settling down too though, or–"

The front door banged open and Carl stomped in, dumping an armful of wood next to the fire. When Ella returned from the bedroom, he scowled at her. Ignoring him, she moved quietly across the room to them.

"Mary's out cold and I don't think Helen will be long. You two need anything?"

"No, thanks." Diane yawned widely.

Ella turned to Carl, who was stacking the wood by the fire. "Want me to take first watch?"

He shook his head. "S'alright. I'll do it." Satisfied with his work, he straightened. "I'm going to patrol the perimeter. Check no one's out there who shouldn't be." He headed for the door. "Wake you in a couple of hours."

When the door had slammed behind him, Diane turned to Ella and rolled her eyes. "Better grab some rest, while you can."

"I'll do my best." Ella suddenly looked exhausted. "It's been a stressful night. And I'm not sure it's over yet."

Faith thought back to their sudden exit from the caves, and the threat that had prompted the sudden exit. "You worried about Ruth?"

Ella nodded. "About all of them. Honestly, I'm not sure what's going to happen. I don't think I can see a happy outcome to all of this, for any of us." She glanced at the closed door where Helen was sleeping. "I just wish things could be different."

"Me too," Faith agreed.

"Anyway, get some sleep, both of you. You need it as much as me."

They fell silent. Diane closed her eyes and, after a few moments, Faith did too. Concerned she might actually fall asleep, she dug her fingers into her palms and held them there until they hurt.

A little while later, she felt Diane's elbow digging into her ribcage. Opening her eyes, she glanced over at Ella.

"I think she's sleeping," Diane muttered, easing herself off the sofa. "But let's give her a good dose to make sure."

Clutching the sleeping solution in her hand, she crept towards the other girl. Ella didn't stir. When she was close enough, Diane eased off the cap. Aiming the can at the other girl, she sprayed a good dose of it into her face.

Startled, Ella shot bolt upright. She stared at Diane curiously, then her eyes went to the spray can. As understanding dawned, a look of horror darkened her face. She sat bolt upright, her hands clutching at empty air.

For a moment, Faith thought they'd blown it. But then, Ella's eyes fluttered closed and she began to topple forwards. Faith was on her feet in seconds. Between them, they caught the older girl and eased her back into the chair.

"What do we do about Carl?" Faith whispered.

"Improvise, I guess." Diane handed the spray can to Faith and selected one of the larger logs from the pile. Swinging it through the air, she nodded. "This'll do." She noted Faith's alarmed expression. "Just in case."

As they crept to the door, Faith glanced back at Ella, already regretting their actions.

"Need to work out where he is," Diane murmured, creeping to the window. "I tried to listen to the patterns of his footsteps. Seems like he does a circuit every ten minutes, then pauses at the front door for a while. Think he's round the back at the moment."

She crept towards the front door and eased it open, wincing as it creaked slightly. They tiptoed through it and pulled it closed behind them. Taking a few steps away from the cottage, they paused to listen.

"Think we can get in and out and be gone before he gets back?" Faith whispered.

Diane shook her head. "We have to deal with him, or he's likely to follow us."

She turned to scan their surroundings. In the darkness, it was difficult to make things out. Faith found she was clutching the can so hard it was digging into her palm. She was just loosening her grip and wiping the sweat from her hands when the slender beam of a flashlight swept around the corner. The shadow of Carl appeared, pacing in their direction but not, as yet, seeing them.

"Wait for it," Diane muttered.

Faith shifted position slightly, angling herself so Carl would pass right by her. Her foot crunched down on some dry leaves and she froze.

"Who's there?" Carl's flashlight spotlighted them both. "What the–?"

He reached for his gun.

"Now!" Diane hissed, shoving her forward.

Faith leapt blindly at Carl, the can of Sleepsol ready. She jammed her finger on the trigger and thrust it at his face waiting to hear the soft shushing sound of the liquid anaesthetic being released.

Nothing happened.

Carl's expression went from confusion to fury in under a second. Like lightning, he sprang forward and twisted the can out of her hand, tossing it aside.

"Don't you dare!" he hissed in her ear as it clattered to the ground.

Like reliving a nightmare, Faith felt the cold muzzle of a gun being pressed against her temple. She froze, searching her mind for something... anything she might do to escape. She tried to wriggle free, but his arms were like steel. Then there was a sudden jolt, and the metal of the gun cut into her skin, as though propelled by some force.

For a moment, she thought she'd been shot. But she knew she hadn't heard gunfire. Then a second blow threw her forward and she landed on the ground hard. She cried out as Carl's body followed, almost crushing her.

When the world stopped spinning, she found she was badly bruised, but still very much alive.

"Are you alright?" Diane's voice seemed to come from far away.

She struggled out from underneath the heavy weight and stared up at her friend. Diane stood over them, her face white, the shaft of wood was still clutched in her hand.

"Did you–?" Faith stared between Diane and Carl. "You hit him?"

"Twice." Diane dropped the wood and bent beside her victim. Pressing a hand to his neck, she nodded. "He's okay, I think. Just out cold." She shot a nervous glance back at the cottage. "We need to leave. In case the others wake up."

Shaking, Faith clambered to her feet. The hard part was over with. It should have been a simple task to open the shed and sneak away into the night. But as they broke into her former prison and she began to gather the provisions—the map, a couple of cereal bars, and a flashlight—she couldn't stop her heart from racing.

The job done, they returned the key to the table inside the cottage. Then, prepared as they'd ever be, they set off through the woods.

As they walked in the direction of the city, Faith tried to keep her thoughts firmly on Sophia. On joining the resistance, working to stop Danforth, and saving her friends. But as the sky grew lighter in the distance, she couldn't stop herself from thinking about those she was leaving behind.

Chapter Thirty-Seven:
Noah

For the rest of the night, the community worked to deal with the aftermath of the attack. Once Flynn had confirmed the danger was over and given the all-clear, the Eremus citizens had begun to emerge from hiding. One group after another had made their way to the central meeting spot, entering with questioning gazes which turned to horror as they saw the bodies.

Jan was dead, and, further up the tunnel, Flynn had found Dane's body lying just outside the entrance to Madeleine's home. He had several bullet wounds in his chest. There was no more evidence of guards, though Flynn hadn't dared to go inside the house itself.

When he'd returned, Flynn had checked on Noah and Paulo before calling Jacob over to talk about next steps. Noah noticed the leader took his time approaching, and wondered if he was angry about the fact that Flynn had been the one managing the rescue. For the first time ever, Jacob had been sidelined, and he didn't like it.

There had been a tension simmering between the two men ever since the meeting with Danforth, and today Noah felt it more than ever. Despite their issues, though, the day's events demanded they work together.

"We need to activate emergency measures." Noah heard Flynn say, rubbing an exhausted hand against his beard.

"Agreed." Jacob's tone was curt. "Even if this was a small group who stumbled upon us by accident, we can't risk another incident like today."

Paulo stepped forward. "Want me to take care of it?"

Jacob shook his head. "You've done enough. I'll send Sarah and Harden."

Paulo opened his mouth to object, but Flynn's hand on his arm stopped him.

"Thanks, Jacob." Waiting until the leader had gone, he turned to Paulo. "I think we can trust them with this. It's in everyone's interest to protect the tunnels."

Noah turned to Flynn. "What are these emergency measures?"

Perhaps noting his worried expression, Flynn met his gaze head-on. "It's nothing to worry about. They'll detonate some small explosives at the end of the tunnel leading to Madeleine's house."

Noah frowned. "Won't that block the tunnel?"

Flynn nodded. "It will. It's not an ideal solution. We've used that house to access the city for years. But right now, we have to conceal the access point."

"Someone will come looking for that patrol." Paulo chimed in. "They have to have an idea about where those guards were when they disappeared. This way, even if *Danforth* were to show up at Madeleine's, she wouldn't find us."

Noah frowned. "I don't understand."

"The explosives will go off very close to Madeleine's house." Flynn eased himself on to one of the benches. "They'll collapse part of the tunnel, so no one can access it. The back of

Madeleine's cellar will also be badly damaged. With any luck, anyone investigating will presume there was an electrical fault or gas leak."

"And no one will be able to trace it back to us?"

"Exactly." Flynn massaged his neck, rolling his head one way and then the other as he spoke. "We lose access, but turn down the heat on the investigation into Madeleine's home. We've other entrances which lead into the city. We'll have to use those instead."

Noah turned to Flynn. "Do you think Madeleine's okay?"

"I hope so." Pushing himself into a standing position, Flynn sighed. "If she is, she'll have concealed herself somewhere well away from her home by now. She'll make contact when she's able."

Spotting Anna entering on the other side of the canteen, Flynn stood up and hurried over to her. He wrapped his arms around his partner and she leaned into him as though he was the only thing keeping her upright. Noah found himself envying their closeness. His ma had been one of the first out of hiding, and had been working hard all day to assess and treat the injured.

Some cases had been more difficult to deal with than others. Since their return, Dan Clark had succumbed to his injuries. Despite all Anna's efforts, the loss of blood from the wound in his shoulder had been too great. He had passed away several hours after they'd arrived back from the tunnels. Noah knew his parents would find it hard to deal with the loss of the man who'd lived in the cave next door to them for so many years.

Mick's injury was thankfully minor and, infections aside, Anna felt confident he would recover. The other raiders had returned with nothing more than scratches and bruises. Most of Eremus seemed to be regarding them as heroes who had foiled a plot to uncover their location. Noah wasn't sure how he felt about their attitude, given the loss of life they'd caused.

Of the seven Bellator guards, the only one who'd survived was the woman who had attempted to retreat. She had been taken aside for questioning, but so far, she wasn't talking. For now, she remained under heavy guard on the far side of the canteen. Noah found himself staring at her, wondering whether her bullet had killed Jan, or Dane, or Dan. Or had she been as reluctant as he had to fire her weapon? She'd certainly surrendered, where the others had been prepared to die.

For the first time, his thoughts returned to Faith as he considered how the Danforth girls might react to another Bellator captive joining them. Glancing around, he spotted Professor Kemp, who his ma had been keeping busy tending to the injured citizens. But the rest of the prisoners were strangely absent.

His heart sank. Where were they? He stood up and went in search of answers, finding he was praying Jacob hadn't *again* made other plans for them without informing the rest of the community.

Spotting Ruth tucking into her dinner, he hurried over. She smiled warmly at his approach.

"Hey. Word in the tunnels is you *single-handedly* stopped those guards getting back to Bellator and blowing the whistle on us."

His face flamed. "Where'd you hear that?"

She pointed at Harriet, who sat at the next table. "Don't be modest." She shook her head. "It wasn't Paulo who saved us, was it? It was you."

"I didn't *fight* anyone. I just—"

"I know what you did." Ruth reached out a hand and pulled him down onto the bench beside her. "Just give yourself credit, won't you? You used your brain to rescue everyone from a terrible situation."

He grimaced. "Not everyone."

"Well, no." She paused to swallow a mouthful of bread. "But there were far more survivors because of your actions. Think about it that way."

"I guess." He shrugged.

She dropped her voice low. "Anyway, I'm sure Faith'll be impressed, when she gets back."

Noah frowned. "Gets back from where?"

"The cottage." Ruth spoke through another mouthful. "You didn't know? Jacob sent Ella and Carl down there with them. To protect them." She rolled her eyes. "Or to stop Danforth from taking them. Guess they should be back sometime soon."

Noah frowned. Jacob was making decisions without consulting the rest of them, yet again. It made him distinctly uneasy. He was about to question his friend further when her eyes moved to someone approaching from behind them.

"Noah!" Turning, he saw Paulo striding towards them, his face thunderous. "Where's your ma?"

Noah turned to gesture to the other side of the canteen before realising his ma was no longer there. "She was here a minute ago. She's maybe gone back to the medcave. What's wrong?"

But Paulo was already gone. Noah followed, but his brother didn't give any explanation until they reached the medcave. Paulo burst in, startling Anna and Kemp, who were counting supplies. "Danforth girls were taken to the cottage last night." He said, with no preamble. "Just heard from Ella. There was some trouble of some kind..."

Noah's heart sank. "What kind of trouble?"

Paulo shrugged. "Not sure. Think maybe her walkie talkie ran out of battery. We only got half a message." He turned to Anna. "But Carl's been injured. Can you come?"

She turned to Kemp. "Can you finish this without me?" Waiting until the other woman nodded, she turned to Paulo. "We'll need others to carry him back. If he can't walk, that is."

Noah stepped forward before his brother could respond. "Me and Ruth'll come."

He thought Paulo might refuse, but he just nodded. "Alright. Be ready in five. I'll round up some of the others."

It was at least twenty minutes before they were ready to leave. By that point, Noah's fists were clenched so hard his hands ached. Paulo had recruited a couple of other male citizens, but Noah knew he was hoping Carl would not be so badly injured as to need carrying. As the six of them set off through the northern exit at dawn, his heart was racing.

The journey through the forest was torture, and he was unable to prevent himself imagining the worst. Over and over, he pictured hundreds of Bellator guards descending on the cottage in the dead of night, the girls inside helpless to defend themselves.

Beside him, Ruth seemed to sense his agitation and didn't speak. But when the cottage finally came into view, she reached down to squeeze his hand. "Try not to worry. It might be nothing."

The small dwelling looked no different than it always had. There was an absence of smoke from the chimney, but there was no sign of a struggle. At first glance, at least, nothing appeared to be broken or out of place.

Paulo readied his gun and instructed the group to surround the building. Hurrying into a position which faced the door, Noah fixed his eyes on it. As Paulo began his approach, it flew open. For a moment, he tensed, but relaxed as he saw it was Ella standing in the doorway.

Her face was pale and her eyes wide. "Thank goodness you're here!" She noticed the gun and shook her head. "No. You won't need that." Her gaze scanned the rescue party until she saw Anna. "It's a medic we need. Come quickly." As Noah's ma and Paulo followed her into the cottage, she continued. "I don't think he's dying, but he was hit pretty hard."

Ignoring his brother's signal to remain in position, Noah moved to the doorway and stepped inside.

His ma went immediately to Carl, who was laid out on the sofa. "How are you?" She bent to examine him. "Ella says you took quite a hit."

Carl's murmur of response was quiet, but he was alive and responsive. That was a good sign.

Noah's eyes searched the rest of the room. The Danforth girls stood at the doorway to one of the bedrooms in an awkward group. He was relieved to see none of them looked injured. Something about the group wasn't right, though.

His eyes searched each face, counted, then flicked back to Ella. She had moved away from Carl towards Paulo and looked stricken.

"I'm so sorry." She dropped her gaze to the floor. "I didn't... I couldn't..."

"What happened?" Paulo asked.

"They drugged me," Ella's voice wavered, "with the Sleepsol. And when I woke up, they were gone. I couldn't find Carl. When I went outside, he was out cold on the ground."

Noah was suddenly aware of Paulo's eyes on him. Behind Ella, the other girls were also staring, their expressions ranging from derision to pity. He could name them all now: Avery, the one with the permanent scowl; Farrah, her friend and follower; Mary, the youngest, devastated by the recent death of her friend; Helen, Ella's companion.

He finished counting. Diane, the girl who'd continually tried to flee when she first arrived, was not with them.

And Faith, who he couldn't begin to describe in a single sentence, was also missing.

He felt someone approach from behind. "They'll be well on their way to the city by now." Numbly, he turned to face Ruth, whose face was creased with concern. "You know she hasn't been happy since Sophia was taken."

He knew she was right. But he couldn't listen to her kind words. And he couldn't bear her pitying expression.

"I have to... have to go." Pushing his way past the group of raiders who had gathered in the doorway, he made his way outside. Hearing Ruth calling after him, he began to run. Paulo's words followed him up into the forest.

"Leave him. He doesn't want company right now."

As he fled, he found himself intensely grateful for his brother's intervention. Paulo had read his mood well. Head down, he began to race through the forest, not thinking about where he was going. He ran full out, dodging low branches and leaping tree roots which jutted from the ground beneath. Only when he could no longer catch his breath did he stop. Leaning heavily against the trunk of a large beech tree, he slid down it until he was slumped on the damp leaves, desperately sucking in lungfuls of air.

All around him, the forest looked the same as ever. The leaves whispered their secrets in the light wind, the sun was rising in the distance, casting its dappled light across the treetops, and a million tiny creatures went about their business.

But something had changed.

Faith, a girl who he hadn't realised he needed, who meant more to him than he'd managed to convey, was gone. And though he loved her all the more for going back, for wanting to rescue her friend, the loss felt like a bullet to his chest.

When they'd first met, they'd been terrified, hostile, prejudiced against one another. Even then, he'd admired Faith's courage, her fierce pride, her loyalty to her friends. Sophia was the reason she'd chosen to return to the city which had treated her so terribly.

He'd dared to hope she might have developed a similar allegiance to him. But how could a boy who she'd known for a few weeks compete with friendships she'd built over years?

His hand went into his pocket, closing around the necklace she'd given to him. Now he knew why. She had been leaving him something to remember her by. He stared into the forest. Unseen in the distance, the city lay sleeping, with no idea that a lost citizen was about to return.

He closed his eyes and rested his head against the trunk of the tree. Their gain was his loss.

Chapter Thirty-Eight: Faith

T he oak doors of the Bellator Library loomed large in the moonlight. As Diane raised her hand to knock, Faith glanced around nervously. It had taken longer than they had expected to reach the city. They got lost several times, despite the maps, and when they'd finally reached the outskirts, it had been dawn.

Too nervous to make their way through the streets in daylight, they'd hidden in the fields surrounding the city. Though they'd seen no one, they had spent an anxious few hours crouching behind a barn and, with nothing more than the cereal bars they'd stolen from the shed, had been famished by the time it got dark.

When they'd begun to creep through the city, they'd almost run straight into a pair of guards making the rounds. Throwing themselves into an alleyway, the two of them had crouched behind some bins. Despite the stench, they hadn't dared to move for some time.

When they had emerged, there was no sign of the guards, but they were terrified of coming across other patrols. Their hearts in their mouths, they'd scuttled across the city streets as fast as they could.

There was no finer sight than that of the old library building. More old-fashioned than many of the others in the city, it nestled amongst skyscrapers crafted from shiny metal and razor-thin glass. Sleek, high-tech constructions, symbols of Bellator's eternal quest for the future. The library stood in stark contrast, a solid, comforting structure.

A perfect place from which to run a revolution, Faith thought.

At first, Diane's knock yielded no response. But as the two girls exchanged worried glances, there was a scraping sound and the door was eased open a crack. From inside, a pair of dark eyes peered at them.

"What do you want?" The woman sounded suspicious.

"We've..." Diane's voice was shaky. "We'd like to come inside."

"It's the middle of the night! We're not open." The woman began to shut the door.

Faith's heart raced even harder. Had they come all this way to be refused entry? She took a step closer.

"We're... students." The eyes continued to gaze, unblinking. "Students who... until very recently... attended the Danforth Academy."

The door cracked open a little further. "Until recently, you say?"

"Yes!" Faith glanced behind her, praying that another patrol didn't appear round the corner. "Until the recent explosion at the hospital. We've been... elsewhere, since then."

Understanding dawned in the woman's eyes. She leaned forward. "Blue door. Round the side. Quickly."

The door slammed in their faces.

Retracing their steps, the two girls headed down the street which ran along the side of the building. When they reached a blue door at the foot of a set of steps, they wasted no time in hurrying down and knocking.

Diane glanced at the street, her eyes wide. "Hurry up!" she muttered under her breath.

This time, they didn't have to wait. The door was unlocked and pulled open immediately. There appeared to be no one on the other side, until a voice came from behind the door.

"Get inside. Hurry!"

Faith pushed Diane through the doorway and followed as fast as she could. Once the door was closed behind them, they turned to face their saviour.

On the other side of the small hallway, stood an older woman with silver-grey hair. Hands on hips, she eyed them suspiciously.

"You're from Danforth Academy, you say?" They nodded. *"Really?"*

"Yes." Diane found her voice again. "Really. We were among the students caught up in the explosion... at the hospital... kidnapped by the Eremus forces."

The woman's eyes narrowed. "And what are you doing here?"

Faith took a deep breath. "We were hoping to join you."

"Join us?" The woman raised an eyebrow. "And what, exactly, would you be... *joining?*"

"Isn't this...?" Faith's heart sank. "I mean, we heard this place was..." she trailed off, despairing.

"It might be." The woman's face softened slightly. "Go on."

Faith straightened. "My name is Faith. Faith Hanlon. And this is Diane King. We've come here because we've just spent several days as prisoners of the Eremus community..."

"Alright." The woman's eyes lit up. "I'm listening."

"We know about Danforth's lies and we want to help... to stop..." Faith ground to a halt in confusion as the woman chuckled.

"Alright. I'm convinced."

"You are?"

"Truth be told, I was convinced as soon as I heard your name." The woman laughed. "We have our spies too, you know. I'm well aware of how important you are, Ms. Hanlon. We were hoping we might get our hands on you at some point."

She turned and began leading them down a steep set of steps. A little disconcerted by the woman's words, Faith had no choice but to follow. They had come this far. There was no turning back. But as she followed the woman, she shivered.

It felt like they were descending into the very bowels of the building. They stopped at a second door. The woman turned as she retrieved a key from a chain around her neck.

"Welcome to the resistance." Unlocking the door, she swung it open and beckoned them into a dark corridor which reminded Faith of one of the Eremus tunnels. "I'm Madeleine, by the way."

Faith remembered Noah talking about the woman who had spent years helping the Eremus community. She was alive, then. He would be glad. Faith found herself wishing she could let him know the woman was safe. It might have lessened the guilt she felt for deceiving him, using him to discover the resistance location. For leaving him.

Locking the door behind them, Madeleine continued down the hallway. Diane shot Faith a nervous smile before joining the older woman. As Faith followed them, she felt like she could breathe again. They had made it. The relief was so intense, her entire body was shaking.

Alongside the relief, though, was a sense that something both exciting and terrifying had begun. She couldn't go back now. Not to the academy to be Danforth's test case, nor to Eremus where Jacob would continue to use her as a pawn in his game.

She was part of the resistance. Here to fight against the secrecy, the corruption, the inequality. Whatever happened, she was on the right side now. She could make a difference.

She thought of Noah. Of where he might be when he discovered she was gone. Would he understand that she *had* to do this? That she was here to fight for him, as much as to fight for Sophia?

Because, she'd admitted to herself as she'd trailed Diane through the forest on her way back to Bellator, she *had* to see him again. But to see him, without facing fear and prejudice from everyone around them, things would have to change. And she wanted to be part of the change.

Ahead of her, Madeleine opened another door. A bright light spilled into the hallway. From inside, she heard the hum of machinery, the tapping of fingers on keys, numerous voices raised in friendly debate. As Madeleine entered the room, Diane turned to wait for her friend.

"This is it," she whispered. "The resistance. You ready?"

Faith nodded as they crossed the threshold together.

Noah would understand. He had to.

Want more?

Want to continue Faith and Noah's story?

Defiance is the third and final book in the Bellator Chronicles.

Get it now!

A forced separation. A risky disguise. A desperate rescue.

Desperate to rescue her best friend, Faith has returned to Bellator. She vows to fight against the Academy's horrific experimentation and is accepted into the resistance. But when the radicals are reluctant to save Sophia, she wonders if she's put her trust in the wrong people.

Back in Eremus, Noah is torn. Things with Faith weren't easy, but he misses her. When an abrupt change in leadership threatens to rip his community apart, he follows Faith to the city. Joining the rebels, he accepts a dangerous mission which might make a real difference – if it doesn't kill him first.

As the hostilities intensify and casualties on both sides start piling up, Faith wonders if they'll ever find peace. And when Noah's assignment puts him in harm's way, she knows she has to act. But the consequences of her actions could be devastating.

With their lives on the line, will Faith and Noah find a way to bring their communities together? And in the brutal final battle, will they have to sacrifice their future to save the people they love?

The third and final book in the Bellator Chronicles, Defiance is filled with intense drama, gripping action, and a pair of star-crossed lovers you'll be rooting for long after lights out. Perfect for fans of The Selection, Noughts and Crosses, and The Handmaid's Tale.

OTHER BOOKS BY CLARE LITTLEMORE

The Flow Series

Flow

Break

Drift

Quell

A drowned planet. A terrible secret. A girl desperate for answers.

In a world where sea levels have risen to unimaginable levels, an isolated society exists. Life in The Beck is tough. Floodwaters constantly threaten existence, and rules must be followed to ensure the survival of the entire community.

Sixteen-year-old Quin knows the Governor is hiding something. When she receives a sudden promotion to the Patrol Sector, she hopes the extra freedom will help her expose his lies.

Life in Patrol is not what she expected, though. The new recruits train hard, and failure is not tolerated. When she attracts the attention of the handsome, mysterious Cam, he warns her that asking questions could get her killed.

But Quin can't resist. She digs deeper, and discovers that there's more to Cam than meets the eye. With her heart and her life on the line, Quin has to decide how far she is willing to go to protect the people she loves.

If you love The Hunger Games, Divergent and The Giver, this gripping dystopian series by Clare Littlemore will keep you up all night.

Author's Note

Thanks for reading Dependence. I hope that you lost yourself in the dual worlds of Eremus and Bellator, just as I did when I wrote the book. I love building relationships with my readers. If you enjoyed Dependence and would like to receive updates when I'm releasing a new book, sign up for my reader's club:

https://clarelittlemore.com/newsletter?signup=dependence

If you sign up, you'll receive a regular newsletter with give-aways, book recommendations, special offers, the occasional free short story, and (of course) details of all my new releases. I promise there will be no spam. I hate spam.

AND WHILE YOU'RE HERE...

You can make a big difference.

Being an indie author, it can be difficult to get my books noticed. And reviews are really powerful. If you liked reading Dependence, please consider spending a couple of minutes leaving an honest review (it can be as brief as you like) on the book's Amazon page, on Goodreads, or similar. It genuinely doesn't have to be long – often just a single sentence is enough to convince someone to give a new author or series a try. I'd be eternally grateful.

Thank you very much.

ABOUT THE AUTHOR

Clare Littlemore is a young adult dystopian and sci-fi author who thrives on fictionally destroying the world with a cup of tea by her side. The tea will often be cold, because her characters have a way of grabbing hold of her and not letting go until the final page of their story is finished. They regularly have the same effect on her readers. Clare lives in the North West of England with her husband and two children.

Come and say hello!
https://www.facebook.com/clarelittlemoreauthor
https://www.instagram.com/clarelittlemore/
https://www.facebook.com/groups/lastbookcafeonearth
https://twitter.com/Clarelittlemore

ACKNOWLEDGEMENTS

This book would not exist without the support of so many people. In the past, I have attempted to list them all, and, inevitably, I always forget someone.

This time, I will simply say thank you to my wonderful editor Beth Dorward for all her hard work and patience, and to my amazingly talented cover designer, Jessica Bell, for continuing the concept for The Bellator Chronicles so beautifully. I also need to mention the fabulous Lyn Blair for her continued support with this series, and Donna Patterson and my mum for their eagle-eyed proofreading.

After that, there are (as always!) too many people to name. So if you listened while I hammered out a complicated plotline, beta read an early edition of the book or encouraged me when I was concerned I'd never finish all the redrafts, thank you. If you brought me endless cups of tea while I tapped away at the keyboard, commented on early ideas for cover designs, or helped me to edit my blurb, thank you. If you proofread the book (sometimes more than once), considered my suggestions for possible titles, or waited patiently until I'd finished the chapter before I helped you with your homework, thank you.

If you bought copies of my previous books and waited for this one without complaint, thank you.

A lot of work goes into writing and publishing a book. And many hands make light work. To anyone who helped me, even just a little, to get this book finished, thank you. You know who you are.

And, finally, to my readers. I hope you enjoy the second installment of the series and will stick with me to the end! Thank you.